A DARK AND TWISTED TIDE

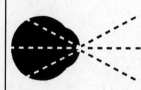

This Large Print Book carries the
Seal of Approval of N.A.V.H.

A Dark and Twisted Tide

Sharon Bolton

WHEELER PUBLISHING

A part of Gale, Cengage Learning

GALE
CENGAGE Learning·

Farmington Hills, Mich • San Francisco • New York • Waterville, Maine
Meriden, Conn • Mason, Ohio • Chicago

GALE
CENGAGE Learning·

Wheeler Publishing Large Print Hardcover.
The text of this Large Print edition is unabridged.
Other aspects of the book may vary from the original edition.
Set in 16 pt. Plantin.

LIBRARY OF CONGRESS CATALOGING-IN-PUBLICATION DATA

Bolton, Sharon.
    A dark and twisted tide / by Sharon Bolton. — Large print edition.
      pages ; cm. — (Wheeler Publishing large print hardcover)
    ISBN 978-1-4104-7294-6 (hardcover) — ISBN 1-4104-7294-9 (hardcover)
    1. Women detectives—England—London—Fiction. 2. Large type books.
    I. Title.
    PR6102.O49D37 2014b
    823'.92—dc23   2014024079

Published in 2014 by arrangement with St. Martin's Press, LLC

Printed in Mexico
1 2 3 4 5 6 7 18 17 16 15 14

In memory of Margaret Yorke,
who was my neighbour, my mentor
and my friend.

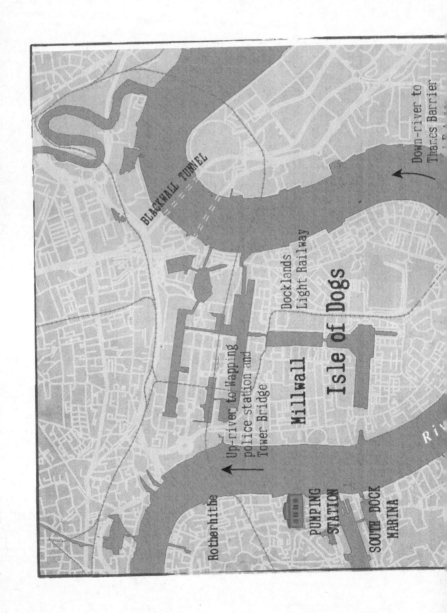

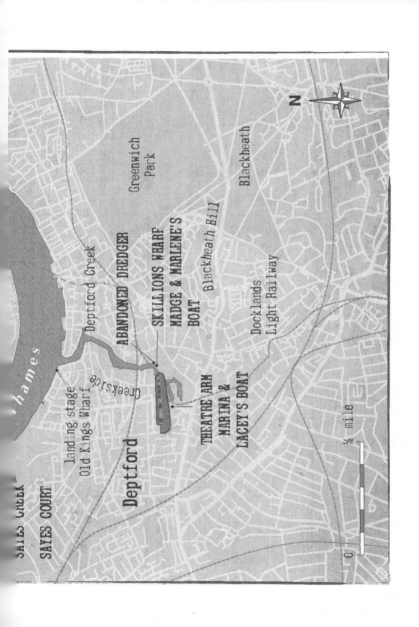

And according to the success with which you put this and that together, you get a woman and a fish apart, or a Mermaid in combination. And Mr Inspector could turn out nothing better than a Mermaid, which no Judge and Jury would believe in.

Charles Dickens, *Our Mutual Friend*

PROLOGUE

I am Lacey Flint, she tells herself, as dawn breaks and she lifts first one arm then the other, kicking hard with legs that are longer and more powerful than usual, thanks to a stout pair of fins. *My name is Lacey,* she repeats, because this mantra of identity has become as much a part of her daily ritual as swimming at first light. *Lacey, which is soft and pretty, and Flint, sharp and hard as nails.* Sometimes Lacey is amused by the inherent contrast of her name. Other times, she admits it suits her perfectly.

I am Constable Lacey Flint of the Metropolitan Police's Marine Unit, Lacey announces silently to her reflection in the mirror, as she dresses in her pristine uniform and sets off for her new headquarters at Wapping police station, taking comfort in the knowledge that, for the first time in many months, a police officer feels like who she was meant to be.

I am Lacey Flint, she says to herself most nights, as she battens down the hatches of her houseboat and crawls into the small double bed in the forward cabin, listening to water slapping against the hull and the scrabble of creatures setting out for the night. *I live on the river, work on the river and swim in the river.*

I am Lacey and I am loved, she thinks, as a tall man with turquoise eyes steps once again to the front of her thoughts.

'I am Lacey Flint,' she sometimes murmurs aloud as she drifts away to the world of what-ifs, could-bes and still-mights that other people call sleep; and she wonders whether there might ever come a day when she forgets that it is all a massive lie.

■ ■ ■ ■

SATURDAY, 28 JUNE

■ ■ ■ ■

1

The Killer

The pumping station sits near the embankment wall of the River Thames in London, close to the border of Rotherhithe and Deptford, like a woman at a dance who has long since given up hoping for a partner. The small, square building has mostly been forgotten by the people who walk, cycle or drive past it each day, if indeed they ever noticed it in the first place. It has always been there, like the roads, the high river wall, the riverside path. Not a striking building, in any sense, and nothing ever happens in connection with it. No deliveries come to the wide wooden doors on one side and certainly nothing comes out. The windows are all sealed with wooden planks and heavy steel nails. Occasionally, someone lingering on the riverside path might notice that the brickwork is a perfect example of Flemish diagonal bond and that the pattern sur-

15

rounding the flat roof is beautiful, in an understated way.

Few do. The roof is above normal sight lines and the nearest road isn't on a bus route. River traffic, of course, is far below. So no one ever appreciates that the pale grey of the building is relieved by bricks of white in a repeating criss-cross pattern, and by uniform pieces of stone set on the diagonal. The Victorians decorated everything, and they didn't neglect this insignificant building, even if few of them would have mentioned its original purpose in polite company. The pumping station was built to pump human sewage from the lower-lying lands of Rotherhithe and discharge it into the Thames. It once played an important role in keeping the surrounding streets fresh, but bigger, more efficient stations were brought into play, and there came a day when it was no longer needed.

If passers-by were curious enough to find a way inside, they'd see that, Tardis-like, the interior is so much bigger than its external framework suggests, because at least half of the pumping station is underground. Two storeys up, the boarded-up windows and the large double door are all high in the walls. To reach them, it is necessary to climb an iron staircase and step along an ornate gallery that runs round the entire circumference of the chamber.

All the engineering equipment has long since been taken away, but the decoration remains. Stone columns rise to the roof, their once-crimson paint faded to a dull red. Tudor roses still entwine at the tops of the pillars, even though they no longer gleam snow-white. Mould creeps up the sides of the smooth brickwork, but can't hide the fine quality of the bricks. Anyone privileged to see inside the pumping station would consider it a minor architectural gem, somewhere to be preserved and celebrated.

It can't happen. For years now, it has been in private hands, and those hands have no interest in development or change. Those hands are unconcerned that a piece of riverside real estate this close to the city is probably worth millions. All those hands care about is that the old pumping station serves a purpose particular to them.

It also happens to be the ideal place to shroud a dead body.

In the centre of the space are three iron plinths, each roughly the size of a modest dining table. The dead woman lies on the one closest to the outlet pipe and the killer is panting with the exertion of getting her

17

there. Water streams off them both. The dead woman's hair is black and very long. It clings to her face like the weed on an upturned boat hull at low tide.

Above, the moon is little more than a curled blond eyelash in the sky, but there are streetlamps along the embankment and some light reaches inside. Together with the glow from several oil lanterns set in the arched recesses of the walls, it is enough.

When the hair is gently lifted, the pale, perfect face beneath is revealed. The killer sighs. It is always so much easier when their faces haven't been damaged. The wound around the neck is ugly, but the face is untouched. The eyes are closed and that is good, too. Eyes so quickly lose their lustre.

Here it comes again, that heavy sadness. Regret — there is no other word for it really. They are so lovely, the girls, with their flowing hair and long limbs. Why lure them away with promises of rescue and safety? Why live for the moment when the hope in their eyes turns to terror?

Enough. The body has to be undressed, washed and shrouded. It can be left here for the rest of the night and taken out to the river tomorrow. Close to hand are the hemmed sheets, the nylon twine and the weights.

The woman's clothes are soon removed; the cotton tunic and trousers are cut away easily, the cheap underwear is the work of seconds.

Oh, but she's so beautiful. Slender. Long, slim legs; small, high breasts. Pale, perfect skin. The killer's strong fingers run the length of the firm, plump thigh, trace the outline of the small round kneecap and go on down the perfectly formed shin, over the spreading curve of the calf. Perfect feet. The high, graceful arch of the instep, the tiny pink toes, the perfect oval of the toenails. In death, she is the absolute picture of unattainable femininity.

A rasping sound. Then a cold, strong hand clutching the killer's arm.

The woman is moving. Not dead. Her eyes are open. Not dead. She's coughing, wheezing, her hands scrabbling around on the iron block, trying to get up. How did this happen? The killer almost faints in shock. Eyes that have turned black with horror are staring. More river water comes coughing out of those pale, bitten lips.

Lips that should not have anything more to say.

The killer reaches out, but isn't quick enough. The woman has scrambled back and fallen off the plinth. 'Ay, ay,' she cries, the sound of a terrified animal. The killer, too, is terrified. Is it all over, then?

The woman is on her feet. Bewildered, disorientated, but not so much that she has forgotten what happened to her. She starts backing away, staring round, looking for a way out. When her eyes meet those of her killer they open wider in dismay. Words come out of her mouth, which may or may not be the words the killer hears.

'What are you?'

And it's enough to bring back the rage. Not 'Who are you?' Not 'Why are you doing this?' Both of which would be perfectly reasonable questions in the circumstances. But 'What are you?'

The woman is running now, looking for a window — which she won't find on this floor — or a door, which won't help her.

She's spotted the upper floor, is heading for the staircase. There is no way out up there — the windows are all boarded, the heavy door can't be opened — but there are skylights that she might be able to break, attracting the attention of people outside.

The killer surges forward, crashing painfully into the iron frame of the steps, catching hold of the woman's ankle, biting hard on the fleshy part of the calf. A howl of pain.

Another hard pull. A squawk, then she comes tumbling down.

The killer has her now, but the woman is naked and slippery with water and sweat. She isn't easy to hold and she's fighting like an eel. The biting and scratching and the continual wriggling are exhausting. The killer's grip loosens. The woman is up. Reach out, grab. She's fallen, slapped down hard on the stone floor, hit her head. Dazed, she's easier to manage. Heave. The sound of flesh scraping along stone. Arms flailing, claw-like hands trying to grab hold of something — anything — but they've reached the smooth, metal pipe that in the old days took the water out of here. Lift her in. Climb after her. Push her along. The pipe is short, not much more than a metre in length.

There is water below, feet away, and gravity is helping now. Lean, pull and — yes — they both hit the surface.

And the world becomes calm again. Silent. Soft and easy.

Easy now. Let go. Let her sink. Let her panic. Wait for her to rise up, to take her last desperate breath, then make your move. Up and out of the water in one massive surge, and down again with your hands around her throat. Then down, down into the depths. Down until she stops struggling. Two of them clasped together. A tight embrace. A good way to die.

■ ■ ■ ■

THURSDAY, 19 JUNE

(NINE DAYS EARLIER)

■ ■ ■ ■

2

Lacey

A single drop of rain falling on the village of Kemble in the Cotswolds is destined to become part of the longest river in England and one of the most famous in the world. On its 216-mile journey to the North Sea, that one drop will hook up with the hundreds of millions of others that wash daily past London Bridge.

Sometimes, as she swam amongst them, Lacey Flint thought about those millions of drops and her entire body shivered with excitement. Other times, the notion of the unstoppable force of water all around made her want to scream in terror. She never did, though. Catch a mouthful of the Thames this close to the estuary and there was every chance it could kill you.

So she kept her head up and her mouth largely shut. When she opened it to snatch in air, because muscles swimming at speed through cold water need oxygen, she relied upon a prior rinsing with Dettol to kill the bugs on contact. For nearly two months now, since she'd bought the vintage sailing yacht that was her new home, she'd been wild-swimming in the Thames as often as tide and conditions allowed, and she was healthier than she'd ever been.

At 05.22 hours on a June morning, as close to the solstice as made little difference, the river was already busy and, even staying close to the south bank, she had to take care. River traffic didn't always stick to the middle of the channel and no boat pilot was ever looking out for swimmers.

The tide was as high as it was going to get. There was a moment at high tide, especially in summer, when the river seemed to pause and become still. For just a few minutes — ten, maybe fifteen — the Thames became as easy to glide through as a pool and Lacey could forget that she was human, dependent on a wetsuit and fins and antiseptic rinse to survive in this strange, aquatic environment and become, instead, part of the river.

A sleek arrowhead of a gull skimmed the water ahead, before disappearing below the surface. Lacey pictured it beneath her, beak open wide, scooping up whatever fish it had spotted from above.

She carried on, towards the jagged black pilings of one of the derelict offshore landing stages that ran along this stretch of the south bank. Built when London was one of the busiest commercial ports in the world to allow larger vessels to moor up and offload their cargo, they had fallen into disrepair decades ago.

Not for the first time, Lacey found herself missing Ray. She missed seeing his skinny arms ahead of her, missed the shower of bright water when he occasionally kicked too high, but he'd picked up a summer cold a few days earlier and his wife, Eileen, had put her foot down. He was staying out of the river until he was well again.

Less than thirty metres to the landing stage. Her senses on full alert, as they always were in the river, something caught her eye. There was movement in the water, over by the bank. Not flotsam — it had been holding its position. There were otters on the Thames, but she'd not heard of any this far down. Other people swam in the river, according to Ray, but higher up where the water was cleaner and the flow more gentle. As far as he knew, he and now Lacey were the only wild-swimmers this close to the estuary.

Slightly unnerved, Lacey struck out faster, suddenly wanting to get past the landing stages, turn into Deptford Creek and be on the home stretch.

Almost there. Ray usually swam through the pilings, a little ritual of his own, but Lacey never got too close. There was something about the blackened, mollusc-encrusted wood that she didn't like.

Another swimmer, after all, directly ahead. Lacey felt the moment of elation that comes from shared pleasure. Especially the guilty sort. She got ready to smile as the woman came closer, maybe tread water for a few seconds and chat.

Except — that wasn't swimming. That was more like bobbing. The arm that, a second ago, had seemed to be waving now moved randomly. And the arm wasn't just thin — it was skeletal. For a second the woman was upright. Then she lay flat before disappearing altogether. Another second later she was back. Maybe not even a woman; the long hair Lacey had seen in the dazzling, reflected light now looked like weed. And the clothes, trailing like a veil around the corpse, had added to the feminine effect. The closer she got, the more sexless the thing appeared.

Lacey drew closer, telling herself there was

28

nothing to be afraid of. She'd yet to see a body pulled from the river. Despite her two months with the Marine Unit, despite the Thames's record of presenting its caretakers with at least a body a week in payment of dues, she'd either been off-duty or otherwise occupied when bodies had been retrieved.

She knew, though, from a briefing talk in her first week, that the Thames wasn't like still water, where a body usually sank and then floated to the surface after several days. The currents and tides of the river swept a corpse along until it got caught on an obstruction and was revealed at low tide. There were sites along the Thames that were notorious body traps, that the Marine Unit always searched first when someone went missing. Bodies that went into the river were usually found quite quickly and their condition was predictable.

After two or three days, the hands and face would swell as internal gases began to accumulate. After five or six days, the skin would begin the process of separation from the body. Fingernails and hair would disappear after a week to ten days. Then there was the impact of marine life. Fish, shellfish, insects, even birds that could reach the corpse would all leave their mark. The eyes and the lips would usually be the first to go, giving the face a startling, monstrous appearance. Whole chunks of the body could be ripped away by boat propellers or hard obstacles in the water. Floaters were never good news.

Very close now. The figure in the water seemed to bounce in anticipation. *I'm here. Been waiting for you. Come and get me.*

Not a recent drowning, that much was clear. There was very little flesh left on the face: a few soggy pink clumps of muscle stretching along the right cheekbone, a little more around the chin and neck. Lots of bite marks. And the river's flora, too, had staked its claim. The few remaining patches of flesh were attracting a greenish growth where some sort of river moss, or weed, had taken root.

Small facial bones, hair still attached to the head, weed that seemed to be growing from the left eye socket. And clothes, although these were usually lost in the river. Except not clothes exactly, but something that seemed to have been wrapped round the body and was now coming loose, trailing towards her, like the long hair. The corpse seemed to be reaching out towards Lacey. Even the arms were outstretched, fingers clutching.

Telling herself to get a grip, that she had a job to do, that a dead body couldn't hurt her, Lacey began treading water. She had to check that the corpse was secure, and if not make it so, then get out of the water and call it in. In a pocket of her wetsuit she always carried a slim torch. She found it, swallowed down the rising panic, told herself that sometimes you just had to bloody well get on with it, and went under.

Nothing. Utter blackness that even the torch's beam couldn't penetrate. Then a swirling mass of greens and browns, light and shadow. Complete confusion.

And the sounds of the water were so much more intense down here. Up above, the river splashed, gurgled and swished, but beneath, the sounds suggested pouring, draining, sloshing. Beneath the surface, the river sounded alive.

Weird, alien shapes appeared to loom towards her. The black, shell-encrusted wood of the pillar. Something brushing her face. Mouth clamped tight — she was not going to scream. Where was the body? There. Arms flailing, clothes stretching out. Lacey ran the torch up and down the suspended figure. The river surged and the corpse was completely submerged. Now its eyeless sockets seemed to be staring directly at her. Christ almighty, as if her nightmares weren't bad enough already.

Don't think, just do it. Point the torch. Find out what's holding it still.

There! One of the strips of fabric was wrapped tight around the pile, anchoring the body in place. It looked secure.

Lacey broke the surface with air still in her lungs and looked past the corpse to the bank. No beach — the tide was too high — but she had to get out of the water. The landing stage above her was largely intact, but too high to reach. Her only chance would be to clamber up on to one of the cross-beams until help arrived. A few yards away there was one that looked solid enough.

She struck out towards it, checking back every couple of seconds to make sure the corpse hadn't moved. It held its position in the water, but seemed to have twisted round to watch her swim away.

The cross-beam would hold for a while. Out of the water, Lacey shrugged off the harness she wore round her shoulders. In a waterproof pouch that lay in the small of her back was her mobile phone; Ray insisted she carry it with her.

He answered quickly. 'You all right, love?'

Lacey's eyes hadn't left the trail of fabric

streaming out from the pier. As the waves rose and fell, she caught glimpses of the woman's round, moon-like skull.

'Lacey, what's up?'

No one was close, but she still felt the need to speak quietly. 'I found a body, Ray. By the old King's Wharf. Fastened round the landing stage.'

'You out of the water? You safe?'

'Yeah, I'm out. And the tide's turned. I'm fine.'

'Body secure?'

'Looks that way.'

'Ten minutes.'

He was gone. Ray had worked for the Marine Unit years ago and knew the significance of a body in the water. Like Lacey, he and his wife lived on a boat moored in Deptford Creek, a nearby tributary. Ten minutes was an under-estimate; he couldn't possibly reach her in fewer than twenty. In the meantime, she had to stay warm.

Easier said than done, wedged between two beams of wood and with the water splashing over her ankles every few seconds. The UK was two weeks into one of the longest heatwaves on record, but it was still early and the sun hadn't reached the south bank yet.

Below, the water sloshed around the piles,

creating mini whirlpools. The dead woman appeared to be dancing, the waves bouncing her playfully, the fabric flying out around her like swirling skirts.

'Hey!'

Lacey almost collapsed in relief. She'd had no idea how tense she'd been. Ray must have flown to get here so — Steady! She felt the beam beneath her give a fraction.

And Ray was nowhere in sight. No small, busy engine chugging its way towards her, no wrinkled old boatman frowning into the sun. Yet, for a split second, the sense of another's presence had been overwhelming. She was sure she'd heard him shout to her.

Lacey stretched up. The embankment was empty. She could hear cars, but at a distance. No sounds of bike wheels or jogging footsteps. There was traffic on the river, but nothing even remotely close.

There he was, at last, coming towards her as fast as his twenty-horsepower engine would take him.

She took the painter he held out and secured the boat before climbing down.

'Put these on.' He threw a bag her way. 'There's a patrol boat up by Limehouse. They'll be here right away. Now, we will not be talking about swimming. You and I were out on the river in my boat when you spotted the body.'

Lacey nodded as she peeled off her wet-suit and hid her wet gear in the bag. Swimming in the tidal section of the river was a byelaw offence. Even if you weren't a member of the Marine Unit.

'Are you OK?' Ray asked, as the police launch approached.

'I'm fine,' she said.

The master of the vessel was a young sergeant called Scott Buckle. He looked over at Lacey and waved.

'Part of the job,' Ray told her in an undertone. 'Won't be the last you pull out.'

'I know.'

'It's a greedy river. People get distracted, a bit careless. It won't give them a second chance.'

Almost a year ago, the river had given *her* a second chance. It had let her go, which was possibly why she didn't fear it now. 'This wasn't the river.' She watched her colleagues prod the corpse with boathooks. 'And they'll not get it with those. It's fastened tight around the pile.'

'You don't know that,' Ray told her. 'No way would you know that unless you'd stuck your head under. Please tell me you didn't do that.'

'She didn't go in accidentally,' Lacey said.

'She's wrapped up tight like a mummy.'

Ray sighed. 'Jeez, Lacey. How do you do it?'

3

The Swimmer

In the shadows, the other swimmer kept perfectly still. Sunlight couldn't reach all the way in here, but the glinting boats with their head-splitting engines sometimes came dangerously close. And they had lights, those men who believed the river was their own. Powerful, searching beams that could find anyone, even in the darkest corner. So keep still, low in the water, eyes down, that was the way. They'd think your head was weed on wood, your arm a broken branch stripped raw by the water and bleached pale by the sun.

Anya had been found. The swimmer could see her now, shroud trailing out into the water, searching for an escape that was a lost hope. Soon more boats would come. They would lift her from the river, expose her poor, ravaged body to the sunlight, prod her, poke her with their fingers and their tools and their eyes.

The woman who swam as though she'd been born in the water was being helped on to one of the bigger boats. They lifted her easily. She looked tiny and slender, despite how strong and fast she was in the river. The breeze caught her hair, already drying in the sun, and it flew out behind her like a bright flag. The men would take her away, too. They thought she was one of them, after all. They had no idea how many secrets she kept from them.

The woman with the bright hair turned and, for a moment, seemed to look directly at the swimmer. It had been close just now. For a moment, only chance had prevented the two of them from coming face to face.

It was all a matter of chance, really. Sometimes it worked in your favour, sometimes it didn't. Given more time — days, even hours — the water would have undressed Anya, the tide and the current left their mark and she would have become just another victim of the river. If the bright-haired woman hadn't swum this morning, Anya probably wouldn't have been found while her story could still be told.

It all came down to chance. And chance would take it forward. Because if Anya spoke to them, they'd find the others too.

4

Dana

'Tell me something. The fifteen-year-old who thinks getting pregnant might inject some meaning into the grubby, state-subsidized existence that passes for a life. Whose permission does she need to reproduce? Or the crack addict, taking it up the arse to fund the stuff that gets more riddled with poison every time? Who signs the form that says *she* can have a baby?'

Dana closed her eyes, as if by doing so she could drown out the sound of her partner's voice. It was over then. No baby, after all. Helen had always had a problem with authority (ironic really, given that she'd made her career in a field that demanded it) and medical authority was the hardest for her to stomach. One of her favourite rants was about the arrogance of the medical profession. She just didn't usually do it in front of them.

Dana opened her eyes and looked at her watch. She'd make the ten o'clock briefing after all. She should have known it would end like this. Well, being thrown out of a fertility clinic would be a new experience.

'We have no powers to determine who out of the general population can or cannot reproduce,' said the consultant, who was also the medical director of the clinic. Trust Helen. If you were going to piss someone off, you might as well start at the top. He was a tall, thin man in his sixties, with large, dark-blue eyes and heavy, black eyebrows. His hair, still thick and slightly too long, was black speckled with grey. The name on his office door read Alexander Christakos.

Christakos's office was directly on the river and the window behind him looked out at the honey and ivory stone, the arched river frontage and the gulls'-egg-blue roof of Old Billingsgate Fish Market. It was a conference centre now, a venue for huge and glitzy events, but in the old days, from this room, you'd have been able to smell the fish.

His voice had just the trace of an accent, but not one that Dana could place. 'You and I could debate the merits of that for some time,' he was saying to Helen, as though it were just the two of them in the

40

room. 'What I do know is that children conceived using donor gametes, and especially those brought up in single-sex households, will have specific issues to deal with as they grow up. It would be irresponsible for us, and for you, to ignore this.'

Out on the river, a Marine Unit launch was passing in front of the Billingsgate building. In the room, Christakos still had the floor.

'A number of issues concern us,' he was saying — and fair play to him for keeping Helen quiet for as long as he had. 'First, the extent to which you've thought through the impact that an unusual conception and upbringing will have on a child. And then of course . . .'

This was their first appointment. Helen had flown down from Dundee, where she worked and lived most of the time, so that they could present a united front. They'd sat in the waiting room with several heterosexual couples, the women flicking eagerly through the clinic's literature as though the secret to fertility might be found on a glossy sheet of paper, the men fidgety and embarrassed, looking everywhere but into the eyes of another person.

'Our philosophy here is that parenting is about love, not biology.' Christakos was determined not to be outdone by a gobby lesbian before suggesting they try elsewhere. Dana could almost have admired him if he weren't about to break her heart. Another police launch heading downstream at speed. She was going to kill Helen.

'Time, commitment, patience, generosity, even humour are important, but love is at the top of the list. Also, a healthy degree of selfishness helps. The patients we accept here very much want to be parents. Now, there is no doubt in my mind that Miss Tulloch wants to be a mother. The question is, do you?'

She didn't, thought Dana, that was the problem. Helen could live her life childless and never feel there was anything missing. She'd only been going along with this for Dana's sake. She'd walk out of here, shrug philosophically and say that at least they'd tried. She'd move on, expect Dana to do the same, and Dana really wasn't sure she could. She wondered how long their relationship would survive, now that Helen had denied her this.

'The truth is I never thought about children,' Helen was admitting now, because Helen didn't know how to lie. Outside, Dana watched a plane move slowly across the sky.

'This is something Dana wants.' As Dana's thoughts drifted, the sound of Helen's voice was fading. 'But I want Dana on any terms. And to pick up on your point about love, if this baby is Dana in miniature, how can I do anything other than adore it?'

Dana's mobile vibrated in her pocket. No reason not to look at it really. Well, that certainly explained the excitement she'd just witnessed on the river. But how . . . ? Never mind, she'd deal with it at the station.

The other two had finished spatting. Christakos was on his feet, offering to shake hands. It would be rude not to, and it wasn't as if she could blame him. It had been Helen's fault.

Dana left the room first, walking ahead along the corridor, wondering how she was going to talk to Helen without screaming at her. *You couldn't do it, could you? You just couldn't keep your mouth shut?*

'We hadn't really thought about the ethnic thing, had we?' Helen paused to let Dana step out of the lift first.

'What?'

'Well, you remember him saying that Indian donors are very rare? We'll almost certainly not find one. Perhaps we can just look for dark hair, dark skin tones. I'd like it to look like you if possible.'

'The Marine Unit have pulled a body out of the river,' said Dana. 'Doesn't appear to be an accidental death. They're taking it to Wapping. Oh, and guess who found it?'

Helen was looking at her watch now. 'I'll be home about six. Look, I may not be able to make the big appointment. Are you OK with that? Me not being there for the conception? I feel as though I should be, it's just . . .'

They passed reception and went out through the heavy glass door. As they left the air conditioning behind, the heat hit them.

'What are you talking about?' said Dana. Helen was looking smart this morning, even by her standards. She was tall and athletic, and always looked good in well-cut trouser suits. Her long blonde hair was swept into a bun at the nape of her neck. She was wearing jewellery, even make-up. The meeting she was rushing off to was obviously important. Much more so than the one she'd just been in.

'Dana, were you listening to anything in there?' Helen side-stepped to let an office worker carrying a tray of coffee get around them.

'Not really,' Dana admitted. 'I tuned out when you went off on one.'

'Yeah, I thought so. OK, I have to go now, so focus for a second. Your period started last Friday, is that right? That means you have to start using the ovulation kit roughly a week today. They'll want to book you in for a scan the first cycle, just to make sure everything's doing what it should.'

Helen had stepped into the road in front of a black cab. She handed Dana a large brown envelope. 'The forms for GP notification and the confidentiality waivers are in here — you need to get them sent off today. Also, the guidance notes on selecting a donor. I do want to be involved in that, because there is no way I want my son or daughter to be ginger.'

Dana was facing directly into the sun now. She blinked. 'He signed the forms?'

Helen was in the cab, about to close the door. 'Of course he signed the bloody forms! We'll be awesome parents. Love you.'

The door slammed shut and the cab sped back towards the bridge. Dana realized she had no idea where Helen was going. She'd been completely mysterious about the reason for her trip down, other than the visit to the clinic. And now she was on her own, in the middle of a London street, with some vague idea that there was somewhere she needed to be, when all she could think

45

about was that, in the last few minutes, her
life had changed completely.

5

Lacey

'You sure about this?' asked Sergeant Buckle.

'I'm sure.' Lacey watched three of her colleagues approach with the body, now decently enclosed within a large, zipped black bag. Their movements were slow and respectful, conversation kept low, mindful of the fact that the jetty at the back of Wapping station was open to public gaze.

On the main arm of the jetty was a small, square building, painted deep blue. Within it were worktops, storage, and a large, shallow steel bath. Each body recovered from the tidal Thames was brought here for initial examination and identification if possible. An unpleasant, unpopular part of the job, it was highly unusual for an officer to volunteer, as Lacey had just done.

'I can easily get someone else,' Buckle tried again.

'Got to do this sometime,' said Lacey. 'And I've seen her already, remember?'

'*It,*' corrected Buckle. 'You've seen it. We don't make assumptions about gender.'

'Delivery for you, Sarge.' The others left and Buckle looked at his watch. 'Right, we've got around twenty minutes before CID get here. Let's see what we can tell them.'

As the sergeant supported the body around the upper part of the torso, Lacey unzipped the bag. She did so holding her breath, but the smell that came out was no worse than a sort of concentration of river water, with a trace of rotting organic matter. The upper part of the woman's body — it *was* a woman, she just knew it — was largely skeletonized, but the cloth binding her was tighter around her abdomen and upper thighs and appeared to have protected the soft tissue in that area.

Buckle had a recorder in the upper pocket of his overalls and he spoke into it, giving the date and time of the initial examination of DB 23, the twenty-third Dead Body to be pulled from the Thames that year. Lacey picked up the digital camera.

'Corpse measures 165 centimetres and weighs just under 70 pounds,' said Buckle. 'Allowing for fairly advanced skeletonization, particularly around the head, upper limbs and torso, I'd say we're looking at the remains of a small adult or teenager.' From a few paces back, Lacey took full body shots of the corpse.

'The size of the frame suggests it's unlikely to be an adult male.' Buckle glanced up and winked at Lacey. She moved up the side of the bath to take close-ups of the head. The weed coming out of the eye socket was vile, like something from a bad science-fiction movie. She was going to get rid of it as soon as she could. She photographed each hand in turn, then did a series of close-ups, starting at the head and moving down the body.

'An unusual feature of this particular body is that it appears to have been wrapped,' Buckle was saying, 'head to foot, in some sort of fabric. Whatever the solution to the mystery, it seems highly unlikely this was an accidental death or an incident of self-harm. OK, let's turn it over.'

Lacey put down the camera and helped Buckle turn the corpse. A patch of scalp with long hair streaming from it was still attached to the skull at the back. Decomposition on this side of the body was less advanced and the flesh of the shoulders and lower back shone red and raw in the bright sunlight.

'This side's different.' Lacey picked up the camera again.

'Probably lay on its back on the river bed,' said Buckle. 'If it was in mud, it would have been harder for fish and the like to get close. They've had a go — look.' He pointed to the left shoulder. 'But only in the last couple of days, I'd say.'

'Any idea how long it's been in the water?' asked Lacey. Buckle had worked with the Marine Unit for several years. He'd have seen lots of floaters over that time.

'More than a month, less than a year. I'll tell you what is striking me.'

'What?'

'It's not been moving around much. Let's get this cloth off to be sure, but I'd say the skeleton's pretty much intact.'

'What's that?' Lacey pointed to the middle of the corpse, where the waist would have been. Buckle bent closer. 'Cord,' he said. 'Tied tight around the waist, possibly to hold this fabric in place.'

'It looks like nylon to me.' Lacey stepped to the foot of the corpse. 'Which means it wouldn't have been eaten away. There's some around the ankles, too. Any up at the head?'

'Not that I can see,' Buckle told her after a second.

'That's why the cloth has stayed in place around the abdomen and legs,' said Lacey. 'It was held by nylon cord that the river life couldn't eat through.'

She looked up to see Buckle watching her strangely.

'Do we take it off?' she asked.

In response he reached behind him and took hold of a large pair of scissors. 'Bag everything,' he told her. 'I'm going to try to get this off without cutting it.' He was tugging at the wrapping around the feet, trying to find a loose end. Lacey labelled two evidence bags and put them down on the counter.

'It doesn't go the whole way up.' Lacey indicated the upper part of the thighs. 'There's a bigger piece of cloth underneath these bandage-type things.'

'And the bandages start again higher up, as though they're keeping the cloth underneath in place.' Buckle slid his hands beneath the corpse's torso. 'Right, I'll lift, you unwind.'

Lacey had unwound almost three feet when something sharp and cold brushed against her hand. She jumped back. 'Jesus, there's something in there.'

Buckle, too, had started. He relaxed a couple of seconds before she did, and they watched the small creatures that Lacey had liberated scuttle across the corpse and try to climb the metal sides of the bath.

'Mitten crabs,' Buckle said. 'The river's full of them.'

Lacey nodded. Chinese mitten crabs, with bodies that could grow to the width of a human palm, had first appeared in the UK in the 1930s, escaping from ships' ballast. With few natural predators, their numbers had soared and they'd done untold damage to riverbanks, harbour infrastructure and native wildlife. Their distinguishing feature being thick, hairy front claws, at low tide they gave a creeping, constantly moving look to the river floor.

Lacey had seen dozens since she'd been living and working on the river. Of course they'd be attracted to decaying flesh. But there was just something about the things — she could count six of them, racing in panic around the bath — that was creepy as hell.

6

Nadia

The river scared Nadia. Even here, high above the city, it unnerved her. The rivers she'd known before hadn't been like this one. In the countryside she'd left behind, rivers were fast and shallow, clear as glass and cold as night. They bounced over rocks and hurried through reeds, splashed and sparkled in the sun, gleaming like star-shine in the darkness. This river was massive: brown as old blood and unthinkably deep.

She'd been staring too long. She leaned away from the telescope and let her stinging eyes rest. This early in the morning, with the wind on her face, her hair flying free and her eyes closed, she could almost believe she was home.

At home, she'd sought refuge in the hills when the noise and anger of her war-beaten country had become too much. She'd fixed her eyes on the snow that frosted them for much of the year, breathed in air that was free of dust and smoke, and told herself that the muffled sounds and distant cries weren't so very far from silence.

Here, on the other side of the world, old habits were proving hard to leave behind and she'd taken to climbing high in this ancient parkland to find air and quiet. Even here, though, it was impossible to get away from the river; telescopes fixed along the highest points made it all too easy to look. It had tasted her, this big, pitiless river, rolled her around in its mouth, getting ready to swallow her down, when she'd been plucked free, like a kitten from the jaws of a hungry dog.

Years ago, Nadia's mother had told her a story of a big, greedy river. In the story, the river remembered everyone who ever came within its clutches. Once it tasted you, it never forgot. You were marked, then, for life, and as the years went by, its hunger for you would grow, until the day came when, in spite of every effort you made to stay away, it claimed you, finally, for its own.

The stinging in her eyes gone, Nadia leaned into the telescope again. Only one police boat left now. Half an hour ago there had been several, their blue hulls and white decks unmistakable as they formed a circle, holding their positions against the tide. The police boats were designed to be distinctive, even to people who'd never been on board one, had never been pulled from the freezing depths like a fish as its strength gives out. The night she'd been saved from the river.

But not forgotten. The river spoke to her in the darkness, as her dreams turned into nightmares in which the water was all around her and the weed and the mud was clinging, pulling her down. It told her then that she would never be free, that one day it would come for her, and the next time there would be no escape.

7

Lacey

'I see you didn't stay out of trouble for long.'

Lacey started. She and Buckle had become so engrossed in the task of unwrapping the corpse that neither had noticed the two men who'd joined them on the jetty. Detective Sergeant Neil Anderson and Detective Constable Pete Stenning of Lewisham's Major Investigation Team. Seeing her for the first time in uniform.

Anderson's stomach was straining against his waistline. He seemed to have put on weight, and he hadn't exactly been a lightweight to start with. In his mid forties, he had thinning red hair, an indistinct chin line and a florid complexion. He was one of those officers who didn't take the stresses of the job in their stride. Stenning, on the other hand, was looking good. Of a similar age to Lacey, he was tall, in good shape. His dark curly hair was held in place with gel and he was wearing an aftershave or cologne that smelled of spice chests.

Back in March, on the brink of leaving the police service for good, Lacey had taken the highly unusual step of requesting redeployment. She'd turned her back on a promising career as a detective, on the hint of an imminent promotion to sergeant, and gone back into uniform. Several colleagues, including Anderson and Stenning, had tried to persuade her otherwise. They'd talked about the unprecedented bad luck that had brought her into the midst of three difficult cases in a row, of the unlikelihood of anything similar happening again in her whole career, had told her she'd be wasted in uniform. And bored witless. Still she'd clung to her decision.

Preventing crime, that was what she needed to do now. She'd patrol the river, inspect craft, check licences, persuade the drunk and the reckless that the water might look inviting but really wasn't that hospitable, and every now and again she'd help haul a body out of it. She'd leave solving the more serious crimes to those who still had a stomach for it.

It was funny how it could be both nice and awful to see people. These two had almost become friends. Almost, because

Lacey Flint didn't really do friends. 'Good morning, Sergeant.' She straightened up and forced a smile. 'Morning, Pete.'

Anderson stepped awkwardly towards her, and seemed about to give her a hug before realizing her overalls were smeared with river water and decomposing flesh. He raised his hand instead. Stenning smiled and mimed blowing a kiss.

The three men exchanged greetings, then Anderson turned to Lacey. 'You OK?'

'I'm fine, Sarge,' she said quickly.

'What have you got for us?'

Out of politeness, Lacey glanced at Buckle, who nodded for her to go ahead.

'Body found in the river just before six o'clock this morning,' she began. 'Found by me, for what it's worth. It was caught around an old wharf on the south bank, just up-river from Deptford Creek. The most unusual feature is that it appears to have been wrapped, head to foot, in that linen-like fabric that Sergeant Buckle is putting in a bag. There was a large piece, roughly the size of a single bed sheet, and then several metres of a much thinner strip of the same fabric. The strips are just over nine inches wide, some sort of densely woven cotton. It's hand-hemmed on either side, not just an old sheet ripped up.'

58

'Male or female?' asked Anderson. 'Young? Old? Dead or alive when it went in?'

Buckle put the evidence bag containing the fabric behind him. 'Very little we can tell you at this stage. No fingerprints left and certainly no identifying marks or documentation. The size of the skeleton and the presence of some long hair remaining would suggest a female, but I can't rule out the possibility of a young Sikh male, for example.'

'She couldn't have been alive when she went in,' said Lacey. 'The burial cloth was wrapped with absolute precision. We can show you photographs when we go inside. That would be impossible if the victim were fighting for her life.'

Buckle frowned but didn't comment upon Lacey's insistence that the corpse was female. 'Also,' she went on, 'there was no evidence of bloodstaining on the fabric. It was discoloured, obviously, but that was the work of the river and the mud.'

'That is a good point,' said Buckle. 'Also, while decomposition is advanced, the skeleton is largely untouched. That is highly unusual for a floater.'

'The tide and current batter them against hard objects, is that right?' said Stenning.

'Causing extensive damage,' agreed

Buckle. 'And that's before you factor in things like boat propellers. After a week, we almost never pull out a corpse with an intact skeleton.'

'She was weighted down,' said Lacey. 'Somehow she broke loose, but the cloth got caught around the pier. Sometime in the night would be my guess, or someone would have spotted her yesterday evening.'

'And your evidence for this?' asked Buckle, who was looking amused now. So were the other two. Well, she couldn't just forget she'd once been a detective.

'The nylon cords around her waist and ankles were to hold the weights in place,' said Lacey. 'The synthetic cord was chosen because it wouldn't get eaten away. We weren't supposed to find her.'

'Is that so?' asked a new voice.

They all turned to the woman who'd crept softly down the gangway. A young, slim woman in a pale-green trouser suit, her shoulder-length black hair lifting in the breeze. 'Hello, Lacey,' said Detective Inspector Dana Tulloch.

'Good morning, Ma'am.' Lacey watched the DI glance down at the corpse then back up at her.

'Are you OK?' Tulloch asked.

'Absolutely,' said Lacey, and wondered if

that had been a fraction too quick and too bright to be entirely convincing.

'You just about done here, Scott?' Anderson, Lacey realized, was glancing from one woman to the other and looking nervous. Not without reason. The last time he'd seen his boss and Lacey together he'd practically had to hold them apart.

Buckle held his hands out in an *it's all yours* gesture, before turning to Lacey. 'You need to get home. I'll see if one of the boats can drop you off. Tide should still be high enough.'

'Actually,' Tulloch was giving that small, precise smile that Lacey had come to dread, 'if Lacey's up to it, I'd like her to come with us to the mortuary.'

Lacey glanced at Buckle. 'Me?' she said to Tulloch.

'Yes. I want to know exactly what you were doing on the river this morning. Shall we go?'

8

Pari

The headaches were getting worse. The pain was bad this morning, had woken her before dawn. Pari had lain with her eyes closed, waiting for the throbbing in her head to reach the stage where she'd have to be sick, or subside sufficiently for her to leave her bed. She still hadn't moved.

The window was open. She never closed it any more. Partly because then the sense of being imprisoned became almost too much to bear, and partly because sometimes, on the breeze, she'd catch a scent — of hot oil, oranges and cardamom, or just the simple smell of frying lamb — that reminded her of home.

Through the open window came the sound of the river. The engines of a powerful boat, orders being called across the water, a noisy gull wanting to know what all the fuss was about.

Pari pushed herself up and climbed on to the bed. She stretched up to her full height, which wasn't great, and pushed her face out of the small wedge of space that was the conduit between the room and the world she'd lost.

Early-morning sun gleamed on the windows across the narrow stretch of water outside, but only those on the upper storey. The creek below her was too deep and narrow for the sun ever to reach the water. But the lower windows acted as dark mirrors and one of them occasionally allowed her to see what was happening on the river.

A boat with a blue hull and a white cabin, holding its position in the river. A police boat.

I'm here! Help me!

The words didn't leave Pari's head. These foreign police wouldn't help. The police in her own country hadn't; why should these? She took one last breath of fresh air, turned back to the room that had greeted her so cheerfully in the beginning, like the down payment on the promise of a better life, and wondered whether she might die in it.

9

Dana

'Those buggers at Wapping been fiddling around with my corpses again?' The pathologist strode into the examination room with a half-eaten fried-egg bap in one hand and a pair of scarlet spectacles in the other. He was a tall, barrel-chested man in his late forties, with thick grey hair and bright blue eyes.

'If it floats, we fiddle,' said Lacey. 'Nice to see you again, Dr Kaytes. New glasses?'

Dana watched Mike Kaytes peer down at Lacey before tucking the glasses into the pocket of his scrubs. 'I suppose I should be grateful you've brought me a complete one for a change.'

For a moment, Dana was lost. Then she realized Kaytes must remember Lacey from the case last summer, when he'd been asked to examine a series of body parts left lying around London. Well, of course he remembered her. Was there a man alive who forgot Lacey once she'd appeared on his radar?

Most women couldn't see it, the appeal that shimmered below the surface of Lacey Flint. They saw a woman who wasn't very tall, who hid her athletic shape beneath loose-fitting, plain clothes, who rarely wore make-up on her perfectly formed but largely unremarkable face, and who kept her long, fair hair tied back or plaited. Lacey Flint, for some reason that Dana still hadn't figured out, didn't want to be noticed. Most of the time, with her own sex, it worked.

'This one isn't complete,' said Lacey, indicating the black-bagged form on the examination table. 'Most of the soft tissue is gone.'

Kaytes bit into his bap and Dana watched the egg yolk ooze perilously close to the point of dripping on the floor. Well, the drain had sluiced away worse things.

'Well, far be it from me to argue with the experts,' he grunted. 'Can you get that bag off, girls?'

The two lab technicians, neither of whom looked under forty, were already waiting by the bagged corpse in the centre of the room. Together, they unzipped the bag and slid it out from beneath the corpse. One switched on the powerful overhead light. The other activated the drain that would make a low, hungry, sucking sound throughout the examination.

The smell of the Thames seeped into the room. Stripped completely of the linen wrappings that Dana had only seen so far in photographs, the corpse seemed small. The head and upper torso were almost completely skeletonized; more flesh clung to the lower extremities.

'I hear you found it?' Kaytes was still talking directly to Lacey. 'Work for the river police now, do you?'

'If David Cook hears you calling his unit the river police you'll be the one needing the post-mortem.' Dana took a step forward, to bring herself more obviously into his sight line. 'I'm DI Tulloch, senior investigating officer. This is Detective Sergeant Anderson and Detective Constable Stenning.'

She didn't expect him to apologize. They had all worked with Kaytes many times before.

'Yeah, yeah. Can you hold this while I get my mask on?' He was actually holding out the semi-masticated egg sandwich towards her.

'I'm vegetarian,' she said.

He looked offended. 'It's egg. Oh, for

God's sake, you take it, Jac.'

The technician held up gloved hands. 'I'm covered in gunk, Boss.'

A pained expression on his face, as though resigned to the incompetence of those around him, Kaytes shoved one end of the sandwich into his mouth and turned to a cupboard. He pulled a disposable mask from a box inside.

'How are you planning to eat with a mask on?' asked Dana. Kaytes turned back, chewing vigorously. The sandwich had disappeared. He pulled on his mask and stepped closer to the corpse. 'I suppose you'd better tell me what you buggers did in that lean-to you call an examination facility.'

'Photographed and measured the corpse,' said Lacey. 'Attempted to take fingerprints but were prevented by the absence of skin on the hands. Removed the burial-sheet-style wrappings, bagged them and sent them away. Set loose a bit of wildlife that had hitched a ride, keeping a couple back for examination. And then we ran out of sensible things to do so we fiddled a bit.'

'Lacey,' warned Dana.

The pathologist was walking from one end of the body to the other. 'So what do you want to know?'

'Name of the victim, cause and manner of death, time spent in the water and a good solid theory about how he or she ended up in the Thames wrapped up like a birthday present.' Dana smiled.

Kaytes continued his slow and deliberate prowl around the corpse. 'Probably female,' he said, 'judging by the height, the size of the exposed bones, the shape of the head and the remaining long hair we can see. No genitalia, but that's often the first thing to go in the water. The soft tissue is still largely present around the abdomen, but we can run X-rays and examine the pelvis later to be sure. Almost certainly adult, given the size, but I can't rule out a well-developed adolescent.'

He neared the head, bent and pushed one gloved finger into the mouth. Unasked, one of the technicians handed him a clamp and then a small torch. 'Now I can,' he said, a few seconds later. 'Wisdom teeth are all through, indicating a probable age of at least eighteen. Once we get the flesh off we can have a look at the long bones. If they're nearing the end of their period of growth, that would suggest someone around twenty-five. The extent of pitting and scarring on the sternal areas can be even more accurate. I'll be surprised if this is someone even approaching middle age, though. The bones are in pretty good nick.'

'What about race?' asked Dana.

'Less easy,' admitted Kaytes. 'Even with more time. There are basically only three racial types that are distinctive in the skeleton — Caucasian, Mongoloid and Negroid — so the best I could do is put it into one of the three. And that's assuming we've got a pure blood — sorry to sound a bit Harry Potter. The difficulty comes with mixed-race subjects.'

'Any initial thoughts?' asked Dana.

'The high, rounded skull, triangular eye sockets and protruding nose suggest Caucasian,' said Kaytes. 'On the other hand, the disproportionately short arms and legs compared to the trunk might indicate some Mongoloid ancestry. Now this is interesting.'

He was looking at the lower arm bone. 'This is a pretty well-developed bone for a young woman. She was quite strong. Possibly evidence of manual labour at some point.'

'Or gym membership,' suggested Lacey.

'Now that's where you're wrong, River Police. Because I've had a good look at her teeth and seen evidence of a couple of extractions. That's pretty basic dental care. No fillings that I could see. And some crookedness that corrective dentistry could have sorted out. I don't think our subject was affluent. And I don't think she's had a couple of decades' access to what little NHS dental treatment is still available in this country. Developing world would be my guess. An immigrant.'

'But a Caucasian immigrant?' said Dana, thinking it wouldn't narrow things down much. A huge chunk of the world's population was Caucasian.

Kaytes inclined his head. 'The X-rays will tell us whether she had a slight forward curve to her femur, again indicating Caucasian. The hair is pretty distinctive. May I?' He stepped up to Dana and, before she had time to think about what he had in mind, reached out to the side of her head. She felt a sharp pricking sensation and then Kaytes was holding up one of her hairs to the light.

'Very good example of Asian hair,' he said, 'although I think you're mixed race, is that right? But can you see how straight it is? Pure black in colour. Quite fine though, that will be the European influence. Now if River Police . . .' He looked expectantly at Lacey.

'I'll do it.' Lacey reached to her shoulder blades where her hair hung in a ponytail. She found a loose hair and handed it over.

'Come to the light.'

They all followed Kaytes to a counter, where he placed the two hairs on a sheet of white paper and angled a powerful lamp on to them. Then he picked up a magnifying glass.

'Max, would you mind?' He indicated that the second lab technician should do something with the corpse. She took up tweezers and extracted a long hair from the back of the dead woman's head, before laying it down on the paper in between Lacey's and Dana's.

'Right, what does anyone see?' asked Kaytes.

'Lacey's is the finest,' said Anderson, 'followed by the boss's. Lacey's also seems to have a bit of curl in it.'

'Classic Anglo-Saxon dark blonde,' agreed Kaytes. 'Dana's, on the other hand, is as straight and black as you'd expect from a woman with some Asian ancestry. Our friend here, though, has hair that's much coarser, longer and thicker than either. I'm thinking Middle East, Indian subcontinent, possibly some parts of Eastern Europe. Probably not the Orient. Still looking like an immigrant. Right, cause of death.'

Following Kaytes's lead, they all moved back to the examination table and gathered around it.

'The way she was so carefully wrapped up suggests she was dead when she went into the water,' said Lacey. 'Struggling of any sort would have dislodged the shroud.'

'Probably.' Kaytes nodded. 'Although she could have been drugged or unconscious.'

'There didn't appear to be any lung tissue left,' said Lacey. 'Which would make it difficult to say whether or not she drowned, wouldn't it?'

'Difficult to say, even with two perfectly intact lungs.' Kaytes turned to Dana. 'I presume you're funding full toxicology screening?'

'Do toxins survive any amount of time in the water?' asked Lacey.

Kaytes pulled an odd face, as though he were thinking about it. Or maybe he just had some egg stuck in his teeth. 'The rate of decomposition tends to slow in water. If she was poisoned, drugged or drank herself to death, we should be able to find out.'

'And if she didn't?' asked Dana.

Kaytes shrugged, as though it were really of no concern to him. 'Well, in that case,' he said, 'you're buggered.'

10

Lacey

Forty minutes later, they were back at Wapping. 'So, we have a young woman, likely to be in her twenties, more accurate age-estimate pending a boiling up of the bones, to quote our friend back at Horseferry Road.' Tulloch looked up from her laptop at the two men across the table and then at Lacey in the small kitchen area on the ground floor. 'Is it me or does Kaytes get worse every time we see him?'

'He does it for effect,' said Anderson. 'The lads back at Lewisham have a sweepstake running on who's going to be the first to land him one.'

'Yeah, well they might want to increase the odds on me.' Tulloch rubbed the back of her head. 'Right. Lacey has kindly agreed to run a Missing Persons Search for us, concentrating on young women who've been reported missing on or near the river in the past two years.'

'What can I get you, Ma'am?' said Lacey. 'Coffee?'

'Do you have decaffeinated?'

Lacey picked up the packet of ground coffee and looked at the sell-by date. 'If caffeine disappears with the passage of time, then yes. I think this came out of a crate that fell off a barge back in the nineties. The tea's a bit fresher. Or orange juice.'

'Freshly squeezed?'

As Lacey shook the small bottle of orange-coloured liquid the sediment spread from the thick glass base upwards. 'I'm not sure it was ever inside an orange. Water?'

'Filtered in any way or straight from the river?'

'Highland Spring,' said Lacey. 'We have three crates of it in the basement. We don't ask where it came from.'

Tulloch gave a heavy sigh. 'Water will do fine, thank you. Right, let's focus for a few minutes, before we leave Lacey to enjoy her new life as a beachcomber. We may never have a cause of death because of the almost complete disintegration of the soft tissues.'

'Has anyone thought of an honour killing?' asked Lacey, as she brought the drinks to the table.

Anderson looked up from his notes.

'Christ, I bloody well hope not.'

No one seemed inclined to disagree. Honour killings were notoriously difficult to solve, usually because entire families, often whole communities, joined the conspiracy of silence.

'Can't rule anything out for now,' Tulloch said. 'Right, I want to hear what Lacey isn't telling us about what happened this morning.'

Lacey stopped in the process of passing Stenning a mug. 'Sorry?'

Tulloch wasn't having it. 'I hate to break it to you, Lacey, but you're not half as good a liar as you think you are.'

'I'm not?' When had that happened? She'd been an excellent liar once.

'No, you have this way of stiffening up, your chin starts to crinkle, and your eyes become just that little bit fixed,' said Tulloch.

'And you drum your fingertips against the nearest hard surface,' Stenning added. 'Table top, worktop, even your own thighs.'

'And your nostrils twitch,' said Anderson.

Lacey shook her head. 'You three are hilarious.'

'We're detectives, they send us on courses.' Stenning picked up his mug. 'You'd probably have done one yourself if you hadn't bailed on us and joined traffic. Christ, was this made with actual coffee or gravy granules?'

'I'll just check.' Lacey turned back to the kitchen area so that they could no longer see her face.

'Never thought I'd see Lacey Flint rejoining the wooden tops,' said Anderson.

'Putting aside Lacey's powers of deception for a moment,' said Tulloch, 'what you three don't know yet, because I had the news from Chief Inspector Cook directly, is that the two pieces of nylon cord that we're assuming tied the corpse to weights on the river bottom didn't fray loose. They were cut, very recently, with a sharp implement.'

A few seconds, while they all thought about it. The corpse hadn't worked its way to the river surface accidentally. Someone had set it free.

'Blimey,' said Anderson.

'So come on, Lacey, out with it.'

Was there any point holding out? Once Tulloch got the bit between her teeth it was only a matter of time. 'What if I said it had absolutely no bearing on the case?' she tried.

'We don't have a case yet, we have a body. And we still want to know.'

Better just get it over with. 'I was swimming.'

'You were what?'

'Swimming. You know, raise one arm, then the next . . .'

'In the Thames?' asked Anderson.

'No offence, Sarge, but do I have to dignify that —'

'Do you have any idea what you can catch in that river?' asked Tulloch.

'Yeah, there was that bloke, that comedian, what's his name? Williams?' said Stenning. 'Swam the entire length of the river for charity. Got the raging trots after two days.'

'I don't swallow,' said Lacey, her eyes hardening.

Anderson was leaning back in his chair, a big grin on his face. 'So are we talking wetsuit, drysuit, or *Baywatch*-style red swimsuit?'

'Inappropriate sexual banter, Sarge.' Lacey got up to return the cups to the sink.

'Lacey, that's ridiculous,' said Tulloch. 'I can't imagine anything more dangerous or irresponsible. You should know better.'

'Yes, Mum,' muttered Lacey, her back still to the others.

'What did you just call me?' Tulloch raised her voice.

'I said yes, Ma'am,' said Lacey.

'No you didn't, you called me Mum.'

'Sorry, no disrespect intended.'

'Oh, I'm used to it. But seriously, you swim on your own?'

'I usually have someone with me, he's just not very well at the moment.'

'I'm not surprised. What has he got? Weil's Disease?'

Lacey turned back to face them. 'There's a comedy club up the road from here. I can see if they have any free slots coming up. In the meantime, it made no difference to what happened this morning, but if you tell Mr Cook, I'll be in serious bother.'

Tulloch was looking troubled. 'It may not be as easy as that, Lacey. How often do you swim in the river?'

'Only since I've been living on the boat, and when the weather's warm enough. Only early morning or early evening, when the river traffic is light. And only at high tide. When it's on its way in or out, the flow is just too strong for it to be safe.' Lacey looked from one face to the next. 'So, to anyone who doesn't know the river, there's no pattern at all. It would look entirely random.'

'But to someone who does, it would be pretty predictable.'

Anderson was scratching behind his ear. 'Hang on, you think someone meant Lacey to find the body?'

Lacey found a chair and sat down on it.

'Was it tied round that pile or just caught round?' asked Stenning.

'The Marine Unit took photographs,' said Tulloch. 'I've been promised them later today. They should tell us how it was fastened.'

'They won't.' Lacey threw up her hands in a surrender gesture. 'I had a look. I went under. It wasn't a bowline or a reef knot. On the other hand, it looked pretty secure. Basically, impossible to say one way or another.'

'Do you always follow the same route?' Tulloch asked.

Lacey nodded again. 'We usually go up almost to Greenland Pier. But we stop a few yards short because it can get quite busy, even very early in the day. So we turn at the lock entrance to South Dock Marina and then head back.'

'Were you on your way out or coming back when you found the corpse?'

'Coming back.' The realization hit Lacey. 'It wasn't there on the way out. I'd have seen it. Shit, it was left there for me, wasn't it?'

Concern washed over Tulloch's face. 'Impossible to know. But for the time being, I'd feel a lot happier if you found a local pool for your early-morning constitutional.'

11

Lacey

'First time in a sewer?' asked Sergeant Wilson, as they approached the tunnel entrance.

'It's been a day of new experiences, Sarge,' Lacey admitted. As they drew closer, she glanced back at the middle-aged man with faded red hair who was steering the small dinghy. Fred Wilson was a Marine Unit veteran of some twenty years who'd pulled Lacey from the river a little under a year ago — and almost thrown her back, he'd been so furious with her for jumping in in the first place. Lacey always thought of Sergeant Wilson as Uncle Fred, because he was Uncle Fred to the man who'd introduced them. One day, she rather feared, she'd call him Uncle Fred to his face.

At the bow was Constable Finn Turner, mid twenties, six foot five, whose gaunt face and thin body fell just a raised eyebrow short of male-model gorgeousness.

Lacey caught hold of the rope-grip as the dinghy was tossed up by a wave. Being aboard small craft always gave her the feeling of being thrown around in a washing machine. On top of that, she was hot. The drysuits worn by the Marine Unit on wet operations were designed to keep their wearers warm. Out of the water, on hot days, warm became drippingly hot.

'Not claustrophobic, are you?' There was sweat beading at Wilson's temples and his face was even redder than normal. As a child, he would have been covered in freckles. In his mid fifties those freckles had merged into a tan.

Over Turner's shoulder, Lacey looked at the gaping hole in the river wall and felt a tickle of anticipation. 'I guess we're about to find out,' she said.

Wilson revved the engine, turned sharply towards the wall, and then Lacey and her two companions entered a long, narrow tunnel that ran under the City of London. The sounds of the Thames on a summer day faded as quickly as the heat and the light. As Wilson cut the engine to an idle, the three officers travelled further into a world few people in London knew existed, even though it was directly below their feet.

A world of strangely distorted sound, of

darkness so intense as to be almost tangible, a world in which only your long-dormant sixth sense might tell you that danger was creeping up behind. The world beneath.

To her surprise, Lacey realized that something was gripping her chest, her breathing speeding up. Was this claustrophobia? Or just the hangover of a memory that needed a little longer to fade? Few people knew this twilight-coloured, subterranean London better than she. There had been times when beautifully engineered, brick-lined tunnels with decorative archways had been as familiar to her as streetlights and traffic signs are to most people. And then, not quite a year ago, in a tunnel very like this one, she'd almost lost everything.

She closed her eyes for a second in an attempt to throw off the sudden urge to jump from the dinghy and swim back towards the sunlight. When she opened them again, it was to see that, behind the sergeant's solid frame, the world they'd left had become a small, hazy circle of light.

Turner turned on a powerful torch at the bow and then, taking that as a signal, all three officers switched on their helmet lights. Being able to see again helped.

At high tide the tunnel they were travelling along would be almost submerged, leaving no room for a boat with three living, breathing occupants. At low water, the river would retreat back down the beach, leaving just a trickle of water flowing from the outlet. This was the optimum time to come in here.

On either side, low down on the arched walls, ran a narrow ledge that was just wide enough to walk along. Beneath them, the water was black, topped with foam, and it smelled of oil, of abandoned cellars, of the trapped water at the far corners of busy harbours.

'I'm guessing trailing my hand over the side at this point probably isn't the best idea,' said Lacey.

'The water in here won't be any worse than the main river,' the sergeant told her. 'This is a storm drain, remember? We don't discharge sewage directly into the Thames.'

'Unless there's been heavy rain,' said Turner, 'when all bets are off on what comes pouring out of here. You should probably wash your hands before you make the tea.'

'What are we looking for, exactly?' Lacey looked up at the perfect arch of the tunnel roof, seeing strange patterns formed by algal growth.

'Items of a suspicious nature,' said Wilson. 'An explosion down here could take out half the financial district.'

'Not everyone would see that as a bad thing.'

'Ladder just ahead on the right, Sarge,' said Turner.

Wilson slowed the boat to a halt. 'You up for this, Finn, or do you want to send Lacey up?'

'If she were wearing a skirt I'd be tempted, Sarge.' Turner stood and reached for a narrow iron ladder that ran up the tunnel wall. 'As it is, I don't want to hang around while she gets an attack of the vapours.'

'You do realize officers have been sacked for less than that?' said Lacey, as Turner sprang from the boat. About ten feet above water level, the ladder disappeared into a narrow chimney. Soon they could only see the lower part of Turner's legs.

'What's he doing?' said Lacey.

'Checking the manhole cover is still in place. Looking for any sign of it having been disturbed recently. Probably pushing it open an inch or so, just to make sure it's still in working order.'

Lacey suppressed a giggle. 'So right now, someone above us could be treated to the sight of Finn popping up like a meerkat?'

'We've just got to hope he doesn't get flattened by a passing car. You heard from our mutual friend lately?'

Lacey felt the familiar stab of excitement. Christ, just the mention of his name. Wilson was talking about Mark Joesbury, his nephew, Dana Tulloch's best friend, and her — what exactly? She was still trying to figure it out.

'Not since early April, Sarge. He's away.'

Wilson gave a quick nod. He knew what 'away' meant. 'Well, when you do hear, his mum wants to know where he put the barbecue tongs last time he was round and his brother needs a word about Lex Luthor.'

It was still something of a novelty, hearing about Joesbury's family. 'Lex Luthor?'

Wilson gave a dismissive shrug. 'Don't ask me, some daft code they invented when they were kids. Probably something to do with cash, given how rich Lex Luthor supposedly was.'

They heard the loud, dissonant clang of iron falling on to stone and Turner jumped back down. 'Hasn't been touched, Sarge,' he said. 'Had to give it a bloody good shove.'

'So,' said Wilson, as they set off again, 'what's the clever money saying about that body of yours?'

'It's my body now, is it?' said Lacey. 'The ancient maritime law of finders keepers.'

'Nah, just the pervs at the station who like

using the phrase "Lacey's body",' chipped in Turner. 'You know, "Have you seen Lacey's body? . . . Lacey's body's getting a bit whiffy in this heat." '

'Where your reputation with women comes from is beyond me,' said Lacey. 'Do you actually have conversations with them?'

'Never found it necessary.'

'Are you OK about it, Lacey?' The sergeant was suddenly serious.

'I'm fine.'

He looked at her carefully for a moment, then nodded. 'How likely are we to get an ID?'

'I wouldn't put money on it,' admitted Lacey. 'CID asked me to run a search of people still officially missing after supposedly going in the river. I found fourteen in the past three years.'

'Doesn't mean they're all dead,' said Wilson. 'Some will have climbed out, wet and embarrassed, and hurried off home.'

'And some will have been swept out to sea, never to be seen again,' said Turner. 'How many were young women?'

'Two,' said Lacey. 'But neither fits the bill. One was a twenty-year-old Nigerian who was seen jumping from London Bridge, the other a bleached blonde who was fooling around on one of the embankment walls and went over.'

'We don't solve them all, you know,' said Wilson. 'I pulled one out myself a couple of years ago. Up Pimlico way. Young woman, almost completely skeletonized. Never did find out who she was or what happened to her.'

'If you can be bothered, you could check the national Missing Persons List,' said Turner. 'Although it's really a CID job.'

'Already done it,' said Lacey. 'Massive number. But once I'd taken out those who were either too old, too young, the wrong ethnic group or the opposite sex, I was left with a hundred and two.'

'It won't take CID long to spot any possibilities.' Wilson cut the engine again and Turner's legs disappeared up a second ladder. 'Then local forces can probably provide DNA samples for matching.'

Turner jumped back down and got into the boat. 'You're up for the next one,' he told Lacey. 'So, if she's been reported missing, we'll know who she was pretty soon?'

'Dana will have it cracked by the end of the week. Brightest officer the Met's had in years, that girl.' Wilson moved them further into the tunnel.

'Bit of a babe as well,' said Turner, as they came to the next ladder and he reached out

88

to hold the boat steady. 'Do you think she just hasn't met the right man yet?'

Lacey climbed on to the ladder.

'Fucking Norah!' Turner practically stuck his fist into his mouth. 'Watch what you're standing on!'

'Sorry, Finn,' said Lacey. 'I guess my eyes haven't quite adjusted yet.'

12

Dana

What on earth possessed the woman to live here? thought Dana, not for the first time.

The tributaries of the tidal Thames had become urbanized over the last few hundred years, morphing into industrial docks with towering warehouses and commercial wharves. Deptford Creek, the name given to the last half-mile of the River Ravensbourne before it met the Thames at Deptford, flowed through a steel and concrete channel that was up to seven metres deep and in places seventy metres wide. Along its length, dark-brick buildings made the walls even higher. At high tide, it was full of water. Other times, it formed a vast, urban tunnel.

At the lock-up yard that was sometimes referred to, in a rather tongue-in-cheek way, as the Theatre Arm Marina, Dana crossed the concrete and found the ladder that would take her down to the twelve boats that were more or less permanently moored there, forming the biggest of Deptford's houseboat communities.

A number of the boats' residents were on deck, making the most of the fresher, cooler evening air. On a large, black-hulled boat in the middle of the rafting sat a young couple, a toddler curled up on the woman's lap. Toys and baby paraphernalia lay scattered around the deck. People actually raised children here? You wouldn't be able to take your eyes off them for a second.

A train went by on the elevated section of the Docklands Light Railway that ran overhead. It was a busy line, and would provide an almost never-ending background of noise.

Lacey's boat, one of the smallest in the yard, was moored on the outside and at the back of the raft of boats, and Dana had to cross several larger vessels to reach it. She clambered from one boat to the next, seeing the flicker of light in one cabin, hearing movement in another, and thinking that they were all nuts. These people had no running water, central heating or electricity. They had tanks that they filled from a hose in the yard every few days and oil-fired generators that gave them a basic level of power. They cooked using Calor Gas tanks. Some of the boats had wood-burning stoves; most didn't. Just carrying groceries home would be a nightmare.

'Evening,' said the thin, sun-tanned man on the boat next to Lacey's as Dana approached.

'May I?' she asked as she climbed down on to his deck, gesturing round the bow of his boat. He inclined his head, silently giving her permission. He held a cigarette in one hand, a beer bottle in the other. As Dana made her way carefully around the cluttered deck, she caught sight of a woman on the boat, watching her through the open hatch. Early sixties, younger than the man. As tanned and as grey-haired as he, but with more body fat.

Lacey's boat was a sailing yacht, built in the 1950s, its hull painted a bright daffodil yellow. Dana stepped down on to what Mark had told her was white-oak decking.

And that tight, pressing feeling got worse again, just at the thought of Mark. It was as if some small creature was clinging to her chest, digging in with claws and teeth. Her foot caught something, sent it skimming across the deck, over the toe rail.

'Damn.'

She leaned over, peering into the gap

between Lacey's boat and the bigger one. A small toy boat lay in the mud, its hull as yellow as Lacey's new home.

'Hold on.'

Without another word, the man on the neighbouring boat leaned over the rail, scooped the toy up with a long hook and held it out to Dana. Trying to avoid the mud, she took it and thanked him.

'Welcome aboard.'

Lacey was in the cockpit, her pale face and hair just visible against the darkening sky. Dana steadied herself on the guard-rail and climbed down.

'Sorry about your toy boat. I didn't see it.'

Lacey peered at the toy. 'Never seen it before. Must belong to the kids in one of the other boats. I'll rinse and return it.'

Like an odd house-warming gift, the small boat passed from one woman to the other.

'I've got white wine in the fridge,' offered Lacey. 'Or tea. Not decaff, I'm afraid.'

'Tea would be great,' said Dana.

Lacey was still in uniform, the simple blue shirt and slacks that the Marine Unit wore most of the time. Her hair was flying around her face in the breeze. Uniform aside, she looked timeless, like a marble statue come to life.

Dana glanced behind. Cabin hatches were

open all around them, and voices would carry. 'Do you mind if we go below? I know it's hot, but . . .'

Lacey took two large strides across the cockpit before swinging round and dropping to the cabin below.

The kettle was being filled as Dana climbed down. She heard the hiss of gas, the sound of a match being struck. Lacey was lifting mugs from a cupboard, finding tea bags, reaching into a box-like fridge for milk, giving Dana the opportunity to look around.

Dana had been in the boat before, but under exceptionally tense circumstances. Last time, she'd hardly been in the right frame of mind to appreciate what was, in fact, a rather beautiful space.

Surprisingly spacious, was her first thought. Her second was that it was a little like being in the private study of an exclusive gentlemen's club. The entire cabin, from floor to ceiling, was panelled in a wood that looked like mahogany. Green-glass lamps glowed gently on the walls and the seats around the dining table were padded brown leather. The small galley on the starboard side was beautifully neat, the chart table beyond it looked like an antique desk, and there was even a glass-fronted bookcase above it. The books, all hardbacks, were a mixture of classics and modern crime. At the far end of the cabin was a door that led to the bigger of the two sleeping cabins. Dana remembered a small, neat double bed enclosed within a wooden frame, the tiniest of wardrobes, a small bedside cupboard. It was all neat and pretty and cosy, but where on earth did the woman keep her stuff?

Lacey was watching her. Had probably been watching for some time. She had a way of moving that was so quiet, so economical.

'I don't have much stuff,' she said, as though she'd been reading Dana's mind. 'What you see here is more than I've owned my whole life before now.'

'That makes you pretty unusual. Most of us are obsessed with accumulating things.'

Lacey moved forward, putting sugar and milk on the table. 'I find the thought of stuff quite claustrophobic. Something of a . . . what's the word . . . tether.'

She served milk directly from the carton, sugar from the packet.

'Some people see possessions as an anchor,' said Dana.

Lacey smiled, before turning back to the kettle. 'I have an anchor. A real one.'

'I suppose on a boat stuff becomes inherently portable. You just set sail and off you go, stuff and all.' Why were they talking about stuff? Why did Lacey always manage to throw her off kilter?

'In theory.' Lacey flicked off the gas. 'But the sails on this boat are in storage, and I wouldn't know how to sail it anyway.'

Dana opened her mouth to say that Mark would, and remembered why she was here. 'Lacey, when did you last see Mark?'

Lacey put the kettle back on the gas burner and turned round. 'Has something happened to him?'

Still an enigma, but so much easier to read than she had been. Dana breathed in the smell of old leather and the faintest suggestion of the perfume Lacey wore occasionally. 'Mark came to see me towards the end of March.'

Lacey leaned back against the chart table as though bracing herself for bad news.

'Shortly after — well, you know what happened in March.'

The smallest nod in acknowledgement. They both knew; neither wanted to talk about it.

'He told me he was off on a case,' Dana continued. 'He had no real idea when it would be over or when he'd be in touch again. Asked me to keep an eye on Carrie and Huck. And on you, incidentally.'

A slight softening in those hazel-blue eyes. 'He said much the same thing to me. Only without the keeping-an-eye-on-people bit.'

'I know he didn't really want to go,' said Dana. 'He felt it was too soon after all the business with the missing boys, not to mention Cambridge.'

'Yeah, he said that to me, too.'

Not surprisingly, Lacey's eyes had hardened again. After three bad cases — four if you counted that business in the park last Christmas — Lacey had been on the point of leaving the police service for good. Lacey Flint, who needed nobody, was starting to need Mark and he'd gone.

But Mark Joesbury was a detective inspector with SCD10, the special crimes directorate that handled covert operations. As one of the senior, more experienced field operatives, he was typically sent in as operations neared their head. Not being available for personal reasons could jeopardize months, sometimes years, of difficult and dangerous work on the part of his colleagues. It would be completely out of character for him to turn down an assignment. It was the sort of dedication that had cost him his marriage and that might now cost him Lacey.

'So what's happened?' Lacey asked.

'Maybe nothing,' said Dana. 'Almost

certainly nothing. But there are rumours flying around and I didn't want you to hear them.'

Lacey turned back, picked up the kettle again and poured. 'Or rather you wanted me to hear them from you.'

Dana smiled to concede the point. 'The rumours are he's disappeared. That no one can contact him. That they haven't been able to for weeks now.'

Lacey brought both mugs to the table. 'Isn't that normal? Isn't that what being undercover is all about?'

'Not really. Whoever's in charge of the operation should always be able to get in touch, if for no other reason than they might need to pull him out.'

'Do they think something's happened to him?'

'No, because he has been seen. He's alive and well, don't worry about that. The rumour is that he's turned.'

'Turned?'

'Turned bad. Joined the bad guys.'

Lacey stared, giving nothing away. Or rather, Dana realized, giving a whole lot away without meaning to. She was thinking about it. There hadn't been the immediate denial, the Mark-wouldn't-do-that protestations.

'Would he do that?' she asked, after a second.

'I don't know,' said Dana, honestly.

'You've known him fifteen years, how can you not know?'

'He's no angel, Lacey. But who is? I've done some pretty unconscionable things in my time to get results. Haven't you?'

'I did some pretty unconscionable things before I joined the police,' Lacey said. 'These days, I try to keep my nose clean.'

Great. Nothing like a constable taking the moral high ground. 'Good for you. But I suspect that puts you in the minority.'

Silence. Dana knew she'd probably said too much. It was a part of the job that most officers understood but few acknowledged openly. Sometimes, it wasn't quite so easy to see the distance between right and wrong. Sometimes, the moral code became blurred.

Nearly fifteen years ago, as young police officers, she and Mark had been staking out the flat of a known drug-dealer. They'd watch him leave the building and hurl a supermarket carrier bag into a rubbish skip. A couple of hours later, they'd taken part in a search of the flat and found nothing. The dealer had stripped his home of every piece of incriminating evidence. It was all in the

99

skip outside and they had no way of tying the carrier bag to him. Mark had pulled back the duvet on the bed and found two short, black hairs. He pocketed them and when they retrieved the bag from the skip, let them slip inside unnoticed.

Unnoticed by everyone but her. She'd watched her friend cross the line and then she'd stepped over to join him. And that had been right at the start of her career. Before she'd even had time to consider just how much integrity meant to her.

The dealer had gone down. One piece of scum less on the street. With no doubt as to his guilt, Dana's conscience had been easy. Noble-cause corruption was the name given to the practice. Planting evidence, telling small white lies, holding back facts to secure the conviction of those you knew were guilty.

It was widespread and, for the most part, did no harm. On the other hand, it was the first step on a slippery slope. How big a step was it from planting evidence on someone you knew to be guilty, to creaming off a few quid from money snatched in a raid? And if you could square that with your conscience — the money was illegally gained anyway — how hard would it be to skim off half a bag of cocaine to sell on yourself? To pocket the two hundred quid and look away when a drunk driver asked nicely? To withdraw a few twenties with the fraudulently obtained credit card?

Most police work wasn't hunting down serial killers and solving heinous murders. It was small and sordid, beating the scum at their own game. Coppers made the best villains. They knew the score. They knew how not to get caught.

And some small spark of light had gone from Lacey's eyes.

'There's also a discrepancy in his bank account,' Dana went on, wishing she could have spared her the most damning evidence of all. 'Several hundred thousand pounds more in there than should be. Far more than he earns in the Met and no way of accounting for it.'

'So what are you saying?' said Lacey. 'That you're all bent and he's just finally gone the whole hog?'

'No, I'm not saying anything of the kind. To be honest, I don't believe it. Partly because I think Mark knows where to draw the line and partly because he's got too much to lose. If he goes off the grid, he'll lose all his friends. Not to mention his son. Not to mention you.'

'How, exactly, did you hear this?'

'One of his mates phoned me. Someone I know from way back. Wanted to know if I'd heard anything. He may be in touch with you, too.'

'I've heard nothing. Since he went, nothing.'

'He should have been transferred out of SO10 before now.' Dana was using the former, but still colloquially popular, name for the covert operations squad. 'The work those guys do is incredibly tough, and no one should stay in the directorate for more than a few years.'

Lacey was nodding. 'They get too close to the people they're investigating. They start to see things from their point of view. They start to care.'

'They make friends. Sometimes they even get involved. Romantically, sexually. They lose the ability to walk away. You know what? If Mark wasn't so bloody good at blending in with villains they'd have moved him too, but it was always one more case, then one more.'

Lacey ran her hands over her face. 'Where will he go, do you think?'

Dana got to her feet. 'If Mark really has gone, then there'll be people who will shelter him. He won't put us at risk. He won't come here.'

Nothing else to be said, really. Dana tried to smile and couldn't quite manage it. She said goodbye and climbed off the boat. In the short time she'd been on board, all traces of sun had left the sky and the creek was starting to assume the gaping, canyon-like presence it acquired after dark.

From the shore, when she turned back, Lacey was nowhere to be seen.

13

Dana

Helen was in the garden, wearing jogging bottoms and a vest top, a sweat-sheen around her forehead. At her side was a pint glass of water, a cold bottle of lager and crisps. It was how she replaced fluid, sugars and salts after hard exercising.

'I expected you back before now,' she said, as Dana came across the decking to join her. 'Busy day?'

'Mad. What about the meeting you were rushing off for? That go well?'

'I know you want to talk about the clinic.' Helen was smiling. 'Did you get the forms sent off?'

Yes, somehow, in between setting in motion a murder investigation and dealing with the news that her best friend might have gone out of her life for good, Dana had found time to complete and post off the forms that marked the next stage in the process that would turn her into a mother. She'd also spent most of her lunch-break moving from one fertility web page to the next.

'You know, a lot of women in our position share the pregnancy,' she said, sitting down and stealing a swig from the bottle.

'Hmmn.' Helen was suddenly intent on the crisps.

'One of them donates the eggs.' Dana put the bottle back down. 'Which are fertilized in vitro and then the embryos are put into the womb of the other partner.'

Helen put several large crisps into her mouth. 'I think that pink thing needs dead-heading,' she said.

Humouring her, Dana looked towards the resplendent rambler rose at the bottom of the garden. It was safe. Helen had no interest in the garden, other than as a place to drink a cold beer and occasionally eat an al fresco supper.

'So Partner A, the one who donates the eggs, is the biological mother, and Partner B, the one who receives them, a sort of surrogate?' said Helen, after at least a minute had gone by. 'Given that you've got me lined up for Partner A, what does that involve exactly?'

Dana watched a butterfly settle on a

purple, bell-shaped flower. 'Well, it would be similar to IVF. You'd have to take artificial hormones that would stimulate follicle development. It's mainly done by injection, but there are some drugs that you just sniff.'

'Yeah, I've come across a few of those.'

'When the eggs are ready,' said Dana. 'God, I sound like Nigella. When the follicles are ready to release the eggs, they're retrieved surgically under a local anaesthetic.'

Helen drank deeply. 'We'd still need a sperm donor.'

'No way round that, I'm afraid. So what do you think?'

Helen put the empty bottle down. 'Sounds hideously intrusive, hugely expensive and generally revolting. Other than that, it's a great plan.'

So did she laugh or get annoyed? That was the trouble with Helen. You could always go either way. 'OK, I just wanted to give you the option.'

Helen tipped her head back and emptied the crumbs from the crisp packet into her mouth. 'I don't need a biological link to this child, you know,' she said, crumpling the bag. 'It'll be enough for me if you have one.'

'I just don't want you to feel left out. It's going to be difficult enough with you in

Scotland and me and the baby down here.'

'Ah, now you can ask me about my meeting this morning.'

She'd known there was something up. 'Tell me about the meeting.'

'Actually it was more of an interview. For a job.'

'Who with?' Dana asked, although what she really wanted to ask was, where based?

'Interpol.'

Interpol in the UK were London-based. Dana thought about it for a second. 'I didn't know you were looking to move.' Helen had always worked in Scotland. She'd built her career in the Tayside Police, had been one of the youngest women in Scotland to reach the rank of Detective Chief Inspector.

'I wasn't,' she said. 'But if I'm going to be a dad, co-mum, whatever, it's not really going to work if I'm three hundred miles away.'

'You'd move to London?'

'I have to get the job first. You have to get pregnant first. Lots of ifs and buts and far too soon to be counting chickens. Now, are you going to tell me what's wrong?'

She could never hide anything from Helen. 'It's Mark,' she said.

■ ■ ■ ■

TUESDAY, 12
FEBRUARY

(EIGHTEEN WEEKS EARLIER)

■ ■ ■ ■

14

Yass

The tide creeps in. It comes slowly at first, like a predatory animal short on conviction. At first the only sign of the water's approach is an almost imperceptible relaxing of the sand. Suddenly it's not as solid as it was. It's relaxing into its component parts, separating, starting to get — floaty. Then the damp becomes wet and Yass knows the time has come to move.

So she moves. She jumps and twists and thrashes. She screams and cries as she hurls her limbs against the hard brick walls around her. She keeps it up until she can do nothing more than sink down, exhausted, on to sand that is softer still.

A few minutes later and the smell around her has grown thicker, more solid. The air smells of salt that has been left too long in the storeroom. Of engine oil. Of a small, decomposing animal. She can smell sweat.

No, that's coming from her. Blood. That's her, too.

She sinks a little deeper into the mud.

She can't see the water. Not yet anyway. It's too dark in here. Black as the night at home when the power failed. Except, just as the stars at home offered a hint of what lay behind the dark cloak, so there is a tiny stream of light finding its way in here.

That's a change. Instantly Yass is moving again, is up, on to her knees. Any change means new information, something she can process. It was night when she was brought here. Sometime after midnight. She'd taken the key that was given her, crept down the stairs, her heart thudding at every creak of the woodwork, and opened the back door. The boat had been waiting.

They'd travelled away, using the oars as paddles, only switching on the small engine as they'd left the house behind. Without speaking they'd travelled up the river, before turning into a brick-lined tunnel beneath the city. A tunnel that had taken them further and further into darkness, until only the torch on the boat had stopped them from being completely submerged in it.

It isn't night any more. There is light coming from somewhere, enough to see her hand in front of her face, were she able to move her hands. She can hear the low roar of vehicles passing overhead. She is beneath the city and the city is awake.

With the knowledge that she's been here for hours comes the realization that she is freezing. The complete lack of light, the damp all around have leached all warmth from her body. Yass is shaking with cold.

She can hear the water now. A steady, rhythmic sucking, the sound of a greedy young animal draining its mother, the hawking and spitting of old men on the street corners. The wall at her back feels colder, wetter. There are trickling sounds all around, as though a dozen taps have suddenly begun to leak. She is kneeling in water.

She tries to stand. Not easy with her hands tied behind her back, but the water is covering her legs now and it is impossible to stay still. Impossible to stand, though, because the rope around her neck simply isn't long enough. She twists round but can't see what the rope is tied to. She pulls against it, thrusting her head forward, feeling the sharp stab of pain from raw flesh that reminds her she's done this many times already.

She shouts out loud. And the soreness in her throat tells her it isn't the first time.

The water is coming in fast, hard waves now. The predatory animal is swollen with courage now it knows that she can't move, can't fight back, is alone down here.

Except she isn't alone. Those are human eyes she can see, just yards away, gleaming in the trickle of light. That pale glow is a human face, the face that brought her here. Yass opens her mouth to beg, although she knows it's hopeless.

Those eyes are here to watch her die.

■ ■ ■ ■

FRIDAY, 20 JUNE

■ ■ ■ ■

15

Lacey

As often happens when exhaustion has been sated, sleep slipped treacherously away and some time in the early hours, Lacey woke up. The boat was moving, bumping and bouncing like a baby in an elastic support swing. The tide was coming in.

In the cabin around her the darkness was utter and complete. There were no streetlights in or near the yard and the boat owners didn't waste their precious electricity keeping lights burning through the night. When the moon wasn't around, or cloud cover was thick, her small bedroom became the impenetrable black of Hades.

Joesbury.

Lacey closed her eyes, feeling tears cold and ticklish against her lashes, willing sleep to take her again. After Tulloch had left, she'd gone straight to bed, refusing to think about what she'd just been told. Since moving to the boat, she'd been sleeping better than she had in years. She loved the unpredictable rhythms of the water, the cheerful slapping of waves against the hull. Even the wind whistling around the few remaining masts in the marina was soothing and she never minded the times when water disappeared completely from this part of the creek, when the boats were beached and skewed at odd angles. She simply rolled against the low wooden frame around the bed, like a child in a cot, and slept soundly.

She'd been angry with him for leaving. He'd phoned in April, asking her to meet him after work, and she'd known immediately there was something she wasn't going to like, because they hadn't been alone for months. He'd been giving her space, seeing her only at weekends or early evenings, and always with his nine-year-old son, Huck, acting as a sort of skinny, cheeky chaperone. And just when she'd started to think that it might be possible after all, that, in spite of everything, there could be a way, he'd gone.

In a pub by the river he'd told her he had to leave the very next day, that a job he'd been on the periphery of for months needed finishing, that no one else could do it. He couldn't tell her where he'd be, what he'd be doing, or when he'd be back. He'd admitted that Carrie, his ex-wife, was furious, that she would divorce him again if she could.

'Huck needs you,' Lacey had said, knowing all the while that what she really meant was, *I need you.* It had hit home. She'd seen his eyes darken, his face tense up.

'If I don't go, kids like Huck might die.'

And what could you say to that? But how dare he take the moral high ground when weeks later he was going to turn?

Did that mean she believed it?

Tulloch believed it. Whatever she might say to the contrary, she believed it and she'd known him for years. She and Joesbury had joined the force together, trained together — she knew him better than anyone.

And who would really be surprised? The service was riddled with officers who were on the make and half the eyes in the Met were blind. Such a fine, fine line, between poacher and gamekeeper.

Tears were coming thick and fast now. Impossible to stop them. Would it even matter? If he turned up with half a million quid in his pocket and asked her to run away with him, to flee to some foreign land and live as fugitives for the rest of their lives, would she?

Outside, on the creek, she could hear soft,

rhythmical splashing.

Impossible. For years now, her job had been all she had. It had meant everything. Upholding the law. Making a difference. Putting things right when they went wrong. She *was* her job. She could not walk away from it.

Splash, splash.

She was not bent, would never be bent. Years ago, as a wild teenager in the sink estates of Cardiff, she'd been in and out of trouble. Schools and local authorities and foster homes had despaired of her. And then, one night, her life had changed irrevocably and a chain of events had been set in motion that would turn her into a different person. Quite literally. She'd lost the person closest to her in the whole world, and the woman she'd been on the brink of becoming had died, too. Lacey Flint had appeared in her place and Lacey Flint was not bent. So if Joesbury came to her, under cover of darkness, and asked her to be with him?

She'd do it in a heartbeat.

Splash, splash.

Lacey sighed and sat up. No one could sleep with this level of misery pressing down on them. Besides, she had a more immediate problem. Someone was swimming round the boat.

Holding her breath, listening properly, she knew she hadn't been mistaken. That controlled, steady rhythm was completely different from the random beating of the waves. It was deliberate, the product of conscious thought. Someone was right outside, in the water.

Joesbury?

Joesbury would climb on to the boat, not swim around it. And yet the thought of him was uppermost in Lacey's mind as she pushed back the quilt and slid soundlessly to her feet. The bow hatch was directly above her, but going up that way would be too obvious to anyone near by.

She kept the boat tidy, the floorboards free of clutter, because she never knew when she'd have to make her way around it in darkness. In the main cabin some light was seeping through the porthole blinds and she could see the reflection off the brass fittings around the walls, the fainter glow of the plastic hatch.

She reached up to the hatch and knew that once she started to move it, whoever was out there would hear and know she was awake. Her torch was on the bottom step. The beam was powerful. It would find anyone in the water before they had a chance to swim away.

But who would be swimming in the creek at this hour? It was ridiculous. And yet, even if that steady *splash, splash* could have another cause, that low-pitched cough she'd just heard couldn't. It was a sound she knew so well, had made herself dozens of times. You opened your mouth at the wrong time, took in a bit of river water and coughed it out quick. Someone not yards away had just spat out water. Someone was out there.

Time to move. The hatch made a rough swishing sound as Lacey pushed it open. She pulled herself up, dropped low in the cockpit and waited.

Above her head a few thin clouds were moving fast, gunmetal-coloured shapes against the coal black of the sky. Across the creek there were a few over-tall, over-thin trees, and their leaves were rustling like the approach of an insect swarm. Below her, the water was moving fast, too, producing sounds as varied as the colours it seemed to absorb on a hot summer's day. Endless noises around her, but the swimming had stopped.

Lacey crouched lower and saw the small boat on the cockpit floor. Red-hulled this time, but otherwise an exact match of the one on her small draining board, waiting to be returned to kids who'd tell her they knew nothing about it. Someone had been on her boat, had left both toys behind.

Leaving the toy where it lay, she looked up. All the residential boats were afloat, but the water was still some way below the edge of the quay. If high tide was due just after six in the morning, it was probably around 3am right now. Over the port deck of the boat she could see starlight bouncing off the moving water. The tide was breaking gently into minuscule white waves, but nothing else disturbed its slick black surface.

Holding the torch up high, she peered over the starboard deck and switched it on. No one hiding between the two boats. Leaving the security of the cockpit, she made her way along the starboard deck, her bare feet making no sound. Nothing at the bow.

She'd been wrong. She must have heard an animal, or just the lapping of the water, after all. There'd be an explanation for the toy boats. Time to go below, to sleep again if she could. Lacey walked back along the deck, jumped lightly into the cockpit and swung herself down into the cabin.

Mark Joesbury was on her sofa, removing his left shoe.

16

The Swimmer

Against the opposite bank, not twenty yards away, a thin, strong arm held tight to the low-hanging branch of a buddleia tree. In the shadows of the bank, in the dark space that no streetlight could ever reach, large eyes blinked. The man was new. The man hadn't been here before. Would he stay?

It didn't feel right. All this moving and looking and shining bright lights in the middle of the darkness. Now there would be talking, maybe for ages. There might be sex.

Watch? The woman never covered her windows. Never seemed to worry about being seen, lying like a princess, hair spread over white pillows, breathing softly and deeply. The man was big and powerful, young like the woman. He'd cover her body like fog on the river, seeping into every curve. Her limbs would reach up like weed, wrapping around him. And their faces. Faces that didn't know they were being watched.

Too risky. The woman was already on her guard. No more tonight.

Later.

17

Lacey

'You're not wet.' Lacey took in Joesbury's dry jeans, a black leather jacket in perfect condition and a white collarless shirt. A canvas rucksack, which didn't look wet either, lay on the cabin floor. He couldn't have swum with a rucksack, could he?

The shoes, both off now, hadn't left a mark. No socks. Feet dry, as far as she could see. Long toes, with small tufts of black hair on each. Why was she staring at his feet? She made herself look up.

'You're not wet,' she repeated.

'Hard to believe CID let you go. Would a cold beer be asking too much?'

He seemed bigger than she remembered, or maybe it was just the confines of the cabin. He'd let his dark hair grow longer again, which always suited him. It softened the lines of his head and face, making him look less of a half-tamed thug. Eyes exactly the same: deep set, turquoise, black eye-lashes. She could never look him in the eyes for any length of time. So she turned, pulled the hatch shut and switched on the cabin light before closing the blinds.

'I heard someone swimming round the boat,' she said. 'That's what woke me up. I thought it was you. And you know I don't drink beer.'

Joesbury was taking off his jacket now, the simple, reasonable action — it was still pretty hot — making her acutely conscious of how little she was wearing. Jogging shorts and a vest — all she ever wore in bed. She watched the white cotton of his shirt being pulled tight against the flesh of his back, saw the dip between two muscles on his shoulders, imagined the gleam of hot skin beneath.

'Swimming in Deptford Creek at three in the morning? I doubt it.' He dropped his jacket on to the sofa. 'I crossed the yard and climbed down the ladder. I was on Ray's boat all the time you were dancing around at the bow. And *I* drink beer. I thought you might have some in on the off-chance.'

'Off-chance of what? You showing up out of the blue when half the Met is looking for you?'

He hadn't shaved in days. The stubble around his chin was just on the brink of becoming a beard. He hadn't washed too recently, either. He smelled of the city, of smoke and hot tarmac. And of the way male bodies smell on warm nights. He was grinning at her, as though his unmasking as a complete villain was amusing. 'Ah, I wondered if you knew. Dana came round, didn't she?'

'A few hours ago.'

The grin was widening and twisting. 'She thinks I'm guilty, doesn't she? Christ almighty, one dodgy arrest fifteen years ago. I could tell you some things about her, you know.'

'She rather did that herself. I've never known her so . . . confiding.'

'That'll be the day. So, do you think I'm bent?'

The words were on the tip of her tongue. *I don't care. I don't care what you've done. I only care that you're here.*

'Et tu, Brute,' he said, and it was impossible to tell whether he was disappointed, pissed off, or still just amused.

'What are you doing here?'

'Need a bed for the night. What's left of it.'

Stay on the offensive. Do not let him know

128

that just the mention of that three-letter word has made it practically impossible to think straight. 'And you couldn't go to your own place because you have the decorators in?'

'I can't go to my own place because I'm not supposed to be me at the moment. I can't go to the doss house I've been sleeping in the last three months because things got a bit tense this evening and I'm keeping a low profile.'

And her brief moment of assertion was passed. 'Mark.' His Christian name still felt odd and presumptuous on her tongue. 'What's going on?'

He took a deep breath and his face was suddenly completely serious. 'The gang I'm investigating know I'm with the police. That was the whole point, they need a bent police officer. They think I'm a uniformed sergeant in Catford who's on the make. Trouble is, they don't fully buy it. They certainly haven't told me what they're planning and I doubt they will until I can win some measure of trust.'

'So why are there rumours flying round that you disappeared? Why are there hundreds of thousands of pounds in your bank account?'

'How the hell?' He shook his head. 'She's

hacked my account again! I can't bloody believe that woman.' He looked Lacey directly in the eyes. 'The money is my brother's. He's sold his house and is doing some creative accounting. As for the rumours, I don't know. Probably a case of Chinese whispers. Maybe someone's seen me around town, put two and two together and made five. Dana's right about one thing — I have been in this game too long.'

He'd been seen around town? 'You've been in London all this time?'

'Closer than you think. I saw you on the river the other night. That lanky twat on the fly-bridge — was that the climber bloke I met in March? The one who calls himself Spiderman?'

'Finn is a member of the line-access team,' said Lacey. 'He's known as Spiderman, I understand, because of his exceptional climbing ability. I haven't seen him in action yet, but give me time.'

Joesbury's right eyebrow went up.

'Please don't do that to me again. I thought I'd lost you.'

Christ, had she really just said that? Joesbury looked as though he didn't quite believe it either. He was stretching out his legs, pushing himself up, and it was lucky the boat was so small, because crossing a decent-sized room right now would have taken far too long.

Yes, that was how he smelled. That was how the skin of his neck felt.

'You know there are any number of cheap, cash-only, ask-no-questions hotels you could have checked into,' she muttered into his left shoulder.

'Well, you've got me there.' His breath was warm against her ear.

'Some of them even come with girls.'

His hands, which had been resting on her hips, moved across her back, holding her closer. 'None of them come with this one.'

His chin was resting on the top of her head now, his arms wrapped tightly around her, and for a while it felt enough, just to be this close, to feel his breathing in sync with hers.

'It feels like a very long time since I've kissed you,' he said, after a few seconds.

'You've never kissed me.' Lacey tried to keep the glee from her voice, to stem the bubbles of excitement exploding in her stomach, and knew she was failing on both counts.

'Bloody well have.' The side of his nose brushed against her temple.

'If you're talking about that night last October, I kissed you, not the other way round. And when I made it clear I had a lot more than kissing on my mind, you went all maiden-aunt on me.'

Three sharp breaths were expelled from his nostrils. He'd actually just sniggered. 'Well, be fair. I thought you were a knife-wielding psychopath and I was next in line for the eviscerating party piece.'

'And now you think otherwise?' She pulled back, tipped her head to look up at him.

He smiled. 'Now, strangely, I find I don't care.'

She was smiling too. 'So, about this kissing business . . .'

He sighed and gave the smallest shake of his head. 'Can't.'

'What?'

'If I start I'll never stop, and what will inevitably follow just can't be a good idea right now. Besides, it's after three in the morning, I've had no sleep, and from what I understand your day hasn't exactly been uneventful.'

Like she'd ever been more awake in her life before. 'What do you know about my day?'

'I still have access to the system. I know all about what happened this morning. Are you OK?'

She opened her mouth to tell him she was

fine and changed her mind. 'A bit fed up with people asking me if I'm OK. Otherwise coping.'

The eyebrow was back up again. 'You can't get away from it completely, you know. The bad stuff. Not in this job.'

She knew that. She'd known that back in March when she'd taken the decision to go back into uniform.

'It's just . . .'

'Just you thought you'd have more time.' Joesbury was nodding, as though he understood completely. 'You knew you'd have to face it again sometime, but you thought you'd have some breathing space. Just a few more months to get your head together.'

'Yeah,' she muttered into his shirt. That was it exactly. She'd been owed a break.

'Tell me about it,' he said, stroking the back of her head.

It was a fair point. The case in March, the one that had ended her career as a detective, had been far worse for him. And yet he'd gone straight on to an undercover job, surrounded by strangers and enemies. He was dealing with everything that she was. Only he was doing it alone and in danger.

'And while I'm on the subject,' he said, 'I'm really not happy about this swimming malarkey.'

'That wasn't in the reports.'

'You live next to Ray Bradbury, whose aquatic activities have been notorious for years, and you were with him when you found the body. I'm not a complete buffoon. No more swimming in the bloody river, OK?'

'When did you get the right to tell me what to do?'

'When I fell in love with you. Now, if you didn't get the beers in, I suppose a spare toothbrush is hoping for a bit much.'

'In the cabinet in the heads. Still in its wrapper. I bought turquoise because it reminded me of your eyes, and if you're still interested there's a six-pack of Carlsberg in the bottom of the fridge. Just on the off-chance. Oh, and your mum wants to know where you left the barbecue implements and your brother wants a word about Lois Lane. Or something like that. What am I now, your PA?'

God, he had a great smile. How could she have forgotten that smile? And was he really, honestly, going to sleep in the other cabin?

It would appear so, because he was bending down, kissing her on the cheek, just above the ear. 'Good night, Flint,' he said, and disappeared.

■ ■ ■ ■

When Lacey woke in the morning, Joesbury was gone. For a moment, she wondered if she'd dreamed the whole thing. And then, on the table in the main cabin, she saw his note. He'd dug his hand in the packet of sugar and let it trickle out between his fingers to draw a single, simple shape on her table top. A heart.

18

Lacey

'I am Lacey Flint and I don't swim in the river any more,' muttered Lacey to herself as she climbed into the canoe. 'I don't swim in the river because it's dangerous and my boyfriend has put his foot down.' She pushed away from the back of the yacht, wondering if the unfamiliar giddiness she'd woken up with — this feeling that suddenly her body was lighter and her head full of space, that the day ahead was awash with wonderful possibilities — could actually be the emotion that other people called happiness.

It was still early and she had several hours before her shift. She could do laundry, shopping, fill the water-tank on the boat and — bloody hell, when had chores become something to look forward to? First, though, the river.

The tide was on its way out and paddling

was hardly necessary. Once she hit the Thames it would be a different story, but one of Ray's golden rules for safety on the water was always to move against the tide when you were fresh, and with it on the way back when you were tired. The other was to stay close to the bank, where the chance of encountering motor traffic was slim and the pull of the tide weaker.

'Good morning, beautiful.'

Lacey was passing Skillions Wharf, one of the creek's other houseboat communities. Leaning over the side of a seventy-foot-German sea-defences vessel was a size-sixteen blonde squeezed into a size-twelve swimsuit. Flesh oozed over the edges of the red fabric at the low neckline, the shoulders and the hips.

'Good morning, Marlene,' Lacey called up. 'You're up early.'

'Haven't been to bed.' Marlene drew deeply on a cigarette that might not contain just tobacco. There was a drink in her other hand that probably wasn't just tomato juice. 'Where's that old tosser you swim with?'

Gravity wasn't doing Marlene any favours. Her breasts drooped heavily and her face had creases that might disappear when she stood upright. Might.

'Got a bit of a cold,' said Lacey. 'Eileen's

put him in dry dock.'

Marlene flicked her finished cigarette into the water and hooked her thumb inside the leg of her suit, pulling it out and away from her body. Lacey caught a glimpse of flaxen pubic hair before she looked quickly away.

'Current's strong.' She let the water take her again. 'Have a good day.'

As she neared the next boat — a massive, long-abandoned dredger moored alongside a gravel yard — Lacey glanced back. Marlene was still on deck, watching her but no longer alone. Her partner, a woman of a similar age called Madge, was standing close behind, and it might just have been a trick of the light, but there was something about the way they were both watching her that seemed predatory.

Telling herself she was being fanciful, Lacey focused on the water ahead, passing the dredger, the pumping station and Hill's Wharf. Each stretch of the creek was named. Ray, who seemed to know them all, had been teaching her. Ray had lived on the creek for over thirty years, had worked on the river for even longer. There was little he didn't know about it. Including its various human residents.

Marlene and Madge were ladies of the theatre. Marlene was an actress, although it was questionable when she'd last had an acting job. Madge was a producer of sorts. Their boat was filled with theatrical memorabilia, according to Ray, mainly photographs of the two of them with various West End stars and props they'd filched from productions over the years.

Under the railway bridge. From this point on, the walls got higher and the creek deeper as it neared the Thames. More wharfs — Normandy Wharf, Saxon Wharf, Lion Wharf. Lacey had come across the creek earlier in the year, when it had been the focus of a series of child murders. Before then, like many other Londoners, even those who lived close by, she'd barely known of its existence. Once an important part of commercial life along the Thames, the creek was now largely forgotten, even by those who owned properties alongside. It was derelict, a borderland owned by no one, attracting no one's attention.

But it was also a wild space, where nature thrived. If the concrete crumbled, if the steel began to rust, if the timber showed any signs of rotting, plants sprang from the weakness and flourished. You had to admire their spirit.

Lacey passed under the Creek Road Bridge and was just a short stretch from the

Thames. She started taking in more air, braced herself for the effort. She'd go as far as the South Dock Marina, maybe a little further — the going would be easier in the canoe. She turned the bend and — oh!

The river was pink, shrouded in mist, the early sun behind her casting its light over London, turning it into a city of coral and smoke. Great warehouses and huge chimneys along its banks were indistinct; like impressionist paintings, they merged together. Birds sat on the water, still and silent as toys in an abandoned paddling pool. The water itself seemed frozen; only the effort Lacey needed to propel herself forward reminded her that it was, in fact, flowing out to sea rather quickly.

This! This was why she had to be out on the river at dawn. Swimming in the water, paddling over it — one way or another, this wasn't something she could miss.

She turned her head to see a small brown rat watching her from an outcrop of concrete. It nudged awake the fleeting memory of a dream that had all but faded. What had it been about? She never dreamed. Eyes watching. Eyes peering down at her. A sense that waking up was important.

Except, had those eyes looked down at her? Or in at her?

In at her. Through the small round window on the port side of the boat, the side that faced the open water. Well, that at least made some sense. She'd woken up in the mistaken belief that someone was swimming round the boat. She'd gone back to sleep — after a pretty eventful half-hour — and dreamed of a swimmer looking in at her.

Lacey realized that her paddling had slowed down, that the river was pushing her back and that she was closer to the bank than she'd planned. She braced herself for a big effort and caught sight of the long, thin strip of white fabric floating towards her.

No, no — oh, for God's sake, it was nothing. Just a strip of fabric attached to a loose piece of wood on the piling of the wall.

On the other hand, she was getting quite close to where she'd found the body yesterday, and if this was a piece of the shrouding that had worked its way loose, she probably should try to retrieve it. She struck out, aiming for the bank, hit it rather faster than she'd expected and grabbed at the fabric. It came loose immediately.

OK, not good. That was the embankment wall she'd just been pushed against.

She struck out hard and the river pushed her back against the slime-encrusted river wall. There was some sort of undercurrent keeping her close to the side. Realizing she was better off going with it for as long as she could to save energy, Lacey let the tide take her back downstream.

Well, this was just great. She'd been swimming perfectly safely for weeks, and as soon as Joesbury put his foot down it was all going wrong. There was probably a lesson there, but in the meantime she was in imminent danger of being sucked into a storm drain.

Except it wasn't a storm drain. It was actually another creek, albeit a very narrow one — far too narrow for motorized craft of any size. Little more than five feet wide, it disappeared between two tall buildings. One of the buildings jutted out into the river a couple of feet more than the other, effectively masking the creek from downstream. Even upstream, you'd hardly notice it unless you were this close.

A second later, Lacey had left the main river. Well, she had kept the canoe to go exploring.

The sense of being cut off from the world, which was always a feature of boating down Deptford Creek, was so much stronger here. Along this creek, tall buildings lined every inch of the banks. Windows in the lower storeys were black and empty; higher up they gleamed in the early sun like squares of gold. Some she passed were barred.

No sunlight made it down to the water. It swirled in dark shapes and shadows around her canoe, pushing her back, fighting her progress. In this narrow, confined space the water was faster and stronger than in her own creek. Were she to turn, or just give up paddling, it would sweep her back with force.

The buildings were changing. The grey of those closer to the Thames had given way to a softer red brick. They weren't as tall. Some of them had doors just above the waterline, and steps leading down to it. Mooring rings lay at intervals along the walls.

There was a sudden burst of light ahead of her. She was about to paddle past the last of the high buildings and in their place, on both sides of the creek, was a stone wall, not much more than two metres high.

The sudden influx of light did a lot to lift Lacey's spirits. And the channel was getting wider. Soon she'd be able to turn. Beyond the walls on both sides of the creek she could see trees. To her left was an orchard. By this time, she'd travelled about a quarter of a mile since leaving the Thames and was nearing the end of the channel. The fresh water that fed it was coming through a sluice.

A slipway ran from beneath large gates in the wall to her right and another boat bobbed against the bank. Of a similar size to her own, it was as different from it in style as could be imagined. The moored boat was made from wood. Its prow had been carved, like the sailing ships of old, into the shoulders and head of a woman with long, flowing hair. Carvings along its length looked like feathers. There were rowlocks, decoratively carved oars and a small outboard engine.

A smaller gate stood just beyond the wide ones, for pedestrian access, and a second narrow slipway led to the water's edge. Lacey pushed past the gates, catching a glimpse of a large stone house beyond the ornate ironwork. At the very end of the creek there seemed to be a turning circle. She spun the canoe and almost dropped her paddle in shock. In front of the narrow gate, which she was certain had been closed a second ago, sat a creature from a fairy tale.

19

Dana

'Right, thank you for coming in early,' said Dana. 'Help yourself to breakfast.'

The team had gathered in Dana's office at Lewisham police station. It wasn't a big room, but they were few in number. The woman in the river had died months ago, there was no real evidence of foul play and, until something changed, resources wouldn't be thrown at them. For now, they were five. Anderson and Stenning, of course, and two other detective constables. Gayle Mizon, a blonde in her early thirties, had taken the spare chair; Tom Barrett, the joker of the pack, his dark skin gleaming like polished walnut, leaned against the far wall with the other two men. All had other ongoing cases. Hence the early meeting.

'Thanks to Det— to PC Flint's prompt report, we know the woman found yesterday is not among those known to have gone

145

missing in the river over the last eighteen months.' Dana picked up her coffee. Mizon was tearing apart a croissant; the men had gone straight for the bacon and egg sandwiches. 'Lacey also went beyond the brief and produced a list of 102 young women, with a compatible ethnic background, who went missing in the UK over a similar period.'

'Girl can't help herself.' Anderson was talking through a mouthful of food. 'She'll be back before the year end.'

'Possibly.' Dana handed him the box of tissues she kept in her top drawer. 'But for now, we have to respect her decision. She's had a tough time of it this last year and she needs to get her head together. We take it from here. We go through this list, find the women in their late teens, early twenties. Contact the relevant forces, get photographs and DNA wherever possible. Tom, I want you to handle that, please.'

Barrett picked up a pot of yoghurt, pulled a face and put it down again. 'Roger that. And if she wasn't reported missing?'

'I'm asking Mr Weaver to fund a facial reconstruction,' said Dana. 'We can do a TV appeal, but it will take some time. I may as well be honest, though — without ID, there'll be very little we can do.'

'Have we ruled out an honour killing?' Mizon had finished her croissant and produced an apple from somewhere. Mizon was never without food.

'I heard there was a survey recently that said two-thirds of British Asians support the idea of honour killings,' said Barrett.

Dana shook her head. 'I read that, too. Just a bit more carefully than you did. What it actually said was that two-thirds of young British Asians support the idea of an honour code. Rather more worrying, I admit, was that around 20 per cent would endorse physical punishment for transgressors.'

'Transgressors being female,' said Mizon.

'So how widespread do we think it is in the UK?' asked Stenning.

'Estimates suggest around three thousand honour crimes per year, although it seems safe to assume there's a lot we don't know about,' said Dana. 'As to deaths, less than a dozen, but still more than anyone would want to see.'

'And an honour crime is . . . ?' asked Anderson.

'Beatings, even torture,' said Mizon. 'Keeping someone locked up, often without food or water. Denying them medical attention. Think of the worst atrocities you've seen inflicted upon abused and neglected children in this country. All of them can be applied to grown or nearly grown women from immigrant cultures who have no one to protect them and nowhere to turn.'

'What I don't need to tell you is that if this is an honour killing, we're unlikely to crack it quickly,' said Dana. 'It can take years to get a case to court. If the physical evidence has deteriorated, and that certainly seems to be the case here, then you're talking months of covert surveillance, cultivating family members, persuading them to turn on their own kin. You can even be looking at witness protection.'

'You know what, Boss? I'm not sure we have an honour killing anyway.' Anderson crumpled his sandwich wrapper. 'That was an elaborate preparation of the body. Who does that for someone who dishonoured the family?'

He threw the ball of cellophane at the bin. 'Victims of honour killings get dumped, don't they? That girl in Kent, wasn't she found in a ditch? If you value your female relatives so little you can put a pillow over their faces, you're not going to take any trouble over handling their remains respectfully.'

Anderson's aim was off. The cellophane lay several inches away from its target.

'But if it wasn't an honour killing,' said Mizon, 'then we have no idea what happened to her.'

Dana picked up the discarded food wrapping and dropped it in the bin. 'The one lead we can follow up is the shroud she was wrapped in. You still OK to work on that, Gayle?'

Mizon nodded. 'How happy are we to treat Lacey's finding of it as coincidence?'

Dana shook her head. 'I'm not. But I've spoken to the dive team who retrieved the corpse and the photographs have been examined at length. It's impossible to say for sure that she was tied to that wooden pile. It could have been coincidence, and do I need to repeat my point about Lacey needing time to get her head together? I do not want her freaked out over this. Let's just hope she stays out of the river from now on.'

20

Lacey

A woman, so old and crumpled that anyone might doubt her sex, were it not for the coral-pink blouse she wore and her very long, greying hair, was staring at Lacey. Her face was that of someone from a hot country who'd spent a lifetime in the sun, and her hands were liver-spotted and wrinkled. She sat in a wheelchair, perched at the top of the ramp, her legs hidden beneath a long, multi-coloured skirt.

'Hello,' she said.

'Hello,' replied Lacey, thinking, what now? Apologize for trespassing? Claim ignorance? Run for it?

'Have you come for breakfast?'

The tide was pulling Lacey back out of the creek. She was having to work hard not to go skimming past the unusually hospitable old lady.

'Thank you, but I was just exploring. I'm

sorry if —'

'I do a lot of that myself. Exploring.'

The woman looked as though getting in and out of her chair would be an effort.

'You'd better moor up.' The woman extended a long hand, with jewels on just about every finger, to point at an iron ring on the slipway. 'You've got about an hour before the water gets too low. There's a lock gate at the creek entrance. With the water this high, I expect you just paddled right over it.'

Well, sometimes you just had to go with the flow. Lacey reached the bank and leaned forward to tie up the canoe, conscious all the while of the woman's gaze on her. Once the canoe was secure, she glanced down at the piece of fabric that had led her here in the first place and realized that it was nothing like the bandages or the sheet that had wrapped the corpse yesterday. This was a man-made fabric, not even white, but a faded pink pattern. A woman's headscarf. She got out of the canoe, noticing the house sign on the wall by the gates. *Sayes Court.*

'I'm Thessa,' the old woman announced once Lacey was on shore. 'Short for something very long and Greek. And you're . . . ?' She waggled long, curving fingernails that were painted pink to match her blouse.

'I'm Lacey. It's very nice to meet you, Thessa.'

'Come on.' Thessa spun round and pushed herself up the ramp at speed, and with a strength that suggested she wasn't nearly as frail as she appeared. Lacey followed and stepped into a buzzing mass of colour.

The garden was large by London standards and laid out as parkland, grassed and interspersed with trees.

Both sides of the path were lined with the slender silver-green leaves and purple buds of lavender bushes. In front of the lavender were tiny white flowers, gleaming like stars against a background of deep green. Beyond it were taller plants that bloomed deep pink, with leaves so huge they wouldn't have looked out of place in a rainforest. Bees and butterflies were everywhere.

'Leave the gate,' called Thessa.

Lacey picked up her pace so that she and the old lady were almost side by side. 'Is this your house, Thessa?'

'Yes,' Thessa replied. 'Been in the family for generations. That's what you're supposed to say, isn't it? Not true, of course. We were dirty immigrants who got lucky and made a pile.'

The house they were approaching looked Georgian, with two main storeys and a series of gabled attic windows. Stretching along most of the back wall was a conservatory.

'This is where I work,' said Thessa, charging in through the open door. 'Come in.'

If I'm offered gingerbread, I'm out of here, Lacey told herself, as she stepped inside the building and the wall of heat hit her like a furnace blast.

Lined along the glass house's central table, set low to accommodate Thessa's wheelchair, were trays of young plants. Others grew from baskets suspended from the ceiling. Around the walls were low counters, similarly filled with plants, except where they'd been cleared as work-stations. Lacey saw knives, scissors, string, pestles and mortars, weighing scales. Beneath the counters were wooden chests with small drawers, each labelled in a handwriting she'd struggle to decipher.

'I'm a herbalist,' announced Thessa. 'What will you have to drink? Elderflower cordial? Damson? Hemlock? . . . Just kidding. The damson wasn't very good last year . . . Still kidding.'

Lacey made a mental note to keep the open door between herself and this strange woman.

'It's too hot for you in here. Come on

through.'

Not sure whether it was a good idea, but strangely compelled, Lacey followed Thessa into a room that wasn't quite a kitchen, but not quite anything else either. There were crude wooden worktops, two huge Belfast sinks and several large fridges, all but one of which appeared to be locked.

To one side of the sinks was a row of tall glass bottles, each containing liquid of a different colour. 'We'll try that one, I think, Lacey,' said Thessa. 'Third from the left. You'll find a jug in the cupboard under the sink and ice in the fridge. The tap water's fine, there's a filter built into it.'

'Elderberry,' said Lacey, reading the label.

'Picked them myself last September. That's the last bottle till the autumn. Now, about an inch in the bottom of the jug, then fill with water. Come on, or you'll miss the tide. I love that, don't you? Miss the tide! Sounds like we're seafaring folk of old, off on adventures to the far side of the world. That's it, not too weak.'

Thinking that, sometimes, eccentrics just had to be humoured, Lacey opened the unlocked fridge and found it full of more bottles, tubs and jars, all labelled in Thessa's sprawling, difficult handwriting. As she added ice to the jug, she saw Thessa rummaging around in several of the drawers. The elderberry cordial, thick and purple in the bottle, turned the palest shade of mauve when she added water.

'To be honest, the wild cherry is a little sweeter,' said Thessa. 'Tray on top of the fridge, glasses in the cupboard nearest the door. And everyone likes the bilberry. But there is something rather special about the elderberry. Seems right for your first visit. OK, if we're done, we'll go outside again. Wagons roll.'

There was a short ramp between the kitchen and greenhouse and Thessa sped down it with glee, spinning her wheels at the last second to avoid hurtling into the glass walls. She went out through a side door.

When Lacey followed, she found herself in a sun-trap. Walled on two sides by the stone of the house and the glass of the conservatory, the paved area faced south-east and Lacey could see across the garden, through the iron gates, down to the creek. The area was filled with the scent of flowers.

'What can I smell?' she asked, as Thessa positioned herself at a small cast-iron table.

'Thyme. The wheels of my chair crush it and release the scent. Come and sit down.'

155

Lacey looked down to see that plants grew along every crack between the paving stones. Some looked like wild daisies, with long, rangy stems and yellow-tipped white flowers. Mostly, though, they were a shrub-like plant, with tiny green leaves and pink or purple flowers. Then different smells took over. Lacey recognized one as lavender; she wasn't sure about the other, but it was making her think of roast lamb.

'Those are chives.' Thessa was pointing towards long thin leaves and a mass of purple flowers. 'I don't crush those. They smell of onions.'

'So what's so special about elderberry?' Lacey sat, wondering if she were really going to drink a homemade brew offered by this strange woman.

Thessa leaned forward in her chair. Her dark eyes weren't brown, as Lacey had thought at first, but the deepest possible shade of blue. 'The elder is one of the most important plants in herbalism. It's like a whole medicine chest in one plant. On the other hand — and this is what intrigues me the most — it's almost universally feared.' She sat upright again and looked round the garden warily.

You old ham, thought Lacey.

The old ham was on a roll. 'Few plants

feature more in legend and folklore than the elder. They used to say that if you were standing near a tree at midnight on Midsummer night, you would see the Faery King ride by. That's tonight, by the way. And almost bound to happen, the moment of the solstice being exactly a minute before midnight.'

'I'll look out for him.' Lacey smiled as she thought of Joesbury in the guise of the Faery King.

'You should.' Thessa had a perfectly straight face. 'I swear that man gets more beautiful with every passing decade.'

'So what are its medicinal properties?'

'Guards against infection. Very good for flu and colds, and helps relieve coughs.'

'I have neither cough nor cold,' said Lacey, 'but I appreciate the thought.'

'You're coming down with both,' announced Thessa. 'Your voice is hoarser than it naturally is, your breathing is shallow, meaning the bottom of your chest isn't working properly because it's fighting off an infection, and you've sniffed four times since you've been here. I bet you're also more tired than usual and your chest feels a bit heavy.'

Complete rubbish. Except, 'I've not been sleeping well lately,' admitted Lacey.

'You haven't been sleeping well for years, not since the great sorrow, whatever that was. Don't tell me, dear, we don't know each other nearly well enough for that yet. But I can give you something.'

She reached into her pocket and pulled out three small bottles.

'Hawthorn tincture.' Thessa twisted the lid from the first and tipped three drops into the jug. 'Made in two stages: from the flowers and the leaves in spring, and then by adding the berries in the autumn. Excellent for the heart and circulation, which you don't need, but also for calming and reducing anxiety, which you certainly do. It also helps with bad dreams and insomnia.'

Elderberry and hawthorn? Didn't sound too bad. If that's what they really were.

'This is linden.' Thessa opened the second bottle and added it to the jug, like the first. 'You might know it as lime. Not the citrus fruit — the English tree. This is made from the flowers. It soothes irritation, boosts the immune system and helps you relax and sleep.'

'I'll be falling asleep by midday,' said Lacey. Not that she had any plans to drink the stuff.

'This last one is mugwort. Not a pretty name, but a very good herb for us women.

It's been used for centuries in healing and magic. It's known as a protector of women and travellers.'

The tops back on the three bottles, Thessa lifted the jug and poured the drink into Lacey's glass and then her own. 'Mugwort's good for female problems. Not that I can see any sign of those, but it's a good all-round tonic. Let's see how you get on with these three. You can take them home with you.' She slid the bottles across the table to Lacey.

'That's very kind, but —'

'Drink up.'

Thessa nodded at Lacey's glass, where the cordial that might or might not be elder-berry had gained the addition of nine drops of heaven only knew what. Was this how dreadful things happened, then? Out of politeness?

'Oh, for heaven's sake!'

Quick as a flash, Thessa picked up her own glass and downed half of it. Then she set it down on the table and looked expectantly at Lacey.

'I'm sorry to be rude,' said Lacey. 'But you are a little unusual and I've never come across a — Oh my God, what's wrong?'

She was up out of her seat, bending over Thessa, who had convulsed in her chair before her head had fallen on to her chest. The old woman was shaking, her arms jerking at her sides, odd croaking noises coming from her throat.

'Thessa, don't be ridiculous,' said a male voice from the doorway of the house.

Lacey spun round to see a tall, dark-haired man in his early sixties watching them with an expression on his face that said he'd seen it all before and it never got any funnier. She looked back at Thessa, who was upright again, grinning.

'Gotcha!' she said to Lacey.

'What is she giving you?' The man had stepped outside and taken a seat beside Lacey. He'd brought his own glass.

'Umm . . . elderberry, hawthorn, lime and mugwort, I think,' said Lacey.

The man shrugged, pulled a face, then poured himself a glass.

He drank and smiled at Lacey. 'I'm Alex. Thessa's brother. Delighted to meet you.'

'Lacey Flint,' she said, to the man with heavy eyebrows and a dark complexion who, at first glance, looked nothing like Mrs Nutty in the wheelchair. He was wearing neatly pressed trousers and an open-necked button-down shirt.

'How novel to have a visitor arriving by boat,' he said. 'Although I rather like it. Puts me in mind of the old days, when the rivers around London were the main means of transport.'

'I live on one of the boats in Deptford Creek.' Lacey picked up her glass and risked a sip. 'We all have canoes or small motor boats. But somebody here has a boat as well.'

'That's Thessa's,' said Alex. 'I've been trying to persuade her that going out on to the Thames is ridiculously irresponsible, but she hasn't listened to me in sixty years and I doubt she'll start now.'

The cordial was rich and sweet, not dissimilar to blackcurrant, but not so sharp. Lacey drank most of the glassful in one.

'A lot of the plants I need grow along the river's edge,' said Thessa. 'Quite a lot of them in Deptford Creek. And I have very strong arms. When your legs are useless, your other parts have to compensate. And there's always the engine if things get hairy. Do you know those skanky old lesbians on that naval ship at Skillions?'

Lacey glanced at Alex. He gave a small shrug as if to say, *don't look at me.*

'Well, I've not heard them referred to in precisely those terms, but I'm aware of two women in their middle years at Skillions Wharf,' she said eventually. 'My neighbour says they used to be actresses.'

'The overweight blonde was a stripper,' said Thessa. 'The butch one was her pimp.'

'Did they empty their septic tank when you were paddling past?' asked Lacey, making Alex snort into his drink. When he stopped spluttering, he glanced at his watch. 'You have twenty minutes to get out of our creek, Lacey, or you'll be spending the day with us.'

Lacey stood up. 'Well, that sounds lovely, but I do have to get to work this afternoon. Thank you very much for the drink.'

'And the tinctures.' Thessa was pressing the three small bottles into Lacey's hands. 'Three drops of each, twice a day.'

'Is that an English accent, Lacey?' asked Alex, as the three of them set off down the flower-lined path towards the creek. A bee settled on Thessa's pink blouse and she let it sit just below her shoulder like a decorative pin. 'You have a lilt in your voice that I can't quite place.'

'I'm from Shropshire,' said Lacey. 'Very close to the Welsh border. People occasionally tell me I sound Welsh.'

'And what do you do?'

'I'm a police officer,' said Lacey. 'I recently joined the Marine Unit.'

'Then I must ask you a great favour. When

you see my sister out in that ridiculous boat of hers, arrest her.'

Thessa giggled in a way that was almost flirtatious. Then she actually started whispering to the bee on her breast.

'Well, I'm hardly setting the best example,' said Lacey. 'But if you avoid the fast tides and stay close to the bank, it's not too dangerous.'

'Not for a healthy young person, maybe,' said Alex. 'But for a mad old woman in her sixties? I suppose I shouldn't complain. If she goes under, I inherit all her money.'

'Changed my will last week,' said Thessa. 'I'm leaving everything to the dogs' home.'

'The canines themselves will handle it more responsibly than you do. Goodbye, Lacey. It was a pleasure meeting you.'

'Come back next Thursday,' said Thessa. 'The herbs need a week to have an impact. But if you just want to chat, come any time.'

Lacey climbed into her canoe and untied the rope. Gallantly, Alex bent low and gave her a gentle push into the centre of the creek.

'Goodbye,' she called, as the returning tide pulled her back towards the Thames. She looked back just before turning the corner. Thessa and her brother were still on the creek side. Alex had crouched down to the same level as his sister and they were deep in conversation. Lacey wondered how she could ever have thought them unalike. From this distance, talking intently as they were, they looked like mirror images of each other.

21

Dana

'The practice of shrouding a body before burial is common to just about every religion and culture,' said Mizon from her place at the front of the room. 'There's even evidence of native North American tribes weaving shrouds out of vegetable material.'

Dana reached up and pulled the window blind shut. A little past noon, the sun had moved round to their side of the building and the temperature was climbing high. In the meeting room were Neil Anderson, Pete Stenning, Tom Barrett and Gayle Mizon. Her inner circle.

Thorough as always, Mizon had projected several images of bodies shrouded for death on to the white screen behind her: grief-stricken nuns carrying a long, thin parcel; the wan face of a child before his head was finally covered; row upon row of white bundles laid out on a tiled floor.

'However people choose to dispose of their dead,' she was saying, 'there will be some ritualistic element to the preparation of the body and that will nearly always include a symbolic washing and then a shrouding.'

'My dad was buried in his best suit,' said Barrett.

'That's become quite common in Western cultures,' Mizon agreed. 'But only recently. Shrouding goes back to the days when clothes were expensive. By putting the deceased into a shroud, the family were freeing up a suit of clothes for another family member.'

Stenning was holding a Coke can against the back of his neck. 'So, does the way she was shrouded give us any clue about her background?'

Two faint, parallel lines had appeared between Mizon's brows. 'That's where it gets a bit trickier. From what I can gather, what we saw really isn't typical of any recognized funeral etiquette.'

'How do you mean?' asked Dana.

Mizon glanced at her notes. 'Jewish burial clothes are called Tachrichim. A tunic, trousers, belt, and a hood and scarf to cover the head. Then the whole body gets wrapped in another large piece of cloth that is effectively the shroud. The Jewish tradition dictates that everyone is equal in death. So Jewish burial clothes wouldn't have zips, buttons, fasteners, or any ornamentation. No pockets, either, because personal possessions have no place in the afterlife.'

'Not Jewish then,' said Anderson.

'Not typically Muslim either,' said Mizon. 'Muslim burial cloths are known as Kafan. Three pieces of cloth for a man, five for a woman. They're not clothes as such, just large pieces of very simple cloth that wrap set parts of the body in a prescribed order. Again, modesty in death is important.'

'Hindus use clothes too,' said Dana, 'with one large sheet to cover the whole body. My mother was cremated in her wedding dress. Which was red, by the way. Of course, all this doesn't mean the victim wasn't Muslim or Jewish or Hindu, just that her body wasn't disposed of in a religiously orthodox manner.'

'People were saying the body was mummified,' said Barrett.

'No,' said Dana. 'Though the way it was trussed up did give that impression. Can you find those first photographs, Gayle?'

They waited while Mizon found the photographs of the corpse taken by the Marine Unit, and then Dana stood and walked closer to the screen.

'You can see that whilst the fabric has largely come away from the upper part of the body, the lower body is still mainly wrapped.' Dana used a pencil to point to the image. 'And if you look around the feet and calves, and then the waist, it does look a little like a mummy, but the way this woman's been wrapped is actually quite different to the Egyptian process.'

'How exactly?' asked Anderson.

Dana nodded at Mizon to explain. 'An Egyptian mummy would be completely wrapped in bandages,' Mizon said. 'Each individual limb, even each finger and toe, would be wrapped separately. You'd be talking hundreds of yards of fabric. On this woman, the bandages were just at certain points — ankles, waist, neck.'

'So, if there's no real link with customs in Islam, Hinduism or Judaism, what about Christianity?' asked Anderson.

'Similar, but not quite,' said Mizon. 'If you've seen images of the shroud of Turin, you'll know it was a piece of fabric just wide enough to cover a body but at least twice the body's length. It would have been fastened in place by some means, quite possibly long thin strips of the same fabric. What we have is one very wide strip of fabric and several much thinner ones that were used to tie the main shroud in place.'

'So, however she died, her body was prepared for burial by someone from a Christian tradition,' said Dana.

Mizon shook her head. 'I'm not sure I'd say that either. Certainly not one of the more contemporary branches because, as Tom points out, Christians these days typically dress their dead in normal clothes. On the other hand, Orthodox Christian burial shrouds are quite ornate.'

Several pictures of shrouds appeared on the screen. They showed arches, the sun's rays, the holy cross, Christian icons, even a resurrection scene.

'No one wanting to conceal a suspicious death would use one of those though,' Dana pointed out. 'They'd be too easy to trace.'

'True,' said Mizon. 'To be honest, Ma'am, I don't think the means of wrapping this corpse was about religious observation.'

'What then?'

Mizon switched the screen off, as though rejecting all the information she'd just shown them. Or maybe she was just getting too hot. 'Some killers display their corpses and some conceal them, isn't that right?'

Stenning's head lifted. 'Those who display them are proud of what they've done. They want us to find them.'

Mizon nodded. 'Conversely, those who don't are ashamed.'

'This woman was wrapped up like a parcel, weighted down and dropped into one of the biggest, deepest rivers in the world.' Anderson, too, was looking more alert. 'I'd say that puts our killer in the ashamed camp.'

'Deeply ashamed,' Mizon agreed. 'I know you don't like us to jump to conclusions too early, Ma'am, but I'd say the shrouding and the dumping in the Thames are about concealment. In other words, shame. I think the bandages were just to make sure the shroud stayed in place. A burial in the ground wouldn't need them, but one in fast-moving water would be much less stable. I think the bandages were to maintain the shroud — in other words, the concealment.'

'So the shrouding gives us no pointers to the killer's background?' asked Dana.

'I didn't say that,' said Mizon. 'He didn't use a couple of bin-liners, fastened tight with parcel tape. The linen suggests a culture that treats its dead with respect. I think our killer is probably someone from an Eastern background, one more domi-nated by religious beliefs and practices than the Western world.'

'I'll tell you what's worrying me more.' Even Barrett was excited now. It took a lot to get him fired up. 'It wasn't driven by panic. It was planned. Careful. It was like —'

Dana never normally stole thunder from a team member. This time, though, she couldn't help herself. 'Like they'd done it before,' she said.

22

Nadia

The sun was low in the sky and Nadia walked quickly. She'd had to queue for the showers, making her late leaving the pool. She'd promised to be back by six because that was when they were leaving and Gabrielle needed the sunscreen.

'You wouldn't mind popping into Boots on the way back, would you?' Always it was the same. 'Can you drop by Sainsbury's? Can you pop into the Body Shop? Can you stop off at Majestic and pick up some wine?' As though Gabrielle felt a continual need to remind Nadia that time off wasn't a right, merely borrowed and subject to being reclaimed at any time.

The class had been busy. She was becoming one of the better ones. The one the instructor sometimes turned to when she needed a demonstration.

'Elbow out of the water first, then stretch

the arm out. You use less energy and move faster. Watch Nadia.'

She could swim front crawl now, with her head in the water, coming up intermittently to breathe and moving at speed. Who would have believed it, months ago, when she could barely manage a panic-stricken dog-like stroke?

Muslim women did not swim. Apart from the few who learned as children, or the very rich with their private swimming pools. It was unthinkable for a Muslim woman to remove her clothes in a public place. But the local authority in Greenwich offered women-only sessions at the local leisure centre, and for two hours a week the pool became a haven for the Islamic or the modest.

It had been one of the hardest things Nadia had ever done, to lower herself into water for the first time. Memories had come raging back: water all around, in her nose, her mouth, her throat. Her chest in agony as burning liquid poured into her lungs. A certainty that she would die, here and now.

It had taken long, long minutes to convince herself that the terror and physical pain were caused by memories, not by anything happening to her at that moment. For most of the first lesson she'd been unable to leave the side, but she'd made herself go back a second and a third time, until getting into water no longer filled her with dread. She'd made herself learn to swim, because she'd known that one day, she and the river would meet again.

As she walked past the box that distributed free newspapers, Nadia automatically scanned the headlines, looking for words she recognized. She'd heard nothing about the body of the woman pulled from the river at dawn yesterday beyond a brief piece on the evening news. The police feared the woman would be difficult to identify and were appealing for help. A young woman, they thought, possibly from the Middle East or the Indian subcontinent, missing for between two and six months. Anyone with any information was encouraged to contact the police.

She didn't have any information.

In the busy shop on the high street she found the sunscreen. 'Be sure to get factor 50,' Gabrielle had said. 'You have to take into account the effect of the sun bouncing off the water.'

It wasn't unusual to pull a body from the Thames, Gabrielle had told her. Most didn't even make it on to the news, just the ones needing identification, or those who'd drowned in suspicious circumstances. Only when the police were appealing for information.

She didn't have any information. She had to get back.

23

Dana

'Helen, it's like shopping on eBay. Only without pictures.'

'Hang on, let me find the same site. OK, I'm logging on.'

Dana closed her eyes and pictured Helen in her home office in Dundee. She'd have taken off the suit she'd have been wearing all day, would be in jeans, or maybe jogging clothes.

With a sudden need to see Helen's face, Dana reached behind her, found the framed photograph that she kept on the bookshelf and placed it just to the left of the monitor. She'd taken it herself — Helen in the garden, not long back from a run. Long blonde hair messy, face red and damp, and a light in her eyes that seemed to say something different every time Dana looked at the picture. Sometimes this picture calmed her when the tightness in her chest was starting to hurt. Not always. 'How was the flight?' she asked.

'Busy,' replied Helen. 'Right, London Sperm Bank. Christ, it's a whole new world, isn't it?'

The London Sperm Bank was a central bank of donated sperm that supplied most of the fertility clinics in London and the South-East. Since accessing its website, Dana had been getting flashbacks to a brief period in her life, years ago, when after inheriting money she'd almost become a shopping addict. Online sales had been the worst, with the impression they gave of there being only a limited time to find and grab the best bargains. She'd get hot and jumpy as a caffeine addict, flicking from one screen to the next, spending recklessly and unable to stop. She hadn't had this feeling in years. 'Find the page where you select a donor,' she told Helen.

'I'm there. Oh my God, you actually have a trolley. It says my trolley is currently empty. Well, I suppose, in a way —'

'Will you focus for a second?' Dana waited for Helen to catch up, her eyes tennis-balling from the photograph of her partner to the drop-down list of men who could father her child. Each entry was identified by a simple icon of a male figure and accompanied by the most basic of details: race, sometimes nationality, eye colour, hair colour, height, skin tone, education and, occasionally, religion. The icons were in different colours. So, did she want a fondant-pink, citrus-yellow or lime-green donor? Helen in the picture was amused, not taking it seriously.

'I cannot choose the father of my child — of our child — on the basis of this information,' Dana said, when Helen in real life was finally looking at the same screen. 'These guys could be child molesters, drug-pushers. They might hang around at Waterloo station on Sunday mornings taking down train numbers. God help us, they might play golf.'

'Just as long as none of them are ginger.'

Silence. And the photograph had that look she always hated, that *So-I've-made-a-joke-at-your-expense,-get-over-it* look. Dana wondered if she might be about to cry. 'We're supposed to be able to pick the father of our children,' she said. 'We choose the man we most love and admire in the whole world and if we're lucky he feels the same way and we make a family together. Other women' (*normal women,* said the voice in the back of her head) 'spend years making this decision. They have a world of data available. I — we — have fewer than a dozen words.'

'It's what we signed up for, hon,' said Helen.

'Did you know that the starfish is one of the few species in the world that can reproduce asexually?'

Silence. She could picture Helen taking a deeper breath, bracing herself to deal with Dana-being-difficult. Sure enough, Helen in the picture was doing the *I'll-keep-my-temper-if-it-kills-me* face.

'Fascinating,' real Helen said. 'But pending the invention of cloning technology, I think we have to be pragmatic. We know these guys are screened for any health issues.'

'Oh, they're screened within an inch of their lives,' said Dana. 'I'm surprised any of them make it through.'

'They also have to have a GP's consent, so if there were any mental-health problems, or even persistent criminal behaviour, we could expect it to be picked up,' Helen continued, speaking slowly, as though to a rather stupid child.

'I guess.'

'And given that remuneration is pretty stingy in the UK, we have to assume their motives are reasonably altruistic.'

'Seems fair.'

'OK, so these are a bunch of healthy, decent guys who are prepared to put themselves through considerable inconvenience, not to mention embarrassment, in order to help others. We could do a lot worse.'

And that was why she loved her. Helen caught her when she was falling. She saw what was important. 'Now let's filter out any who don't have at least a bachelor's degree,' she was saying now, ever the practical one.

Dana smiled at the photograph that had transformed back into what it normally was: a picture of a wise, warm woman.

'OK, how about Donor 68? Dark-brown hair, brown eyes, 1.78 metres, medium skin tone, postgraduate degree.'

'He's Scottish,' said Dana, looking at the blue icon.

'Perfect,' said Helen.

24

Lacey

'Hard to starboard . . . Bloody hell, woman, slow down . . . No, you missed it. OK, take her round . . . No, reverse won't work against the tide. Take her round . . . Bloody women drivers.'

'No disrespect, Sarge, but back-seat drivers are worse. I've got it.'

'OK, ease back on the gas, tad to port, hold her steady and . . . Yes, well done, Finn.'

Great. Against a fast-moving tide, in rapidly disappearing light, she'd pulled the launch up alongside a piece of floating debris and held it steady for several seconds. Turner, on the other hand, who'd done nothing more than stretch out one overlong arm and lift it out with a boat hook, got the credit. Sighing audibly, Lacey put the engine into neutral.

'*Marine Central. Can you confirm your loca-*

tion, please?'

Wilson leaned across Lacey and spoke into the mike, giving their location as just up-stream of Tower Bridge. 'Go ahead, MP,' he told the call dispatch centre at Lambeth. Inside Lacey, anxiety started nibbling. They were practically at the end of the shift. She didn't want to be delayed, not tonight, not when someone might be waiting for her back at the boat. What was it, a minute before midnight, when the Faery King appeared?

'We've been getting reports of a small, unlit craft, heavily occupied, proceeding up-stream in the region of the Blackwall Pier. Suspected illegal immigrants on board. You are asked to find and hail. Marine Lower unable at present. Local police informed. Proceed with care.'

'Take the port bow,' Wilson told Turner, heading for the fly bridge. 'Lacey, once I'm up there, you go on starboard. I want you both clipped on.'

With a sinking feeling — they were unlikely to finish on time now — Lacey hooked her safety line on to the base of a stanchion.

'Hold tight,' called the sergeant.

Travelling with both tide and current, an unpowered craft would move fast; the Targa flew across the surface of the river. They bounced as they hit higher waves and spray

182

soared up around them, sparkling like crystals in the boat's lights. Warm waves of air buffeted Lacey's face as the elegant columns and domed towers of the old Greenwich hospital grew closer with every wave they cut through. As Lacey's hair started to come loose, she turned her head to tuck it back in place and saw a tiny light at water level on the south bank. She wobbled, almost overbalanced, and grabbed the guard-rail. The light was still there, and just the faintest outline of something moving against the bank.

As they neared the entrance to the docks, Wilson cut back the engine, keeping it low and quiet, revving just enough to hold them in the river. To the port side of the boat, where Turner was keeping a lookout, there were lights and bustle. The docks on the Isle of Dogs never really shut down for the night. To starboard, though, it was a different story. Lacey looked across the water to where the Millennium Dome glowed orange and gold, its upright supports gleaming like hot metal. The area around it was largely in darkness.

'I think we've been here before, Lacey,' said Wilson, in a voice just loud enough to carry down to his two juniors. 'Stay on board this time, won't you?'

Lacey smiled, acknowledging the private joke, the reference to the previous autumn, the night she'd met Sergeant Wilson. She'd been invited by Joesbury to take a river trip with his uncle Fred and his crew. It was supposed to be a chance for her to get her nerve back on the river after a near drowning. Instead they'd been thrown into a chase for a dinghy with four occupants, three men and a girl, trying to enter the country illegally. The immigrants' boat had overturned and all four had gone into the water. So had Lacey. It had been a thoughtless, reckless act, and she'd been in serious trouble over it. But she'd probably saved the girl's life.

'Happy to stay dry tonight, Sarge,' she called up.

The boat fell silent as they held their position. Lacey tried not to look at her watch too often.

'We've missed them, haven't we?' said Turner eventually.

'Almost certainly,' replied Wilson. 'Ah well, better go through the motions, I suppose.' He turned the boat, heading for the docks.

'Sarge?'

Wilson eased back on the throttle and peered down at Lacey.

'Just a thought,' she said. 'But what are our chances of finding them in the docks?'

'Bugger all of nothing,' said Wilson. 'They'll have tied up and scarpered.'

Lacey hesitated for a second. Did she really want to go down this route?

'So we don't have much to lose if we try something different?' she said, mentally kicking herself even as the words came out.

Over the roof of the cabin, Turner was watching her with interest. 'Does this involve getting wet? Because I've heard the rumours about you.'

'Ditto.' Lacey didn't take her eyes off the sergeant. 'Suppose I said that on the way here, I saw a small light and movement over near the south bank, just in front of the naval college. Would it be the end of the world if we went to take a look and didn't find anything?'

Wilson was silent for a second, no doubt calculating the time it would take for a small-engined craft to make its way around the curves of the south bank. 'It's going to take twice as long to get back if we're hugging the south bank,' he said.

It was a good point. And she'd done her duty by suggesting it. When the men decided to go straight back, she wouldn't be the one to argue.

'Nice night for it,' said Turner.

Trust her to pick the one night he didn't have a date.

With a heavy sigh, Wilson turned the boat round in the river and drove directly south until they were close to the bank just in front of the naval college.

'I'm in your hands, Lacey,' he said. 'What's the plan?'

It was her own fault; nothing to do but give it her best shot. 'They can't have gone much further up-river. There just wasn't time. So they'll be somewhere close. They'll know we're here and that we can outrun them, so I'm guessing they're clinging close to the bank, trying to sneak past us. So we have to go in after them.'

'I'm finding this plan strangely exciting,' said Turner.

'They may even have tried to pull up on a beach,' said Lacey. 'If there are any cars around Greenwich town centre, they could usefully go on standby.'

As Wilson spoke into the radio, Lacey joined Turner on the port bow. He crouched beside her and they peered into the gloom beneath the river walls.

'I'm not running this boat aground, Lacey,' said Wilson. 'You two will have to keep your eyes peeled.'

Slowly, the Targa made its way up-river. No one spoke. The grandeur of the Regency buildings fell away and as they steered around Greenwich pier Lacey and Turner leaned out over the water, searching its depths.

'There's a police car on Thames Street,' said Wilson. 'Just waiting for instructions. As am I, incidentally.'

'Can you cut the engine for a second, Sarge?' asked Turner.

'Not for long,' said Wilson, as the engine died. 'What is it?'

Turner held his forefinger up to his lips. 'What's the depth here?'

Wilson glanced at the instrument panel. 'Metre and a half. Not enough. If I run this thing aground I'll never hear the end of it.'

'Lacey, you got the light?'

Lacey held the torch close to her chest, watching Turner's face. 'What've you seen?' she asked.

He didn't reply, but his eyes didn't leave the south bank.

'They'll be looking for a ladder,' he said. 'They're closer than we are, so they'll see it sooner. Sarge, is there any chance you can —'

'No.'

'Is there a reason you're no longer clipped

187

to the boat?' Lacey asked Turner.

'I'm relying on you for light in the right place at the right time,' he replied. 'And possibly a brisk rub-down in a warm room later.'

'Dream —' Lacey began.

'Ten o'clock.' Turner jumped to his feet and over the side.

'What the bugger!' Wilson pulled the boat into reverse, clearly terrified at the thought of catching one of his officers in the propeller. 'Lacey, where is he? Get that light on him.'

'Keep the light on the wall!' shouted Turner from somewhere in the water. Lacey flicked the beam on to him, making sure he was on his feet and moving forward, then aimed it back at the wall, where she was pretty sure at least one dark-clad figure was trying to climb up from the beach. She found Turner again, just steps away from the shore, and shone the beam at the water's edge to give him something to aim at. Then up at the wall again. More than one figure trying to climb the ladder.

Behind her, she could hear Wilson on the radio, informing the car up on Thames Street that one — two — possibly more suspects were climbing the river-wall and would appear just east of the Victoria and

Norway Wharf.

'One male, one female,' called Lacey, watching dark hair fly out around the head of a slender form. A much bigger person was already over the wall. 'Female is young, Asian, at a guess. Second male on the ladder now. Older. White, medium height. That's three suspects.'

Turner was running across the beach. He reached the ladder and sprang up it, practically leaping over the small day-boat tied to one of the lower rungs. He was at the top a second after the third suspect cleared it.

'Police! Stay where you are!' they heard him yell.

'Be bloody careful up there!' shouted Wilson, before informing Call Dispatch that one of his officers was chasing suspects in a southerly direction away from the — 'He's got him. Hold that light steady, Lacey. Suspect apprehended at the Victoria and Norway Wharf by a Marine Unit officer who is bloody lucky not to be floating out into the North Sea right now. Can we have some assistance, please? Bloody kids'll be the death of me. Two more suspects on the loose. One Asian male, one Asian female. Assistance would be appreciated.'

'He's got back-up, Sarge,' said Lacey. 'He's OK.'

On the embankment, two uniformed officers had come to Turner's aid. The suspect
was pushed to the ground and cuffed.

'Well done, Lacey,' said Wilson.

'Finn's the one we have to thank.'

'Silly bugger needn't think he's coming
back on this boat. He can soak a patrol car.'

25

Pari

'I think of you when the first snow falls,
I think of you when the last star fades.
You are my strength, you are my kindness,
Never leave, oh never leave my heart.'

Pari wasn't sure whether she was awake or
not. Her mother had sung that song for as
long as she could remember, had probably
sung it over her cradle when she'd been a
baby, had sung it as she'd cleaned other
women's houses, as she'd baked bread, as
she'd sat and watched the sun sink below
the rooftops of the city.

The song of a woman in her middle years,
pining for the village boy she'd left behind,
her lost love. The daftest song imaginable.
Because women from Pari's country didn't
fall in love. They couldn't afford to. Her
countrywomen, the lucky ones, married an

honest, kind man and learned affection for him.

She'd been dreaming, of course. Dreaming of her mother again, of home. Except she was awake now. She could see the dark room around her, feel the sweat at her temples, between her breasts. And somewhere, outside her room, maybe below her on the water, someone was singing a folksong from home.

26

Lacey

It was decided to be impractical to get Constable Turner back on board the Targa. He would accompany the land team back to Greenwich police station, where the apprehended suspect would be held overnight and interviewed in the morning.

When Wilson and Lacey arrived back at Wapping, Chief Inspector Cook was waiting for them. Lacey felt an uncomfortable tug of nerves in her stomach. The boss was never usually here at this hour.

'Can I have a word, Fred?' He turned to Lacey, apparently having second thoughts. 'You too, love,' he said uncharacteristically. 'Come on down.'

Lacey followed both men into Chief Inspector Cook's office at the front of the building.

'I had a phone call half an hour ago.' Cook leaned back against his desk. 'Scotland Yard are keeping it under wraps for as long as possible, but it can only be a matter of time before it gets out.'

Wilson and Lacey sat in the easy chairs Cook kept in his office.

'There was an incident in Catford early this morning,' Cook went on quickly. 'A couple of green young coppers tried to arrest some suspects wanted in connection with terrorism offences. Silly buggers should have waited for back-up. One of them got shot in the chest. He died an hour ago.'

'What's that got to do with us?' asked Wilson.

Lacey already knew.

'The other constable recognized the shooter. He's been working with him for the last three months. A uniformed sergeant at Catford, supposedly.'

Lacey tried to remember how far away the lavatories were, and whether she'd make it there before she threw up. Cook handed Wilson a photograph.

'Sergeant Mick Jackson,' he told him. Lacey didn't need to look. She knew the alias Joesbury used on undercover jobs.

'He was undercover,' she said, to no one in particular. 'Pretending to be a bent copper.'

'Undercover or not, you don't shoot a fellow officer.' Cook's look of sympathy had gone now. 'The two arresting officers weren't armed. I'm sorry, both of you, but there's a warrant out for Mark Joesbury's arrest.'

27

Lacey

Lacey walked across the yard, alert to any sign of movement, any hint that someone might be waiting in the shadows.

The tide was out. Some time in the last couple of hours, her boat had settled in the mud, making that sound, somewhere between a squelch and a sigh. She always liked to hear it in the middle of the night, found it soothing, restful. Next time, though, it might sound like someone suffocating.

He'd shot someone? Killed a young constable who'd had the nerve to attempt an arrest? And this just hours before showing up on her boat? Had she missed him washing the blood off his hands?

She had a long climb down to the first boat. It was late, not far off midnight. All the lights were out on this boat and the next.

There was no coming back, not when you killed a fellow officer.

He'd told her he was innocent. He'd looked her in the eyes and lied. Or had he just said the minimum he thought he'd get away with? Had he only come to her, rather than to Dana or any of his mates, because he knew she was the one who wouldn't ask questions, the one most anxious to believe whatever he told her?

Her phone ringing. Joesbury? There'd be some explanation, there had to be.

'Lacey, it's Dana.'

'I don't believe it.' Too loud. She was on someone else's boat, she had to be quiet. She had to watch where she was walking or she'd fall overboard.

'Are you OK?'

'No, I'm not OK. I don't believe it.'

'Lacey, calm down. Where are you?'

She stepped on to her own boat and leaned against the forestays. 'I'm home. I just got back. It isn't true, is it?'

The sound of Dana catching her breath. 'I'll tell you what I know and that's not much. The operation Mark was involved in was something to do with national security. It was a joint initiative with MI5.'

'What, like a terrorist threat, Al-Qaeda or something?'

'Possibly. I think some sort of attack on London was being planned, and Mark was supposed to be an enabler, someone who oiled the wheels. Half of this is what I've surmised myself, you understand?'

'Go on.'

'He was spotted last night by some uniformed officers. Doing what, I haven't been able to find out. He resisted arrest and shot one officer in the chest. Emergency services got to the kid pretty quickly, but the bleeding into his chest was too extensive. Scotland Yard are trying to keep it quiet to give themselves time to find him. Or for him to give himself up. If he gets in touch, you have to make him do that, Lacey.' Dana muttered goodnight and hung up.

'Lucy!'

Lacey looked up at the woman who'd appeared on the next boat. Ray's wife, Eileen, appeared to believe that names she'd never heard before couldn't possibly be real, and that the young woman who'd been her neighbour for the past few months must be called something more conventional than Lacey. Lucy was her favourite. Lizzy sometimes. Even Stacey or Tracey occasionally.

Eileen had been in bed, and was wearing a quilted purple dressing gown around her ample frame. Lacey could never see her and Ray together without thinking of the old nursery rhyme about Jack Sprat eating no fat and his wife eating no lean. She was bigger than her husband, taller, with a greater body weight. With wheezy asthmatic breathing and a smoker's cough, she struggled with simple actions like getting around the boat and climbing ashore. In her day though, according to Ray, she'd been an excellent swimmer. Far stronger and faster than he.

'Were you here a few hours ago?' she asked Lacey. 'Around seven o'clock? On your boat?'

'No. I've just got back.'

Eileen frowned. 'Well, someone was. Expecting visitors?'

Yes, she had been expecting visitors. One in particular. Had he been, after all? 'Not especially,' she said. Calm. She had to act calm. 'Did you see who it was?'

'I didn't see anything.' Eileen glanced uneasily over at Lacey's boat. 'I felt your boat move against ours, the way it does when someone steps on it, and I heard clattering around in the cockpit. It didn't sound like you, so I came up for a look. No one around.'

It couldn't have been Joesbury. He wouldn't come back. Not when the news of what he'd done was out. Lacey carried on, heading for her own boat.

199

'Hang on a minute,' called Eileen. 'Whoever it was, they didn't come across our boat first.'

'They must have done. There isn't another way.'

Eileen pointed emphatically at the bow of her boat. 'Nobody walks over my boat without me hearing it. Whoever it was must have come by water.'

Lacey turned to look at the creek. 'There's no boat there now,' she said.

'I didn't see a boat.' Eileen sounded annoyed. 'Or hear one. I came up top pretty quick, it didn't take more than a minute or two. There wasn't time for a boat to turn the corner.'

Silence. A train passed overhead. Lacey looked towards the point where the Theatre Arm met the main creek. A small, fast boat would probably turn the corner in a couple of minutes. But a fast boat would have an audible engine. Unless it had coincided with a train going past.

'Where's Ray?' asked Lacey.

'In the pub. Want me to call him?'

'Let me just have a look.' Lacey stepped on to her own boat.

It *had* been Joesbury. There was his calling card on the floor of the cockpit. She counted quickly. Three shells, two pieces of green glass, one piece of blue, all polished smooth by the water, a broken fragment of a teacup, still bearing the pattern of a tiny pink flower, and several smooth white pebbles. Thirteen small objects arranged in the shape of a heart.

'It all looks OK,' she called back over her shoulder. 'Cabin's locked up. Thanks for waiting up.'

'Are you sure you don't want me to call Ray?'

Lacey glanced towards the pub. 'He won't thank either of us for that. I'm fine, thanks, Eileen. Get back to bed.'

She unlocked the boat as Eileen disappeared into her own cabin. 'Hello?'

The air in the cabin had that tightly pressed concentration of leather, toiletries and river water it always assumed when it had been shut up all day.

'It's me. Are you there?'

No answer. There'd be some trace of him, surely? If he'd been here for an hour or more, she'd be able to smell him. That faint cologne he sometimes wore. His shampoo. The warm, salty smell of a hot male body. She knew the way Joesbury smelled. Lacey breathed in deeply through her nose. Nothing.

A minute later she'd checked everywhere

— even the sail locker beneath her bed — and found no trace of him. Now she was back on deck, unable to cope with the warm, close air below. She sat and stared at the heart.

He'd been here and left a sign that only she would recognize as being his. If Eileen were right, he'd come by boat, which wouldn't be unusual in itself. Joesbury knew boats. His grandfather had been an officer in the Marine Unit, and he and his brother had spent much of their childhood clambering on and off police boats. It would be nothing for him to drive a boat up the creek and moor alongside her yacht. But if he'd come by boat, why hadn't Eileen seen him driving away?

Shells, pebbles, river-polished glass. How had he found time to collect these little treasures?

Beyond the heart shape on the cockpit floor were the two toy boats that had mysteriously appeared on her yacht. Had Joesbury brought those, too? Quirky little gifts were hardly his style.

This wasn't Joesbury.

Now where had that come from? That voice in her head, as loud as if someone sitting right behind her had spoken? As if there were anyone else in the world who would

come to her boat, surreptitiously by river,
leave her a heart and then vanish.

28

Lacey

Lacey was filthy. Unable to stay on the boat, she'd pulled on waders and walked the short distance down the creek to see if Marlene and Madge had seen anyone approach the Theatre Arm earlier. They hadn't. She'd insisted on walking home, despite their warnings that the tide was coming in, that it was getting dangerously dark and that she'd be much better off staying the night.

They'd been right. The tide had been coming in quickly and she'd slipped. Now, as she climbed aboard her own boat, she was caked in mud. Giving a quick look around to make sure no one could see her, Lacey slipped off her shorts and T-shirt. She climbed back down the ladder to the narrow dive platform a couple of feet above the water line and pulled the swim shower from its socket.

Misery was like mud, she thought as she

turned on the water. It was greedy and jealous, grabbing hold and sucking you down. Misery stank like mud. It got into your eyes, making them sting and smart, and into your throat, drawing it closer and tighter so that you wondered how you'd ever breathe again.

The big difference being, of course, that you couldn't strip down to your underwear and wash away misery under the shower at the back of a boat.

She held the nozzle high with her eyes closed, letting the water wash over her, feeling the mud stream down her body and back into the creek. She moved her head this way and that, knowing she'd need to shampoo it when she went below, but at least this would get the worst of the mud off, and — for the love of God, what had just crawled across her hand?

Lacey dropped the shower and opened her eyes. Hanging above her head was a roughly tied bag of linen, about the size of a grapefruit.

Linen?

It was hard to tell, but the fabric looked similar to the one the river corpse had been wrapped in. And that wasn't a grapefruit in there — that was something alive.

The makeshift bag billowed out and then in again, bumps forming at the top, where it had been tied loosely, and at the bottom, where most of its contents were gathered. The constant movement of whatever was inside was working the ties loose. Just as Lacey realized she was directly underneath it, the bag broke open.

The crabs tumbled out, many of them striking her wet body, hitting her feet as they landed on the platform, before disappearing into the water.

29

The Swimmer

She was back. Safe. Her strong, shining body washed clean, her footprints still visible on the back of the boat. Others were coming, the light-flashing, rough-shouting, electric-screaming ones, so keep low, keep still, keep to the shadows.

It had been close, just now. Lacey had been distracted by a noise on the old dredger, spinning round in alarm, her feet sliding beneath her, falling flat. It was a miracle that she hadn't hit her head in the fall, that she hadn't drowned in the mud, never mind the tide, coming in fast and angry like an avenging army.

Beautiful, bright-haired Lacey could have drowned in the creek tonight. Her body could have been picked up and washed out into the river, and what a waste that would have been. Because there were other plans for Lacey. Other plans entirely.

Something was tickling the swimmer's arm. It was a small crab, its funny little fists clenched up tight like those of a boxer.

'Good job,' whispered the swimmer. 'Now, go play.'

■ ■ ■ ■

Sunday, 23 March

(THIRTEEN WEEKS EARLIER)

■ ■ ■ ■

30

Samira

'I'm going to get a job in a carpet shop,' says Samira, by way of an experiment, to see if she will be hushed again. No reply. They must be far enough away now. 'That's my plan,' she goes on, encouraged by the silence at the stern of the boat. 'Carpets are what I know. It was my job at home. Making carpets with my mother. Since I was five or six years old.'

The driver of the boat doesn't reply, but the engine revs and they pick up speed. To Samira it feels encouraging, not that she ever needs encouragement to talk, but she sees in the gathering speed, the growing bubble of water at the bow, the trail of white at the stern, a means of getting to her new life faster.

The river surges over the bow and she feels a pang of alarm. She isn't used to boats. There are no oceans in her country and her home was nowhere near a lake. Not counting the night, several months ago now, when she arrived, she's never been in a boat before.

She looks back, but the house she crept out of minutes earlier can no longer be seen. The keys that were thrown to her lie gleaming in the bottom of the boat, close to the driver's feet.

'When I got here, I thought they wouldn't like me. I have this thing with my spine, you see. It's round when it should be straight and they kept asking if I was born with it. If it was a problem in my family. And I told them it was, but we aren't born with it, it comes from leaning over the looms all day. None of the men have it. Just the women. The men have better lungs than we do, too, because they're not breathing in carpet dust all day long. I told them that and then they were worried about my lungs. They did all sorts of tests. That's why I had to stay there so long, I guess. They had to do the tests.'

She's talking too much. She always does when she's excited. Or when she's nervous. Or bored. All the time, really. 'Samira, stop talking for just a few minutes,' her mother would beg. 'My ears are hurting.'

'Where are we going?' she asks, suddenly conscious that they've moved much closer to the river's edge, and that the wall beside them seems immeasurably high and dark.

'Not far now,' says the driver, steering them directly into the wall.

Samira clamps one hand over her eyes. With the other she holds the boat tightly, bracing herself for the shock of a collision that doesn't come.

When she risks looking again they are beneath the wall, travelling away from the river through a narrow, arched tunnel. Were she to stand up in the boat, she would be able to reach the brick ceiling. Were she to stretch out, plank-like, along its width, her fingers and toes would brush the slime-damp walls.

'Where are you taking me?'

'To the city. If we don't go in here, we have to travel much further along the river and that's not safe in this small boat.'

That makes sense. Samira tells herself to be calm. That it will be over soon.

'My sister died,' she says, and wonders why she should think of that right now. 'That's why my mother sent me away. My baby sister died because my mother gave her too much opium. It's how we keep the babies quiet. We give them the tiniest piece of opium in sugar water so that they sleep and we can work. But she didn't wake up and my mother said she didn't want that life for me any more. She said I had the chance of something better and that I should take it.'

The engine dies; the boat has stopped. The driver is tying it to an iron ring in the tunnel wall. Samira climbs out and walks towards the light.

She hears — or maybe just feels — the rush of air behind her. Then nothing.

■ ■ ■ ■

SATURDAY, 21 JUNE

■ ■ ■ ■

31

Lacey

Yet another metal gate clanged shut. Sometimes, as she stood in line, Lacey wondered whether it might be the same gate, its hollow, dissonant echo broadcast on endless replay throughout the series of buildings. The sound was symbolic, somehow, another reminder that they were leaving the world behind.

Another instruction was called and the queue moved forward again, deeper into the smell of boiled food, engine oil and industrial-strength disinfectant that was characteristic of every prison Lacey had ever been in.

Sometimes, it seemed that every step deeper into the high-security facility at Durham seeped a little more of the life force out of those making the journey. Colours faded, voices grew muffled, shoulders slumped. Something in the process of queueing to enter a place that so few would ever choose to visit leached the life out of this crowd of women, children and a few grey, limp men.

More hands probed her, coldly impersonal, less intrusive than the whiff of humanity around her. Another corridor. Another check of bags and pockets. More forms to sign. Another half-hearted protest over an imagined grievance and they'd reached the visitors' room. As one, the visitors began moving around with the resignation of those who'd done this many times before.

Lacey found a table in the centre of the room as the prisoners filed in, each wearing the violet tunic that distinguished them as the crowd that wouldn't be going home any time soon. They were as dull and drab as their surroundings, more shadowy even than the people who'd come to visit them.

And then she came. Twelfth in line, yet separate somehow from the others. She walked with her head held high, her shoulders back, either not seeing or pretending not to notice the sideways glances, the lulled conversations, the nods and whispers. She was the celebrity presence, the one they all talked about, the one they felt they knew, the one they wanted to get closer to, if only they dared.

She was young, in her mid twenties. Her long, toffee-coloured hair was clean, although it needed a good trim. She wasn't tall, but was so slim and had such great posture that she gave the impression of being so. Her skin was clear and her eyes still bright; the notoriously poor prison diet hadn't impacted upon either yet. She was vivid and beautiful, infinitely more alive than everyone around her, and in her presence you never for a moment forgot that she was a killer.

Lacey called her Toc, although it wasn't even close to being her real name. She came up to Lacey's table, rested her cheek on either side of Lacey's for a second, then held her tight for a second longer. 'Hey, you,' she said, before stepping back and smiling.

'You need to get off that boat,' Toc said, some time later. 'Just for a while. Just till this is sorted out.'

The visitors' room was noisy. It always was. There was nothing soft in the fixtures or furnishings to soak up sound, and the endless posting of instructions, of rules and regulations, of notices of rights and responsibilities on the walls around them almost seemed to add to the incessant noise. They both had to lean forward across the table, to speak a little louder than felt comfortable.

'I don't know for certain that there is a "this" yet,' Lacey said. 'And even if there is a "this", the "this" in question may never be sorted out. I can't just abandon the first home I've ever owned.'

Toc frowned and blinked. 'Gimme a minute to process that.'

'We have no proof that the corpse in the river was left specifically for me to find. And no proof that whoever left the bag of crabs on my boat had anything to do with the corpse. The bag was just an old linen napkin. Probably somebody's idea of a joke; someone who heard about the examination of the body and knew I jumped when the crabs came scuttling out. Coppers have a very sick sense of humour. It's practically in the job description.'

'And, of course, if you move away from the creek, a certain turquoise-eyed DI won't know where to find you.'

No one knew her better than Toc.

'OK, back to crustaceans,' said Toc. 'What did the police say? You did call the police?'

'I called Tulloch. It didn't seem serious enough to call out uniform, but of course she disagreed, so the whole of the marina was like a scene from *CSI Miami* until daybreak.'

At the mention of Dana Tulloch, Toc's eyes had narrowed. Lacey waited a little nervously. Tulloch had been Toc's arresting officer.

'So what was the conclusion of the Met's finest?'

'Well, to say she's not happy is putting it mildly. She actually wanted to take me home with her, and settled for leaving a couple of uniforms in the yard. So I spent what little was left of the night dreading that you-know-who would emerge from his hiding place and get arrested.'

'If he was there in the first place.'

'Who else would leave me the heart?'

'Why would Joesbury leave you a bag of smelly crabs? Or a couple of toy boats? It's not as though you have a bath to play with them in.'

Lacey shook her head. 'He wouldn't,' she said. 'Not the crabs anyway. I had two visitors yesterday. If this keeps up, I'll be complaining about my hectic social life.'

Toc gave the polite smile the remark seemed to need. 'OK,' she went on, 'let's say Lover Boy came round, left his calling card and scarpered, and that crab man, or woman, came later. Crab man is who we should be worrying about. Joesbury wouldn't hurt you. Crab man is a different kettle of fish entirely.'

Lacey couldn't help but smile. 'I'm loving these mixed seafood metaphors.'

Toc wasn't about to be distracted. 'I'm not sure Joesbury did leave you that second heart. What time does a man on the run have to go beachcombing? If someone else left the bag of crabs, someone else could have left the heart and the boats.'

Lacey shook her head. 'Not possible. The heart was a personal thing. Like a secret message.'

'What if someone has been sneaking around your boat, saw the heart that Butch Boy left you in the cabin and thought it would be funny to play with your head a bit? And I'm really not happy about the floating corpse that, in the biggest river in the world, just happened to stray directly into your path.'

Lacey said nothing.

'And you know what's worrying me more? Because you didn't tell the boys in blue about the second heart —'

'I couldn't.'

'Yeah, yeah. But because you didn't, they won't take the whole thing as seriously as they should. They'll go with the

222

coincidence-followed-by-practical-joke
theory.'

She was right. She usually was. Lacey
dropped her head into her hands. 'Why me?'

'It has to be someone you know. Or rather,
someone who knows you.'

Lacey looked back up. 'Why do you say
that?'

'Strangers don't come into the yard,' Toc
said. 'From what you've told me, those gates
are locked half the time. To have seen Joesbury's artistic creation in sugar, they'd have
had to get into the yard without being chal-
lenged, cross at least three boats and then
peer down through your cabin window.
They'd be conspicuous, to say the least.'

Lacey said nothing. She could tell Toc
most things, but . . .

'What?'

'There's a window on the other side,'
Lacey admitted. 'The creek side. The night
he stayed, just before he arrived, I thought I
heard someone swimming round the boat.'

Toc gave an incredulous smile. 'Nobody
in their right mind swims in that river.'

Lacey waited.

'Sorry. Lots of people enjoy a bracing dip
in the sparkling waters of the Thames and
its South London tributaries. Could have
been anyone.'

'It could have been someone in a boat.'

'Still conspicuous,' said Toc. 'Unless it's someone who's often seen in the water there.' She leaned back in her chair. 'I'm getting a bad feeling about this.'

'You and me both.'

'Could there be fingerprints on those bits of glass and shell?'

Lacey thought about it. 'Could be.'

Visiting time was coming to an end. The drinks station had closed. The prison officers were looking at their watches, tapping people on the shoulders.

'I can't believe he's just gone,' said Lacey.

'If I were giving him the benefit of the doubt, I'd say he decided you'd be better off without him. Associating with a known cop-killer won't exactly improve your promotion prospects.'

'Visiting you every fortnight has hardly put me on the fast track.'

'Well, that's your call.'

Even Lacey knew when she'd gone too far. 'Sorry. Uncalled for and irrelevant. I've no desire to be on the fast track.'

Toc softened. As people were starting to say goodbye she reached over again. 'I'm really sorry, Lacey,' she said. 'Just when everything was starting to work out.'

For a second, the noise level fell. And then

a toddler ran shrieking across the room. Her mother, in a prison tunic, got up to retrieve her. Lacey felt her nose stinging, her jaw starting to ache. She couldn't cry. She never cried.

Toc was watching her intently. 'People kill for all sorts of reasons, you know.'

'Seldom good ones.'

'That's a matter of opinion.'

'No, it's really not.'

Toc's gentle, hazel-blue eyes could turn cold in an instant. They couldn't argue. If she lost Toc, she really did have no one.

While Lacey waited, not sure what to say to make things better, Toc seemed to force herself to relax.

In the six months since she'd been sentenced, Lacey had been slowly coming to terms with the knowledge that if you cared for someone deeply enough, you could deal with just about anything they'd done. It *was* possible to love a killer, and in the circumstances, that might prove to be no bad skill.

SUNDAY, 22 JUNE

32

Lacey

Lacey took a deep breath and told herself to hold it together for just a few more hours, because that was how she was dealing with life right now, in hourly chunks. With gloved hands she emptied the contents of the freezer bag on to the work counter. The day shift was over and Wapping police station had fallen quiet.

She switched on the desk lamp and picked up a magnifying glass. The pebbles, the shell, even the broken crockery were all hard, non-porous surfaces. Whoever had touched them would have left some prints behind. The experts could find them easily, but this was hardly a job she could send to the fingerprint specialists.

She picked up each pebble in turn, twisting it under the light. There were several partial prints but nothing that would be definitely identifiable. Nothing on the shells either, or on the broken pieces of glass.

She was in the basement, a room with no external windows. Lacey changed the light configuration and went back to the worktop.

There, on a triangular piece of green glass, the ridge pattern of a print was fluorescing in the ultra-violet light. A large print, probably from a man's hand. Lacey studied it carefully, then flicked the overhead lights back on and referred to the reference book she'd found earlier.

Patterns in fingerprints were largely referred to as whorls, loops and arches. Arches were ridge-lines that rise in the centre to create a wave-like pattern and were either plain or tented. Only around 5 per cent of all pattern types were believed to be arches. Loops were made up when one or more ridges doubled back on themselves, and were sub-divided depending upon whether the ridges flowed towards the thumb or the little finger. About 60 per cent of human fingerprints were made up of loops. Whorls were circular patterns, either concentric circles like a bull's eye or continuous like a spiral. Thirty-five per cent of patterns contained some form of whorl.

The pattern she'd found on the green glass was a plain arch. The ridge lines ran from left to right of the print, rising slightly towards the tip of the finger and then falling again. A very distinctive print.

Encouraged, Lacey found the second bag she'd brought, the one containing the two toy boats. It was a matter of seconds to find several prints, all compatible with the one on the piece of green glass. Whoever had left the heart had also left the boats.

Reaching into her bag once more, Lacey took out the turquoise toothbrush that Joesbury had used when he'd stayed over and that he was the only person to have touched. Under the ultra-violet she could see marks along the handle, but nothing measurable. Then, at the head of the brush, just below the bristles, one very clear print that had probably come from his thumb. She directed it towards the light, held up the magnifying glass to be sure, but there was no mistake.

The print on the brush was completely different. A double loop. Ridges running from the bottom left corner to form a loop that overlapped with one originating in the top right. Whoever had left the heart in the cockpit of her boat, whoever had brought the boats, it hadn't been Joesbury.

33

The Swimmer

The swimmer rose to the surface roughly twenty yards away from Lacey's boat. The last of the marina's residents had gone below some time ago. All seemed quiet.

Slowly. Lacey is wary now, on edge. Her nervousness as plain as daylight when she came back to the boat earlier. She's holding herself differently, her shoulders high, her weight forward on the balls of her feet, as though ready to run. She's never still any more, her head turning, her eyes searching for something she wouldn't necessarily recognize if she saw it, her nerves anticipating fears she can't even begin to name. Lacey is afraid, and a frightened Lacey is a dangerous one.

Hearing, seeing nothing, the swimmer moves forward through the still, cold water, into the shadow of the hull, to the stern of the boat. The swim ladder is down, as it always is. The swimmer reaches up, takes hold of the bottom rung and then the next.

Several of the hatches are open to catch the night breeze. Careful now. A noise below. Lacey awake, after all.

From the bow cabin comes the sound of a heavy sigh. It escapes into the night, hovers like mist above the boat before drifting away across the creek. The night it leaves behind has chilled. It was the sound of misery.

The swimmer waits for the weeping that will surely follow such a sigh, but hears nothing other than a creaking of wood, a rustling of cotton sheets.

When no further sound comes, the swimmer reaches forward and places the small, plastic, blue-hulled toy boat on the flat door of the stern locker.

A twist, a jump, a gentle splash and the swimmer is gone.

MONDAY, 23 JUNE

34

Lacey

'There's people-smuggling and people-trafficking,' said the civil servant, a bland-looking man in his early thirties whose name badge read Dale. 'People use them interchangeably but they mean something quite different, you know that, don't you?'

Lacey was at Lunar House on Marsham Street, headquarters of the UK Border Agency, the government body with responsibility for managing immigration into the United Kingdom. That morning, Chief Inspector Cook had announced a desire to be brought up to speed on the whole business of people-smuggling. He wanted as much background as possible before he organized resources. Consequently, Lacey, the newest member of the team and the only one with a background in CID, was off river duty for a couple of days.

The room she'd been shown into was grey.

Grey walls, grey furniture, grey carpet. Even the lukewarm coffee she'd been served was grey.

'I think so,' she said. 'People-smuggling is consensual. The people concerned want to access another country without the necessary permissions. The smugglers help them do it, for financial reward.'

Dale dropped his head and tapped something into the laptop in front of him, as though Lacey had made a point he wanted to remember. His limp, mousey-brown hair was thinning at the crown. He suffered from dandruff and smelled of medicated shampoo.

'People-trafficking, on the other hand, is altogether darker,' Lacey went on. 'The people themselves are the commodity. Usually women and children — they're brought illegally into a country and then sold. People-trafficking is effectively the slave trade.'

Dale looked up. 'You've not been with the Marine Unit long, have you? I just wonder why Chief Inspector Cook assigned you to this.'

Lacey took a deep breath. 'About three months.'

'I suppose it could be your background as a detective,' Dale went on. 'I'm not sure

I've met anyone before who's chosen to go back into uniform. Quite a few who were obliged to, but that's another matter.'

The question was left hanging in the air. Which was exactly where it was going to stay. Lacey spotted a splash of coffee on the table and, without thinking, touched it with her index finger and drew a heart.

'So, what's puzzling us, Dale,' she pressed on, 'is why anyone would choose to bring illegal immigrants up the Thames. For one thing, it's an extremely busy patch of water. The chances of being seen are very high.'

'Yes, you'd think so.' Dale's eyes were fixed on the heart she'd drawn.

'Of all the routes illegal immigrants could take into this country, why this one?'

'Well, that's another misconception,' he drawled. 'Most illegal immigrants aren't smuggled in in the depths of night. They come into the country perfectly legally, with a work or study visa, and quietly stay behind when the permit runs out. That's the real immigration problem this country faces, trying to find all these people and send them home. Not the odd boatload sneaking up the Thames.'

Christ, if this bloke were any more laid back, he'd be asleep under the table. 'I understand that. But in the last year, I've personally witnessed two boatloads coming up the Thames. According to records at Wapping and anecdotal evidence, there have been several other sightings. The one I was involved with last October could have ended very badly. The boat the people were travelling in overturned. We had to pull them out of the water.'

Dale started pressing keys on the laptop again. 'I've got it,' he said after a moment. 'First of October, just east of Greenwich, wasn't it? Now that's interesting. Three of the occupants weren't illegal immigrants at all. Only the woman was.'

'What happened to them?'

'The three men were all known to the police, all had records,' said Dale. 'They were charged, found guilty and sentenced. They're in Wormwood Scrubs, eligible for parole in a couple of months.'

'So that gang has been out of action for nearly a year?'

Dale shook his head. 'I wouldn't read anything into that. These gangs employ any number of gofers and the people at the top never get their hands dirty. If whatever they're doing is lucrative, someone else will have stepped in.'

'What about the girl?' A sudden flashback to that night last October. The cripplingly

240

cold water, a desperate woman trying to pull her under.

'Nadia Safi. According to this, she was sent to a hostel that takes in victims of trafficking. I can give you an address.' He wrote something down on a Post-it note.

Lacey took it. An address in London.

'You made an arrest on Friday night, I understand. Did you learn nothing from him?'

'Nothing,' Lacey admitted. 'He insisted he was alone in the boat and that he was just out for a spot of night fishing. Absolutely wouldn't budge. We charged him with having an unauthorized craft on the river and causing a danger to other shipping, but that was all we could get him on.'

'Frustrating.' Dale nodded sympathetically.

'Tell me about it. But I still don't understand why they're coming up the Thames.'

'I'd say their initial destination is somewhere along the river,' said Dale. 'Otherwise it hardly seems worth the extra risks.'

'What are we talking about? A brothel with a river view?'

'Hardly. More likely to be some sort of holding facility. You know, a derelict building, maybe a lock-up somewhere. There's still a lot of waste land and abandoned buildings along that stretch of the south bank. Somewhere between Greenwich and Rotherhithe would be my guess. Probably closer to Greenwich, if anything. Bringing them right into the city seems too risky.'

Somewhere near Deptford Creek. Near where the body was found.

The body of an immigrant?

'I hope you find them, Lacey,' said Dale, who didn't look remotely laid back any more. 'If women are being trafficked, they'll be kept in conditions that would have the RSPCA baying for blood if it was happening to animals. They'll be half starved, probably ill, and frightened out of their wits. And that's while they're still in transit.'

Lacey felt a sudden urge to get up, out of the chair and the building, to get moving. 'It gets worse?'

'Oh yeah. And if you've seen two, the chances are there are a whole lot more.'

35

Pari

> Dear Mother,
> At last I have time to write to you. I have been a little poorly, but am much better now.

Pari put the pen down. Her mother had always known when she was lying. Would she be able to tell now, across thousands of miles? And was it less of a lie, or more of one, if it were written down?

> This city is bigger than I could ever have dreamed. Every day I see something new.

That wasn't a lie. Every day Pari saw huge stone churches and elegant buildings like palaces, gleaming towers made of jewel-coloured glass. Always something new, and really no need to tell her mother that everything she saw was on television; that

243

her only real view of this massive, alien city had been the night she'd arrived, along the dark river that ran through its heart.

But I should not have believed the people who said this country would be cold. Since I have been here, the sun has shone hot and strong most days, like our springtime. All the time, I am warm as bread from the oven.

Also true. Pari put her pen down. She was burning hot and it had nothing to do with the weather outside. Her room was actually quite cool. When she laid her forearms or her forehead against the whitewashed walls, it filled her with wonderful numbing coolness that never lasted quite long enough to make her feel better.

She had a fever. In a little while, if she felt well enough, she'd stand in the shower and let the water run cold; anything to stop the fire that was smouldering away inside her, getting hotter with every hour that passed.

My English is so much better already. I'm talking to lots of people, improving all the time. The different accents can be confusing, but I am getting used to them.

That was true too, or almost true. A few weeks ago, when she'd first arrived, Pari could barely understand the simple sentence construction and continual repetition of the toddlers' TV programmes. Some days now, if she wasn't feeling too bad, she could follow the news.

I'm sorry I haven't written before now, I've just been so busy.

It had never occurred to her to ask. She'd been amazed, just now, when they'd agreed. 'I want to write to my mother,' she'd said, expecting the immediate refusal that had followed all her previous requests. 'Of course,' they'd replied. 'We're only surprised you didn't ask sooner. Perhaps you can write her a sentence or two in English. Think how proud she'll be.'

That was hardly likely. Pari's ability to read and write her own language was limited. In her home province, most girls left school when they reached puberty. Even in the university city, they probably had half the school hours that the boys had benefited from, and less than half the teachers' attention when they were there.

She was glad, though, even for the little time she'd spent in school. Education was

important, they kept telling her here. She'd
need to be able to speak English well by the
time she left.

Soon now, I will be leaving this place
and going to my new home and job.
Then I will send you money. I will find
a way to send it safely. They tell me this
letter may take a few weeks to get to you,
so I will try to think of you at the next
new moon, opening my letter and reading all my news.

All my love,
Pari.

36

Dana

When her phone rang, Dana started, as though she'd been caught doing something she shouldn't. She looked round and spotted an area near the wall where she'd be out of the way. Selfridges baby department. An hour to kill on the way home from work and this was where she'd ended up.

'Ma'am, it's Lacey. I've had an idea. I wanted to run it past you, is that OK?'

Dana looked back at the rows of babygrows, patterned with rabbits, mice, butterflies. 'Go ahead.'

Lacey talked fast, the way she often did when she was fired up about something. 'You know how sometimes several ideas come together at once, and whilst none of them make sense individually, when you put them together, suddenly it all looks different?' she began.

The lift opened and three women came

out. One was heavily pregnant. 'I think so.'

'OK, we have a problem of illegal immigrants coming into London via the Thames,' Lacey went on. 'I've been involved in two cases, and there are others on record at Wapping. The two I witnessed involved young women, probably from somewhere in the Middle East or Asia, which suggests people-trafficking, probably for the sex trade.'

Lacey was almost certainly right. The sex trade was like the drugs trade, an ongoing, ever-present problem. The more beautiful of the women would typically start out in private harems, the property of one man, who would be pretty generous about sharing with his friends. The girls would be passed round, forced to take part in orgies, used to make pornographic material. Nothing much would be out of bounds.

The less attractive would go to brothels where they'd be expected to service several clients nightly for twenty to fifty quid a time, of which they would see nothing. They'd quickly become hopeless drug addicts. They'd die, very young, in squalor. Met sources suggested that there were more than nine hundred brothels in London alone.

'OK,' Dana said, because to say anything

else would probably take too long.

'I was at the UK Border Agency earlier today,' Lacey rushed on. 'They think there could be some sort of holding facility on the riverbank around Deptford.'

'It's possible.'

A toddler ran squealing past Dana.

'Right, now, according to Dr Kaytes, the dead woman I found in the river at Deptford was an immigrant. A young woman, possibly from somewhere in the Middle East or Asia.'

Dana spotted a door and made for it. 'And you're thinking she was part of this people-trafficking operation you think is going on up the Thames?'

'It's possible, isn't it?'

She made it to the lift lobby. Silence fell. 'Perfectly possible. But still quite a stretch at this stage.'

'I know that. But do you remember that DI Joesbury and I were involved in an arrest last October? A young woman called Nadia Safi, who was entering the country illegally? She was picked up in the company of three men with a history of people-trafficking. They're all in the Scrubs right now.'

Suddenly Dana was more interested. 'And the woman?'

'This is where it gets interesting. I've just left the hostel where she lived for a few weeks, but as nothing really traumatic had happened to her — well, not that she was admitting to — she was sent to a detention centre in Kent. I just called them. They were cagey about giving me details, but once I started talking about warrants, they did admit that someone had sponsored her.'

'To do what? Run the London Marathon?'

'Illegal immigrants can be released into the care of others, for a limited time, as long as they prove they have the means to look after them and agree to put them on a plane home at the end of the given period. This bloke turned up, claiming to be a relative of Nadia's and agreeing to look after her for a couple of weeks and then take her to the airport. He did. He had photographs of the two of them together, including at the airport, and a receipt for her plane ticket back to Iran, which is where he claimed she came from. Trouble is, she never boarded the plane.'

'It was a set-up?'

'Probably. But he's claiming ignorance. Says he has no idea where his wife's second cousin is, and the Border Agency have no means of proving otherwise. It seems to me someone went to a lot of trouble to keep her in the country. So why is she worth so much and to whom?'

'You think she was destined for the same place as the girl you pursued on Friday night?' said Dana.

'Two gangs smuggling young women up the Thames,' said Lacey. 'How likely does that seem?'

'Not very.'

'So I'm thinking we need to find this Nadia.'

'Probably easier said than done if she's somewhere in London's underbelly, but I'll get people looking into it tomorrow. Thank you, Lacey, that is actually very helpful.'

'There's something else.'

Dana smiled to herself. 'I'm all ears.'

'The same day I found the body, last Thursday, I was talking to Sergeant Wilson — you know?'

'Uncle Fred, I know.'

'And he mentioned finding a young woman's body about a year ago.'

'Lots of women end up in the Thames, Lacey.'

'I know, but what if that's the problem? What if, because there are so many, we don't see the connections when they're there?'

'The connection being . . . ?'

'Young, female, illegal immigrants who are murdered. Dana, what if there are more of them?'

37

Lacey

What if there are more of them?

In the last five years, 415 bodies had been pulled from the tidal Thames and taken to the shallow bath not far from where Lacey was sitting. Typing 'unidentified' into the search facility soon reduced the 415 cases down to just thirty-five. Thirty-five people who'd been pulled from the river in the last five years remained unidentified. She only needed the women. She ran another search and the thirty-five reduced to fourteen.

But God, it was hard to concentrate. The heatwave was showing no sign of abating and Wapping police station was an old building, in which air-conditioning meant opening a window or turning on a fan. She stood up, wafted the open neck of her shirt, retied her ponytail and sat down again.

According to the post-mortem reports, four of the women had been over fifty, taking the group down to ten. Two of the ten were of African or Caribbean origin, one was Oriental.

Seven left, thought Lacey. What else? She got up, left the room and found herself heading for the jetty that took her down to the water. One of the unit's fast-response boats had just left its mooring and was skimming over the water like a dragonfly. Lacey watched as the RIB followed the course of the river. The RIBs had a top speed of 45 knots. It wouldn't take long for it to reach the lowest curve of the river where Deptford Creek emerged and a body, long since hidden, had finally found the surface again.

And that was the next search: length of time in the river. Her corpse had been in the water for several months, according to the pathologist.

Back inside, she ran another search, this time ruling out bodies that had been found quickly after being immersed. Three of them had been pulled out of the water after two weeks or less. That left four.

Four unknown young women who'd spent some months in the water before floating up to be found.

Found where?

Going back the furthest in time, to four

and a quarter years earlier, Jane Doe 645/01 had been spotted by anglers and pulled out of the water near Putney. That felt too far west. Jane Doe 322/92 had been found two years earlier beneath Pimlico Bridge and was probably the body Sergeant Wilson had referred to. Was Pimlico still too far west? Possibly.

The third on the list had been pulled out at Limehouse ten months ago, making her a possibility. The fourth had been found two months ago near the entrance to the South Dock Marina.

So she was left with two. Lacey opened the file reports on each to see if there was anything else she could learn. The Limehouse lady had been in the water several months. Soft tissue was almost completely gone but her skeleton had undergone minimal damage. The woman from the marina, similarly, had very little soft tissue but a skeleton that was largely intact. She wrote their case numbers on a Post-it note.

Together with the one she'd found, that gave her three young, unidentified Caucasian women who'd been in the water for some months but whose skeletons displayed little damage. Neither of the two she'd just found had been recovered with clothing of any kind, but that was to be expected.

Clothes disappeared very quickly in moving water.

A voice behind her made her jump. 'Haven't you finished for the night?' Sergeant Buckle was standing by her desk.

'Yeah, I'm just going.' As Lacey logged out of the programme, Buckle wandered over to a filing cabinet in the corner.

'Sarge,' she said, 'where do we keep the pictures of dead bodies?'

Buckle took off his glasses and rubbed his eyes before replacing them. 'I beg your pardon?'

'The files on the bodies we pull out of the river. I know we have basic details on the system but I was wondering about photographs, the actual reports made out at the time.'

'Didn't have you down as the ghoulish type, Lacey.'

'What if that woman we found last week wasn't the only one?'

Buckle's eyebrows appeared over the top rim of his glasses. He folded his arms and waited.

'I've been searching through the system,' she admitted. 'I was looking for similar cases and it's just possible I've found two.'

'How long ago?'

'Not long at all. Ten months and two

months.'

'Young women, unidentified?'

'Caucasian, been in the water long enough for soft tissue to have gone, but skeletons largely intact.'

Buckle stood up. 'Come on,' he told her.

Lacey followed Buckle out of the room and into another, where three sergeants had their desks. Buckle took keys from his own desk and unlocked a filing cabinet against one wall. Lacey handed over the Post-it note with the case numbers and waited. There were footsteps outside the door and then both Fred Wilson and Finn Turner came in.

'Nobody got homes to go to?' asked Wilson.

'Nancy Drew here has a hunch she wants to follow up.' Buckle held out a file and carried on looking, leaving her to explain.

'Probably just being daft,' she said. 'But I was thinking about what you said the other day, about how you found a young woman in the river who was never identified.'

'I imagine there are a whole load of blokes found in the river who are never identified,' said Turner. 'Or are they not important?'

'Now, now, children. Here we go.' Buckle carried two files across to the nearest free desk and put them down. He opened one, Lacey the other.

'Oh, nice.' Turner caught a glimpse of the photograph clipped to the inside cover of Lacey's file.

'Looks a bit like you first thing in the morning,' said Wilson.

'Sarge, I told you, that was our secret.'

'My team found this one.' Buckle was flicking through the Limehouse lady's file. 'I've got no real recollection, but I have processed a few in my time here. Some superficial damage, it says, dents in the skull, a couple of fingers missing.'

'How did you find her?' asked Lacey. 'Where was she, exactly?'

'Between the river wall and the piling of an old pier.' Buckle stared at the report and the photograph for a few seconds longer. 'She'd got trapped there as the tide went out.'

Lacey was looking through the second file. The body had been found floating around in rubbish that collected near a moored fuel station, spotted by a yachtsman who'd gone out to fuel up early in the morning. It was more badly damaged than the one in Limehouse. One hand was missing, and several ribs broken.

'Long dark hair.' Turner had been reading over Lacey's shoulder.

Lacey was looking at the photograph.

'What's that?' She let a finger hover above the woman's left ankle.

'Hard to say,' said Buckle. 'Could be a broken bone, bit of rubbish.'

'That's a piece of fabric,' said Lacey. 'Look at the frayed edge. In fact, I'd go as far as to say it's linen.'

38

Dana

The garden was at its best on summer evenings, after the heat of the day had woken the scents of the flowers. Being in the garden at the end of the day had become something of a habit for Dana. Even after the worst of days, she found it soothing. There was an exception to every rule, she supposed.

'Bloody Lacey Flint.' She ran a hand over her eyes.

'Tell me about it,' replied David Cook. 'None of the men can concentrate when she's in the room. She has daft pillocks like Finn Turner jumping into the Thames just to impress her and now she's got a bee in her bonnet about more bodies. And that's before we get on to her little habit of taking morning dips in the ruddy river.'

'You're not supposed to know about that.' Dana couldn't help a smile.

'We all bloody know about it.' Cook seemed incapable of keeping his voice down. 'Guys on early patrol have their ruddy binoculars permanently focused on the entrance to Deptford Creek. Christ, does she have any idea what people catch in that water?'

'Have another beer, Dave.'

Cook reached out and helped himself from Dana's cool box. The sky was finally starting to deepen in colour.

'So, if I followed you correctly,' said Dana, when Cook had opened and poured his beer, 'Lacey and the Scooby Gang found two more unidentified women who've been pulled out of the river in the past twelve months. Definitely young?'

'Neither over thirty, according to the post-mortems.'

'Both Caucasian, had little soft tissue, suggesting they'd been in the river for some months, but relatively intact skeletons, which would normally suggest they hadn't,' continued Dana.

'What we would expect to see in a corpse that had been trapped somewhere.'

'Or weighted down,' suggested Dana. Cook inclined his head.

'Both in a similar part of the river to the one Lacey found?'

Cook drank deeply. 'Limehouse and South Dock Marina. The Scoobies found two others, apparently, but they ruled them out because they were up west. Most significantly, the one at South Dock had very long dark hair and a piece of white fabric wrapped around one ankle.'

'How soon can we see this piece of fabric?'

Cook had a narrow briefcase with him. He pulled out a small, square plastic bag and put it on the table.

'Looks very similar to me.' Dana picked up the bag and held it up to the fading light.

'I signed it out earlier,' said Cook. 'We haven't taken it out of the bag yet. It will need to go back to the lab for testing, but it does look exactly like the sheets and wrappings we found on the one last Thursday. There's even a bit of hand stitching.'

'Shit,' said Dana.

'My thoughts exactly,' agreed Cook, before ducking sharply. 'Friggin' hell! What was that?'

Dana smiled. 'A bat. They nest in the trees just over the way. I quite like them.'

Cook was looking around in alarm. Several small, dark shapes had appeared, flitting around the trees and rooftops. 'Each to their own. But it leaves us with a bit of a dilemma.'

'There's no dilemma, Dave. We have to search.'

Cook sighed and dug into his bag again. He brought out his laptop and logged on. After a few seconds of delay, he pulled up a map showing a section of the Thames.

'Speaking purely hypothetically, if we start at Limehouse and finish just beyond Deptford Creek, we're talking five miles of river, Dana. Not far off a quarter of a mile wide at that point.'

'You're just being grumpy because I'm going to blow your underwater search budget out of the water. Pun not intended.'

Cook got up and walked a few paces into Dana's garden. 'These tiles must take some upkeep to keep the moss off.' He looked down at the smooth and shiny pale-grey stones that covered the patio and the steps down into the lower part of the garden.

'There's a chemical for everything these days,' said Dana.

'Lucky you don't have kids,' he said. 'They'd break their necks clambering over those concrete boxes.'

He was coming back. 'I can't justify anything until we have the results back on the fabric comparison. If there's no match, that's probably the end of the matter.'

'Fair enough.'

He sat back down beside her. 'And Lacey thinks there's a connection to our illegal-immigrant problem,' he said after a second.

'So I understand. Is it possible?'

'Everything's possible. Whether it makes sense is another matter.'

'Bringing illegal immigrants up the Thames doesn't make sense,' said Dana. 'Unless they're heading for somewhere very close to the river. In which case, dumping the bodies when they're done with them would be relatively easy.'

'Aye, but what are they doing with them? I know the sex trade is the most likely, but if that's the case, these girls have a value. They're not going to have been dumped after a few months' work.'

'Maybe they died on the job,' said Dana, thinking back to her conversation with Lacey. 'Some men have very odd tastes. From what I understand.'

'Proving anything is going to be bloody impossible,' said Cook. 'You'd better start hoping this search never gets approved and, if it is, that we don't find anything. Because if we do, it will be Homicide's budget that gets blown out of the water. Pun very much intended.'

■ ■ ■ ■

FRIDAY, 4 APRIL

(ELEVEN WEEKS EARLIER)

■ ■ ■ ■

39

Anya

She's made a terrible mistake. This isn't a way out. This is the river, vast as an ocean and black as impending death. Water explodes in her face, mountain high, surging with uncontainable power. Everything has turned to water. Anya feels it hit her like a speeding car, throwing her into the wall behind. She cannot see the sky, the lights, her own hand. The storm has come from nowhere.

The whole world is sinking. Blows come from all sides. Her eyes burning, she sees nothing but a swirling mass of black, grey, brown.

The wall at her back stretches up for ever, water pouring down it. Anya rubs her eyes, looks up, left, right, searching for a ladder, for a break in the endless, deadly-smooth surface.

Movement. Clutching at the weed-slick

wall, Anya turns. The boat appears, flying up into the air like a spark in an ice-cold fire. A hand stretches out. Desperate, she grabs it.

And now the water has swallowed her whole. This is how it feels to drown, this ferocious tugging at your hair, this tearing of your limbs. She clings to the side of the boat.

The engine can barely be heard against the sound of the waves crashing all around her and yet Anya has a sense that it is trying. That the boat and its driver are trying to save her.

She was wrong to be afraid. Stupid to leap from the boat, to try to find her own way out of the endless dark tunnel. That has always been her trouble — her inability to choose a course of action and stick to it. The boat slips once more into the partial shelter of the tunnel and Anya feels as though she might be able to breathe again soon. The water still dances like a dervish all around them but at least in here it's contained. They hit one wall, then the other, surge up towards the roof, but then they move on and the sounds of the storm grow fainter. Anya starts to wonder if maybe she isn't about to die after all.

The driver reaches out, pats her head.

Anya thinks she is about to be pulled aboard, but instead a rope fastens tight around her neck and the boat picks up speed.

'You were right to be afraid,' says the driver.

■ ■ ■ ■

Tuesday, 24 June

■ ■ ■ ■

40

Dana

'Mike, what a surprise.'

'Really?' Kaytes paused on the threshold of Dana's office. 'I thought they'd phoned up from the front desk.'

'Indeed they did.' Dana rose to her feet, wondering if politeness was wasted on this man. 'But the surprise has stayed with me for the full four minutes it took you to get here in person. Come in.'

Kaytes stepped through the doorway. 'I brought lunch.' He was holding up a bag from one of the big sandwich chains. 'Roast vegetables and cream cheese. For me too. Just in case you're one of those vegetarians who can't be in the same room as meat.'

'That was very sweet of you. Please sit down.'

Kaytes collapsed into Dana's chair as though he'd walked up several floors instead of one, and tipped the contents of the bag on to her desk. 'Mind if I tuck in? Badminton match last night. Always eat like a horse the next day and I've got to cut open a suicidal dental hygienist at two o'clock.' He pulled the wrapper off one of the sandwiches. He'd brought orange juice too, and crisps.

'So did you just fancy some company?' said Dana.

Kaytes had a corner of his sandwich in his mouth. 'Don't flatter yourself. I got the toxicology report.' His face screwed up into an expression of extreme distaste.

'Something wrong?' enquired Dana.

Kaytes appeared to be chewing painfully. 'Bit slimy.' He blinked his eyes rapidly before taking another bite, a smaller one this time, as he dug one hand into his briefcase and pulled out a thin plastic folder.

'The fact that you're here in person,' said Dana, 'suggests there might be something out of the ordinary.'

'Blood and sand, what is in my mouth?' Kaytes swallowed hard and then pulled a long piece of maroon vegetable matter from the remainder of his sandwich. He held it up to the light.

'That would be aubergine,' said Dana. 'Eggplant if you're American.'

'Looks like something I might find in my

sluice.' Kaytes leaned over the desk and dropped the rest of the sandwich in Dana's bin. 'Thank God for crisps.'

'Toxicology?' prompted Dana, once Kaytes had opened the packet and emptied half of it.

'Yep, I'll leave it with you, obviously, but it was a bit odd. Not something I've come across before, to be honest.'

She leaned back in her chair. 'All ears.'

Kaytes opened the file and studied the first page for a few seconds. 'Well, as you know, we didn't have a lot to work with, owing to the advanced state of decomposition. The internal organs had gone, meaning we were relying on muscle and connecting tissue, which simply isn't as reliable.'

Dana waited.

'Well, first of all it was interesting because of what wasn't there,' Kaytes went on. 'Of course, they looked for traces of alcohol, and the usual range of commonly available drugs, such as amphetamines, barbiturates, benzodiazepines.'

Dana nodded. Kaytes was reeling off the list of substances a toxicology investigation typically tested for. The laboratory would have tried to find traces of cannabis and cocaine, of the opiate drugs, typically morphine and heroin, and the chemically produced ones such as Ecstasy. It would also have looked for paracetamol and organic solvents. 'Find anything?' she asked.

'Not a sausage.' Kaytes was sprinkling crisp crumbs all over the report. 'That's not to say we can rule them out categorically, but if she'd been a drug addict or died of alcohol poisoning, I'd be surprised if nothing had been absorbed into her tissue.'

'So now we get to the interesting bit?'

Kaytes turned the page. 'We do indeed. Because one of the girls — Max, I think — had the bright idea of sending off a hair sample. You remember she still had some attached hair, very long and black?'

'I do remember the conversation about hair,' said Dana. 'Perhaps your yanking a handful from my head gave Max the idea.'

'Very possibly. In many ways, hair is ideal for toxicology testing. The day may come when it takes over from blood, urine and soft-tissue testing completely.'

'How so?'

'Substances disappear from urine quite quickly, from blood after days or weeks, but hair offers a much more permanent record. Every centimetre provides, very roughly, a record of the previous thirty days. And it doesn't deteriorate. So when you consider that our subject's hair was nearly two feet long, that's a long period of history we've got.'

'And?'

'First up, it seemed to confirm everything the tissue analysis had told us. No evidence of substance abuse. The woman was actually pretty healthy. But one bright spark at the lab had a good idea. She'd been reading about the case and had been struck by the notion that it could be an honour killing. She started thinking outside the box about what could lead to a so-called honour killing — typically, it's sexual misbehaviour on the part of the woman. So she did a few more tests, off her own bat, and found this.'

Kaytes turned the page round to face Dana.

'Human chorionic gonadotropin,' read Dana. 'Now why does that ring a bell?'

Kaytes gave her an odd, searching look. 'In laymen's terms, it's the hormone produced by the fertilized egg in the uterus. The over-the-counter pregnancy kits are designed to detect the presence of hCG in the urine.'

'She was pregnant?'

'Not necessarily, and without the key internal organs there's no way to know for sure. hCG can also indicate the presence of some cancerous tumours. But in a woman of that age, pregnancy seems most likely.'

41

Lacey

Lacey tapped lightly on the door of the incident room at Lewisham and slipped inside. 'It's a lead,' Tulloch was saying. The large room was largely empty, everyone out enjoying the sunshine. Just Sergeant Anderson, Pete Stenning, Tom Barrett and Gayle Mizon were gathered around Tulloch, who looked up and smiled.

'Good afternoon, Lacey, thanks for popping in. OK, as I was saying, if our victim was registered with a GP, there will be some record of her pregnancy. We can contact surgeries, ask them about immigrant women who visited in the past eighteen months and who have since vanished.'

Lacey pulled a chair from behind a desk as Tulloch looked at the faces around her. 'Yes, I know, a long shot,' she admitted. 'But we haven't got much else.'

'Could have been a pregnancy out of

wedlock,' said Mizon. 'That wouldn't go down well in some cultures. Or the result of an adulterous liaison. Big drama. Family disgrace. Death before dishonour.'

Tulloch was on her feet now. 'Seems a bit extreme, but I'm not sure we can rule anything out. Gayle, can you find out how many surgeries we'd be talking about in London? Maybe talk to one or two, see what sort of reaction you get. I'd like to get going with it today, if we can.'

She looked across at Stenning. 'How are we doing with tracing Nadia Safi?'

'Her photograph's been sent round every station in the Met. We've got her up on all the People Wanted websites. We know she hasn't left the country officially. No record of her at immigration.'

Anderson gave Lacey a wink. 'What about these two extra bodies Lacey and the Marine Unit have found for us?'

Lacey sat up a little straighter. This was why she'd been asked to come along. They'd found something. She'd been right.

'Mike Kaytes had a look through the post-mortem reports earlier this afternoon,' Tulloch told them. 'Mainly to see if they could be immigrants, and to see if he could spot any similarities with the woman Lacey found last Thursday.' She paused.

'Don't keep us in suspense,' said Anderson.

Tulloch seemed to give herself a little shake. 'Sorry, I find myself needing to take a moment after dealing with him these days. Anyway, it seems Limehouse lady isn't connected. She was blonde, had some pretty expensive dental work and, the clincher for Dr Kaytes, breast implants, one of which was still attached to the body. And frankly, if I could wipe from my memory his comments on that one, I would, believe me.' She stopped again, and this time looked directly at Lacey.

'The other one, though, found at South Dock Marina, is a different matter. Certain similarities between that corpse and the one retrieved last Thursday lead Kaytes to believe the earlier body is also an immigrant.'

She glanced down at his notes. 'Minimal dental work, well-developed bones in the arms and, of course, the long black hair. He's sent off a hair sample to see if it shows the same trace chemicals as in Lacey's friend, but it'll be a while before we hear. In the meantime, though, it seems a good idea to keep an open mind.'

'Any news on the linen?' asked Mizon.

'Yes, thanks for reminding me. We've had

the report back on the fragment found on the body at South Dock Marina, the one we think could be connected. Not entirely conclusive, unfortunately. It's linen, of the same style and weave to the shroud covering Lacey's corpse, but not the same batch.'

'So where does that lead us?' asked Anderson.

Tulloch found a chair and sat down heavily. 'We're going to search the Thames.'

42

Pari

Pari wasn't getting any better. Soon, they kept telling her, soon. These are very powerful drugs we're giving you, they're bound to make you feel a bit worse before you get better, but they are working. Soon you'll be fit as a fiddle.

Pari wasn't sure what a fiddle was, or why she should want to be like one. She just wanted to feel well and strong again. But it wasn't just headaches any more. Her stomach had started to hurt badly, there were pains in her back and parts of her body had swollen. And she was getting a feeling, more and more often, that the blood in her veins was hotter, moving around faster than it was supposed to. It was even harder to deal with than the headaches and the cramps, this sense that blood was never where it was supposed to be: sometimes up in her head, making it pound with heat and noise;

sometimes pooling in her ankles, swelling them to the width of young trees.

'Pari, thank God you're not as puny as you look,' her mother used to say. 'Does nothing wear you out?'

Pari was no longer sure whether she'd give anything to see her mother's face again, or whether she'd die of sadness were her mother to see her this ill.

'Pari, darling, no one can clean my home like you do. When you leave, it shines like pearls.'

These last few days her head had been full of voices from the past. Of the women she'd worked for, who'd liked her and praised her. Of the one woman, rich and educated, who'd set in motion the train of events that brought her here. 'It is your right, under the law,' she'd told Pari's mother, whilst Pari had listened in awe to her stories of women's rights, which had seemed as far removed from reality as the fairy stories she'd heard as an infant. 'Your father's farm should be shared equally between you and your brother. He has no right to it all. You must ask him for your share.'

For a moment, Pari didn't see her own face in the mirror, but that of her mother. It had been a kind face, a little like a faded rose, before Pari's uncle, enraged by his sister's unreasonable demands, had beaten it to a bloody, blackened mess.

'It's that girl of yours who's put these ideas into your head!' More voices from the past. Pari put her hands up to her ears. 'That ugly whore of a daughter. I'll kill her with my own hands when I see her. I'll drown her in the trough.' Pari had cowered outside, listening to her mother's sobs, knowing he meant it. Knowing that if she stayed, she'd die.

A sudden cramp bent Pari double. What was happening to her? They told her it was nothing. That the sharp pains, the headaches and dizziness, the swelling were nothing more than a bug, picked up on the long journey, coupled with the effects of unfamiliar food.

But she'd never felt this ill in her life before. Even when there was barely enough food to keep the family alive. When her mother had gone from house to house in their city, begging for work to feed her children, when Pari had joined her mother, scrubbing and polishing and sweeping for entire days. She'd never felt this bad.

And today, hours had been lost. She'd woken in the early evening, able to remember nothing since she'd been brought lunch at noon. She'd woken stiff and sore, groggy and stupid from sleep, to find the walls of her room shimmering and dancing as though they were alive.

What were these people doing to her?

■ ■ ■ ■

THURSDAY, 26 JUNE

■ ■ ■ ■

43

Lacey

The garden at Sayes Court had embraced midsummer. The lavender edging the path had been in bud a week ago; today the small purple flowers were fully open. Bees, lolling and bouncing from stem to stem, seemed almost drunk with pollen. The small, white flowers closest to the path were spreading across it now, softening its hard edges, whilst the taller plants behind had grown even taller. They leaned towards Lacey, as though their heavy pink blooms were weighing them down.

'Hello!'

When no answer came, Lacey stepped inside the conservatory. Bees, butterflies and other insects had strayed in here, but the heat was exhausting them. They clung limply to panes and leaves, or swayed heavily through the air. The room had been watered recently; drops still shimmered on foliage and the air was full of the scent of damp vegetation.

There was a sound behind Lacey of wheels on concrete and she turned to see Thessa rolling up the path. This morning, her long hair was plaited and wrapped around her head. She wore a turquoise blouse and a long multicoloured, striped skirt that covered her feet. Her jewellery was heavy, fashioned from silver and turquoise.

She beckoned to Lacey. 'Come here. Into the light. Let me have a good look at you.'

Amused, Lacey did as she was told. 'Are you alone this morning?' The house behind her had an empty feel about it.

'Yes, Alex is at his clinic,' said Thessa. 'Now keep still.'

Lacey put her hands behind her back and raised her chin a fraction.

'The cold didn't break out, did it?' Thessa had a note of triumph in her voice.

'I wasn't convinced I had a cold in the first place.'

A butterfly hovered for a second above Thessa's hair, then made for the fresh air outside. 'But you have been sleeping better, don't deny it.'

'Well, that is true,' said Lacey. 'But I've been having some very vivid dreams.'

'Frightening or sexual?' Thessa leaned closer.

'I'm only complaining about the frightening ones.'

'That'll be the mugwort.' Thessa was nodding knowingly. 'It does have that side effect sometimes. Especially with people of a sensitive nature.'

Lacey was starting to feel uncomfortable under the intensity of Thessa's scrutiny. 'Nobody's ever described me as sensitive before.'

'That's because you direct most of your energy into hiding who you really are. If you'd stop that, your health would improve no end.'

'I always think of myself as being pretty healthy.' Lacey's sense of unease was building. 'I'm one of the fittest people I know.'

Thessa shook her head emphatically. 'Ninety per cent nervous energy. You'll burn out before you're forty if you carry on. I think I might cut out the mugwort and give you something else. Something for boosting confidence and self-esteem. You need that rather badly. I'm amazed I didn't see it last time.'

'Now you're making me glad I came.' Lacey stepped back into the doorway of the still room, if only to get out of the light and put the unsettling conference to an end.

'We should go through.' Thessa ushered Lacey on ahead. 'It's much cooler inside and I have to finish a job before lunch.'

Spread out on the worktop in the cool, dark room were chopping boards, knives, a pestle and mortar, several pre-labelled empty bottles and two distinct bunches of soil-encrusted roots.

'I'm making a cordial of dandelion and burdock,' said Thessa. 'I've got three patients waiting for it, but I had to wait for the moon to be on the wane to harvest the roots. Really doesn't work otherwise.'

'Dandelion and what?' said Lacey.

'Burdock. The roots closest to you. You're probably too young to remember the fizzy drink, dear, aren't you? Dark-brown, very sweet, sparkling.'

'Are you sure you're not thinking of Coke?'

Thessa pulled her face into something close to a scowl. 'No, dear, I'm not thinking of any of the brand names of the substance properly known as cola. That has entirely different properties. Dandelion and burdock was a popular fizzy drink about thirty years ago. Very distinctive taste. You can still buy it, but these days the flavours are artificially produced. I make the real thing.'

Lacey looked into Thessa's eyes, but if the twinkle was there she couldn't see it. 'I'm not sure I'd know a burdock if I saw one.' She looked down at the shrivelled brown roots, like carrots that had been too long in the bottom of the fridge.

'Can't miss it,' said Thessa. 'For one thing, it's everywhere, and for another, it's very good at attaching itself to passers-by. It has a sort of thistle-head or bur that detaches and clings to clothes and animal fur. It's also known as the Velcro plant because the chappy who invented Velcro got the idea from looking at the thistles.'

'Well, I admit, Velcro is pretty useful.'

'Velcro Schmelcro,' snapped Thessa. 'There are records of burdock treating cancer back in the Dark Ages and leprosy in the Middle Ages. Henry VIII was given it for his syphilis.'

'Did it work?'

Thessa's face took on a prim look, as though a king's venereal disease was an improper subject for levity. 'I believe it relieved the symptoms, but didn't cure the underlying cause. And the plant is currently the subject of clinical trials to test its efficacy with cancer and HIV.'

Lacey nodded at the small, brown roots. 'I'm impressed. And the dandelion?'

'Almost as good. And they're perfect partners, because dandelion is a diuretic, expelling all the wastes away through the kidneys and the liver.'

'What can I do?' asked Lacey.

'You can peel the roots,' said Thessa. 'Then give them a good scrub under the tap. No, use the blue peeler — that one has chickweed on it.'

Lacey picked up a root and ran the peeler down it. Yep, just like peeling an old, limp carrot.

'Good girl,' said Thessa. 'When you've done that, you can chop them up small and then do the same with the dandelion roots. I need about five hundred grams of each. The scales are in the corner. You don't have many friends, do you?'

'I'm sorry?'

'I see a terrible sense of loneliness hovering over you.'

Lacey concentrated on the peeling. 'I'm quite a private person.'

'And there it is again, that veil. You know who you remind me of, dear? The women from my part of the world who wear those long, flowing robes to hide themselves.'

'I thought you and your brother were Greek.'

'We're not talking about me, Lacey. I

never wore the burka. You do. We can't see it, but it's hiding you all the same.'

The peeling done, Lacey carried the burdock roots to the sink and ran the tap. She couldn't remember when she'd last washed a vegetable. 'What will you do with them next?' she asked Thessa, who was clattering around in a cupboard under the other sink.

'I'm going to boil the roots, then strain the liquid,' Thessa told her. 'Then I'll add sugar and boil again until it's dissolved. When it's cool, I can bottle it. How's your appetite, dear?'

'Fine,' said Lacey.

'Hmm, you don't cook fresh food much, do you?'

'Are you planning to give me a bill for all this free consultation?'

'If I billed you, it wouldn't be free, would it? That's good. Now, can you chop them nice and fine, like slicing carrots for a stew, if you ever slice carrots.'

Lacey checked the width of the slices she was producing and started cutting thinner. 'You're very judgemental, you know that?'

'Next time you have a headache, dear, eat a few dandelion flowers. But only when the sun is shining, otherwise they'll be too bitter.'

'How long have you been a herbalist?' asked Lacey, as she finished chopping the burdock roots and carried the dandelion roots to the sink.

'These forty years,' said Thessa. 'Alex and I both went into medicine, but he took the conventional route and I deviated.'

'Do you ever work together?'

'Good lord, dear! Did you ever meet a Western doctor who would have anything to do with alternative medicine? It's little better than witchcraft to most of them. Thank you, that's lovely. I'm going to boil them up later when it's cooler, so they can stay there for now. Can you help me with some raspberry leaves?'

Lacey agreed that she could, and the two women left the still room.

'I think I'm going to take back the mugwort and give you a tincture of hops instead,' said Thessa, as they went out into the sunshine again. 'It's a very useful sedative. The only disadvantage is that its oestrogen-like compounds do tend to increase the female libido, and that can't be good for you with your man playing fast and loose the way he is.'

Lacey wondered if it were possible for body temperature to drop, purely at the sound of someone's words. Or whether it just felt that way. 'What do you know about my man?' she asked, trying to sound light-hearted, as though the question were amusing.

'Not a sausage. Which I'm having for lunch, incidentally, if you'd like to stay. But I can spot a lovesick girl a mile off.'

'Do your patients come to see you here?' Anything to take Thessa's attention away from her.

'No. Alex feels very strongly that our home is private. I have a couple of rooms just off Harley Street. You look surprised, dear. You can't imagine a mad old fool like me on Harley Street, but you'd be surprised what some people will pay for health. I treat a lot of young women with fertility problems. Between three and six months it usually takes me, to get their cycles as regular as the moon. I try to synchronize the menstrual period with the new moon, if I can. Egg follicles grow best when the moon is waxing.'

There didn't seem a lot to say to that, so Lacey stepped back to let Thessa precede her under an archway of vines into a fruit garden. The first beds were strawberries, scattered with tiny, white flowers and already glistening with fruit. They passed gooseberry bushes, then redcurrants. The raspberries, on their tall, spindly stems, were plentiful, but small and green.

'Just the leaves today, dear,' said Thessa. 'The new ones grow high on the bushes and I can't reach them.'

'Dare I ask what you do with raspberry leaves?' said Lacey.

'I make tea. Even you must have seen raspberry-leaf tea in the supermarkets. Of course, mine is much stronger. I give it to my successes. It's wonderful for strengthening the uterus before giving birth. Damn it!'

The basket of leaves had slipped from Thessa's lap. Lacey bent down, gathered up the leaves and returned them to the basket before offering it to Thessa, who seemed to be in pain.

'Are you OK?'

Thessa took hold of both legs just below the knee and tugged at them. For a split second Lacey caught a glimpse of wrinkled bare feet, pressed very close together, before Thessa smoothed her long skirt to cover them again.

'Can I do anything?' said Lacey.

Thessa shook her head. 'Physician, heal thyself, huh? If there's a plant that can help me, I've yet to find it.'

Lacey carried on snipping leaves. 'Did you have an accident? Sorry if I'm being nosy, but you seem so — well, so lively. You don't seem like someone who's spent her whole life in a wheelchair.'

'That's a very sweet thing to say, dear, but I have. Something went wrong with my legs in the womb. We are twins, Alex and I, so maybe there just wasn't enough room for both of us.'

'I'm sorry.'

'That's why my little boat is important. On the water, I'm the same as everyone else. If we lived in the country, I'd probably ride a horse. As it is, I need my time on the water. It makes me feel normal. But I expect you know all about that, dear. The never-ending effort to appear normal.'

■ ■ ■ ■

17 MAY

(FIVE WEEKS EARLIER)

■ ■ ■ ■

44

Badrai

The small ball of cork comes hurtling through Badrai's open window and lands with a noisy clatter on the floor. Badrai doesn't move. Somebody would have heard that, surely? She waits.

Bad things happen to women in this house.

Outside, the sound of a helicopter, but in the distance. Traffic on the nearby roads. Voices somewhere. This city is never silent. The water is high, lapping softly against the walls of the house, and against those across the creek. When she arrived, Badrai was hardly able to believe the way the houses grew out of the water. Surely they'd just dissolve, rot away and crumble down into the river? Those first weeks she had trouble sleeping, expecting to wake at any moment and feel that sickening, landslide-like movement beneath her as the house and all its occupants sank into a wet grave.

The house is still. If someone did hear the metallic clatter of the ball and its attached keys landing on her floor they aren't rushing up here to stop her leaving. They are listening, biding their time, waiting to see what she will do.

Nothing. Do nothing. Throw the ball back, close the window, jump into bed and pull the pillow up around your ears. Trust the people who are taking care of you. They say you will leave soon, that there is a job and a home waiting, people who will help you. They say it so many times: as soon as you are well. Trust them.

Bad things happen to women in this house.

Without a sound, Badrai crosses to the window and looks out. The boat is just feet below her. The sky is thick with clouds and there is no light in the creek. The boat is no more substantial than a dark shadow on the surface of the water. Only the pale face of the driver is visible.

No urgent commands. No gestures. No signs of impatience. No attempts to convince. It has all been said already.

Bad things happen to women in this house.

Does she believe it? She didn't want to.

The room is so clean and comfortable, the food so good. The people taking care of her so kind.

But the crying she hears when the house has fallen quiet for the night? The shouting of women whose requests are denied. The locks that are always turned? The pain in her stomach and back, which never seems to go away?

The boat is waiting. It won't for long.

Badrai picks up the cork ball. Two keys. One of which she already knows will fit the door to her room, the other the back door of the house. She lifts the key and slips it into the lock. She listens for as long as she dares. All is still.

Five minutes later she is stepping down into the boat. The driver smiles.

■ ■ ■ ■

FRIDAY, 27 JUNE

■ ■ ■ ■

45

Lacey and Dana

'Good afternoon. I'm afraid there's an operation in progress ahead. We're going to have to ask you to take a detour. What do you draw?'

The master of the tugboat gave Lacey the dimensions of his boat.

'You should be fine,' she told him. 'Can you make for that line of red buoys and steer between them and the shore? At St George's Stairs you're clear again.'

'What's going on?'

'Just routine, Sir. Thank you for your cooperation.'

The tugboat moved off up-river and Sergeant Buckle, up on the fly bridge, steered them towards the next boat heading their way. In spite of emails sent out to all craft that regularly used the Thames, in spite of frequent messages on the Thames shipping channels, a lot of vessels didn't seem aware that half the river was closed for much of the day.

'Any time you want to get involved, just say,' she muttered to Turner, who was reading the *Daily Mirror* in the cockpit.

He didn't bother looking up. 'We both know they'll be a lot more lippy if I try and boss 'em about. Cute girlie in uniform and they bend over backwards.'

'I'll assume you didn't intend that to sound as obscene as it did. How do you think they're getting on?'

Turner handed over the binoculars he'd forcibly removed from her twenty minutes earlier, when she hadn't been able to take her eyes away from the operation half a mile up-stream. She adjusted the focus and fixed them on Sergeant Wilson's Targa, the lead boat in the operation. It was directly in the middle of the channel, feet away from the lead dive boat. Tulloch and Chief Inspector Cook were in the cockpit, Wilson on the fly bridge.

On the dive boat she could see the skipper, the sergeant in charge of the dive and other team members milling around. One officer, wearing the customary black diving suit, was getting ready to go down, his orange, spaceman-like helmet on the deck close by. He was being hooked up to the multicoloured air-supply tube and to the harness that would keep him anchored to the boat all the time he was below.

Turner spoke, making her jump. 'So where do we think these women are coming from? Middle East covers a big area.'

Lacey bit back her irritation. She didn't want to talk. She wanted to watch and worry. 'Could be bigger than that. According to the staff at the hostel I went to, some of the people we see trafficked could have come here legally. We could be talking about any of the poorer countries in the European Union. Other parts of Eastern Europe. They also talked about a big influx of people from the Stans. You know, Afghanistan, Kazakhstan, Uzbekistan.'

'And they're being brought here for what? The sex trade?'

Lacey put the binoculars back to her eyes. 'Probably. Although the Border Agency said we shouldn't rule out organ-trafficking. It's very rare in the UK, but not unheard of.'

'Jeez, what sort of organs?' Turner was actually looking down at his genitals.

'Nearly always the kidneys. People can manage with only one, so no messy dead bodies to deal with.'

'Yeah, but we do have messy dead bodies, floating about all over the place, so it can't be about kidneys.' Turner was looking smug.

'Unless they took both.' Lacey looked at her watch. The operation was planned to last for six hours. Given that rainfall had been unusually low throughout the Thames catchment for three weeks now, water levels in the river were as low as they were ever likely to get. 'If there ever were a good time for such a foolhardy operation, it would be today,' David Cook had told them during the briefing earlier. He hadn't tried to hide that he was glaring at her specifically.

'How will they do it?' asked Dana.

'Basically, in circles,' Cook told her. 'You see that yellow buoy?'

Dana turned to the buoy close to the adjacent dive boat.

'And the other two. Both next to dive boats?'

Dana looked and nodded.

'Keep watching — any second now you'll see a diver go down below each of them,' said Cook. 'The buoys are weighted to the bottom with a straight line coming up to the surface. The weight marks the starting point. The divers will swim around the weight at a two-metre distance. When they complete the circle, they'll move away and swim around it again at a four-metre distance, gradually widening out until the three of them are practically touching each other. That way, we'll cover the whole area before we're done.'

'Is it dangerous?'

Cook shook his head. 'They need to know what they're doing, but I'm not unduly worried about safety, not on a day like this.'

Dana looked up at the sky. The day seemed fractionally cooler than they'd all grown used to. 'What sort of depth are we talking about?'

'About seven metres in the middle. Depth's not the problem here so much as the fast movement of the water and the visibility.'

'Visibility being?'

'With the naked eye, zero. With strong searchlights they'll be able to see a few inches. Largely they're working on feel. I don't envy them. You never know what you're going to touch next.'

Dana looked over the side. Seven metres wasn't much deeper than an Olympic diving pool, and yet for well over a thousand years people had lived and worked on this river. There could be anything beneath them.

'Ma'am, we've got the visual link up and running. Do you want to come and see?'

At the chart table in the cabin, a young constable sat in front of a computer monitor. Dana stepped closer, conscious of Cook directly behind her. The screen showed swirling shapes of a green so deep it was almost black, occasionally interspersed with pinpoints of razor-sharp light.

'Does one of the divers have a camera?' she asked.

Cook leaned closer. 'These pictures are coming from the RV. Remote-controlled vessel. Bit like a mini submarine. Darren here is controlling it.'

The young constable's gaze never left the screen.

'On the surface those torch beams will stretch a hundred metres,' said Cook. 'Down there, less than one.'

Dana watched the dull glow of the torch beam. Particles of sand and grit floated across the screen, giving the impression that the RV was moving through soup. It was very close to the river bed. Shapes emerged from the gloom, vague and indistinct. Intermittently, a diver's gloved hands came into view, creeping hesitantly along the bottom like a slow-moving river creature. Every time he touched something, a fine spray of silt sprang upwards, almost destroying what little visibility there'd been.

'What's down there?' Dana muttered, not really intending that anyone would answer.

'Nobody knows for sure,' Cook told her. 'Lot of building material — bricks, stones, stuff that's fallen off bridges or riverside buildings over the years. Anything heavy that's fallen off a boat. Any amount of stuff people have deliberately tried to get rid of. Unless it runs dry, we'll never know. Even if we invent lights powerful enough to be able to see, most stuff will be covered in silt.'

'So even if there are more bodies down there, the divers could swim straight over them and never know.'

'Well, I like to think they won't be that easily fooled. But it always was a long shot, you know that.'

'I do.' Dana looked down-river towards Lacey's boat. A couple of times during the last half-hour she'd seen the glint of binoculars. It seemed safe to conclude that Lacey was as nervous as she was. Lacey, though, wouldn't be the one to carry the can when it all went wrong.

'What are you hoping to see down there?' asked Turner, coming up beside Lacey on deck. She'd been leaning against the guard-rail, staring down into the depths. River traffic had eased and the crew had taken a short

315

break. Lacey took the coffee Turner was holding out to her.

'You look like one of the legendary mariners of old,' he told her.

'Under the spell of a mermaid? Being lured to a watery grave by the siren sound of her song?'

He caught her mood and went along with it. 'I think women were largely immune to the magic of the mermaid.'

'Let's hope so.' Lacey straightened up and followed Turner back to the cockpit just as Buckle was wiping ketchup from his mouth.

'Another coffee, Sarge?' offered Turner.

'Aye, go on. You two realize we're going to take a whole load of grief if that lot don't find anything today, don't you?'

'The linen matched,' said Lacey. 'The sample we had in storage from a corpse retrieval two months ago was the same as the fabric wrapping the body we pulled out a week ago. That's way beyond coincidence.'

Neither man looked convinced.

'The woman found at South Dock Marina was likely to have been an illegal immigrant,' she tried again.

The other two exchanged a sceptical look.

'I don't flatter myself they're doing this to keep me happy.' She nodded towards the three boats at the centre of the operation.

'How much does an operation like this cost?'

'I dread to think,' said Buckle.

'So Mr Cook and DI Tulloch would never have authorized it if they didn't think we'd find something.'

'It's a massive river, Lacey. We're searching a fraction of it. There could be a dozen down there and we might never find them. What are the chances, realistically?'

Lacey closed her eyes, feeling her face tighten. The chances were low to non-existent, everyone knew that. She wouldn't officially be held responsible if the search turned up nothing, but it would be pretty clear what everyone thought of her.

46

Nadia

The *Cutty Sark,* one of the last great British sailing ships, always made Nadia think of a tethered goddess, or a magnificent bird with its wings clipped. She liked to close her eyes when she was in its vicinity and imagine it in full sail, cutting through a rising storm, the scantily clad witch at its prow laughing in defiance of the weather. Instead, it was held captive in a dry dock, sails in storage, for tourists to crawl over.

It was also very close to the river. From the tip of Greenwich Reach, the old ship could see all the way to the city in the west, to the skyscrapers of Canary Wharf directly ahead, and to the Millennium Dome in the east. In the sun, the Thames was gleaming blue. It was nothing more than a mirage, Nadia knew, a sleight of hand, the reflection of the sky. The sun had only to slink behind a cloud and the water would revert to its normal state of moving, greedy, liquid mud.

Fazil was sitting on the edge of one of the concrete flower-beds. Nadia pulled her scarf up around her head, hiding the sides of her face. She kept her eyes down until she drew close.

'Uncle.'

It was a courtesy title. Fazil was a distant relative, hardly family at all, but older than she. He wasted no time, pushing a folded sheet of paper into her hand. 'The police are looking for you. What have you done?'

Nadia opened it to see her own picture. She had to stop herself looking round, as though even here, already, there would be people pointing.

'We printed it off the police website,' Fazil was saying. 'Your picture is everywhere. I can't protect you from the police. Why are they looking for you?'

The police would arrest her. Send her home. Or back to the house on the river.

'I don't know. I swear. I've done nothing wrong.'

He leaned closer. He smelled of mint and tobacco. 'You think they care? Just being here is wrong to them.'

He was holding out a plastic carrier bag. 'Jaamil sent you this,' he said. 'It's not easy for us to help you.'

Nadia took the bag. 'I'm very grateful.'

'Did you bring the money?'

Nadia handed over banknotes. Fazil counted them twice. 'Not as much this week.'

'I broke a plate. I had to replace it.'

He nudged the carrier bag, causing the plastic to rustle against his hand. 'Straight away,' he said, pointing to a door some twenty yards away. 'Or I won't be responsible. I'll be here next week.'

Nadia said goodbye and walked over to the ladies' lavatory. Five minutes later, a burka-clad woman, her face entirely covered, emerged. She passed briefly through the evening crowds and disappeared.

47

Lacey

In her bedroom cabin, Lacey changed into shorts and a T-shirt, then pulled her hair free from its pins. She found sneakers and climbed back up top. Ray was in the yard, chatting to one of the other boat owners. She could hear Eileen clattering about below. Good, she really didn't want to talk.

'It's not over,' Tulloch had told her, as the search had finally been called off and she and the MIT had said their goodbyes. 'The pregnancy gives us a whole new lead. If she was treated in this country, she's traceable.'

The water was high, lapping against the hull of Lacey's boat, gleaming an uncharacteristic blue beneath the evening sky. A family of swans sailed elegantly around the Theatre Arm. The younger ones had just a trace left of the grey plumage of cygnets. Lacey reached into the sealed box where she kept dried bread and biscuits and threw a handful overboard.

The woman's pregnancy wouldn't help. The chances of an illegal immigrant seeking medical attention early in her pregnancy were slim to non-existent. And, failed search aside, vulnerable young women were still being smuggled up the Thames, probably before being sold into modern-day slavery. Lacey had met such women in the past, girls who were a very long way from home, who quickly became dependent upon alcohol or drugs, living from one fix to the next, willing to do anything to stave off the beatings, to bring on oblivion. She'd joined the police force to help such women. And yet, on the brink of a transfer into one of the specialist units set up to deal with victims of rape and abuse, she'd left CID, going back into uniform, knowing that all her colleagues, however sympathetic they might be, thought she'd wimped out.

Shit, she *had* wimped out.

She got up, climbed down the steps at the back of her boat and clambered into the canoe. The swans were still hanging around and as she pushed away they followed her, like some sort of queenly escort, down the water. At the end of the Theatre Arm her little flotilla turned left into the creek. Lacey paddled past Skillions, lifting her hand to

Madge and Marlene on deck. Madge raised her phone and appeared to be taking a photograph of Lacey and the swans.

She'd wimped out. Trouble was, turning her back on the difficult stuff hadn't helped at all. It had just come looking for her again.

Women were being brought up the Thames and kept somewhere along its banks. Somewhere derelict, where no one would think to look. Somewhere without power, water or comfort of any kind. They'd be locked up, twenty-four hours a day, hot, starving and terrified. And this misery was probably within a mile of where she was right now.

The flow of water was pushing her close to the abandoned dredger on the right bank. She raised the paddle and reached out to fend it off. Touching the cold, slimy hull, she heard something move inside.

The water whisked her past before she had time to think. She dug the paddle in and turned on the spot.

The old ship had been abandoned years ago, presumably because the cost of moving it outweighed the inconvenience of having it moored alongside the gravel works. No one should be inside it.

Somewhere derelict, where no one would think to look? Somewhere without power, water or comfort of any kind?

She made for the bank and caught hold of a mooring ring to steady herself in the tidal flow. Tucked away between the dredger's hull and the wall was a small boat, not much bigger than her canoe, but with an engine.

Lacey moved closer. The boat seemed to have been used recently. No rainwater in the bottom. No rust on the metal fittings. The engine looked clean, there were even traces of oil. She looked up and saw a boarding ladder that had been hung over the side of the dredger to allow access to the deck.

Someone was on board.

For several seconds, Lacey sat thinking. Did she call it in and risk being labelled an attention-seeking drama queen, or check it out herself first? Either way was risky. Finding her phone, she tapped out a message to Ray:

Checking the old dredger at Enfield gravel yard. Call out the cavalry if I don't check in again in fifteen.

She sent it and waited. Not for long.

Fifteen and counting. Be bloody careful.

Ray had her back. She tied her canoe

alongside the motor boat and climbed up to the empty deck.

Around 150 feet long, she assessed quickly, and 30 feet wide. She was at the stern. What was left of the crane was forward of the centre deck; the wheel house was at the far end, just behind the bow. Below her feet would be the hold, a vast storage space. If a large number of people were being held together, the hold would be the most convenient, if most uncomfortable place to keep them. To access it, she'd have to find a way below.

She crept forward slowly, her sneakered feet making no sound on the steel deck, an odd feeling of unreality creeping over her. All around her, the evening was so normal. Deepening blue sky, traces of gold light, birds, voices, traffic, and yet below her feet an unknown environment.

Even up top, there were too many hiding places: several storage crates, behind the crane, inside the wheelhouse. The boat rocked against the enormous tyres that rimmed its hull and something moved below. Twelve minutes before the cavalry set off.

No one hiding behind the crates, nor behind the crane, but discovering nothing unsettled her more. If she had to face someone, better to do so up here, where she had room to move, where escape was relatively simple. Once she went below, it would be another matter entirely.

The wheelhouse, too, was empty. The iron steps that led below were to the port side of the cabin. This was where it got tricky. She hadn't even brought a torch. All she had was the minuscule light on her mobile phone.

Attention-seeking drama queen or reckless, maverick idiot? No-win situation.

Lacey crept down the steps. The door at the bottom opened silently and through it she could see the cabin that served as galley and relaxation room for the crew. Plastic, padded seats around a Formica table. A blackened range cooker. Pans still hanging from hooks on the walls. Coke and beer cans on the floor. The cabin smelled of creek mud, of rotting vegetation, of bilges.

Most of the interior of the ship, including the hold, lay behind her, towards the stern, but ahead of her, beneath the bow, was a door and she had no choice but to check that first.

Nervously, not liking to move away from her exit, Lacey stepped past rotting charts and log books piled high on a table, past a mould-stained pin-up of a topless model with 1980s hair, past a pack of playing cards scattered over the floor. The door was oval-shaped, small and narrow. Lacey pushed at the handle and it opened noisily. She jumped, spinning on the spot, waiting for an answering sound: a cry for help, investigating footsteps. Her heart beat out the seconds as she waited. Ten minutes before Ray set off.

The stench coming from behind the open door, the unmistakable mixture of harsh chemicals and organic material, told her she'd found the heads. She shone the thin light around to make sure. Two cubicles. No one hiding. Letting the door close softly, she moved back through the galley, past the steps and into the narrow, dark corridor that took her, inevitably, towards the hold.

The ceiling was lower here. There was a ventilation shaft only inches above her head. Cabins on either side, four in total. She walked forward, glancing to the right, to the left, seeing nothing. Eight minutes before Ray set off. A lot could happen in eight minutes.

In the last cabin, something gleamed in the thin torch-beam. Torn, clear plastic. The wrapper from a pack of litre-sized bottles of water. Skin prickling with anticipation, she stepped into the cabin. Something about the air in here, whilst not fresh exactly, was different from that of the rest of the ship. A sleeping bag lay on the narrow berth. And there was a gym bag in the corner of the room, a huge torch by the bed.

And something she recognized on the folded sweatshirt that was serving as a pillow. A pale-blue scrunchie. Hers. One of several she used to tie her hair back into a ponytail. Definitely hers — she remembered the way the seam had started to fray. Whoever was camping out here had been on her boat. Had helped himself to a very personal souvenir.

Two thoughts, fighting for attention. The first — get out now. The second — too late.

She spun round to see the dark silhouette of a man in the cabin doorway. A very large man.

'I'm a police officer.' The most aggressive, confident, assertive thing she could think of.

'No shit,' replied Joesbury.

48

Dana

The room into which Dana and Anderson had been shown wasn't quite a laboratory, nor yet an artist's studio, but somewhere in between the two. Several computer monitors were on sleep mode and each displayed wallpaper that depicted the human head, slowly revolving. Images on the walls were likewise of the human head, some modern, some ancient.

There were skulls in display cabinets, skulls on the worktop that ran two lengths of the room. There had even been a human skull on the coffee table in the reception area.

Apart from Dana and Anderson, there were three other people in the room. The woman who'd met them at reception, who was also the director of the facility, and two men working at desktop computers.

'Before we go any further, I would like to

give you some idea of the limitations of the technique,' the director began. 'All too often people are disappointed because I can't say, this is it, this is what she looked like.'

'I understand,' said Dana, although she wasn't sure she did. She'd committed a significant part of the budget to the facial reconstruction of the body Lacey had found in the river. If it took them no further forward . . .

The other woman looked as though she rather doubted it, too. 'What does work invariably well is when we have a suspected identity. If we have a photograph of someone who could have been the victim, the process of matching it to skeletal remains is relatively straightforward and conclusive. But that's not the case here.'

'It's not,' said Anderson. 'We have absolutely no idea who she was.'

'OK, so what we did with your subject,' continued the director, 'was first of all to carry out a full examination of the skeleton. We needed to be sure in our own minds that the details we'd been given in terms of sex, age and race were reasonably accurate.'

'And were you?' asked Anderson.

'As far as age and sex are concerned, yes. Definitely a young female. Race is always a bit tricky, but taking the bone structure and the remaining hair into account, somewhere in the Middle East or South Asia seems the most likely.'

She reached down and lifted a thermally controlled box from under the worktop. 'This is your skull. We'll be returning it to you now, there isn't any more it can tell us.'

Anderson took it and put it down softly by his side.

'The first thing we do when attempting a reconstruction is to reattach the mandible to the skull,' the director went on. 'Then we clean it, and repair any visible damage with wax. We photograph each stage. Here you are.'

She tapped some buttons on a keyboard. A second later, Dana was looking at the skull on the computer screen, cleaner and neater than she'd seen it previously.

'At this point we make a cast that subsequently forms the basis of the reconstruction.' The director flicked to a new screen that showed a clay-like substance being smoothed over the skull. 'We build it up using data based on average tissue thickness for any given age, gender and racial group. In this case, we were particularly lucky that there was already some soft tissue remaining. This gave us much more to work with than we would otherwise have had. This next photograph shows you the pegs in place.'

The image on the screen was now displaying several dozen small, thin tubes, a little like matchsticks, jutting out from the skull at intervals. Several where the lips would be, another at the nub of the chin, one on the tip of the nose, a line along the cheekbone.

'So then you fill it in?' asked Dana. 'You just smooth clay along the skull until the pegs can't be seen any more?'

'Good God, no.' The director looked shocked. 'If we did that, the final bill would be a lot less, I promise you. We build the face up muscle by muscle. The thickness and length we make them depends upon the average data we have, the actual tissue sample we took and the small clues on the bones that tell us where muscle tissue was attached. That way, the face builds up slowly, but hopefully accurately. We insert eyes, attach ears and work on any indicated scars or abnormalities. The last thing we do is choose skin colour and attach hair. Are you ready to meet the lady you've been trying to help?'

'We are indeed,' said Dana, conscious of a nervous tickle in her stomach.

The director took a large blue box from

the worktop and carried it to the podium in the centre of the room. She placed it on top and unfastened the lid. The box's sides came away separately and fell down to reveal the modelled head within. The sculpture was of the head and shoulders of a young woman with an emerald-green scarf around her black hair.

Wow, thought Dana.

'She was gorgeous,' said Anderson.

'Yes, I think she probably was,' said the director.

The sculpture's face was oval, widening at the jawline and with a rounded, pronounced chin. Her nose was longer and wider at the tip than would normally be compatible with perfect beauty, but it was balanced by full lips and strong eyebrows. Her eyes were dark, kohl-rimmed with thick lashes.

'Now you understand that a lot of subjective decisions led us here,' said the director. 'Based on the hair she could have been Indian, Pakistani, Bangladeshi, Sri Lankan, or, coming further west, from Turkey, Morocco, even Greece, but something was whispering Persian to me.'

'Modern-day Iran,' said Dana.

'Yes, or possibly Iraq, or one of the Stans. For one thing, the lower part of the face is quite pronounced — wider than you might see in India or Pakistan — and whilst the nose is notoriously difficult to reconstruct, there were indications that on this lady it was longer and wider towards the bottom than is average.'

'Beautiful eyes,' said Dana. 'Not large, compared to some of her other features, but lovely all the same.'

'Yes, almond shaped. You see it a lot in people from the East. And the eyes we can be reasonably confident about, because their shape is largely determined by the shape and slope of the socket. I've given her brown eyes, of course, because that's far and away the most common colour in that part of the world.'

'I feel as though we should give her a name,' said Dana.

'Yes, she rather had that effect on us too,' said the director. 'We've been calling her Sahar. It's the Persian name for dawn, because that's when you found her.'

49

Lacey

Lacey stared at the man she loved, would always love, whatever he'd done. There was just enough light coming down the stairs for her to see him. He hadn't shaved in days. His clothes looked as though they'd seen several days of wear.

'I should arrest you,' she told him.

Joesbury's eyebrow went up. 'Try it,' he countered. 'Might be fun.'

Something about the half-twist of his lips hit her harder than anything. After everything he'd done, he could laugh at her.

'I don't know who you are any more.'

'You're putting us both at risk by being here,' he said. 'I need you to leave now and not come back. Promise me?'

So cold. Had she fallen in love with a man who didn't exist? 'I think you lost the right to extract promises from me when you killed a man.'

She could never look him in the eyes for long. Even here, when there was barely enough light to see them properly. Even here, where they were little more than a glint in the darkness. When Joesbury made a noise in the back of his throat, somewhere between a sigh and cough, and stepped towards her, she backed away, almost falling on to the bunk.

'When I was on the brink of the worst thing that could happen to anyone,' he said, 'you asked me to trust you. Do you remember that?'

Three months ago. A winter night. A bridge over the river. The man she adored on the point of despair. And he was asking if she remembered?

'I couldn't think straight. I didn't know how I was going to make it through the next hour and you asked me to trust you.'

Joesbury, collapsing in front of her, sobbing. Was that the sort of thing she could forget? Ever?

'You gave me no reason, no hope, just demanded unconditional trust. Ringing any bells for you?'

She snapped at him, 'Of course I remember.'

'Good. Then you'll also remember that I did.'

He had, too. *Do you trust me or not?* she'd said to him. *Because if you do, you have to let me go.*

He'd let her go.

'I still trust you. So I'm going to tell you what nobody else can know. Not even Dana.'

That pounding noise might be her heart beating.

'Police Constable Nathan Townsend is as alive as you and me. Probably with a much better chance than either of us of staying that way, given the way you're carrying on.'

She'd heard the words, but the processing of them took a little longer. 'What?'

'Alive and well. Or rather, alive with a very sore shoulder and seriously pissed off with me.'

'You shot him.'

'Yes, that I do admit. If I hadn't shot him, someone else would have done and they'd probably have been aiming to do a lot more damage. I shot the daft git to keep him alive, although I doubt he'll see it that way.'

'He's alive?'

Something in Joesbury's face softened. 'Alive and under guard at a convalescent home somewhere in Northumbria. Whilst the people I'm investigating think I'm a cop killer, they're more inclined to believe I'm on their side. And for the time being, it's very important they think that.'

It couldn't be true. She could not let herself hope. 'I don't believe you.'

'Has there been a funeral? Have you seen his weeping mother on television? Has there even been anything on the frigging news?'

'You haven't killed anyone?' Shit, that was hope, wasn't it? You just couldn't keep it down for long.

Joesbury sighed. 'I haven't killed anyone. I'm an undercover police officer on an excruciatingly difficult job and starting to feel a bit sore that the women in my life can give up on me so easily.'

She sank down, the fabric of his sleeping bag smooth and slippery beneath her bare thighs. At her surrender, something in Joesbury's stance seemed to relax. There was a softening, a warming about him.

'I've imagined you many times in my bedroom. Never quite like this.'

The cabin wasn't much more than six feet long. Could he even stretch out his legs? 'You're actually living here?'

When he sat down beside her, she took his hand, holding it tight between both of hers.

'The people I'm dealing with need to believe I'm on the run,' he said. 'On the other hand, I can't leave London and lose the chance of finding out what they're up to. I need to lie low. I thought about this place the other night when I was with you.'

She could smell sweat on him. Unwashed clothes. She thought about the cavernous space all around them, the darkness, the smell. 'All this time, you've been just across the creek?'

Those turquoise eyes were warm now. Even in the dark of the cabin, she knew it. 'I creep on deck when it gets dark,' he said. 'Look for the lights on your boat.'

Something was going to happen. Something she'd dreamed about so many times. Was she ready for it?

'I should go.' That was nerves talking. Leaving was the last thing she wanted to do.

'You should.' He ran a finger up the bare skin of her arm.

'I'm putting you in danger.'

'From the moment I first laid eyes on you.' The finger had reached her neck. His hand cupped the back of her head.

'Anyone could see my canoe outside.'

His face was very close now. 'Disaster,' he said.

She closed her eyes. So many times, alone in the dark, she'd imagined Joesbury's lips on hers. It had never been like this. Who would have thought he'd be so gentle, that his lips would stroke hers so softly, brushing against first one and then the other? She'd imagined his hands pushing her roughly against a wall, his body heavy, crushing hers; never that his fingers would twist round in her hair, pulling her closer, or that the tips of his fingernails would feel so smooth running up her back.

'Lacey!' Someone was banging on the hull. 'Lacey! Are you in there!'

Joesbury was on his feet, out of the cabin. Needing a second longer to get her head together, Lacey followed him.

'It's Ray,' she whispered. 'I told him where I was going.'

Joesbury's shoulders dropped as the tension left his body. He adjusted the waistband of his jeans and sighed. Then he shook his head. 'Better go call off the dogs,' he told her.

She pushed past him, ran up the stairs and across the deck. Ray was steering his way around the stern of the dredger. Another couple of seconds and he'd see Joesbury's boat.

'I'm fine,' she called down. 'False alarm. Sorry.'

Saying nothing, Ray gave her a wave and

turned his boat around.

Joesbury was on the steps, just out of sight. She ducked down to join him.

'There's something I need to ask you. That night you stayed over, you left a heart on the table. That was you, wasn't it?'

Joesbury's eyes narrowed. 'I couldn't find a pen. Why, who else —'

'Sshh. Did you come back the next day and leave another one?'

Bewildered was quite a good look for him. He looked younger, rather cute, when he was baffled. 'I haven't been back since. It's too risky for both of us. What's going on?'

She stepped down until their faces were level and kissed him, lingering against the skin of his face for just a second longer than felt wise. 'I have to go. Can I at least phone you?'

He was holding her again. 'Phone calls leave a trace. Too risky.'

She sighed, could almost see her breath wrapping itself around his neck. 'Any chance this will be over soon?'

'God, I hope so.'

If she kissed him again, she'd never stop. Lacey turned, ran up the steps and across the deck. As she climbed over the side and back down to her canoe, she looked back. The deck of the old ship was empty.

50

Lacey

As the sun disappeared behind the old mill building and the golden light started to fade, Lacey was sitting on the deck of Madge and Marlene's naval ship at Skillions, thinking about toy boats, shapes made out of pebbles and glass and whether she'd boxed herself into an untenable corner by not mentioning them sooner.

And yet there was no way of telling Tulloch about them now without explaining why she'd kept quiet for so long. *I'm going to tell you what no one else can know. Not even Dana.*

Three toy boats now. One yellow, one blue, one red. What the hell was all that about? She took another sip of the gin mojito she'd been offered on arrival, which was definitely a lot stronger than she'd been promised. Ahead, she could see the Theatre Arm, her own boat rocking against its moorings. If she turned her head to the right, which she was trying not to do every couple of seconds, she could see the dredger. And you know what? She was not going to worry about toy boats. She was not going to sweat the small stuff. Not tonight.

'What are you doing tomorrow, Lacey? Would you like to come and have lunch with Alex and me?'

Lacey turned to smile at the old lady by her side. Just minutes after she'd got back from the dredger, Thessa had pitched up in her small, pretty motor boat, hammering on the side of Lacey's yacht, insisting they'd both been invited to a party by the skanky old lesbians and there was no way she was going alone. When she'd run out of arguments, Lacey had locked up her boat and climbed down. The two of them had motored across and then Thessa had been hauled aboard by means of a harness and pulley, with every appearance of having done it many times before. Madge and Marlene had even produced a wheelchair for her.

The party was small but noisy. Around two dozen people, all of whom seemed to work in the theatre, and many of whom looked as though they'd come straight from a performance. Also, to Lacey's surprise,

Eileen, Ray's wife. There was no sign of Ray. A little further along the deck, a wind-up gramophone was playing Buddy Holly tracks and a small, thin person of indeterminate sex was swaying to the music.

And Thessa had just invited her to lunch.

'That's really kind,' she said, 'but tomorrow I have to be on a train to Durham.'

'Long trip. I expect that takes most of the day. Or do you stay over?'

'No, I always come back the same day. Four hours there, four hours back, one hour in the visitors' suite.'

She waited for the question that didn't come. Thessa wasn't entirely lacking in tact.

'I visit a woman in Durham prison, the high-security wing,' Lacey said. 'She was given a life sentence for murder in January.'

'Someone very close to you?'

Lacey nodded.

Thessa swirled her drink, letting the ice chink against the sides, waiting until it stopped moving. 'It isn't your fault, you know. What she did.'

Being with Thessa was like playing paintball with the SAS — you never knew when the next strike was coming, only that it was inevitable and that it would be bang on target. Lacey opened her mouth to say, of course it isn't, I fully understand that, everyone takes responsibility for their own actions.

'Well, actually it is,' she said instead. 'But I don't go out of guilt or as any sort of self-indulgent penance. I go because seeing her makes me happy.'

'Is she family?'

Lacey had to remind herself to breathe. 'Why would you think that?'

'I can see love in your eyes. And tears.'

Ah, now she was on slightly safer ground. 'I never cry.' She half smiled, half glared at Thessa.

Who did exactly the same thing back. 'They may not fall, but they're there all the same.'

'Drink up, ladies.' Madge had stolen up behind them. 'You have six hours before the tide goes out and you're trapped here.'

In spite of the heat, Madge was dressed like a gangster from the prohibition era, with a wide-striped suit, red shirt and black tie. A trilby was perched on her short hair.

'Please don't give Thessa any more alcohol,' said Lacey. 'She's driving me home. Not to mention herself.'

'We're skinny dipping later.' Madge was giving Lacey the sort of look she normally only saw on the faces of drunken men in pubs she raided. 'See if we can catch the mermaid.'

Thessa snorted. 'If that's a sexual euphemism, you're wasting your time. Lacey's in love. With a man.'

Madge squeezed herself down on to the bench next to Lacey. 'I can't believe you've lived on the river since the old Queen died and you don't know about the mermaid.' Her voice was slurred, her eyes not quite focused.

'I don't know about the mermaid,' said Lacey. 'But didn't the old Queen die quite recently?'

'She doesn't mean the Queen Mother,' said Thessa. 'She means that hairy old drag artist from the Duke on Creek Road.'

'It's practically a local legend.' Marlene had crept up without them noticing. As had Eileen. 'The beautiful dock-worker's daughter who fell in love with a pirate. When he was hanged at Neckinger Creek she threw herself into the water in despair, but such was the power of her love that she lived, and grew a tail. And now she's doomed to swim the waters of the creek and the Thames for all eternity, looking for her lost love.'

Lacey's eyes couldn't help straying to the dredger, just yards away from them.

'She's been seen lots of times,' said Marlene.

'Yes, but it's always a bloke who knew a bloke who'd seen her one night, usually after a few in the Bird's Nest,' said Eileen as Marlene strode away towards the main cabin, tottering on heels that seemed far too high for the deck of a boat.

'Don't give me that. Even Ray's seen her. He told me so himself.' Madge leaned even closer to Lacey. 'He was out fishing one night, about twenty years ago. He saw a mermaid sitting on one of those old timber piles near the railway bridge.'

Eileen laughed cynically. 'Gazing into a mother-of-pearl mirror and combing her hair?'

'When his boat got closer, she dived into the water and disappeared,' added Madge.

'He was drunk.'

'Ray would never go out on the water drunk,' said Lacey.

'He was drunk when he told the story,' insisted Eileen. 'He saw a seal.'

Lacey realized that Thessa had fallen quiet. 'So have *you* seen her?' she asked.

Thessa shrugged. 'I've seen odd things. Usually in the creek, sometimes in the main river. Very early in the morning, or late at night, just occasionally I see what looks like

347

a face, staring at me.'

For some reason, the story seemed more credible when Thessa, ridiculous old ham that she was, was telling it. The dancing twinkle had completely gone from her eyes.

'Seals,' said Eileen. 'Or an old football bobbing up and down.'

Thessa smiled.

Marlene had come back, carrying a large photograph album. She handed it to Lacey, already open at a page containing press cuttings going back years. Dolphins in the Thames, seals in the Thames, porpoises, even a small whale in the river. At some time over the past few decades, most species that passed close to the Thames Estuary had lost their way and found themselves in the heart of the city. Most, sadly, didn't find their way out again.

'Go down a bit further,' Marlene told her. 'There you are.'

She was pointing Lacey towards an article from the *Illustrated Police News* dated 1878. THE MERMAID AT WESTMINSTER AQUARIUM, said the caption. The story covered the new attraction at the Royal Westminster Aquarium: a manatee.

The manatee, Lacey read, was a sea-dwelling animal from the South American continent, believed to have given rise to the legend of the mermaid, the beautiful half-human, half-fish creature that lured sailors to their deaths in perilous seas.

'They're also known as sea cows,' said Marlene. 'They have very long flippers at the front, which could look like arms at a distance. And they have the wide, strong tail that mermaids are supposed to have. Mind you, how anyone could look at one and fall in love is beyond me. Even after several months at sea and a bottle or two of the strong stuff.'

She had a point. The manatee was a large, cumbersome creature without even the cute, humanoid face of the seal.

'They're native to South America,' said Lacey. 'And Florida. They couldn't live in the Thames, could they?'

'You wouldn't think so,' said Marlene, 'but Ray used to tell some odd stories. It's no good looking like that, Eileen, you know he did. Odd tracks, massive birds disappearing in split seconds. You get talk of crocodiles every few years. People release their exotic pets into the river all the time. Maybe they don't all die.'

'It's too cold,' Eileen scoffed.

'Maybe they get lucky,' said Thessa. 'Find a drain near warm pipes. Hole up until the cold weather passes.'

'I'd rather believe in the mermaid,' said Lacey. 'It's a nice story.'

'Yeah, woman falls for a bloke, he turns out to be a wrong 'un, she drowns herself and spends the rest of eternity as a fish,' said Madge. 'Just like a fairy tale. Who needs a top-up?'

'Why do you love the river so much, Lacey?' asked Thessa, when Madge and the others had wandered away. 'Every time your thoughts drift, you stare at it.'

Lacey hadn't been looking at the water at all, but at the hull of the abandoned dredger, wondering if he could hear the music, whether he was watching them right now. Thessa was right about one thing, though. She did love the river.

'I always loved swimming. I swam in the sea when I was a child. We didn't live too far from the coast.'

'Yes, Shropshire's well known for its beaches.'

The realization of her mistake was like a physical shock. Lacey had completely forgotten that she'd already told Thessa she was from Shropshire. It was the first time, ever, that she'd made such an error.

'I expect you mean you stayed with relatives who lived near the beach,' said Thessa. 'Go on, dear.'

She'd been let off the hook. No choice, really, but to go along with it. 'Well, I swam competitively at school. It was about the only thing I was really good at. And then, about a year ago, I nearly drowned in the Thames.'

The others had returned, gathering round to listen. Everyone loved a police story.

'We were pursuing a suspect,' Lacey said. 'This was the early hours of the morning. I chased him on to Vauxhall Bridge and my colleagues came the other way. We thought we had him trapped. Only he grabbed me and pulled us both over the side. It was a surprisingly long way down.'

Gasps of shock, faces intent with interest.

'I had surveillance equipment sewn into my clothes, a tracking device, so the Marine Unit pulled me out,' said Lacey. 'He wasn't so lucky. His body was found several days later. I know it sounds daft, but I like to think the river took care of me.'

'That means you can't ever drown,' said Marlene. 'That's the legend among watermen. If you cheat death in the water, the river loses its power to harm you.'

'Claptrap,' said Thessa. 'Of course you can drown. Don't you dare take silly risks.'

The story over, some of the others drifted away again. Eileen and Madge stepped towards the rail and looked down into the water.

'I've been trying to decide what month you were born, Lacey,' said Thessa. 'May is a possibility, like Alex and me, which would make your birth flower the Lily of the Valley.'

Lacey smiled.

'Hmm, I don't think it's as late as August, somehow,' said Thessa. 'So I'm going with June or July. July, I think. Larkspur.'

'I was born in December,' said Lacey.

Thessa screwed up her face. 'A carnation? I don't think so, dear.'

'I'm sure Lacey knows her own birthday, you daft old trout,' Madge called back over her shoulder. 'Anyone for a skinny dip?'

'Eileen doesn't approve of swimming in the creek,' said Lacey, smiling at her neighbour. 'She's pretty much clipped Ray's fins.'

'Only because the silly old sod's too old to cope with the Thames,' said Madge. 'Besides, who do you think got Ray into wild-swimming in the first place? Swims like a fish, our Eileen.'

■ ■ ■ ■

SATURDAY, 28 JUNE

■ ■ ■ ■

51

Lacey

'Ok, let me get my head around all this crap,' said Toc. 'You pull the body of a woman out of the Thames and decide she's an illegal immigrant.'

'With reason,' said Lacey.

'Yeah, yeah. You find records of another body, pulled out two months ago, that may or may not have been an illegal immigrant — no way of knowing — so you decide there's a whole load more of them at the bottom of the Thames and persuade your bosses to mount a multi-operational, massively expensive search that turns up zilch. Lacey, at best they're questioning your judgement, at worst they're writing you off as a bit of a loon.'

'Way to make me feel better.'

'I'm not trying to make you feel better. For a police officer living under a fake identity, you are not exactly keeping a low profile.'

Lacey looked round in alarm. 'Why don't you just send a memo?'

'I thought the whole point of going back into uniform was to stay clear of the high-profile stuff. Keep your head down, concentrate on being a good, solid copper.'

'It was. I just can't —'

Toc was making her *I give up, I just give up* face. 'I know. You never could. OK, let's see what we can work out. Give me that pad.'

Lacey had brought a notepad and pencil into the room with her. She pushed them across the table. Toc wrote the number one in a bold, heavy hand.

'First problem,' she said. 'Mass ethnic graveyard at the bottom of the Thames.'

'Glad you're finding this funny.'

'Even if you're right, there's nothing you can do. The search has happened. It found nothing. So unless you're planning to stick on a wetsuit and snorkel and go down yourself, that avenue is closed. Agreed?'

Lacey had a brief flashback to the seconds she'd spent under the water, looking at a floating corpse. 'Agreed.'

'Next, you have a gang smuggling young women up the Thames and keeping them somewhere near Deptford Creek, but not on the old dredger because that has treasure of a different sort entirely in the hold.'

Far better not to react when Toc was in this mood. Just let her get it out of her system.

'So is Tulloch the Terrible looking for this holding place?'

'She's got people on to it,' said Lacey. 'But it's a big area and she doesn't have a lot of manpower. It's going to take time.'

'You might want to tell them you've already checked the old dredger.'

'Christ, I didn't think of that.'

'Lucky you've got me on the case, then. But this is something else you have to leave to Tulloch and the team. If they're short on manpower, you're on your own, working when you're off duty. You can't search the south bank by yourself.'

'You're making me feel like a spare part.'

'Are you going to tell Tulloch you've seen Joesbury?'

'I can't. I promised I wouldn't tell anyone. I've already broken my promise by telling you.'

Toc beamed. 'So instead of confiding in a trusted senior officer in the Met, you blab to the most notorious serial killer of the twenty-first century? Love it.'

'Anything else on this list of yours?'

Toc drew a large, thick number three.

'Nadia Safi. Someone who could shed a whole load of light on the mystery, but who is still missing. Is Tulloch looking for her, too?'

'The whole of the Met is looking for her, but she clearly doesn't want to be found. I've got a picture somewhere.' Lacey reached into her bag and found the photograph of Nadia Safi taken shortly after her arrest the previous year. Toc peered over.

'Oh, look at her,' said Toc. 'She's a Pashtun.'

52

Dana

Dana's eyes were glued to a computer monitor, not two feet from her head, trying to make sense of the mass of grey matter on the screen. She lay on her back, her knees raised, a pink blanket over her bare legs, horribly uncomfortable.

'There we are,' said the nurse who had been guiding the probe inside Dana. 'We're starting to see the eggs now.'

I'm not, thought Dana.

The nurse pointed to the screen. 'The round, black shapes,' she said. 'I suppose they look like holes more than anything else, if you're not used to seeing them. Oh, that's a good one. I'll just take a measurement.'

Dana watched, mystified, as the nurse marked the largest of the black holes with two tiny crosses.

'Yes, that's probably the one. Although you can never be sure. I could scan you again tomorrow and the picture could be quite different. The main thing is, everything's as it should be and you should ovulate some time in the next day or so. Now, you're using ClearPlan, is that right?'

On the basis of several packets in her bathroom cabinet, Dana agreed that she was.

'When you get your FSH surge, you need to phone us,' the nurse continued. 'We'll book you in for the following day. It's important you keep that appointment. I know it's difficult for you professional ladies, but the eggs don't wait and once we've taken the sperm out of storage, we can't put it back. You'll still get charged for it.'

'I understand.'

'You get yourself dressed, then we'll have a chat about it.'

When Dana emerged from behind the screen, the nurse had a file open on the desk in front of her.

'Right, the lab have confirmed the donor you chose, you'll be pleased to know. Let's see. Economics graduate. Works in finance. Quite sporty. Keen on rugby, athletics. Always a good sign, I think, when they're active.'

'Is he kind to animals?' asked Dana.

The nurse blinked. 'Sorry?'

'Does he have a good sense of humour?'

The nurse smiled carefully. 'The donors choose how much information they give us. We know a little about what he looks like. He's just above average height. Slim build. Dark hair, brown eyes.'

Is he married? Does he have a family already? Why is he donating his sperm? If he works in finance, it can hardly be about money. This man and I are going to have a child together. How can I not know these things?

'You know, since anonymity has been taken away from donors, the numbers have dropped considerably,' said the nurse. 'Some months we don't have enough to treat all our ladies.'

The subtext being, I'm lucky and should behave in a suitably grateful manner, thought Dana. Where's Helen when I need her?

53

Lacey

'She's a what?' said Lacey, looking at the photograph of Nadia Safi.

'Pashtun. Biggest ethnic group in Afghanistan, something like 40 per cent of the population. But there are quite a lot of them in the neighbouring countries as well.'

Afghanistan?

'Tulloch phoned me on the way up,' said Lacey. 'They've had the reconstruction done of the woman I found. They think she might be from Iran. Are those two countries close?'

'They share a border,' said Toc. 'So it's quite likely there'll be Pashtuns in Iran as well.'

Lacey looked again at the photograph on the table. 'Is it significant?'

'Could be. The Pashtuns are quite beautiful to Western eyes. Very similar to Europeans in terms of bone structure, but with darker hair and skin colour. Quite often they have blue eyes.'

'Blue-eyed Asians?'

'This girl's are pretty light, look. A bluey-grey, I'd say. They're certainly not the black you normally expect in people from that part of the world.'

Lacey turned the photograph round. She hadn't noticed it before, but now it was pointed out, the girl in the photograph did have unusually light eyes.

'There was a famous photograph of an Afghan girl on the cover of *Time* magazine about twenty years ago,' said Toc. 'She was only about fifteen years old but she was really quite astonishingly beautiful. Mainly because of her striking green eyes.'

'The woman in the Salvation Army hostel I visited talked about Afghanistan,' said Lacey.

Toc was shaking her head sadly. 'One of the worst places in the world to be a woman. I've not heard of large numbers of female immigrants from there, but you certainly couldn't blame them.'

Lacey's knowledge of foreign affairs was confined to what she caught on the late evening news or read in the weekend papers. 'I thought things got better when the Taliban left. That there was a new constitution, that

363

women had equal rights.'

Toc shrugged. 'I think they have improved. But all things are relative. Most women there are still illiterate. Female life expectancy is still the lowest in the world. More women die in pregnancy and childbirth there than almost anywhere else, mainly because so many women marry as children.'

'I hadn't realized.'

'People believe what they feel comfortable believing.' Toc's voice had got louder. It always did when she felt strongly about something. 'I'm not saying the government there isn't trying to do the right things, but you can't change society overnight. Most women have no idea of their rights so don't know how to complain, and in the unlikely event that they do, they're rarely taken seriously. Half the women in Afghan prisons have been convicted of so-called moral crimes.'

'And a moral crime is what, exactly? Adultery? Promiscuity?'

Toc gave an incredulous look. 'I doubt many would dare. More likely running away from an abusive husband or being sexually molested. The women in rural areas suffer the most. They can't travel outside the home without a male escort. Fewer than half go to school. They're usually forced to marry very young, often to a man much older.'

Lacey shook her head, slightly in awe. 'How do you know all this stuff?'

'I read newspapers. Watch TV. Lot of time to kill in here.'

'OK, I'm getting the picture,' said Lacey. 'So we can expect these women to jump at the chance of a better life?'

'It can't be that simple. These women have no money, no passports, half of them can't read. They're as innocent as children in the ways of the world. It simply isn't possible for them to leave Afghanistan without help.'

'But quite possible that if they were offered help — say passage to a country where they'd be safe, help finding a job and somewhere to live when they get there — then quite a number would be tempted?'

'Yes,' Toc agreed. 'I imagine an awful lot would leap at that. Christ, talk about out of the frying pan.'

A toddler ran close, careering off their table and on down the room. His mother shot past and scooped him up. On her way back to her own table she paused to glare down at Toc, who returned the foul look with a beaming smile.

'I want to try and find Nadia Safi,' said Lacey. 'She could really kickstart the investigation. Any thoughts on how I might do that?'

Toc was leaning back on her chair, looking smug. 'I'd have thought you were the expert on tracking down young women in London.' Her smile widened. 'You spent eight months looking for me, remember? Very nearly found me as well.'

Lacey sat back in her chair and smiled back at Toc. 'I did, didn't I?'

54

Pari

The firing was getting closer now, the heavy thud of large guns striking the walls around her home, the breaking of glass. She could see daylight beyond. A few more strikes and the wall would be down. She'd be free. Boom, tinkle, tinkle.

Pari woke just in time to hear the splash as something struck the water below her window. She lay still, dreading the nausea that crippled her when she was awake these days.

Had there been singing? That old folk song, just before the thudding had made her dream of gunfire?

There it was again. The soft thud that had seemed so much louder in her dream, followed by the sharp rattle of metal against glass. Then the splashing again. Curiosity getting the better of her, Pari got out of bed.

The room was dark. Only the faintest slivers of moonlight ever found their way inside. She couldn't hear anything, but something told her that the world around her wasn't entirely asleep. Somewhere, not very far away, people were awake. Something was happening.

When Pari put her face to the window, the buildings across the creek were almost entirely black. A missile — small, round — was flying up towards her. It hit the wall below and dropped down again.

Standing on a chair, she could see something in the water below. Impossible to see exactly what — just shapes and movement. The missile was flying up again, catching on the partially open window directly below hers. It was a set of keys attached to a ball. Pari watched a small hand reach out and close around the keys.

She stayed where she was until her back started to hurt, then climbed down and sat on the bed, listening and waiting.

Traffic from somewhere quite distant. A siren. Shouting, again very distant. The normal sounds of London. Then a door being softly closed.

No one moved around at night. It didn't happen. The prison warder — Pari had long stopped thinking of her as anything else — valued her sleep. And that hadn't been an internal door. Pari climbed up again, leaned out of the window once more and looked down.

Vague shapes. Pale colours against the black of the water. The gleam of skin, the graceful fall of long hair. Then a gentle, rhythmical splash. A boat was moving away from the building. Someone had left.

Pari returned to her bed, lowering her throbbing head carefully. For the first time in many weeks, she felt hope.

Someone had just got out.

Someone was helping them.

55

Lacey

What on earth am I doing? Thought Lacey, as she stepped down from the bus. She wasn't a detective any more, she'd only recently been signed off as fit for duties and there was no way she'd be allowed to take part in undercover work. Plus her credibility in the Met had probably hit rock bottom. Maybe that was it, the need to claw something back. She couldn't don a wetsuit and dive the Thames, she couldn't search a five-mile stretch of the south bank, but she might just be in with a shot at finding Nadia Safi.

She took a moment to get her bearings. The Old Kent Road in South London was notorious. There were over a dozen brothels and massage parlours on this section of the street alone, many tucked away below or above fast-food outlets. Catching a glimpse of her reflection in a shop window, she pulled the headscarf a little further around her face. Eyes down, submissive body language: she was a scared young woman in a foreign country.

Arriving back in London after visiting Toc, she'd gone straight to a tanning salon for an all-over bronze look. Before coming out, she'd darkened her hair, avoiding the garish blue-black that would give it away as artificial, settling instead on very dark brown. Her darker skin threw the whites of her eyes and the hazel-blue irises into sharp relief. She'd drawn a fine kohl rim around her eyes and darkened her lips. In the dark of the street and the artificial lights of the buildings, she knew she had a chance of passing for a Pashtun woman.

The first place she went into had a small reception area with whitewashed walls and plastic seats, a dusty plastic palm tree pushed into one corner. On the chipped coffee table were several used plastic cups. Lacey raised her eyes from the floor and met those of the fifty-something white woman behind the counter.

Speak slowly. Lots of pauses, as though searching for the words. She didn't risk trying to fake an accent.

'Can you help me, please? I am looking for my sister.'

The woman shook her head and breathed in through her cigarette. Lacey took the photograph of Nadia Safi out of her bag and put it on the counter. 'Her name is Nadia.' The woman wasn't looking at the picture. She was staring at Lacey, her mouth twisted into an amused smile. Knowing that a woman would be more likely to spot hair dye and a fake tan, Lacey reached quickly into her bag again.

'Please.' She put the scrap of paper on to the counter and picked up the photograph of Nadia. 'I have a phone. If you know anyone who might know Nadia, please?'

As Lacey turned to leave, in the glass of the front door she saw the woman screw up the scrap of paper and sweep it on to the floor. You win some, you lose a lot more. She'd done this before, spent months of her life searching London for a young woman who didn't want to be found. It was like fishing. Scatter enough worms on the water and sooner or later one of them would be taken.

The second place she tried — on the face of it a massage parlour — had an elderly bloke behind reception and two women in the waiting area. From the way they were dressed and made up, Lacey assumed they were workers.

'Go home, love,' one of them advised her when, with downcast eyes, she showed them the photograph. 'This is no place to be out at night.'

Next, a kebab shop. A young Asian man behind the counter. 'Never seen her,' he said, in an accent that told Lacey he was British born and London raised. 'Where are you from?'

'Kunduz.' Lacey named a province in the north of Afghanistan, close to the Tajikistan border. 'She's my sister,' she repeated, indicating the photograph.

'You got papers?'

Lacey flinched, dropped her eyes. 'I don't want trouble. I just want to know that she's well.'

'How'd you get here?'

She backed away, closer to the door. 'We travelled together. We were separated at Calais.'

'You got a place to stay?' The look in his eyes was becoming acquisitive. Time to move on. Lacey took out the scrap of paper with her phone number, scurried to the counter and left it behind. The door chimed behind her as she stepped out on to the street again.

'You speak very good English for an Afghan

woman.'

'I went to school.' Lacey kept her eyes on the dust-strewn floor. 'I was one of the lucky ones.'

The man leaning against a cheap plastic bar was West Indian, middle-aged and overweight. 'Do you need a place to stay?' he asked her. 'Any money?'

It had been the same everywhere. Either they wanted to recruit her, or they did their best to ignore her.

'I just want to find my sister.' Lacey put the card with her phone number down in front of him. He reached out, tried to grab her hand. 'We're looking for nice girls here. Do you want a job? Steady work.'

Lacey stepped back, away from the counter. 'If you think of anyone who might have seen her, please phone me.'

By three o'clock in the morning, she'd had enough. Last time she'd done this, she'd been ten years younger and she'd been looking for someone she cared about. Nadia was just a name, a photograph and a damp memory.

Her phone was ringing. Not her own phone, which was back on the boat. This was the cheap, throw-away mobile she'd bought earlier. Her heart was suddenly beating loud and fast, exhaustion forgotten.

'Hello?'

'I know where she is.'

The green illuminated sign advertised EXOTIC GIRLS, the red neon beneath it said PEEP SHOW. More signs, as if the purpose of the establishment weren't sufficiently clear, advertised pole dancing and striptease. As Lacey approached, three men in business suits, two of them Japanese, the other their British guide, were admitted by the over-weight doorman. The voice on the phone had told her to go round the back.

She looked quickly in her bag, to check that the text message she'd sent to her own phone back at the boat had gone through. She'd texted exactly where she was going and why. If anything happened to her, sooner or later her phone would be checked. As insurance policies went, it was hardly fully comprehensive, but it was better than nothing.

The alley she was expected to walk down was very dark. She could barely see the other end of it. She pulled out her phone again and dialled 999.

'Emergency services.'

'I just saw a girl being dragged into a strip club on Argyle Street,' said Lacey. 'Just off the Old Kent Road. There were three men with her. It looked like she was being forced. I think she needs help.'

Less than a minute later, she was walking down the alley. The average police response time in this part of London at this time of night was fifteen to twenty minutes. In a case of possible abduction, the constables responding would tread cautiously. They wouldn't go charging into a strip club without back-up. They'd look around, talk to the doorman, wait for reinforcements. It was seventeen minutes past three. She had time.

At the end of the alley, a dark-skinned, dark-eyed man was waiting for her in an open doorway.

'Where is Nadia?' said Lacey from several feet away.

'You need to come inside.'

Fifteen, twenty minutes. Still a big risk.

'Is she here?' She'd be expected to be frightened. Frightened would look convincing. A step closer. Glance into the yard behind the door. She was probably looking very convincing right now.

'I don't want to go in there.'

'Up to you. Do you want your sister or not?'

Lacey stepped forward. When she was

close enough to reach, the man grasped her shoulder and pushed her inside. The door closed behind them and a bolt was pulled. Shit!

The yard was surrounded by high walls on three sides and a narrow three-storey house on the other. It smelled of Indian food, of stale beer and even staler urine, of bins that hadn't been emptied in a while. There were lights on in the house. The man pushed her towards the back door.

Filthy kitchen. At least a dozen milk bottles showing varying shades of yellow, curdling milk. A recycling box overflowing with beer cans. A stack of pamphlets in Urdu on the worktop. From somewhere inside the building she could hear the monotonous drone of cheap European pop music. Three more men in the kitchen, two of them white, one Asian.

'Check her bag,' snapped the man who'd met her in the alley.

Lacey's bag was pulled from her shoulder, its contents tipped on to the worktop beside her, but she'd spent enough time with Joesbury to know that, when working undercover, you carried nothing that might identify you. In the bag were her phone, an umbrella, a few cheap items of make-up, a bus ticket and a few coins.

'Who are you?'

Eyes down. An illegal immigrant would be terrified. The man talking to her, the older of the two white guys, stepped forward and thrust a hand under her chin. 'I said, what's your name?'

'Laila.'

She tried to drop her eyes again. He held fast. *Stay calm. Think back to when you did this before.*

'Laila what?'

'Just Laila. Please, I only want my sister.' She turned to the man who'd brought her in. 'You said you knew where she was?'

The other Asian man spoke. 'Muslim women don't wander the streets on their own at this time of night. What are you, some sort of whore?'

'She's my sister. She doesn't have anyone else.'

'Where are you from?'

Lacey looked at the men in front of her. Two of them could easily be from South Asia. She couldn't panic. There were any number of languages and dialects in that region. They couldn't possibly know them all.

'They told me not to say,' she replied. 'I don't want to go back. I just want Nadia.'

'What if we told you we do know Nadia,

and she's told us she doesn't have a sister?'
This was the other white guy, the younger
of the two, in a brown leather jacket and
with a tight woollen cap over his dark hair.

'If she told you that, she's trying to protect
me. Is she here?'

'Hold on to her.'

The older white man turned and left the
room. At least ten minutes before help
would get to her. Eight minutes before she
had to get out of here, or risk being taken
into custody. Shit, this was not going well.

'I want to see my sister or I want to leave,'
she told the man who'd brought her in, the
one who was now leaning, bouncer style,
against the back door. He straightened up,
not about to let her through without an
argument.

'Bring her upstairs.'

The boss was back. Two of the others
reached out for her.

'No!'

Lacey was being backed up against the
counter. She could brace herself against it,
kick out with both legs. With only one bloke
she'd have a chance. With four, none at all.

'You think I'm alone? I have a friend who
will call the police if I'm not out of here in
two minutes.'

She was grabbed and pushed forward, out

379

of the kitchen, into a narrow corridor. Oh, what the hell had she done? She was alone, in a strip club that probably doubled as a brothel, the prisoner of four men, and the music was so loud that she wouldn't hear the sirens and no investigating police officer would hear her.

The stairs they went up were filthy, the carpet old and worn. The light-bulb above them was broken. On the first floor another man was waiting. He opened a door at the far end of the corridor and pushed Lacey in.

The man behind the desk looked to be in his early sixties, with thick, greying hair and a large hooked nose. His eyes were dark brown, his skin suggested he might be mixed race, or very fond of foreign holidays.

The door slammed shut and the noise of the music faded just to the point where it no longer hurt. The arms holding her fell away and she was left in the midst of a circle of unfriendly eyes like a captive animal. She had to hold it together. The police would be here.

'You have thirty seconds to convince me you're from Bongo Bongo Land or I'm making plans for you,' said the man with the hooked nose and the cruel eyes. He glanced at the man behind her in the brown jacket. 'Know her, Beenie?'

Lacey was turned to face him.

'No.' Beenie kept his eyes on her as he shook his head. 'That one I would remember.' He let his eyes trail down to her feet and then up again.

'Could she be one of your lot?'

Beenie screwed up one side of his mouth. 'Can't be. No female officer would be allowed round here at night without back-up. And if she had a team with her, they'd be in here by now.'

One of your lot? Beenie was a cop. What the hell had she walked into? One of the men walked to the window and looked outside. If he saw anything to alarm him, he didn't mention it.

'So if she isn't the filth, who the fuck is she?'

'If you want my best guess, I'd say a PI,' Beenie replied. 'Maybe that girl she claims to be looking for has a family after all.' He turned to the doorman. 'Have you searched her?'

'Nothing in her bag.'

'I didn't ask about her fucking personal effects, I said have you searched her?'

Shake of the head.

'Then I guess it's your lucky night.'

Lacey stood, impassive and unconcerned,

as if she was going through airport security, as male hands ran along the length of her body. Her back, arms, legs. Everywhere.

'Nothing.'

Hook Nose was losing patience. He stood up, leaned over the desk towards her. 'OK, enough fucking around. What are you doing here?'

Probably time to drop the submissive act. Beenie had given her an angle, maybe she could use it.

'I'm looking for Nadia Safi,' she told him. 'Does it really matter whether I'm her sister or not? She has people who care about her, who'll pay my bill. If you haven't seen her, just say so and I'll leave you in peace.'

'Who do you work for?'

'Myself.'

Hook Nose sat down again. 'So what do we do with her?'

'Can you dance, darling?' said the white man who'd brought her up here.

'There's a room free upstairs,' said one of the Asians. 'Want to try her out first, Rich?'

The man behind the desk, Rich, seemed to be thinking about it. Beenie had been picking at his nails, feigning complete indifference. He looked up. 'Sorry, guys, you can't keep her. She won't be working alone, whatever she might tell you. She'll have

382

people who'll come looking. You don't need that sort of attention right now.'

'What then?'

'Let her go.'

'Just like that?'

'Show her the family album. She looks like a woman who values her face.'

Rich crinkled his eyes at Lacey for a second before reaching inside his desk drawer. He brought out a cheap-looking photo album and beckoned her closer.

The first page showed a woman whose face and neck had been badly scarred. Her flesh rose in lumps and ridges like the surface of the moon. 'Acid,' said Rich. 'She got clumsy, pulled a bottle down on herself when she was trying to run away before we'd done with her.' He turned the page. More dreadful injuries. 'Silly girl set fire to herself,' said Rich. 'You have to be careful with saris. Especially the cheap ones. All that nylon is very flammable.' Another page. 'Cut off her own nose, can you believe that?'

'I've got the message,' said Lacey.

Rich ignored her, turning the page again. A woman whose face had been cut either side of her mouth, creating a scar that was a hideous mockery of a smile. As Lacey closed her eyes, the phone rang. Rich picked it up.

'There's a police car outside,' he said a

moment later. 'Two officers watching the building very closely.'

'I have to be out of here,' said Beenie. 'I'll get rid of her. My car's out back.'

They hurried from the building, Beenie pulling Lacey along by the hand. Down the stairs, back along the corridor as someone started banging on the front door, out into the yard and then the alley. Beenie led her to a dark saloon car parked a few yards away. He jumped into the driver's seat and was almost moving before Lacey was properly inside. They reached the end of the alley, turned on to the main road and sped past the club. Two patrol cars were parked outside, their occupants still discussing the possibilities of admission with the doorman.

Driving down the Old Kent Road, Lacey watched Beenie's eyes in the rear-view mirror. For a second he looked up, but his expression told her nothing. I'll get rid of her, he'd said. Get rid of her how? The street was getting quieter, they'd left most of the lights behind. They were slowing. Beenie indicated and pulled over. Lacey turned to see where they were.

Outside an all-night minicab firm. He was putting her in a cab?

Less than a minute later, Lacey was in the back of a car that smelled of cigarettes and cheap air-freshener. Beenie leaned in and handed over a twenty-pound note to the driver, whom he'd greeted by name.

'She'll tell you where she wants to go,' he told him. 'Take her straight home.' Then he turned to Lacey. 'We see you in this neighbourhood again, love, and it won't be a minicab we send you home in. Got that?'

■ ■ ■ ■

SUNDAY, 29 JUNE

■ ■ ■ ■

56

Pari

'How did she get out? How the hell are they getting out?'

'Don't look at me.'

Pari felt too bad to wake up. Sleep was sometimes the only way to push the pain to one side. Even then, it never really went away completely, always invading her dreams, turning them dark.

'Who else am I supposed to look at? Who else was here all night?'

'What are you saying? That I let them out?'

They were speaking too quickly for Pari to catch more than a few words, but the fear behind them was clear. The people who looked after this place never normally raised their voices.

'Well, someone is doing it. He's going to go berserk.'

'Then he needs to fix it.'

'What's that supposed to mean?'

'Ask him. It's his call.'

Pari opened her eyes. It was no longer dark in the room. Morning.

'Oh, you'll tell him that, will you?'

'Can you tell me how they're getting out?'

'That's nine we've lost now. Nine who've just wandered out by the back door. They're not doing that by themselves.'

No, they're not, thought Pari. Someone is helping us. Soon, it will be my turn.

57

Lacey

The tide was out, the yacht had settled into the mud and Lacey could no longer see the deck of the old dredger. She really had no idea how long she'd been just sitting here, staring out across the water. She'd slept most of the morning and spent the afternoon trying, and largely failing, to find something useful to do. It was going to be one of those wasted days. The sooner it was over with, the better.

God help her if Joesbury found out what she'd done last night.

At the faintest sound behind her, Lacey realized that she wasn't alone. Eileen had climbed into the cockpit of the next boat and was sitting watching her. But when Lacey smiled, opening her mouth to say something, she was no longer sure the older woman was looking at her. Eileen's eyes were fixed in her direction, but they weren't actually focused. Eileen seemed lost in thought.

Below, a phone was ringing. Lacey got up, swung herself down the steps and stopped. Her usual phone, on the table, was silent. The ringing was coming from the bag she'd carried along the Old Kent Road the previous night. The number was withheld.

'Hello?'

Silence on the line. Through a starboard side hatch, Lacey could still see Eileen. There was something different about her this afternoon. She was wearing a dress the colour of the ocean and her hair was loose. Her strong face was made up, giving her a glamour that hinted at the woman Ray had married all those years ago. In the tight-fitting dress, she didn't seem nearly as big as she usually did. Quite shapely, in fact. Still silence on the line, then —

'Why are you looking for me?'

A woman's voice. Broken English. Heavily accented.

'Is that Nadia?' Lacey turned away, so that the unusual sight of a glamorous Eileen wouldn't distract her.

'You are not my sister. Why do you tell people you are my sister? What do you want?'

'I'd like to meet you. Can we talk, please?'

'I have nothing to say.'

So why had she phoned?

'I'll come alone,' Lacey said. 'I just want to talk. You've nothing to be afraid of, I promise.'

Silence. Was it even Nadia Safi? It could be anyone. She looked back up through the hatch. Eileen was combing her hair now, that faraway look still on her face. Long hair reaching her shoulders. Grey, but still soft. Not wiry, the way older people's hair often became.

'Where are you now?' Lacey spoke softly, conscious that Eileen could probably hear her. 'I'll come and find you.'

'Why?'

'I think you can help me. I might be able to help you.'

Lacey held her breath.

'Kensington Gardens. By the statue of the little boy. In an hour.'

58

Nadia

The park was full. An ice-cream van was pumping out far more heat than the product it was selling could hope to soothe. Dogs and children ran, adults followed as best they could. A juggler looked ready to melt, he was sweating so much.

Nadia walked through the Italian Gardens at the northern edge of the Serpentine, the colours of the flowers muted and dull through the grille she wore over her eyes. The burkas worn at home were pale blue, and supposedly bad enough, but nothing could be worse to wear in the heat than this oppressive, suffocating black.

She glanced back. Fazil was by the gate, one of his sons further inside the park; another would be close by. It had been their idea to meet the woman from last night, to find out who she was, what she wanted. Nadia set off along the water's edge, the ground cracked and dry beneath her sandalled feet, her hands wafting the dark folds to allow some air to reach her face. The statue of Peter Pan lay ahead.

Several people were near it. A man intent upon his mobile phone. A mother rubbing ice cream from her toddler's shirt. A woman looking west towards the palace. Young, judging by her shape and posture, long dark hair loose down her back. A bicycle lay at her feet and she was wearing the green and white striped shirt she'd mentioned on the phone. This was the woman who'd walked the length of the Old Kent Road claiming to be Nadia's sister.

As if any of Nadia's sisters would dream of doing something so reckless. As if any of them would care enough.

She turned, looked directly at Nadia, her face registering nothing. Fazil had been right about meeting here. All around the park, black-clad women walked, sat and talked, pushed buggies, only their hands showing a glimpse of the person within.

The woman in the striped shirt turned again, spinning a slow, lazy circle. Nadia stepped on to the grass so that her feet made no sound. When she was close enough, she spoke the name she'd been told on the phone.

'Lacey?'

The woman turned. Nadia stepped back in alarm. This was a terrible mistake. She had to get out of here.

'Nadia, is that you?'

Nadia began to hurry towards the gate. Footsteps behind her told her she was being followed. Then the English woman jumped in front, stopping her from moving forward. 'I know it's you,' she said.

'You're the police,' said Nadia. How could she have been so stupid? How could Fazil not have realized?

Lacey held up both hands. 'I'm alone. No one knows I'm here.'

Was she telling the truth? Impossible to know. Nadia turned her head, cursing the tiny grille that made her vision so limited. She saw Fazil, who would withdraw his protection completely if he knew she was talking to the police.

'You were on the river,' she said. 'That night last year when the boat overturned.'

Lacey nodded.

'You came in for me,' said Nadia. 'You, not any of the men.'

'They were at the other side of the boat. They didn't see you.'

'You think they would have jumped in the water for someone like me?'

396

'Actually, you'd be surprised. And I was fastened to the boat. I was never in any danger.'

'You were when I tried to stand on your head to get out.'

The policewoman smiled, showing teeth that were small and the colour of fresh cream. 'I'd really like to ask you some questions,' she was saying now. 'Can we sit down for a while?'

Nadia's voice dropped to a whisper. 'They are watching us.'

The policewoman didn't look round, didn't react in any way. 'Who? Who is watching us?'

'I have to go. They cannot know you are police.'

Lacey was looking directly into Nadia's eyes, as though the grille wasn't there. 'Come with me now. I can keep you safe. Come and testify. We'll look after you.'

Did she really think it was that easy?

'Will you look after my family, too? Thousands of miles away. Can you keep them safe?'

Lacey was clearly too honest to make promises she knew she couldn't keep. She stepped back and shook her head, exaggerating the gesture. 'Tell them you're not who I'm looking for. Tell them I'm a private investigator, they'll know what that means, and that I made a mistake. Tell them I won't be bothering you again. Then call me. We'll talk when you're alone.'

Slowly, Nadia raised her veil. She kept the edges close to her head, so that only Lacey could see her. The policewoman had dyed her hair since the night last October. Even soaking wet, Nadia knew it hadn't been this dark. Her skin was darker too, as though she'd spent months in the sun. Only her eyes were the same.

'You would have asked to see me,' she said. 'To be sure I'm not who you're looking for. Thank you for saving my life.'

She dropped the veil again and set off. She didn't look back.

59

Dana

'Ma'am, we lost her.'

'You are kidding me!' A woman had come to them of her own volition, had met with one of them, and now they'd lost her? Dana turned on the spot, looked up and down the Bayswater Road. No burka-clad woman had come out of the shopping centre this way. Up the road, at the entrance to the park, she spotted Lacey, who'd followed Nadia at a distance, trusting in her colleagues to keep her in sight. 'Are you sure?' Dana said into her radio.

Stenning sounded out of breath. 'Do you have any idea how many burkas there are in Whiteleys shopping centre at this time of year?'

'Keep looking.' With less than an hour's notice, the only members of her team Dana had been able to get across London were Stenning and Mizon. They couldn't even cover all the exits. 'We can't lose her. She's all we've got.'

As the words came out of Dana's mouth, she knew it was hopeless. Nadia had gone.

60

Lacey

'Penny for 'em?'

Lacey jumped. Ray was in the cockpit of his boat, smoking, an open can of beer at his side. From somewhere below, she could hear Eileen humming quietly and tunelessly to herself. The two of them hadn't gone out for the evening, after all. She wondered if Eileen were still in her sea-blue dress, and what on earth had possessed the woman to get herself all dressed up with nowhere to go.

'Didn't see you there, skulking in the shadows,' said Lacey as she made her way around the port deck of his boat.

He blew smoke up into the air. 'Too hot to go below.' There was practically no breeze on the creek tonight, and the smoke hung above Ray's head, almost as though he were in an enclosed space. She could see Eileen's comb and mirror beside the beer can.

'You been working?' he asked her.

'Wild-goose chase,' Lacey admitted. A big, black, billowing wild goose, who'd got clean away. And some time tomorrow she'd have to explain to Tulloch about her unofficial undercover activities along the Old Kent Road.

Exhaustion getting the better of her, she wished Ray a good evening, opened the hatch and went below. The cabin was hot, as she'd expected. It was going to be a long, sticky night. She slipped off her shoes and went into her bedroom. The cabin was small enough for her to take in everything from the doorway, and neat enough for her to be able to spot anything out of place.

Crabs.

Three of them, on her bed. All alive, two still and glossy brown against the plain white duvet cover, the other moving slowly and gracelessly along her pillow. For a second, Lacey watched them, not quite believing her eyes. There was something almost surreal about the long spindly legs and oversized claws on her spotless bed linen. Then she left the cabin, found a high-sided dish and tongs in the galley and went back.

'Crabs,' she said to Ray, a second later, when she was back in the cockpit.

402

'I can see that,' he said.

'On my bed,' she added.

He flicked cigarette ash over the side. 'Not something you see every day.'

Lacey leaned out over the stern, upturned the dish and watched them disappear.

'How did they get there?' asked Ray, when she'd straightened up again.

'I have no idea. I left the cabin hatches open but crabs can't climb a smooth hull, can they?'

'Not to my knowledge. Mitten crabs, were they?'

Lacey nodded. They were, to her knowledge, the only crab resident in the Thames.

'Lot of them about,' said Ray.

'Ray, have you been here all evening?'

He nodded. 'Nobody came past me. Any more down below?'

'Not that I could see. Maybe I've got a hole somewhere and they found their way in.'

'If you've got a hole somewhere, you'll find out at high tide.'

'You're right. I'll give you a yell if I need a bail-out. Goodnight.'

Lacey went below again, unwilling to admit, even to herself, how jumpy she felt. On the scale of one to ten, mitten crabs were hardly disturbing intruders. But it really wasn't that likely they'd found their own way in here. So, could she call Tulloch and report three intruders of the crustacean variety? Did she want to be the subject of crab jokes down at Wapping for the next six months? Better to sit tight. Ray and Eileen were within shouting distance.

The boat rocked and rolled, with its bumpy, irregular, oddly soothing rhythm. Around the creek, the air was full of sound. Tidal London had remembered that some wind was the norm and the masts and high buildings were a mass of sighs and whistles. The A2 hummed with the occasional passing car, and a nocturnal bird screeched at the loss of a catch. Inside the cabin, all was quiet.

Lacey stirred, not quite asleep, conscious of being overly hot. There was sweat between her breasts and at the nape of her neck. She grabbed the pillow and turned it, then pushed the duvet further down the bed. It was far too hot to sleep with the hatches shut, but after the little surprise of earlier she hadn't wanted to be open to the elements. She turned again, and the darkness in her head grew deeper.

She was riding her bike down a long, dark tunnel, which was part creek, part Greenwich foot tunnel, and part something that belonged entirely to dreams. Crowds of veiled women lined her path.

Her head was itching. She reached up, scratched, turned over again.

Joesbury was staring down at her. He lowered his head and her eyes closed. She waited for the moment when his lips touched hers. His eyes again, outside the boat, staring in at her through the cabin window.

Lacey's own eyes opened, saw the hatch black and empty, and closed again.

She was in the water, swimming fast and going nowhere, in the usual way of dreams. Veiled women were behind her, drawing closer with every stroke, their long scarves floating out across the water, reaching, wrapping, dragging. Those veils, so long and light, so very deadly, running the length of her body, stroking, tickling.

Tickling her foot.

With a sudden, sharp awareness, Lacey sat up, crying out in confusion. She kicked hard and the creature that had been making its way along her foot fell to the floor of the cabin. She could hear it — clatter, clatter, clatter — along the polished wooden boards.

She found the bedside light, then sprang into a ball on the bed, convinced the things were everywhere.

They weren't. She ran her hands over her head, her shoulders; knelt on the bed and twisted this way and that. She bundled the duvet into a heap and pushed it against the cabin wall. Only then did she lean over the side of the bed to find the crab she'd knocked to the floor.

It was huge, its body a good three inches across and its legs stretching to eight or nine inches. There was weed attached to its right, rear leg, and one of its claws was much bigger than the other. It had been crawling all over her while she slept.

She had to stop shuddering. It was only a crab. Apart from a nasty nip, it couldn't hurt her. Lacey looked round. The hatches, one on each side of the cabin, were closed, as was the larger one above her head. The crab must have arrived with the others earlier, hiding out until it could emerge safely under the cover of darkness.

God, it was huge, easily the biggest of the four. And she had searched every square inch of the boat. There was nowhere a creature like that could hide.

Then she remembered. The large hatch above her head could not be opened from outside, but the smaller side ones could.

Clatter, clatter, clatter. The crab was trying to climb.

Ridiculous to be scared. She swam amongst creatures like this all the time. She'd never minded crabs, quite liked their comic, scuttling ways. And yet this one — she risked peering over the edge of the bed again — there was something almost predatory about the way it was making repeated attempts to scale the smooth wood of the bed frame.

Jesus, where was the man in her life when she needed him?

Before she could change her mind, she swung her legs over the side, picked up the crab and leaned across the bed to open the port hatch.

The creature's legs thrashed. Its claws reached for her. Lacey thrust her right hand out of the hatch and dropped the crab on to the deck. She closed the hatch and fastened it tight.

'Lacey.'

The voice was so soft, so close, that for a second Lacey thought there was someone in the cabin with her.

'Lay-cee.'

There was someone outside. On the boat, almost certainly — they were too close to be anywhere else. She reached out and switched off the light.

Clatter, clatter. Tap, tap, tap. The crab was scuttling along the deck. A pause, then a splash. It was back in the water where it belonged.

Lacey felt along the shelf that ran around the cabin wall and found her watch. Three forty-seven in the morning. It would be getting light soon. Not soon enough.

Who could be on her boat at nearly four in the morning? She didn't recognize the voice, couldn't even tell whether it was male or female. It had been low-pitched, croaking.

A tapping noise. Not the crab this time. The crab was back in the water and that had been heavier, more deliberate, like knocking on a door.

Tap, tap, tap. Someone was tapping on the side of the hull. Lacey picked up her phone. Ray, the reliable insomniac, answered on the second ring.

'What's up?' He kept his voice low, even though he'd told her previously that Eileen and he slept in different cabins, his at the stern, hers at the bow.

'There's someone on my boat.'

He didn't ask her if she was sure, or suggest she might be dreaming. He told her to give him a minute and hung up. Knowing the cabin was in darkness, that anyone watching from outside would see nothing, Lacey got to her feet, found her sneakers and pulled on a light sweater. She made her way into the main cabin and, when she could hear Ray opening the hatch of his boat, did the same with hers.

She stood in the cockpit, looking around, aware of Ray doing exactly the same on his boat. The tapping had been on the port hull, but there was no one on deck. No place to hide either.

'You been upsetting anyone?' asked Ray, when she'd filled him in.

Where would she start? 'No one who knows where I live.'

'Never a wise assumption,' said Ray. 'It always surprises me how many folk know where I live. Your bed is under the port-side hatch, isn't it?'

Lacey agreed that it was.

'If the crab was dropped through the other side, you would have heard it banging on the floor.'

'I guess.' That meant the intruder had been on the river side.

'Did you feel the boat rocking? Hear any footsteps?'

'No. Just the voice. And the tapping.'

Ray was already on her boat. He stepped

up on to the port deck and shone his torch in the water.

'You think they slipped over the side?' Lacey was having to look behind her every other second.

Ray ran the beam along the length of Lacey's boat, from the bow to the stern. 'What say we have a look around?' he said.

Five minutes later, Lacey crouched in the bow of Ray's motor boat as they made their way around the community of house boats. Ray hadn't turned on the engine, was relying instead upon muscle power to propel them along. The dripping of water from the oars as they were raised, a gentle splash as they dipped into the river were the only sounds they made, and these were more than drowned out by the slapping of waves against hulls, the wind keening around the masts and the distant and occasional hum of a passing car.

In spite of the sweatshirt she wore, in spite of the warmth of the night, Lacey couldn't stop shivering. She'd been on the river at night many times before, but always within the secure environment of one of the Targa launches. This felt very different. So low in the water, so close to the inky blackness that flowed around them, so much a part of the

410

briny, oily smell that rose like steam from a boiling saucepan. And so vulnerable to whatever was out there.

It had been Ray's unquestioning acceptance that she'd been right that had unnerved her the most. And also, that he hadn't considered for a moment searching the yard. They'd come straight out on to the river. Quite who or what he was expecting to find was another matter.

Not so long ago, Joesbury had drawn a heart shape in sugar in her cabin. The next day someone had copied it using shells and pebbles and had thrown in a linen bag of crabs for good measure. Toy boats had been left for her to find on three separate occasions. Someone was watching her. Playing games. Someone who'd come back. Someone who was out there now.

They'd reached the point where the creek met the concrete beneath Church Street. Ray steered the boat under the shelter of the bridge and the gloom deepened. Water drizzled from the steel plates overhead, the dripping unnaturally loud. There was a scurrying on the bank as they disturbed a riverside creature. Then they were out again, gliding smoothly along.

There was movement everywhere. Water splashed against the bank, trickling down again to join the river. The breeze stirred leaves and branches. Particles of mud and dust tumbled down. And every so often a creature — rat, vole, another one of those blessed crabs — scurried from sight into the mud.

A sudden sound above them made them both jump. A large bird was passing overhead. Too stocky to be a gull, it flew in low and fast, its wings fanning a current of air over Lacey's face. She'd swung the torch upwards and now lowered it again, letting it sweep across the water in front of them.

Eyes staring back at her, not fifteen yards away.

Lacey's hands gripped the torch, pinpointing its beam on the small, round shape in the water. A head. Human? Possibly. No doubt about the eyes, though. Large and gleaming, reflecting back the light of the torch. A sleek head, which might have hair floating around it. Or it could be just a trick of light on the water.

'Ray.' The boat moved closer with every stroke of the oars. 'Stop rowing. Turn round.' He did what she told him. They both watched the head in the water, which didn't move. There was something almost hypnotic about those huge, pale eyes.

The bird was back, screeching overhead,

breaking the spell. The head disappeared. Lacey leaned forward in the boat, trying to find it again.

'Steady on.' Ray sounded more unnerved than she'd heard him before. 'We don't want to go in. Not now.'

'Ray, where did it — ?'

'Keep still. And keep quiet.'

Lacey regained her balance and began sweeping the light across the creek, from one wall to the other, her heart beating so fast and so hard it seemed to be in danger of rocking the boat. She had to calm down. The torch-beam was powerful enough to reach each bank, but they were almost at the main channel now and the flow of water was less predictable. And much faster.

'I think we're done,' said Ray.

He avoided her eyes as he turned the boat and began rowing towards the marina. It would take them several minutes to get back. Lacey turned once again. There was no way she was turning her back on the creek. Not for a second.

The Bradburys' boat was twice the size of Lacey's but, unlike hers, hadn't been de-signed with comfort in mind. The main cabin was large but the walls were the bare charcoal-grey metal of the hull. It smelled of tobacco and fried onions, and of water left too long in the bilges.

Ray was fumbling around inside a free-standing cupboard. None of the furniture she could see had been designed for a boat. It was ordinary household or office furniture. It didn't work somehow, giving the room the look of a floating furniture store. When he'd straightened up, he put a bottle and two glasses on the table in front of her.

'Drink this,' he told her. Lacey reached out and accepted the glass gratefully. She breathed in the fumes and took a sip. Rum. Ray was a waterman. Of course he'd be a rum drinker.

'Won't we wake Eileen?' she asked quietly.

'End of the world wouldn't wake Eileen.' He pulled his own glass closer. The bottle sat between them, like a scene from a pirate movie.

'You saw it, didn't you?' she asked him.

Ray didn't take his eyes from hers. Just let his head fall and lift again. He'd seen it.

'What the hell was it?'

He flicked the glass up towards his mouth in the manner of someone planning to down it in one, but when it was lowered again on the table, very little seemed to have gone. Lacey copied him, letting the spirit sit on her tongue until it burned.

'My best guess?' he said. 'A seal.'

'It didn't look like a seal.' Lacey put her glass down, empty, on the table. 'It looked human. Ray, I've heard the talk about the creek mermaid. I just assumed they were drunken fishermen's tales. After tonight, I'm not so sure.'

'There are seals in the estuary,' said Ray. 'Not as many as there used to be, but you do see them occasionally up this far.'

Lacey reached out and poured herself another measure of rum.

'Seals have very human faces, Lacey. Big eyes, cute little noses.'

'I doubt a seal could have filled my boat with crabs. Or tapped on the side of the hull. Or called out "Lacey".'

Ray didn't reply.

'We have to report it,' she said.

Ray rolled a cigarette and knocked it lightly on the table top. 'Probably. But let's just sleep on it for now. From what I hear, you're not exactly flavour of the month at Wapping right now. How do you think your governors are going to react when you say you saw a mermaid?'

Lacey finished her second drink.

'Go on,' he said. 'Get back to bed. I won't sleep any more tonight and I always enjoy a sunrise. I'll make sure nothing bothers you.'

61

The Swimmer

In the creek, the swimmer watched the lights on the boat. Through the cabin window was movement, darker shapes against the glow of the lamps. Moving closer, it might be possible to hear what they were saying. Closer, close enough to touch. Between the two boats. Risky, but sometimes . . .

Time was running out. Another girl was going to die soon. Another one of those beautiful, long-limbed, smooth-skinned girls.

A raised voice inside the cabin. Lacey. The name was like a flower. Lacey was the most beautiful of them all.

They couldn't swim, the other girls. All that flaying, screaming, thrashing. They were easy meat. They screamed as they went under, water pouring into their gullets, and then it was all over. Not Lacey, though.

Lacey was strong. Fast. She was born to be in the water. Lacey would fight. Or flee. Either way, Lacey wouldn't be easy.

Lacey was the one.

■ ■ ■ ■

MONDAY, 30 JUNE

■ ■ ■ ■

62

Lacey

Lacey woke just as dawn was breaking. For a moment she was disorientated, then remembered she'd curled up in the stern cabin because its two tiny portholes were impossible to open from the outside. She'd wrapped the duvet around herself and had overheated, but at least she'd slept.

Tap, tap, tap.

It was back. Whatever had woken her in the night had come back. She sat up, banging her head on the low roof. The knocking was coming from the main hatch.

'Lacey.'

Ray's voice. He was at the hatch, agitated. 'Lacey, I'm coming in.'

The hatch started to slide open. Lacey got up on legs that hadn't had nearly enough rest. As she opened the cabin door, she saw Ray's tanned, wrinkled face peering down at her from the cockpit. Every line on it seemed to sink with relief when he saw her.

'Thank God for that.' He held out a hand. 'Come on, love. Let's get you out of there.'

Still groggy, Lacey looked round. 'What? What's happened?'

'I need you off the boat. Right now.'

The boat looked normal. It wasn't on fire. She checked the floor quickly. No water.

No crabs.

'I'll just get —'

'No!'

She'd been about to go into her own cabin to get clothes, had half stepped along the floor towards it. And yet, she could see now, there was something different about the room she usually slept in, not as much light coming through the bow hatch as there should be.

'Ray, you're scaring me.'

Ray made a quick, urgent gesture with both hands, a *get-up-on-deck-now* signal. 'You're going to stay close to me and we're going to walk across to my boat,' he said. 'It would be really good if you kept your eyes on your feet.'

That noise sneaking its way up her throat was a whimper.

'It's only just become light enough to see,' he was saying, as she climbed the steps and stepped out into the cockpit, not taking her eyes from Ray's.

'I think it must have been there for most of the night,' he went on. 'Maybe strung up while we were out on the water.'

It was behind her, whatever it was that Ray didn't want her to see. There was nothing out of place at the stern. The thing was up at the bow, above the cabin where she usually slept.

'Try and keep your voice down,' Ray was saying, as if making sound of any kind wasn't completely beyond her. 'The police are on their way. I really don't want people seeing this if we can help it.'

They'd stepped on to the starboard deck. Ray's boat was a large stride away. The air around them was still cold. The sun hadn't appeared yet.

Ray held out his hand. Lacey took it and stepped from one boat to the next. When she was safely on his boat, she turned round.

The first thing she noticed was the linen-wrapped corpse, dangling from the mast of her yacht. One of her halliards had been hooked on to the twine that was wrapped around its neck and it had been hoisted aloft. Its feet just brushed the port hatch. Then she saw the crabs. Dozens of them, climbing the legs of the corpse, scuttling around her boat, as though it had become their natural home.

63

Dana

'We need to find you somewhere else to live for now, Lacey. You can come to me tonight. Until we sort out something longer term.'

Silence in the small, eclectically furnished cabin of the Bradburys' boat.

Dana braced herself for a fight.

'You can't stay here. Even you must see that. We've gone way beyond coincidence now. Whoever is killing these women has got you in their sights. God alone knows how you manage it.'

Lacey sighed, got up from the table and nearly knocked over a coffee cup. She crossed to the porthole and looked out. Over her shoulder, Dana could see the yellow yacht. The body had been removed. SOCOs were crawling all over the boat, just as the crabs had done earlier. It would be days, maybe longer, before Lacey could live on it again.

'And why, *why* didn't you tell me about those toy boats sooner? This has been going on for well over a week.'

Over in the galley area, Ray and Eileen were talking quietly. Eileen, still wearing a purple dressing gown, turned to face them. 'You can stay with us, Lucy. We've got plenty of room.'

'I don't think so,' said Dana. 'It's very good of you to offer, but it's not fair to expect you to be responsible for Lacey's safety.'

'But this swimmer the two of them saw last night is more likely to come back if she's still living here,' said Eileen.

Another look between Ray and Lacey. What weren't these two telling her? As if the story hadn't been daft enough. Someone tapping on Lacey's boat in the small hours. The two of them going out on the water to investigate. A dark figure in the creek that disappeared as they'd looked at it and might have been a seal, neither of them were entirely certain. Oh, and crabs. Lots of crabs.

'That is true,' said Lacey. 'I can be seen on and around my boat during the day once SOCOs have finished with it, just sleep here at night.'

Dana thought about it. She could have a

heavy detective presence in and around the yard. The Marine Unit could increase patrols around the creek.

'We'll see,' she said in the end. 'Let's see what the post-mortem throws up.'

64

Dana

'Finally, the River Police give me one they haven't buggered about with first.' Kaytes pulled on his gloves and looked around at the six police officers. 'Pretty sizeable crowd for a mortuary. Come to find out how it's done, have we?'

Dana glanced across the room to where David Cook and Lacey stood side by side. Both remained still, staring at the body, oblivious to Kaytes's banter.

'She was found this morning on Lacey's boat,' said Dana. 'Given that, technically, she was found on water, she was taken to Wapping police station, where she was weighed, measured, photographed and entered on to the system. I particularly requested that no examination of the body take place until she was brought here.'

'She?' Kaytes pulled at his nose. 'Know something I don't?'

'It's a woman.' Lacey's eyes went briefly to Kaytes. 'From somewhere in the Middle East or South Asia. No disrespect, Dr Kaytes, but we all know that.'

Close to Lacey, Mizon was nodding. Neither Anderson, Stenning nor Cook showed any sign of disagreeing.

'Yeah, well, you're probably right,' muttered Kaytes. 'OK, let's all have a good look. Feel free to tell me your thoughts, people, but I want considered opinions, not hysterical assertions. Are you listening, River Police?'

Once again, Lacey didn't rise, just stepped closer and continued her slow, careful appraisal of the body. Around her, others followed, Dana last of all.

The slender form on the gurney was still wrapped in linen, the fabric stained the brown of the river silt. Algae had covered swathes of it, giving it a dull, greenish sheen, and the marine creatures had begun the process of making it their own. Ragged holes gaped around the face and neck, more on the abdomen. Dana felt a surge of excitement. This one hadn't been in the river long. This one would have more to tell them. There would be fingerprints, her internal organs would all be present, any wounds would be obvious. They would know whether or not she'd been pregnant.

'OK.' Kaytes turned to his colleagues, Max and Jac. 'Let's have a proper look, shall we? Who's got the scissors?'

The two lab technicians began the process of removing the linen wrappings. They found the knots at the neck, midriff and feet and snipped them away first. When everything was loose, Kaytes got involved, lifting the head, shoulders, waist and legs as the technicians unwound the bandages and bagged them carefully. The shroud beneath was a large, square piece of fabric, large patches of which were still white. At a nod from Kaytes, Max found the loose edge beneath the corpse's left side and raised it. The woman beneath was revealed.

'She looks like Sahar,' said Mizon, referring to the woman Lacey had found in the river just over a week earlier.

'She looks like Nadia,' said Lacey.

She looked like both, thought Dana. The dead woman's features were strong and regular. A high forehead, strong nose. Her eyes were open, large and pale in colour. About twenty years old, was Dana's best guess. Her breasts were high and small, her hips narrow and angular, her waist tiny. Her legs were long and a little on the thin side. The dark triangle of pubic hair had been neither trimmed nor shaved. There was fine, dark hair on the lower part of her legs and lower arms. The hair on her head was black and very long.

'She wasn't stabbed, or shot,' said Stenning. 'There's barely a mark on her.'

'We still need to turn her,' said Kaytes, 'but I'm inclined to think you're right. Jac, can I get a light up here, please?'

As the powerful light illuminated the woman's head, everyone moved a step or two closer to the top of the gurney. Kaytes took out a surgical comb. He began moving it through the woman's hair, gently parting it at inch-wide intervals across her head. 'No obvious major head injury. OK, let's turn her.'

He and his two assistants, with the skill of long practice, slid their hands beneath the woman's body and turned her on to her front.

'Pete's right,' said Anderson. 'No sign of blunt-force trauma at all.'

'She couldn't have drowned,' said Lacey. 'She was practically gift-wrapped. She must have been dead, or at least immobile, before they did that to her.'

Kaytes had found a magnifying glass and was looking through it at something on the woman's neck. Then he walked back down the body until he was directly above her left hand. The skin around her hand looked like a thin glove about to slip off. Kaytes frowned and leaned over to check the other hand.

'Was she strangled?' asked Dana. 'Or suffocated in some way?'

Kaytes gave her a small smile. 'Possibly. Turn her back, please, girls.'

'Look,' he said, a few seconds later, when the woman was once again staring up at them. 'See these marks just above her collar bone?'

'Looks like something was wrapped round her neck,' said Anderson. 'Strangulation then?'

'Could be,' said Kaytes. 'The mark goes all round to the back of her neck and it doesn't look like a post-mortem wound to me. And there are marks on both hands that could be defence wounds. We need to be very careful with the hands, girls. We could very well find our perp's DNA tucked away under the fingernails.'

'They're Pashtuns.' Lacey had both hands wrapped round a coffee mug, as though she needed the warmth within it. 'There's no way of knowing now, but I'll bet Sahar had pale eyes. Nadia has. So has this one. Young, beautiful women from Afghanistan or some-where very close.'

The team, together with David Cook and Lacey, were back at Lewisham police station. The post-mortem would continue for several hours. They'd left Kaytes and his team to it.

'We do need to talk to this Nadia Safi,' said Dana. 'Whether she's involved or not, she's all we've got for the moment. Which is why you're joining the team again, Lacey. You're our only link with her.'

Lacey looked sharply at Cook, who nodded his head. 'I've said it's OK,' he said. 'We can cover your shifts until it's over. Which I hope it will be soon, by the way. We've got a busy few months ahead.'

As Dana watched, a gleam lit up Lacey's eyes. For all that she had insisted upon her need to go back into uniform, Lacey wanted to be involved with this case. She wanted to solve it. She was still a detective, however much she might try to pretend otherwise.

At that moment, the door swung open and Mizon walked in. 'Report back from fingerprints,' she announced. 'Three different sets of prints on those toy boats, including yours on the yellow one, Ma'am, and Lacey's on all three. More significantly, though, another very distinctive print that we also found around the winch on Lacey's boat, one that matches, exactly, the third set.'

Dana sat up a little straighter, saw her movements mirrored by those around her. 'The winch used to haul the body up the mast?'

'The very one. Seems little doubt that our perp has a personal interest in Lacey and has been paying her visits for some time. Unfortunately, as his prints aren't on the system, we're no closer to knowing who he is.'

'What about the latest victim?'

Mizon shook her head. 'Sorry, Boss. Her prints aren't on record either.'

Around the table were collective sighs of frustration. 'Couldn't be that easy, could it?' said Dana. At that moment, her phone started ringing. It was Kaytes. He wanted them back.

The pathologist steered them towards a small, windowless meeting room that smelled of stale coffee and cleaning fluid. He didn't sit, just took up a position at the far end of the table. 'She wasn't pregnant. I'd be inclined to say she'd never been pregnant. The uterus was small, just what you'd expect to see in a young woman who's yet to start the whole messy process of sprogging.'

Dana pulled out a chair and leaned on it. Another lead gone.

'Any major organs missing?' asked Mizon.

'All present and correct. I made a point of checking the kidneys.'

And another. Dana sat down.

'I don't think she was strangled,' Kaytes went on. 'For one thing, the hyoid bone was intact. We'll have to wait for toxicology reports, but there are no signs of the most common forms of poison.'

'So how did she die?'

'We may never know for certain. But the clever money at the moment says she drowned.'

'That's impossible,' said Lacey immediately.

'Good to see you're keeping an open mind, River Police,' said Kaytes.

'Open mind or not, I can see Lacey's point,' said Anderson. 'Unless she was drugged to immobilize her before they trussed her up.'

'On the contrary, I think she put up a bit of a fight,' said Kaytes. 'There are wounds on her hands and lower arms, some scratch marks and faint bruises. The sort that can develop in minutes, because I think minutes were all she had. There's also a small wound on the skull, just above the back of her neck. And the mark around her neck that you all saw. They all indicate to me that somehow, possibly with some sort of restraint around her throat, she was held under the water until she drowned.'

'There's water in her lungs?' asked Stenning.

Kaytes nodded. 'There is. And it's Thames water. The mixture of fresh and salt water is quite distinctive. Not that that in itself proves anything. If a corpse is underwater for any length of time, water can seep its way into the lungs and stomach.'

Kaytes stretched, put both hands behind his head and arched his back. There was a lecture coming. 'You know, don't you, that we can usually only suggest drowning as the cause of death either if someone saw it happen or we've managed to rule everything else out. If our toxicology reports come back clean, then my conclusion will be that this young woman most likely died as a result of being forcibly submerged in the River Thames.'

'After which, she was removed from the river, shrouded, attached to weights and then dropped back into the Thames somewhere around Deptford Creek,' said Dana.

'Seems reasonable to me,' agreed Kaytes.

'Seems seriously weird to me,' said Anderson.

'But what you really all want to know,' Kaytes went on, 'is whether the woman found this morning, the one River Police pulled out of the Thames last week, and the one found at South Dock Marina two months ago have enough in common for them to be the subject of a joint investigation. Basically, do we have three unconnected deaths, or three linked by common circumstances? Is that fair?'

'Exactly,' replied Dana. 'We already know they were found in roughly the same stretch of river. We know there was a good chance that at least two of them were weighted down, given that their condition was consistent with their not moving around too much.'

'We also know we're covering a time period of less than a year,' said Lacey.

Kaytes nodded. 'Very likely, River Police. Right. All under thirty. I'd go as far as to say all under twenty-five, judging by their teeth and bone development. All three had long, black hair, suggesting Middle Eastern or Asian origin. None of them showed any sign of sophisticated dentistry.'

'No obvious cause of death, other than

what you've just told us?' asked Anderson.

'No sign that any of them were shot, stabbed, or hit over the head with a blunt instrument,' said Kaytes. 'Unlikely they were strangled, because the hyoid bone is intact on all of them. The post-mortem reports on the earliest one shows no sign of her having ingested any poisonous substances. I don't like to get ahead of myself, but it looks likely all three were forcibly drowned.'

'The shroud clinches it though, doesn't it?' said Mizon. 'The fact that two, possibly three, of them were shrouded is beyond coincidence.'

'I think so,' said Kaytes. 'You have a highly unusual serial killer, ladies and gentlemen. One who likes his work wet. Very wet.'

65

Lacey

'It's still bonkers,' argued Anderson, as he'd been doing for most of the afternoon. 'We're talking about a major operation. First you've got to find these good-looking Afghan girls with blue eyes. Then bribe them to leave their homes and travel thousands of miles with men they don't know across a major land mass, including the length of Europe. Then you have to smuggle them into Britain somehow.'

'Not somehow, Sarge.' Lacey was finding it surprisingly easy to be back at her old desk in Lewisham nick. 'We know exactly how. They're coming on a ship to Tilbury, being offloaded there, and then brought up the Thames by small boat.'

Anderson's complexion had been getting steadily redder as the day went on. He sighed. 'I stand corrected. We have some idea of the last couple of miles of a several-thousand-mile journey. We're positively brimming over with information. I'm starting to wonder how we managed without you, Lacey. But to get back to my point, it all smacks of big business. Nobody goes to all that trouble unless there's money to be made.'

'Nobody's disagreeing with you, Sarge,' said Mizon. 'But this money-making venture, either by design or accident, is resulting in some of these women dying.'

'And that's where we go slipping off into the Twilight Zone,' snapped Anderson. 'Because they're not just being dumped, they're being wrapped up like Egyptian mummies. That suggests something ritualistic to me, something twisted.'

'Because smuggling women across the planet and holding them captive isn't twisted?' said Mizon.

'I'm not saying it's nice, just that there's a logical point to it. Money. There is no logical point to how these women are being disposed of. And that's before we get on to the whole business of Lacey's stalker. It's all seriously weird.'

Nobody argued.

'Well, I'm glad we're clear on that,' said Stenning. 'Hush up now, she's on.'

The others turned to the TV set that had

been playing quietly in the background. The early evening news had just begun and the lead story was of the body that had been found on Lacey's boat earlier that day. A reporter was doing a piece to camera outside New Scotland Yard.

'The Metropolitan Police have confirmed not only that they are treating the death of the woman found at Deptford Creek this morning as suspicious, but that they believe her death may be linked to two similar cases in London within the last twelve months.'

The scene switched to the press room inside. DI Tulloch, Chief Inspector Cook and Detective Superintendent Weaver sat at the top table facing the reporters.

'We believe these young women are being recruited somewhere in the Middle East.' Tulloch had changed for the press conference and was wearing a pearl-grey suit with a deep-pink blouse. 'We believe they are being tricked into leaving their homes, possibly with the promise of a new and better life in the West. They are being brought into the country illegally, and kept prisoner. Then something terrible is happening to them. We believe three women have died in this way in the last year. There could be many more. There could be more young women at risk even now. If you know anything at all that can help us, please get in touch.'

'She has a natural authority, doesn't she?' said Mizon to Lacey.

'She does,' agreed Lacey. 'How much of it is the clothes?'

'They help. But I think it's also about knowing you're always going to be the brightest person in the room.'

A phone in Lacey's bag was ringing. Both women looked at each other. Then Mizon's eyes went to Lacey's usual mobile, still and silent on the desk between them. They'd hoped the press conference would flush out Nadia Safi, encouraging her to make contact again with Lacey. They just hadn't expected it to happen so soon.

Conscious of the room around her falling silent, Lacey found her phone. *Number withheld,* said the display screen. Just as it had the last time Nadia had called.

'Hello?'

'Do you still want to talk to me?'

'Of course.' Lacey nodded at her colleagues. 'Are you OK?'

Nadia hesitated just for a moment. 'I'm fine. I saw the news just now. Is it true? That three women have been killed?'

'At least three. Something terrible is happening to young women just like you. Can you help us?'

'Yes,' said Nadia. 'I think I can.'

66

Lacey

Greenwich Park was languid, heavy with the weight of the summer's heat and over five hundred years of history. Flower stems in the ornamental beds seemed barely able to hold up their blooms.

In running clothes, because what could be less conspicuous in Greenwich Park than a jogger, Lacey ran up the perimeter hill. As the slope levelled off, she slowed to get her breath, and to give what breeze there was the chance to cool her off.

Nadia, no longer wearing the burka but the traditional Muslim shalwar kameez, with a headscarf around her dark hair, was waiting on the steps of the General Wolfe statue. She was taller than Lacey remembered.

The park below and around them was busy. Everywhere Lacey looked, people walked dogs, played with children, threw balls at each other or just lazed around on blankets. Nadia had told her to come alone and had promised to do the same, but in this wide-open, crowded space there was no knowing one way or the other.

Lacey certainly hadn't kept to her word — that would never have been allowed, and the park was liberally sprinkled with plain-clothed police officers. On the way up, she'd passed Stenning and Mizon sprawled on the grass sharing a can of diet Coke. An operations van in a nearby street was listening to every word she said via the wires inside her running vest. Lacey stopped a couple of feet from Nadia and let the drinking flask she'd been carrying drop to the ground. It rolled towards the other woman, who stooped, retrieved it and handed it back to Lacey.

'Thanks.' Lacey tucked it carefully back into the strap around her shoulders. They now had prints to compare against those already on the system. They would soon know for certain if this were the same woman who'd been arrested last October.

As though neither knew how to begin, they turned to look at the view: the medieval deer park, a layer of white stucco Regency splendour below, then a sliver of urban river, topped off with twenty-first-century skyscrapers.

'At least up here it feels like there's some

air,' Lacey said to the Canary Wharf tower.

Nadia continued to stare ahead. She was older than Lacey remembered, and her skin had the fine lines of a face that had spent much time in the sun. 'We should keep moving.' Nadia turned suddenly and moved away. 'It will be safer.'

Feeling a chill that had nothing to do with air movement, Lacey fell in step beside her as they set off east. What to ask first?

Back in the van, Tulloch was uncharacteristically silent.

The two women passed beneath a short canopy of trees and suddenly the air around them was filled with sound. Leaves rustling, birds chattering and fighting, even the heavy scampering of a squirrel.

'Do you need any help?' Lacey began. 'I know you're in this country illegally, but if you're the victim of crime there are people who can help you.'

'Ask me again later,' said Nadia. 'What do you want to know?'

'Can you tell me where you're from?'

Silence.

'I think you're from Afghanistan,' said Lacey. 'I think, back home, someone offered to help you travel to the United Kingdom. I think you were probably told there'd be a job waiting for you, that you could earn good money and send it home to your family. If I'm wrong, it would be really helpful if you told me so.'

Nadia was looking to her right, away from Lacey, at a tree so wide around the girth as to seem hardly younger than the park itself. 'Such old trees,' she said. 'What are they? Do you know?'

Lacey didn't need to check. 'They're oaks. Most of the trees here are. It's a very old park.'

'In my country, too, we have old trees.' Nadia picked up the pace again. Importantly, she hadn't denied being from Afghanistan.

'I think they chose you because you have pale skin and eyes and because you're beautiful. I think you're not the first and you won't be the last. But, here's the tricky bit, I think some women like you who've been brought into this country have been killed.'

Lacey waited, giving Nadia time. The path had brought them to the prone form of the oldest tree in the park and the only one to merit its own protective railing. The empty husk of Queen Elizabeth's Oak.

Nadia was looking at the sign in front. 'What does it say?'

'It says that Henry VIII used to meet Anne

Boleyn by this tree,' said Lacey, before re-alizing that the names would probably mean nothing to this girl. 'Henry was a very famous king of England. He was married, but fell in love with a young English girl called Anne. He stopped at nothing to make her his queen, but when she didn't give him a son, he turned against her. She was executed when she was just thirty-five years old.'

'Did she have a daughter?'

'Yes,' said Lacey. 'Elizabeth. She became a very great queen.'

'I had three daughters.'

'Where are they?'

'With their father. I haven't seen them for three years.' Nadia turned back to the fallen tree. 'He killed her? She was a queen and he killed her? I thought this country was different.'

Lacey opened her mouth to point out that Henry and Anne had lived five hundred years ago and realized that to a woman who'd lost three children, half a millennium would be a detail. 'What happened to you?' she said instead.

Nadia pulled her scarf higher around her head. 'I married when I was fifteen. To the eldest son of a government official. It was an important marriage. I was told how lucky

I was. I think I even believed it. At fifteen, you don't think of much beyond having a good and kind husband, lots of healthy children, earning the respect of your husband's family. Do you?'

At fifteen, Lacey had thought of stealing cars, of driving them at speed around empty car parks at night, of torching them in the dock area of her home town. Of the boys with their gelled hair and hungry eyes. Of the lies she could tell her foster families and, very occasionally, of what would happen to her when she was too old for local-authority care. This woman and she probably weren't going to find much common ground. 'I guess girls are the same all over the world,' she said.

'My first daughter was born less than a year later.' Nadia reached out and, without seeming to know what she was doing, tore the head off a tall, daisy-like flower. She began tearing petals off it and throwing them to the ground. Her hands were surprisingly large, calloused and tanned. 'My second just over a year after that. My third nearly two years later. Three beautiful healthy girls. I was allowed to finish feeding my youngest before he divorced me and sent me back to my family.'

'For having girls? Are sons really so

important?'

The remains of the flower were scrunched in Nadia's hand. 'You have no idea what it's like in my country. A family without sons has no security, no future. A family without sons is nothing. A woman without sons is worse than nothing.'

'But you were young. You couldn't have been much more than twenty. You were obviously capable of producing healthy children. Why didn't you just try again?'

Nadia set off again quickly. 'Because my mother-in-law wanted to be rid of me. We have a custom in our land. When a girl is about to be married, her mother gives her a handkerchief. Often embroidered, often with lace. It is very special. But I wasn't told what to do with it. That night, after my husband and I had been together, he looked for evidence that I'd been a virgin.'

Lacey thought for a moment. 'He looked for blood?'

Nadia nodded. 'There wasn't any. The sheets were clean. He was supposed to take the handkerchief, you see, to my family the next day, as proof that they'd given him a pure bride. I was supposed to put it between my legs to collect the blood. But he couldn't do it. So I was disgraced. My family were broken by the news, my husband's family lost all respect for me.' She turned, and for a second there was such fury in her cold, silver eyes that Lacey almost stepped away. 'I was fifteen. I'd never left home alone. I'd worn a burka since my first period started. How could I not be a virgin?'

'Not all women bleed when they lose their virginity,' said Lacey.

'If I'd known what that handkerchief was for, how important it was, I'd have taken a knife into bed with me. I'd have cut myself without him knowing. I'd have made sure there was blood. My whole life depended on it and my mother didn't even tell me what it was for.'

'But you stayed together,' said Lacey. 'You had children.'

'If I'd had sons I might have been forgiven. But my mother-in-law saw each girl as a sign that God was cursing me for my impurity. She told my husband he would never have sons while I was his wife. So I was sent back to my family. He took another wife. She gave him a son within the year.'

'And your daughters stayed with him?'

'Children in Islam belong to the father. But they will never be happy. They won't have the best food or new clothes like the children of his new wife. When they're old enough they'll be married to unimportant men and will have no respect in their husband's families. No one will love them. Yet here I am, on the other side of the world, and my love is slowly killing me.'

Finally, Nadia turned to look at Lacey properly. She was a beautiful woman, clearly an intelligent one, all but crushed by the oppressive culture she'd been born into.

'Just over a week ago I found the body of a young woman in the Thames,' said Lacey, sensing an advantage. 'This morning, we found another woman just like her. We haven't been able to trace either of them, and that makes me think they came into the country illegally. The other night, I was out on patrol and we nearly caught a group of people coming up the Thames in a small unlit boat, just like you did. The two girls and one of the men got away. I was hoping you might be able to tell me what's going on.'

As Nadia set off again, Lacey followed. The path was taking them lower and Lacey caught the scent of roses, of dry earth and warm bark, as though the scents of the park were hovering close to the ground, like early mist.

'How did you know I was looking for you?' Lacey asked. 'When you contacted me last time? Who gave you my number?'

Nadia said nothing.

'Was it the men who brought you here? I don't want to put you in danger, Nadia. Look, come with me now. I can keep you safe.'

Nadia shook her head. 'I don't know whether they were involved in that or not. They said not. But I can't just disappear. I can't risk them hurting my daughters.'

Of course. It was how they controlled these women. Threats against the families back home. Whether the threat was real or not didn't matter; it only mattered that the women believed it.

A crackling in Lacey's ear told her that DI Tulloch was running low on patience. 'Why don't you tell me what you can?' said Lacey. 'Start with what happened when you left the hostel.'

'I was taken to a house,' said Nadia. 'It was a large place, but I only really saw my room. They kept me there for a long time. Several months, I think, but it was hard to keep track.'

Lacey heard Dana catch her breath.

'And what happened to you in those months?'

'Nothing. They said I had to wait until the paperwork was ready. And until they'd made arrangements for my job. So I waited.

I ate the food they gave me, watched television, slept a lot. It was dull.'

Not what any of them had expected to hear.

'They didn't hurt you in any way? Make you do anything you didn't want to?'

Nadia shook her head. 'I know what can happen to women like me. I know what a risk I took coming here. I'm one of the lucky ones.'

'Were there other women in the house?'

'I think so, but I didn't see any of them. I just heard voices from time to time. Occasionally someone shouting. I'm not sure everyone else was as patient as me.'

'You were kept prisoner there? The other women too?'

'I suppose so. I did ask to leave one day. They said I couldn't. That until the paperwork was sorted out, I'd be sent home. But I wasn't badly treated. When I got ill they looked after me. I had doctors, nurses, medical treatment.'

'You were ill?'

'Yes, several weeks after I arrived there. They said it would delay my release. That no one would want to employ me unless I was healthy.'

The ear piece started crackling again, but Lacey was already there. 'Ill in what way?'

she asked.

Nadia looked puzzled. 'I'm not sure. They said it was quite common for young women from my part of the world. That I just wasn't used to English food and water. English germs. They were right in a way. I did get better. And then I left.'

'Lacey, try and find out where she was kept,' Dana Tulloch's voice whispered in her ear.

'It was dark when I was taken there,' said Nadia, when Lacey asked her. 'And the same when I left. All I know is it was somewhere in London. The houses were tall. I couldn't find it again.'

'Did your room have a window?'

'Yes, but the glass was — I'm not sure what you would say — cloudy?'

'Opaque?' suggested Lacey. 'It lets light through but you can't really see anything. We use it in bathrooms a lot.'

'Yes, exactly, like bathroom glass. I knew there were other buildings close. And also, I was quite close to the river. You can tell, can't you, when you're near water? There's a smell in the air. And boats sound different to cars.'

'Did they take you there by water?'

A shadow appeared on Nadia's face. She let her head fall and rise in confirmation.

'They did. But if you want me to remember the journey, I really don't think I can.'

'Anything you can tell us — anything at all.'

'I'm sorry, but you have to understand how frightened I became of water. After what happened to us, that night you pulled me from the river, I couldn't think about water without feeling as if I was going mad.'

'That's understandable. It was a pretty terrifying experience.'

'But not the first, for me. Not the first time I nearly drowned.'

Lacey waited. Nadia seemed about to say more, then shook her head.

'It was years ago,' she said. 'The details aren't important. But because of it, water terrified me. I know they took me to that house by water, and brought me away by water. But I was so frightened both times, I just kept my eyes down and my scarf around my head.'

Lacey felt a surge of disappointment. It was possible they transported the girls by water to disorientate them, to make it harder for them ever to explain where they'd been. If that were so, it had certainly succeeded in Nadia's case.

'You didn't look where you were going?'

Nadia was shaking her head. 'No. I must

have seen a few things, but when it was over I tried so hard to forget it all.'

'I understand, really I do. But anything you do remember, anything at all, will be very useful to us.'

'There was something else. Something I never really understood.'

'What was that?'

'There was a woman. She was outside, I think. I heard her through the window.'

'A woman doing what?'

'Singing,' said Nadia. 'She used to sing to us.'

67

Dana

'Big house in Blackheath, Ma'am.' Barrett had just got back from tailing Nadia Safi to the place where she lived. 'In its own grounds with remote-controlled access gates.'

'OK, these are the options,' said Dana. 'We can bring Nadia in, make her our responsibility, but if there's nothing more she can tell us about the people who brought her here or where she was kept, we could be putting her or her family at risk for no good reason. We can also bring in her current employers, see if we can find out who's supplying their illegal staff, but again we risk putting the gang on full alert and not necessarily gaining much. Or we keep Nadia as a contact. She's given Lacey her number now, so at least we can get in touch if we need to.'

'I honestly think she's told us all she can

for now,' said Lacey.

'Exactly,' said Dana. 'For now. She may see one of the gang at the house. Something else could come up. I'd also really like her to give you a hair sample, Lacey.'

'A hair sample?'

'Yes. I want to find out what medication she was given while she was in the riverside house. Has anyone here ever heard a real doctor talk about English germs?'

Silence while everyone thought about that.

'They could just have been trying to use language a new immigrant could understand,' said Mizon.

'Possibly,' admitted Dana. 'But who were these doctors and nurses? Nobody pays house calls these days unless the patient's practically at death's door. And how come they weren't asking questions about these young women under house arrest?'

'Not real doctors?' said Lacey.

'They could have been anyone, giving her anything,' said Dana. 'All the other girls in the house as well. Lacey, can you ask her for a hair sample? She can pop it in the post to us if she's worried about meeting you again.'

Lacey nodded, as Dana glanced at her phone. 'That was uniform,' she said. 'The search of Deptford Creek and its surrounds begins at dawn tomorrow. If anyone's hiding out near the creek, we'll find them.'

68

Lacey

By six in the evening, the sun had lost much of its strength, but the ground seemed to be radiating back the heat it had absorbed during the day. Even Ray and Eileen's boat, with the benefit of the creek's breezes, had been unbearably hot and it had been a huge relief to get off her bike and step inside the green shade of the Sayes Court garden.

The circular wrought-iron table she'd been shown to was on a raised deck to one side of the house. The surrounding buildings blocked the view of the river, but Lacey could see the treetops in the orchard across the creek. Tiny apples, pears and plums, as fresh and green as the miniature grapes on the vine growing overhead.

'Are you ready to tell us what's troubling you?' Thessa gave Lacey that odd, sideways glance she liked to use a second after she'd thrown a difficult question her way like a

461

hand grenade.

'Tell her to mind her own business.' Alex, approaching from the house, was carrying a large tray. 'You never know, it might work for you.'

'I imagine when you work in the medical profession other people's business inevitably becomes your own.' Lacey smiled at Thessa. 'It's similar in the police. And then in social situations, it becomes a little difficult to switch off.'

'If that's your best attempt at a polite ticking-off it's not going to work.' Alex put the tray down on the table. 'She's far too brazen to be warned off by subtleties. Help yourself. All cold, I'm afraid. We've both been working all day, but the bread is very fresh and that Brie looks like it's about to run off the plate.'

'It looks great,' said Lacey. 'It really was very kind of you to ask me over. And what's this we're drinking?'

There was an unopened bottle of Chablis on the table, condensation running down it like raindrops on a window, but Thessa had mixed another of her cordials and, given the heat of the evening, they'd started with that.

'Blackberry,' said Thessa. 'With a few drops of truth serum.'

'Do tuck in, Lacey.' Alex passed her a plate. 'And just ignore her. Although I have to confess to being rather curious about the incident at Deptford Creek today.'

'You saw it on the news?'

'Thessa was out in that paddle-boat of hers and saw the police on the river. I'm surprised one of you didn't run her under. She called me and I kept an eye on the local news for the rest of the day.'

'Then you'll know we found a body,' said Lacey. 'Not the first of its kind. There was another just over a week ago, one that I found when I was out swimming.'

'You swim?' Alex looked genuinely shocked. 'In the Thames?'

'I did,' admitted Lacey. 'Haven't since then. I'm thinking of giving it up completely.'

'Yes, please do. No one should be swimming in that river. That's probably what happened to the two poor souls you and your colleagues found.'

If only. Lacey leaned forward and added bread, cheese and cold chicken to her plate. As she settled back, she caught Thessa glaring.

'What?'

Thessa's eyes went pointedly to the mixed salad in a carved wooden bowl.

'Silly me.' Lacey leaned forward again. 'This is a work of art, Thessa.' The salad was sprinkled with flowers, tiny cherry tomatoes and small, jewel-like fruits and berries. 'Looks too good to eat.'

'Nevertheless.' Thessa watched, lips pursed, until Lacey had loaded up her plate and begun the process of putting leaves in her mouth.

'You'd make a good mum.' Lacey was wondering how much of the green stuff she had to force down before she could spread that rich, runny cheese over bread that looked as though it had been baked with walnuts. 'Of course, you could be already. I shouldn't assume.'

Silence fell like a shower of summer rain. The breeze from the river seemed to have changed direction. She couldn't hear the usual river sounds of traffic and water fowl. Instead there was a soft, almost musical sound, like water flowing.

'Can I hear a fountain?' she asked, when the silence became uncomfortable.

'Yes, it's coming from Thessa's Koi pond at the front,' said Alex. 'There's quite a collection in there. And to answer your question, neither of us have children.'

Lacey kept the smile steady on her face.

'I married very briefly, not long after we

arrived in the country,' he continued. 'It didn't last long and I wasn't inclined to try again.'

'There's a bond, you see, between twins,' said Thessa. 'Especially identical ones. A closeness that I imagine anyone would find it difficult to break into. Alex's wife always felt like the odd one out, I think.'

It was on the tip of Lacey's tongue to ask whether they'd all three lived together in this house and, if they had, which of them really — honestly — had thought it would be a good idea.

'But you can't be identical,' she said. 'Identical twins have to be of the same sex.'

'Of course they do. I think my sister was just making a general remark. What about your family, Lacey? Where are they?'

This was why she didn't have friends. Friends asked questions to which there were no easy answers. Lacey stole a glance at Thessa, who was intent on the contents of her glass, but whose ears were practically flapping.

'I don't really have any family,' she said.

Thessa looked up. 'Everyone has a family. Even us, although the chances of our ever laying eyes on any of them again are pretty slim.'

'I was taken into care when I was quite

465

young. When I grew up, I lost touch with my foster family and I have no idea about my real one. There's just me, I'm afraid.'

'Until you marry and have a family of your own,' said Alex. 'Which can't be very far away, I'd imagine.'

'Yes, how is that young man of yours?' said Thessa. 'Behaving himself any better, is he?'

Lacey smiled patiently.

'Oh, you'll tell us everything in time. They always do.'

'They?'

'My sister has pet projects,' said Alex. 'Patients, usually. She won't rest until she's worn them down physically and spiritually with her combination of pills, cordials and relentless intrusion into their private lives.'

'I consider myself warned,' said Lacey. 'But the young man in question works away a lot. He's away at the moment and I've been rather surprised by how much I'm missing him.'

'He'll be back,' said Alex. 'Unless he's a complete buffoon.'

Lacey smiled. Alex had fallen into the habit of paying her gentle compliments over the past couple of weeks. Normally, compliments from men meant a sexual interest that she was always very careful to guard against, but she never had that feeling from

Alex. His compliments were always respectful. They were almost paternal — yes, that was the only word for it. It was something new in her experience, the unquestioning, unconditional approval of an older man.

'That's not all, though, is it?' said Thessa. 'The sadness in you goes so much deeper than just missing your man.'

Lacey glanced at Alex, wondering if he were going to jump in again, but he was unusually silent.

'I was a detective,' said Lacey, 'up until a couple of months ago. It was all I'd wanted to be since I was young. But this time last summer I got involved in a very difficult case. I ended up right in the thick of it. After that, I was sent away on a job. It was supposed to be just routine surveillance, but it turned out to be anything but. I nearly died.'

She looked from Thessa to her brother. Two sets of large, dark-blue eyes were unwavering. They were good listeners, these two. Too good.

'I came back to London on the verge of leaving the police for good,' she said. 'I was a wreck. And the last thing I needed was another bad case, so of course that's exactly what I got.'

'You weren't involved in the South Bank murders, were you?' said Alex. Lacey nodded. 'Dear me. They were particularly distressing.'

'I'll say,' agreed Lacey. 'So I gave up my career as a detective and went back into uniform. I just want to patrol, uphold law and order on the river, help keep London safe. I know that sounds a bit cheesy, but it's all I can manage right now.'

'So what went wrong?' asked Alex.

'I found that body. A week ago. And, as luck would have it, it wasn't a suicide or an accident. It was something much worse. Then, this morning, another one popped up, practically on my doorstep.'

'But you can't be involved, surely?' said Thessa. 'CID or Special Branch or the Flying Squad will handle it now?'

'No prizes for guessing who gets her knowledge of police operations from the television,' said Alex.

'The Major Investigation Team at Lewisham are dealing with it,' Lacey explained. 'But they have co-opted me back on the team because, like it or not, I seem to be involved.'

'And that's a problem in itself?' said Alex.

Lacey nodded. 'I can't be involved and I can't not be. How screwed up is that? Sorry to be so self-indulgent, it's really not like me.' She looked pointedly at the jug of cordial. 'You weren't kidding about the truth serum, were you?'

'You're a lot stronger than you think you are,' said Thessa, without hesitation. 'Midsummer babies always are.'

'I was born in December,' said Lacey. 'I'm sure we've had this conversation.'

'Whatever. The important thing is, you're not on your own. Not any more, anyway. You're quite right, you know. I would make a very good mum.'

'Sometimes my sister is beyond ludicrous.' Alex was shaking his head. Then he stopped, reached over and gave Lacey's hand a quick, almost furtive pat. 'And sometimes her instincts are absolutely spot on.'

69

Dana

'So how did it go?'

Dana looked up. In the reflection of the bedroom window she and Helen made eye contact. Suddenly stiflingly hot, Dana reached out and pulled the sash window open. The effort made her robe loosen. She waited for the breeze to cool her skin. It didn't come. Outside the air was still and heavy.

'I lay on my back in a small cubicle with my knees in stirrups and a nurse syringed the sperm of a complete stranger into my uterus,' she replied. 'If I think about it too carefully, I feel the start of physical revulsion.'

The frown line between Helen's brows had deepened. Even feet away, reflected in the glass, Dana could see it, like a short, vertical scar on her partner's face. 'Did it hurt?'

'A bit. Not as much as childbirth, I imagine.'

Helen was moving closer, but slowly, as though nervous of approaching too fast or too suddenly. It was unlike her, this sudden uncertainty. 'I guess a big case will help take your mind off things over the next couple of weeks.'

Outside, Dana could see a small brown bird on the lilac tree in the next garden. It started singing, a shrill, sweet sound of summer. Funny, that against the background of one of the biggest, busiest cities on earth, against cars revving, horns sounding, people shouting, this tiny bird was the clearest thing she could hear.

'Except I can't help thinking this case is about pregnancy,' she said. 'Lacey and the others suspect some twisted branch of the sex trade, but I'm less sure.'

'No trace of that hormone, whatever it was, in the woman you found this morning,' Helen reminded her.

The bird was a song thrush. Smaller than a blackbird, with creamy yellow breast feathers, speckled with grey. It seemed to be singing directly at her now.

Helen's eyes dropped to the spot just below Dana's waist where the edges of her robe touched. 'Want me to bring a drink up?'

'I shouldn't.' Dana's hand went instinctively to her belly.

Helen raised her eyebrows. 'Don't you think it's a bit soon to start acting the pregnant woman?'

Suddenly inexplicably angry, Dana stepped closer to the window and looked down into the garden. The song thrush had gone. Just the sound of traffic now, an aeroplane passing overhead, an argument in the garden next door. Nothing out there as loud as the noise in her head.

'Guess that wasn't the most sensitive thing to say right now.' Helen had moved forward too, was directly behind her. Dana kept her eyes down. 'It's just not in my dour Scottish nature to count chickens before they're hatched.' Helen never wore perfume, and yet somehow the smell of her skin and hair always made Dana think of summer mornings.

'Are you angry with me?' Helen's breath tickled Dana's ear.

'Yes.'

'Why?'

Dana took a deep breath. 'Because I have to spend hundreds of pounds and beg for help from total strangers who couldn't care less about me, not to mention suffering untold humiliation, just to get something that every other woman on the bloody planet takes for granted. I'm angry with you because you don't have balls.'

Behind her came the sound of a breath being taken and slowly released. 'I can think of a few guys in Dundee nick who might take issue with that.'

Still, Dana didn't, couldn't, look up. She'd had no idea how much rage was inside her. 'Children are supposed to be created out of love. Ours — if we're lucky enough to have any — will be conceived with a pair of stir-rups and a syringe.'

From somewhere a breeze had arrived. It crept its way inside Dana's robe, stroking her skin.

'No man ever loved his wife more than I love you,' said Helen. 'I'd say the rest is just detail.'

As the breeze cooled Dana, she felt herself calming down. It had just been the heat. The heat and the frustrations of a case she didn't believe she'd ever solve. She felt the tension in her body give way, come tumbling down like the bricks in a child's tower. Either Helen had moved closer or Dana had leaned back. She could feel the warmth of her partner's body through the cotton of her robe and it felt good. The cool of the breeze, the warmth of Helen and somewhere in between maybe, just maybe, the start of something new and incredibly special. Whatever unorthodox route it had taken to get here.

'Do you want to get married?' Helen asked, her fingers brushing the side of Dana's neck.

Dana held her breath, ran the words over again in her head, making sure they really were what she thought she'd heard. And then a giggle rose in her throat. 'Are you proposing?'

'Well, someone's got to make an honest woman out of you.'

The robe was at her feet. Helen's fingers were running slowly up her right arm. Goosebumps responded immediately, turning her arms into a mass of pimples. Helen loved that, she knew, loved the feel of her dark hairs standing to attention. Sometimes, she ran her hands over Dana's body just close enough to touch the hairs. Sometimes, she made love to her for long, long minutes before really touching her at all. She was three inches taller than Dana, just tall enough to have to bow her head to kiss the side of her neck.

'Yes,' Dana said, closing her eyes. 'Let's get married.'

70

Lacey

Lacey said goodnight to Alex and then, accompanied by Thessa, walked round to the front of the house, where a narrow path led through a small, neat garden to the high metal gates and perimeter brick walls. The cooling temperature had intensified the scents of the garden, the rich, heady perfume of old-fashioned roses and the strong sweetness of jasmine. Thessa had been chatting, her usual mix of local gossip, folklore and nonsense, pointing out plants and flowers, when she stopped her chair abruptly, just ahead of Lacey's bike.

'There!' She was pointing towards the back of the flower bed, to the tall, spiked columns that grew against the wall. 'Blooming in your honour. Aren't they beautiful?'

Lacey looked at the spears of blue, lilac and white flowers, standing proud amidst the mass of greenery and colour. 'They're delphiniums, aren't they?' She smiled at Thessa's quizzical look. 'I like flowers. I used to hang around the flower market a lot, when I lived in Kennington.'

Thessa looked politely impressed. 'Do you know their common name?'

Lacey didn't, but she could hazard a guess. 'Larkspur by any chance? Goodnight, Thessa. Thank you for a lovely evening.'

She bent to kiss her friend on the cheek, the first time she'd ever done so, but at the last second Thessa pulled back.

'I read up on that woman in Durham prison you were telling me about, dear. I didn't mean to pry, but I remembered the case and I was curious.'

'It's all a matter of public record.' Lacey straightened up and stepped back from Thessa, conscious of her chest suddenly constricting.

'It was a sad story. Those poor girls.'

'We don't concern ourselves too much with the why.' Lacey picked up her bike and switched on both lights, although it wasn't nearly dark enough to need them. She bent to check the tyre pressure, although she'd never known it need attention. 'We leave that to the defence.'

'And yet, being a "why?" sort of person, I found myself deeply curious as to what would turn a perfectly normal girl into a killer.' Thessa moved away, her chair crunching across the gravel. Lacey felt a moment of relief that was soon over.

Thessa's wheels stopped turning. 'There was a particularly insightful feature in one of the Sunday papers. I don't know if you read it. Two sisters, brought up in care, subjected to a horrible attack one night, denied any level of justice.'

She'd positioned herself directly ahead of Lacey on the path. There was no getting past her.

'According to the story, the younger sister, Catherine, went completely off the rails, ran away from home, lived on the streets and then died in a river accident. She'd been living in a houseboat on the creek, not so very far from where you are now. Such a coincidence, I thought.'

Lacey tried to look up, got as far as the blue and lilac pointed columns of flowers.

'The older one couldn't get over her sister's death.' Thessa was relentless. 'She spent years plotting her revenge. She turned herself into a killer, constructed an elaborate and deadly plan and put it into action. Killed four women, nearly got a fifth, too, but she was caught. Does that just about sum it up?'

'I knew Victoria Llewellyn a few years ago.' Lacey had found her voice at last. 'We were friends for a while. That's why I was able to track her down, how I persuaded her to give herself up. It's why I've kept in touch.'

'Yes, I gathered you were the unnamed young constable instrumental in her arrest. And I'd probably have left it at that if there hadn't been such a clear photograph of her accompanying the article. My dear girl, the resemblance is unmistakable.'

Lacey watched Thessa's strong, brown hand reach out and break off a column of deep blue flowers. Resting her hands back on her lap, she began to twirl the stem in her fingers and Lacey wondered if she'd ever be able to smell garden flowers again without feeling sick.

'I simply couldn't understand why nobody else has spotted it. But as Alex is fond of pointing out, not everyone sees what I see.'

Surprise gave Lacey the ability to make eye contact. 'You've discussed this with Alex?'

For a second the shine in Thessa's eyes grew dull. 'No. These days Alex and I have more secrets from each other than I'd have once thought possible. But that's why you dress the way you do, isn't it? Hiding under those ugly baggy clothes. Why you never wear make-up, and always keep your hair tied back. Do you wear sunglasses when you go to see her, so that no one will spot that your eyes and hers are identical?'

She had to get a grip, put a stop to this once and for all. 'You have quite an imagination, Thessa. And that's a very entertaining theory, but Catherine Llewellyn is dead.'

'Yes, yes, very clever. But someone who swims the way you do would have no problem surviving a river accident.'

'I'm not Catherine Llewellyn.' Seeing no alternative, Lacey picked up her bike, stepped into a flower-bed and strode round Thessa. A rose thorn tore into her bare leg. She ignored it, put her bike down and pushed it along the gravel, making more noise than was necessary.

'I know you're not, dear. I did a bit more digging, you see. I found the girls' birthdays. Catherine was a Valentine baby, born on 14 February.'

Thessa was having to raise her voice now, as Lacey was almost at the gate. 'Victoria, on the other hand, when do you think she was born?'

She'd reached the gate. She pushed it open with one hand.

'The ninth of July.' Thessa's voice came

drifting towards her like the tendrils of a poisonous plant. 'Midsummer. Her birth flower is the Larkspur.'

■ ■ ■ ■

TUESDAY, 1 JULY

■ ■ ■ ■

71

Lacey and the Swimmer

Joesbury was gone. The cabin he'd been sleeping in was empty, with no trace, not even a lingering scent, that he'd ever been in it. It was stupid to be disappointed, really; better by far that he'd gone. By tomorrow night Deptford Creek would be crawling with undercover police officers. In the morning, the Met would begin a systematic search of all the creekside properties. Lacey switched off the torch and let the faint light from the stars guide her back up on deck.

For a moment she stood in the shadow of the wheelhouse. Back at the Theatre Arm, all looked still. There was a uniformed constable in the main cabin of Ray and Eileen's boat, another on Lacey's own boat. It hadn't been easy, to creep out of the hatch above her borrowed bunk, cross the boat without making any sound, and climb down to where she'd left her canoe, ready

for a quick getaway. There were police officers in the yard, too, but she'd dressed in
black and was pretty certain no one had
seen her. It had been a risk, just one that
had felt worth taking. Except he'd already
gone.

Suddenly weak, she sank down on to the
deck of the dredger and laid her aching
head against the cold metal wall of the
wheelhouse. She simply hadn't allowed
herself to think about how much she'd
wanted to see Joesbury until she'd discovered it was impossible, and now the trembling that she'd managed to keep at bay
since she'd left Sayes Court was creeping
up on her. For so long, she'd thought Joesbury would be her nemesis, the one who
would drag her secrets to the surface and
blow apart her carefully constructed life.
How had she not seen the real danger?

She had to get back. Lacey pulled herself
to her feet and set off towards the stern of
the dredger. The creek was different tonight.
It had its moods, like the Thames, like any
living thing, and the only word Lacey could
think of to describe its present one was frac-
tious. The minor currents were odd, for one
thing. There were more of them, some
seeming to run completely against the tide.
At one point on the way over, she'd felt

herself being pushed downstream. Closer to the bank, there had been small whirlpools and eddies.

Light. A sudden flash of a torch-beam across the channel, roughly beneath the old power station. Lacey stopped in mid stride. It could have been a reflection, a light from a boat on the main river bouncing off the steel plating of the creek walls. Somehow, though, it had seemed too bright for that.

There it was again. Definitely a torch. The beam probably couldn't reach her here, but even so, Lacey kept very still. It was at water level, probably in a boat.

Back in her canoe, Lacey let grumpy little waves smack hard against the hull while she tried to decide what to do. She had her mobile phone, police radio, a camera and binoculars in the small waterproof bag between her shoulder blades. A light on the creek at this hour was worth checking out, surely? Maybe just get a bit closer?

She loosened the rope and began paddling, keeping close to the bank. At Dowell's Wharf a small inlet offered shelter and a mooring ring. Holding the canoe still in the water with the paddle, she tied herself up.

The walls here were the highest along the creek, rising up yards above her, cutting out all light. On the other hand, they were protecting her from the wind and the rougher waves. The water moved more slowly in here, seeming almost still in comparison with the swift flow in the main channel. It was a good place to lie in wait.

The swimmer looked towards the boat. It was close now, too close to risk the torch again.

Had Lacey seen the light or not? Surely she had, or she'd have gone back to the marina, not be hiding up in that tiny inlet, barely visible against the dark of the bank. Oh, she was a creature of the river all right, whether swimming or in that little boat of hers. She moved around silently, at speed.

Nothing more to be done. Lacey would either see the boat or not. If she did, she would follow it.

And if she followed it, she wouldn't be the only one.

The swimmer started breathing heavily, taking on more and more oxygen, getting close to the point of hyperventilation, knowing that a fast, hard swim was coming and determined to be ready.

All around Lacey there was noise, the incessant drone of London, but after a few seconds it became surprisingly easy to tune out, to hear instead the sounds of the river. The low, constant grumble of water moving between high, hard walls, the swirling, splashing and sucking as the current hit the bricks just in front of her before bouncing away again. The tiny waves that smacked against the hull of her canoe. And the scuttling of creatures around her. One such, mistaking the smooth hull of the boat for the river wall, climbed up and started clack-clacking towards her. Lacey knocked it back into the water with the paddle. It might be some time before she felt comfortable around mitten crabs.

Slowly, she raised her binoculars and immediately saw the boat. Small, wooden-framed, with a modest outboard engine. Two, maybe three passengers. No movement of water around the engine. One man at the stern was looking out towards the Thames, another at the bow holding on to the river wall to keep them in place. The third passenger sat in the middle, a scarf wrapped around her head.

Hardly daring to move, but knowing she had to, Lacey reached into her shoulder pack and tapped out a message on her phone:

Urgent assistance needed. Where are you?

Her usual crew would be on duty on the river right now. Finn Turner always kept his phone close, in case one of his numerous girlfriends tried to get in touch.

Then a reply came in:

Not far from your place. What's up?

The small boat was moving.

Possible illegal immigrants in Deptford Creek. Two males, one female. Small motor boat, heading out to Thames now. Can you intercept?

That would have to do. Lacey cast off and began to follow. The boat, about ten yards in front, turned the bend and went out of sight. Lacey paddled hard and in another second had turned the same bend. The boat had vanished.

No sign of her colleagues. Nothing on her phone.

Lacey sped towards the mouth of the creek, keeping close to the left bank. She hit the Thames and, in spite of all her experience on the water, had to fight hard not to give way to panic.

The full force of the tide swept her up, pushing her on towards the city, and the river seemed so much wider in the dark, she could barely see the north bank. But there was the boat, about fifteen yards in front. Sometimes, it was just all about muscle. Head down and paddle.

They were using their engine again, but slowly, hugging the shoreline, slinking in and out of the shadows. They probably weren't going much faster than she, but she'd tire soon. Where the hell were Fred and Finn?

Then, almost from nowhere, came the sound of engines so loud she thought she was about to be run over. A large boat was heading straight for her, lights shining out like beacons. Lacey grabbed her own light and switched it on, then began paddling hard out of the way.

'This is the Metropolitan Police. Stay exactly where you are.'

The sergeant's voice. The Targa was almost level, she could see him at the fly bridge, the lanky form of Turner on the port side. Another officer in the cockpit. As the boat drew level, Turner's eyes caught hers for a second, then they'd gone past, were gaining on the small motor boat.

'Cut your engines and wait for us to reach you. Do not attempt to get away.'

The wash from the Targa's engines reached her, picking her canoe up and spinning it round. She paddled hard to correct it, but the second wave hit her and she almost went over. Her phone fell into the bottom of the canoe. Ahead, the Targa was lighting up the river. They'd picked out the small boat, were gaining on it easily. They'd look for her just as soon as they could but she wouldn't be their priority.

OK, what were her options? She was more or less opposite the entrance to South Dock Marina. Conscious of getting tired, knowing it would be a safer place to wait, Lacey paddled over and tucked herself in the lee of the nearest yacht, a forty-foot Moody. Then she found her radio.

'Constable Flint requesting urgent assistance,' she managed, a split second before the world turned upside-down.

This was it, the swimmer knew. This was the moment. Such a chance would not come again. Lacey was below the surface. She had to be found quickly, before she had a chance to get her bearings. Speed and courage were needed now. Lacey was strong and fast. The swimmer had to be stronger.

■ ■ ■ ■

Lacey was beneath the surface, trapped inside the canoe. She forced her mouth shut and swung her body to one side.

The canoe wasn't moving. She was stuck upside-down in the water. What the hell had happened? Again, she swung herself to one side. She had to get out. She was still holding the paddle. Keeping it in her right hand, she pushed herself free with her left.

For a second, after breaking the surface, she could do nothing but gulp in air and spit out water. The canoe was just out of reach, still upside-down. Lacey looked round quickly. No one in sight.

Still clutching the paddle, she began swimming towards the canoe, but as she reached out the smooth fibreglass hull bounced away.

Then something was dragging her down. Lacey went below the surface in an instant, with no breath in her lungs. She kicked down and broke free, but immediately was grabbed around her shoulders.

Survival instinct kicked in. Lacey twisted, struck out with the paddle and her free fist. Her buoyancy aid was pulling her towards the surface, the weight clinging to her legs trying to get her down. There was light in the water. The torch had fallen from the canoe, was sinking to the bottom, illuminating the river bed, which seemed alive with mitten crabs.

And the linen-wrapped corpses on the marina floor.

She broke the surface again, bracing herself for the next attack. Nothing. No face bearing down on her. No wiry arms reaching out. She was, or appeared to be, completely alone.

From out on the main river came the sound of an engine. If one of the Marine Unit boats was looking for her, they wouldn't think to come in here and she no longer had a phone or radio. The sound was fading again.

Without stopping to think, Lacey abandoned her paddle and set off in a fast crawl towards the Thames. Her canoe had disappeared, she just had her buoyancy aid to keep her afloat, but spending another moment near whatever had attacked her was impossible. She would have to take her chances in the river.

How long had she been in the water? Five minutes? An hour? She'd cheated the river once, which meant she couldn't ever drown. Claptrap, Thessa had said, of course you can drown, don't take silly risks.

She was getting colder, and slowing down. She was no longer sure she could feel her feet and the tips of her fingers were going numb. The buoyancy aid was keeping her head above water, but the waves were bouncing into her face and every few seconds she dipped below the surface again.

The massive circular edge of the landing stage that marked the entrance to the creek was in sight, gleaming like a beacon in the moonlight. It had the look of a prehistoric temple, of a wooden henge rising out of the water. Why was it suddenly so much harder to concentrate? Why were her thoughts drifting off in random directions?

The Targa was coming back. Impossible to mistake that high-pitched drone. And this time it was looking for her, no doubt about it. Travelling slowly, but relentlessly, the flashlight in the bow sweeping left and right in the water.

The beam settled on her face, blinding her, but getting out of the water was all she could think of right now. The boat drew closer. The buoyancy aid tightened around her chest and she felt herself being lifted. The water was falling away, she could see it swirling beneath her. A second later she was on the hard, cold deck of the boat, conscious only that it felt good to breathe freely, and that the man who held her was warm.

'Look, Sarge!' Finn Turner's voice was gleeful. 'I caught a mermaid.'

72

Dana

'The divers are back up,' Chief Inspector Cook told Dana, as he put the phone down. 'They're pretty certain there are two bodies. Wrapped like the other two we found and weighted down at the neck, waist and ankles.'

Three hours after the arrest of the two suspected people-traffickers and their human cargo of one, two and a half hours after the frantic search to find the body (alive or dead, and frankly either would do) of Constable Bloody Flint, Dana had assembled her team at the station. SC07, the specialist division that dealt with people-trafficking, had been informed and had agreed to her retaining operational control for now.

Two more corpses. Together with the two Lacey had found, and the one pulled out of the river weeks ago, she had five dead women.

It would be getting light soon. The search of the marina bed had been conducted in darkness. Which might now prove to be no bad thing. 'How secure are they?' she asked.

'What?' Cook's heavily lidded eyes seemed sleepier than usual.

'Are they going anywhere in a hurry?'

'I really don't think I want to know what's on your mind,' Cook said. 'And far be it from me to tell you your job, but shouldn't you be cordoning off that marina and getting started on the boat-to-boat search?'

Yes, she probably should. That would be doing it by the book, and if in doubt, one always did it by the book. Except —

Dana turned to where Lacey was sitting quietly in the corner of the room. She wore borrowed clothes and her hair had dried in long, stringy tendrils. She'd managed to get hold of a laptop and her attention was fixed on the screen. Dana raised her voice.

'OK, thanks to PC Flint and her unfailing disregard for procedures, we appear to have found the body stash. What we can't necessarily assume is that we've also found the centre of the operation.'

'I'm not following,' said Cook. 'And I hope you realize there's a limit to how long I can leave a couple of corpses bobbing around in South Dock Marina.'

Dana glanced at the clock again. Time seemed to have speeded up. 'Dave, the suspects your officers arrested tonight — thanks to PC Flint and her unauthorized stake-out — may not have been heading for the marina. Who hides bodies within yards of where they're being killed?'

'Fred and Rosemary West,' said Barrett.

'Yeah, thanks, Tom. But if you have a yacht, how likely is it that you'd dump a body over the side in the marina? You wouldn't. You'd take it out into the middle of the channel, or closer to the estuary. I'm not sure our gang have any real connections with the marina other than using it to store bodies.'

'Also,' added Lacey, 'anyone with half a brain would realize there are CCTV cameras around the marina. And all the berth holders will be known and registered. It's just too big a risk.'

'Not everyone's approach to risk is as cautious as I'd like, Lacey, but I take your point.'

'I think they're transporting the bodies around in a small boat,' said Lacey. 'Something that can sneak past the cameras at the riverside entrance. A boat that may have no connection to the South Dock Marina.'

'Well, I suppose that does make some

sense,' Cook grudgingly admitted. 'If they're using a small boat, maybe one with a small engine, they won't want to risk motoring out to the centre of the channel.'

'The tide's too strong and there's too big a risk of being mown down in the shipping channel.'

'So,' said Cook, 'if they can't dump the bodies in the middle, which would be the ideal place for them, they need another area of deep water that isn't affected by tides.'

Lacey sat back. 'Marinas.'

Cook rubbed his eyes. Being dragged from his bed in the middle of the night didn't suit him. 'God help us if we have to search every dock and marina in the city.'

'I don't think we will, Sir,' said Lacey. 'Small boat, remember? They're not travelling far. And there's another thing. Look what I found.'

She turned the laptop round to face the rest of the group. They were looking at the website of one of the natural history publications, a feature on Chinese mitten crabs. 'This was in *The Ecologist*. It seems they're a particular nuisance around marinas. Possibly because edible rubbish thrown from boats encourages the little wiggly things that they eat. Anyway, they're a notorious problem at South Dock Marina. I think the crab business was a bit of a game on the part of my stalker. You know, throwing a clue in our faces and seeing how long it took us to work it out. The toy boats, too. Where do you find a lot of boats together? A marina.'

Around Lacey, heads were nodding.

'I think South Dock Marina is where the bodies are dumped, and the holding facility, whatever it is, will be somewhere near by,' she went on. 'We're closing in.'

'Which brings us to the problem,' said Dana. 'Once it gets out that we've found two more bodies, and arrested the three in the boat tonight, the operation will close down or move on. We'll never find who's doing this.'

Cook sat down heavily. 'I can't do it, Dana. We'll have been spotted there tonight. People will start asking questions. We'll have the press down there before you know it. And that's before we get on to the fact that Lacey was attacked there and only just escaped with her life.'

'More by sheer luck than operational competence,' snapped Dana.

Lacey gave her a weak smile.

'My point is —'

The door to the meeting room opened and Stenning and Anderson entered. 'The girl still isn't talking,' Anderson said. 'The interpreter's tried both main Afghan languages and a couple of dialects and got nothing out of her. We can try other languages in the morning, but frankly she could be from anywhere in the Middle East.'

'She's a Pashtun,' said Lacey, picking up the photograph again. 'Just like the others.' Dana found herself nodding. Even the standard police mugshot couldn't disguise the girl's appeal. She was striking, with fair, almost European skin, bright blue eyes and dark brown hair.

'She looks quite a lot like you with your Bollywood makeover.' Mizon turned the photograph towards her.

'Neither of the two men are saying anything either yet,' said Stenning. 'Although both of them do have some knowledge of English. What's pretty obvious is that they're scared.'

'Will they talk, do you think?' asked Cook.

'Probably,' said Stenning. 'But I can't see them being major players. They can probably tell us where they were going to take the girl, but other than that . . .'

'That's something in itself, though,' said Anderson. 'We get a warrant, a dawn raid should throw up something. In which case, we need to get moving. Once it's known that these guys have been picked up, they'll start covering their tracks.'

'Except, if Nadia was telling the truth, nothing illegal happened to her while she was with these people,' said Lacey. 'She was looked after, given a nice room and plenty of food, medical attention when she got ill, and then the job that she'd been promised.'

'So, if we raid the place, wherever it is, and we come up with nothing, that's it,' said Dana. 'We might get some minor convictions for people-smuggling. The operation will move somewhere else and we'll never know what was going on.'

'People-smuggling is hardly a minor offence.' Cook looked offended.

'It's not murder, though,' said Dana. 'Lacey's right. We're no nearer knowing what they're doing to these women and why some of them are dying.'

'Pity we can't let them go ahead and put a bug on her,' said Stenning.

'Yeah, that'll work.' Anderson stifled a yawn.

'It might.' Mizon was still looking at the photograph of the girl from the boat. 'How old would you say she is?'

'Difficult to tell.' Stenning leaned over her shoulder. 'Late teens, early twenties.'

'She's about five foot four, right?' said Mizon. 'Weighs about eight and a half stone?'

'What's on your mind, Gayle?' said Dana.

'Whoever picked her out back in Afghanistan or wherever wouldn't have sent a photograph through, would they?' said Mizon. 'They won't want any sort of paper trail. I'll bet whoever is expecting her was just told it would be a young, good-looking girl, dark hair, light eyes.'

'If you're suggesting we send someone in undercover, we'll never get it organized in time,' said Dana. 'I can talk to SO10 tonight, but the chances of them having a young Asian officer available are practically non-existent.'

'So you're saying we'll never find a young, dark-haired female officer with light-coloured eyes and experience of working undercover at short notice?' said Mizon.

Suddenly, every eye in the room was on Lacey.

Lacey

It felt to Lacey as though she was the only person in the room capable of being still, of remaining silent. Everyone else was fidgeting, talking too fast, too loud, all at the same time. Tulloch was on her feet, striding from one side of the room to the other, the way she invariably did when she was stressed. 'I am not risking the life of an officer on a half-baked, ill-considered, reckless operation,' she announced. 'We're not discussing it any further.'

'No disrespect, Ma'am,' said Mizon, 'but there's no harm in considering every possibility. Lacey can pass for one of these women. She already has. She convinced half the occupants of the Old Kent Road the other night. If Mr Cook can give us twenty-four hours before he brings those bodies up, it might just be enough.'

Enough, thought Lacey. It wasn't enough,

then, that she'd had corpses strewn in her way, strung up from her boat. It wasn't enough that someone had wanted her to be the next one. Funny, how she hadn't been able to see that until now.

Tulloch was leaning against the far wall, her arms folded, glowering.

Anderson had the floor. 'I'm not saying I agree with Gayle, but presumably SO10 can fit us out with surveillance equipment. We'll know where she is at all times. The minute she's worried, we can pull her out.'

Cook held up one arm to get attention. 'I definitely don't agree. Lacey's my officer and my responsibility, when all's said and done. But just for the sake of argument, we can put teams on the river in unmarked vessels. We can be seconds away from her, all the time she's in there. I'm still not saying I think it's wise. It's too rushed.'

They were going to let her do it, Lacey realized. This was noise, bluster. They were going through the motions, but when it came to it, they didn't have another option.

'Exactly,' snapped Tulloch. 'And how will we get the two men to play ball?'

'Offer them a deal,' said Mizon. 'They make a phone call, now, to whoever they were due to meet, saying they were held up and they'll try again tomorrow. Tomorrow night, with a close but discreet police escort, they take Lacey and hand her over. Then they come back into custody until the operation is over. In return for their co-operation and for testifying, they get lenient treatment.'

'All they have to do is wink, or pass a note, and Lacey ends up at the bottom of the Thames,' said Tulloch.

Like she hadn't been there before. *Hello, river bed, looks like you won, after all.*

'If there's any winking or note-passing, we get her out of there,' Mizon was arguing. 'We'll practically be camped out on her doorstep. Look, I'm not saying it's ideal, but it might be the best chance we have.'

And there was that brief moment of silence, as though she'd ordered it.

'Gayle's right,' said Lacey. 'It is our only chance. You all know it, you just don't want to ask me to do it.'

'Do you speak Pashto?' said Tulloch, eyebrows raised. 'Or Dari?'

'There are forty languages in Afghanistan,' said Lacey. 'What are the chances of the reception party being fluent in all of them? Not that I'm saying it's a good idea, you understand.'

'Well, I'm glad we're agreed on something,' said Tulloch. 'Because even if you idiots can talk me into it, Weaver will never agree.'

'Can I talk to her? The girl we picked up tonight? Can I have some time with her?'

'Why? To work on your cover story? It's not happening, Lacey.'

'I'd like to talk to her without the interpreter and the solicitor, just her and me.'

'No. That would be highly irregular.'

Lacey sighed. 'She hasn't requested a solicitor, Ma'am, and she hasn't even acknowledged the interpreter. There's no reason why we shouldn't ask them to leave. Gayle can come in with me, if you don't want me to be alone.'

'Lacey —'

'I know, Ma'am. We all think it's a bad idea. So we need to find out what we can, while we can.'

'Oh, do what you bloody well want. I give up.'

'I think you can understand me.'

Gayle was right, Lacey thought. She and the girl across the table did look alike. The other girl was probably younger, but spending more time outdoors in extreme temperatures had coarsened her face. Her hair was long and dark brown, her eyebrows finely drawn and her eyes the colour of cornflowers just as their freshness starts to fade.

They'd had her moved to the family room, a more relaxed space than the interview rooms, a space where they normally interviewed children or vulnerable people.

'I think you're from Afghanistan.' The girl looked steadily back at Lacey, almost without blinking. 'And that you were told there would be a job for you here. Maybe looking after children or helping a rich Western woman with the housework. You expected to be able to send money home to your family. So you must be able to speak some English, or you'd never have considered coming.'

Lacey waited, for any sort of reaction. The other woman's eyes dropped to the untouched mug of coffee on the table. Lacey glanced to one side and got a reassuring nod from Gayle.

'I think your journey here took a long time,' she said. 'That it became uncomfortable, maybe even frightening. I think you began to wonder if you'd made a mistake, but you were told it was too late to change your mind. I think the men who were bringing you here changed. They started to threaten, instead of persuade. They told you that you had no choice. That your family would suffer if you made trouble. I think

509

you're probably terrified right now.'

She waited again, looking for something, anything, in those blue eyes. OK, time to step it up a bit.

Lacey opened the folder in front of her and turned it so the girl could see the photograph of Nadia Safi. 'What I need you to understand is that you're actually very lucky.'

Blue eyes darted down and lost interest. She'd clearly never seen Nadia before.

'This is Nadia Safi,' said Lacey. 'She was very lucky, too. She arrived in England last summer. From Afghanistan, like you. She's working with a family in London now. Of course, she could be sent home at any time because she's still here illegally. She's probably little more than a slave, but no one hurts her. She has food, somewhere to live. She's a lucky one.'

The girl was looking bored now. Lacey opened the folder again and pulled out two more photographs, laying them face down on the desk. She turned the first over.

'We call this girl Sahar. This is what we think she looked like when she was alive.' She turned the other photograph. 'This is what she looked like when we pulled her out of the river. She wasn't so lucky.'

The girl had looked quickly at the photograph. The shock on her face had been genuine. Her eyes were down now, fixed on the table top.

'I'm sorry to upset you. But you need to understand how serious this is.' Lacey took out a photograph taken at the last post-mortem, of the corpse found strung up on Lacey's boat. Then another, taken from the Marine Unit files, of the woman pulled from near the South Dock Marina two months previously.

'Three dead women. All your age, all from your country, all brought into the UK just as you were. All exactly like you. So here's where we make a decision. When you leave police custody and go into the United Kingdom's immigration system, the men who brought you here, the men who are doing this, will find you again. They found Nadia and they'll find you. You're too valuable to them to let go. You may be one of the lucky ones, like Nadia. Or you may not.'

'Lacey,' said Gayle, 'I'm really not sure she understands a word you're saying.'

'Oh, I think she understands just about every word I'm saying.' Lacey didn't take her eyes off the girl. 'But I'll slow down, because this next bit is important. In a few hours, I'm going to take your place. I'm going to wear clothes just like yours and I'm going to let the men who brought you here take me to where they were going to take you. I'm going to pretend to be a young, terrified woman from Afghanistan. Only I won't have to pretend to be terrified. That will be for real. We call it undercover work. I'm going to put myself in danger because I don't want any more girls from your country to die. That's what I'm going to do. How about you?'

She waited. The girl held eye contact steadily. Lacey could hear Gayle breathing at her side. She gathered together the photographs and stood up.

'Interview terminated at 04.23 hours.' She went to switch off the recording equipment.

'You haven't asked me anything,' said a voice from behind her. 'All you've done is talk at me. If there's something you want to know, ask me.'

74

Dana

Dana pulled the photograph of the three dead women up on to the screen of her laptop.

'We're going to charge you with murder,' she told the dark-skinned young man across the table. 'We have three bodies of illegal immigrants. We have contacts in Afghanistan, we're going to find out who these women were and we're going to trace them to you. More importantly, we have a woman who was brought in last year, who didn't end up at the bottom of the Thames. She can identify you.'

The man sat stony-faced, not reacting. Beneath the table was a different matter. His left leg was vibrating with nervous energy. It was making the whole side of his body shake.

'You'll probably serve thirty years,' she said. 'Your friend, on the other hand, will get off lightly. Because he's cooperating.'

Just the hint of a glower beneath those heavy brows.

'He's talking to my sergeant right now. I wouldn't be surprised if he's already told him where you picked the girl up and where you were heading tonight.'

She reached out and picked up her phone. The screen was empty, but he couldn't see that.

'My sergeant wants to see me,' she said. 'I think it must be over. We need someone to help us with an operation. But we only need one of you. It'll be the one we trust the most. The one who's cooperated.' She got up and closed her laptop.

'What do you want to know?' asked the man.

'It isn't happening, Lacey,' said Dana, when she and the team were once more in the meeting room. 'You may have taken maverick operations to a whole new level, but I don't take foolish risks with the lives of fellow officers. Your sun-tan is clearly fake, your hair is obviously dyed and your skin is classic English rose. And just in case you'd forgotten, whoever is killing these women knows who you are. He tried to drown you earlier. All I'd be doing by sending you in is making it easier for them. "Here's Lacey. I've gift-wrapped her for you." You know what, I'm actually tempted.'

'If we let this chance go, we'll never get another one,' said Lacey.

'I know that,' said Dana. 'Which is why, against all my better judgement, I'm going to agree.'

It was as though someone had poured ice-cold water over the girl. Dana watched, half amused. Lacey liked to talk tough, she was exceptionally brave and would do it, no doubt at all, but she'd been badly scared recently. Scratch the bravado and terror was only just beneath the surface.

Dana watched her reach out for a coffee mug that was long since empty with a trembling hand. She drew it back quickly, before anyone could see, and Dana was suddenly reminded of why she liked this young woman so much, why her best friend had fallen in love with her.

'Right.' Anderson jumped to his feet. He was ashen. He, too, liked Lacey. 'We'd better get moving. I've got someone from SO10 coming over to talk us through what to expect. Lacey, are you sure about this? Because if you're not . . .'

'Keep your knickers on, Neil,' said Dana. 'Lacey isn't going undercover. I am.'

75

Dana and Lacey

They waited for the tide. It had to be high, the two men had explained, plenty of water, but not flowing too fast. At a little-used jetty on the south bank just east of Greenwich, Aamil climbed into the boat first and stepped to the front. He was the younger of the two men, the muscle. Raashid was at the tiller. Dana stepped in last. Only one member of the Marine Unit, Sergeant Wilson, wearing jeans and a sweater, had accompanied them down to the jetty. Fred looked as unhappy about the job as everyone else. He'd squeezed Dana's shoulder just before she'd climbed down, but as the engine fired up at the second attempt, he couldn't manage more than a tight-lipped smile.

They left the bank behind and Dana turned away from the still figure of Fred on the jetty, knowing that, finally, the reality of what she was doing was about to hit home. There had hardly been time to think, over the last few hours. Maya, the girl they'd picked up the night before, had given her the rudiments of a cover story. She was twenty-five years old, a childless widow from Takhar province whose dead husband's family had refused to care for her. They'd sent her back to her own family, who hadn't been too keen on the idea either. With her future in Afghanistan looking bleak, she'd jumped at the chance of a new life in the West. As a young girl, she'd spent several years in school before the Taliban had clamped down on female education, hence her rudimentary knowledge of English.

The clothes Lacey had bought for her trip along the Old Kent Road — cotton trousers, tunic and headscarf — had been pronounced perfectly acceptable by Maya. She'd even offered advice on the simple cotton underwear women from Afghanistan favoured. In the canvas bag at Dana's feet were her possessions, based on what Maya had had in her own bag. Lacey had spent the day in Brick Lane doing her best to replicate them, and had found a change of clothes, some simple toiletries with eastern labelling and photographs of Dana's supposed family back home.

Dana had also spent time with a detective sergeant from SCD10, who'd come over to give her some tips on how to behave. He'd set a time limit of 24 hours maximum on the operation, a timescale David Cook had reluctantly agreed to. Any longer, the sergeant had said, would expose her to unnecessary risks. Twenty-four hours hadn't seemed long back at Lewisham, but now, just a few minutes into the operation, it was a different story.

She hadn't told Helen. Helen was back in Dundee, and wouldn't necessarily think it odd if she didn't hear from Dana for a day.

Helen would have argued that it was foolish. Too great a risk. That Dana was neither trained in undercover work nor properly prepared for the operation. She'd have been right.

Fighting off a sudden urge to panic, Dana turned to look back over Raashid's shoulder. Fred had disappeared, but somewhere in the gloom of the river was an unmarked RIB, staffed by officers from the Marine Unit and an armed sergeant from SO10. In a few hours they'd be replaced by another identical unit and then later by a third, each working an eight-hour shift. They were her protection. They wouldn't go more than a hundred metres from her until she was safely back with them. If she pressed her panic button, they'd be the first to respond. It would have been good to be able to see them, just to know they were definitely there, but that was impossible.

It was all about trust, going undercover, the sergeant had told her. You had to trust your back-up was there. She did trust Neil, in charge of the operation in her absence, she trusted David Cook and his officers. But how Mark had done this for the last ten years was beyond her.

Across the river, close to the north bank, would be the Targa that was currently the command centre of the operation, although that would move back to Lewisham as the night wore on. Every available craft belonging to the Marine Unit was out on the river tonight, with the specific instruction to stay well clear of Deptford but to be ready to respond if necessary. She was as safe as it was possible to be and it was about time she started feeling that way.

Around her neck was a cheap-looking metal locket that appeared to be sealed shut. It was particularly important that no one succeeded in opening it, because it concealed a tracking device. As long as she wore it, her colleagues would know where she was. If the plan went wrong, she had to open the locket and break the device. That would be the signal to get her out.

She wasn't wired. They'd discussed bugging her and it had been considered too risky. Aamil and Raashid both were, though, and as long as she was with them, anything she or they said would be heard by the surveillance team.

They were passing Greenwich now, hugging the south bank. She couldn't imagine how Maya and the others had felt, on this cold, massive river, with no idea of where they were heading or what would be waiting for them, without even the most basic protection of the life-jackets that Cook had absolutely insisted that she and the men wear.

'If I lose you in the river, that's my job and my pension,' he'd told her when she'd tried to argue that it might make the reception committee suspicious. 'This is not negotiable.' Dana had taken one look at his face and realized it probably wasn't. Chugging along now, watching waves break over the bow, realizing how low in the water she was, she was glad he'd put his foot down.

The huge circular structure that marked the entrance to Deptford Creek was getting closer. She could see the differing flow in the river as the creek water hit the Thames.

She wrapped the headscarf closer to her head as they went on.

They couldn't be too far away now. So far, the two men had done exactly what they'd been told. The tricky part would be when they arrived. She'd watch them closely. Any sign at all that they were trying to alert others to the police surveillance and her instructions had been clear. To break the tracking device, get her head down and wait for rescue. They were slowing down.

'We go in here,' said Raashid behind her.

'That's Sayes Creek,' said Lacey, on the control boat. 'I know that piece of water. It's very narrow. There's only one turning point, about a quarter of a mile up, near a big house called Sayes Court.'

On the computer monitor, they watched the red dot that was Dana move up the narrow creek. The small boat went the full length, turned outside Sayes Court and then set off back again, Dana still on board. About a hundred yards from the entrance to the Thames, the boat stopped moving. They'd moored up.

'Thank you,' they heard Dana saying over the wires attached to her two escorts. 'Goodbye.'

'Be quiet,' a woman's voice answered.

'People are asleep.'

'She's going in,' said Anderson.

Dana was led up the narrow, concrete river steps and inside the building. She heard the boat engine firing up and glanced back. Aamil and Raashid were at the entrance to the creek. A second later she was inside and the door closed behind her.

A dimly lit corridor, painted a pale beige colour. Two doors on the left. At the end of the corridor, stairs going up. Outside, she'd counted four floors, including one that seemed to be slightly below the water line. A tall, narrow building.

So far, so good.

Outside, the crew on the river would already be in touch with their colleagues on land. They'd put an unmarked car in the street outside. They'd use thermal-imaging equipment to find out how many people were in the building. They'd think about accessing the buildings on either side, to see if listening devices could be implanted. They were close. Even if it didn't feel that way. The woman guiding her along the corridor had spoken to her. She'd stopped, had turned round, was waiting.

'What is your name?' she repeated, enunciating every word, as though used to people whose grasp of English was weak.

'Maya,' said Dana.

The woman looked at Dana. Then she let her eyes run up and down, taking in her face, clothes, even shoes. Earlier in the day, Dana had run cooking oil through her hair to make it look as though it hadn't been washed recently. Before getting into the boat, she'd rubbed dirt into her hands and fingernails. Her appearance was convincing. She had black hair, coffee-coloured skin, even the light-green eyes that were common among Pashtun women. It would be her voice, if anything, that let her down.

Dana spoke Hindi and Arabic, and could adopt a regional accent that would fool most Westerners. Native Afghans, on the other hand, would be a different story.

'Say as little as possible,' the SO10 sergeant had told her. 'Act dumb. When you do speak, keep it to short, simple sentences and pitch your voice low.'

Finally, the woman seemed satisfied. 'Follow me,' she said.

Dana was shown into a room on the top floor that her sense of direction told her would face the creek.

'May I take your bag?' The woman was holding out her hand. Dana hesitated. She'd expected this. They would be bound to check what she'd brought with her, but no one would willingly hand over every possession they had in the world, would they?

'You'll get everything back,' said the woman. 'But we do need to know what you have with you.'

Dana held out her bag. The woman put it behind her against the door. She took a step closer to Dana and held her arms out by her sides.

Telling herself that getting bolshie would hardly be convincing, Dana submitted to being patted down, airport-security style. The woman found the money belt in seconds. She slid her hands under Dana's tunic, unfastened the belt and looked inside.

The team had reproduced, exactly, what Maya's money belt had been carrying, a mixture of Afghan notes, euros and sterling. The woman peered into each of the three pockets, zipped them back up and returned the belt to Dana. Not interested in money, then.

'You should shower and change,' said the woman. 'I'll take your clothes for laundry. And I'll get you something to eat.'

Dana watched her guide leave the room. She was a woman in her fifties, about five foot seven and well built, wearing what looked like medical scrubs. Her hair was short and iron grey, her face sallow and coarse, but relatively unlined. Dana would know her again, would be able to identify her if necessary. The door closed and was locked on the outside.

'The team are in place outside,' said Detective Superintendent Weaver, when Lacey and Detective Sergeant Anderson arrived back at Lewisham. 'East Street, built in the late seventeenth century. Originally warehouses and offices for shipping companies. Some of the properties are offices now. A couple are residential.'

'Do we know who owns the building?' asked Anderson.

'Registered to a company with an overseas head office,' replied Weaver. 'It will take time to track them down.'

Lacey watched the small red dot on the screen that was DI Tulloch. They had the bodies, they had the place where the women were being taken. They had at least some of the people involved in the operation.

It wasn't enough.

Unable to stop herself, Dana ran to the door and pulled the handle. She was locked in. But, honestly, what had she expected?

She'd learned a lot already, already the risk had been worth taking. And nothing bad had happened. She still had the lifeline round her neck. She just had to do her job and that meant finding out as much as she could about where she was.

A room, roughly ten feet by eight, resembling nothing so much as a private hospital room, although it would be difficult to say exactly why. There was no medical equipment, the single bed had a simple wooden headboard rather than a metal frame, and yet there was something about the tiled floor, the absence of pictures or ornamentation of any kind that looked institutional. There was another door that led to a small bathroom with basin, loo and shower. A few rough, white towels, a thin robe and some surprisingly nice toiletries. She was expected to be clean and presentable.

Back in the bedroom were a table and chair, a cabinet beside the bed, a TV on a cupboard and a tall chipboard wardrobe. In the cupboard were magazines and a few books aimed at students of the English language. Also some English-language DVDs. The occupants of this room were expected to improve their English while they were here. Which rather suggested they had a future beyond it, didn't it?

There were clothes in the wardrobe. Leggings, T-shirts, long cardigans, long loose skirts, underwear and pyjamas, all in plain, dull blues and browns. None of them even remotely alluring. These were simple, modest clothes. They were all clean and ironed, but none had the crisp newness of clothes that have just been taken out of their packaging. Someone else had worn these clothes.

Dana took out pyjamas and a thin cotton robe, conscious that she was almost certainly being watched. Surveillance technology was extremely sophisticated and readily available, she'd been told earlier by Mark's colleague. Cameras could be plastered into walls and ceilings, their lenses concealed as something as innocuous as large screw heads. Until she left this place, she had to assume that everything she did, everything she said, could be overheard or seen, and that meant she had to behave as though she had nothing to hide.

She walked to the window, because that seemed like the most natural thing to do. And yet the world beyond the opaque glass was black. This must be the creek side of the building. On the street side, there would be more lights. More of a sense of space beyond the window.

She'd been told to shower and change, to have her own clothes ready for laundry. Maya would probably have done that, so she had to as well.

The water was hot and the shampoo they'd provided had a heady scent of musk roses that reminded Dana of Turkish Delight. They'd included conditioner, too, and body moisturizer. Whatever plans were in store for these girls, they were being looked after. So far, Nadia's account had been accurate.

When she'd rinsed her hair, Dana dressed quickly and went back into the bedroom. She wasn't wearing a watch — Maya hadn't been — but estimated it was close to midnight. She should be tired. She *was* tired, but to sleep in this strange place, with no idea why she was here or what would happen to her? Was that possible?

Footsteps outside. She backed up against the bed, her hand going to the locket around her throat. Break the chain, drop the locket on the floor and stamp down hard.

Not yet, not yet. It might be nothing.

The door opened and the smell of food wafted in. The woman who'd met her carried a small casserole dish on a tray. There was also a half-litre bottle of water, an apple and a banana. The woman put the tray down, picked up the dirty clothes Dana had left on the chair and half smiled at her.

'Wait!'

The woman turned back in the doorway, her smile already gone.

'What will happen?' said Dana.

'Eat and sleep. Tomorrow, you'll see the doctor.'

Then, as though wanting to be away before any more questions could be hurled at her, she strode out and locked the door again.

Tomorrow she'd see the doctor. Why did that send a chill around her heart?

'That woman, Nadia Safi, I want her bringing in. First thing in the morning,' said Weaver.

'Is that wise, Guv?' said Anderson. 'The last thing we want to do is draw attention to the operation.'

'She's been where Dana is now. She can tell us exactly what's happening to her.'

'She's in a room on the top floor.' Lacey was sitting with the technician at the monitor. 'There are four other people in the building. Two of them haven't moved in the last hour, so I'm guessing they're asleep. One of them seems to be in the room next to DI Tulloch's, the other on the floor below. The third person is doing most of the moving around — it could be the woman who met the boss at the door. The other seems to be confined to the ground floor, but is moving, so not asleep.'

'What's Dana doing now?' said Weaver.

'Very little. She's been moving quite a bit — you know, wandering to the window, maybe going to the bathroom. She's been still for about four minutes now, so she may be trying to get some sleep.'

'Which is exactly what we should do,' said Anderson. 'Nobody got much kip last night and this could go on for another twenty-four hours.'

The sergeant was right. The surveillance equipment would be monitored all night. If anything happened, they'd know about it.

Nobody moved.

'She isn't moving, she's asleep,' said Anderson.

'No, the locket isn't moving,' said Weaver. 'She could be anywhere.'

'With respect, Sir, that just proves you're too tired to think straight. There's a red and orange glow on the thermal-imaging camera that is a warm, healthy body in exactly the same spot as the tracker. Not wishing to put too fine a point on it, if that healthy glow starts to look a bit blue, then we can panic. For now, she's fine.'

76

Dana and Lacey

When Dana woke in the night, it was with the immediate thought that she hadn't expected to sleep, and yet she felt strangely rested, if a little groggy. Had the food she'd eaten been drugged? If so, it had been with a sleeping draught only, no harm done.

She'd heard something. Something had woken her, and yet now there was complete silence, as though, around her, everyone slept.

The room wasn't as dark as she remembered it being when she'd switched off the light, and a pale-grey glow surrounded the window. She got up and pressed her face against the glass. Yes, definitely getting light out there, and if she listened hard, she might be able to hear early-morning traffic on the river. So the day was coming. She'd survived the night.

The doctor will see you. Christ, she wanted

to see the doctor like she wanted a hole in her head.

The table and chair she'd pushed against the door before getting into bed were still in place. They'd have made useless barriers, but the sound of them scraping along the floor would have given her a couple of seconds. And there was that noise again. Listening to it properly, it was definitely the sound that had woken her, just an hour or two before her body was ready to be woken. The sound of someone crying near by.

When Lacey woke in the night, it was to the sound of the tide coming in. It sounded different on Ray and Eileen's boat. A soft movement in the main cabin told her that the officer guarding her was still on board. She sat up, opened the hatch above her head and climbed out.

The air around her was heavy with the chill of night and the moon was a sliver of cheese, about to fall below the horizon. High tide would be in about an hour. Her own boat swayed gently on its moorings, rocking and pitching in time with the bigger boat at its side. They looked like two drunk dancers, clinging together on the dance floor at the end of the evening.

Lacey crept forward until she could sit on

the edge of the cabin roof and look out at the water. She could see quite well. It couldn't be long till dawn.

Some time during the day, the operation at Sayes Creek would come to a head. With luck and a fair wind they'd get DI Tulloch out safely and find out what had been going on. They'd make arrests, close the operation down. The bodies bobbing on the river bed at South Dock Marina would be brought to the surface, identified and, eventually, laid to rest properly. It would be over.

Except why, when the ongoing criminal operation depended upon the bodies not being discovered, had someone been practically hurling them into her path? She'd assumed the killer was playing games, had chosen her as a conduit to the police, as a means of taunting them, but did that really make sense? What little they knew of the set-up suggested something big and organized. Professional. Generally speaking, professionals with big sums of money at stake didn't play games.

It was surprising how quickly one lost track of time on the river. There was something almost hypnotic about the relentless flow of the water, broken only by debris that was big enough to be seen and pale enough to catch the starlight.

Sudden movement on the water made Lacey jump, as a dozing bird was disturbed and flapped its way to safety. The sky was definitely getting lighter. The sounds of avian panic faded, the ruffles in the water settled and for a moment the incoming tide moved smoothly. Then, about twenty yards from the boat, the rounded shape of a human head emerged.

■ ■ ■ ■

WEDNESDAY, 2 JULY

■ ■ ■ ■

77

Dana and Lacey

Dana was in her bathroom. The crying was coming from the next room. The tone and strength of the sobs suggested a woman. She bent and saw the pipework beneath the washbasin.

Tap, tap, tap.

No response. No break in the crying. Dana got up again, ran into the bedroom and found the spoon from dinner the night before. They hadn't given her a knife. Back in the bathroom, she tapped three times on the pipe. And again. The crying stopped. Three more taps. Silence from the next room.

'Hello?' tried Dana, just as footsteps sounded in the corridor outside.

She heard someone enter the next room, a low exchange of conversation, the rattle of crockery, then the door being closed and locked. Dana sat on her bed and waited.

Her own door opened and the woman from last night entered, carrying a breakfast tray. She had Dana's clothes over one arm and her bag over the other.

'Thank you,' Dana risked.

'Did you sleep well?'

Dana nodded. In the brighter light, the woman had an eastern European look about her. Her eyebrows were dark, her skin sallow, her eyes dark and rather deep set. There might also be a trace of accent about the deep voice.

'You should get dressed,' said the woman. 'I'll be back in an hour.'

'A car's just arrived outside the house,' Lacey told her two colleagues. 'Looks like other people are arriving.'

The Marine Unit had been on the river since before dawn: Sergeant Buckle, Finn Turner and Lacey in a small dinghy hovering near the entrance to Sayes Creek. Buckle was at the helm, Turner sat at the bow. Lacey was monitoring radio activity.

She hadn't gone back to bed after seeing the swimmer again. Before she'd had a chance to call the officers on duty, the head had disappeared.

While she'd been staring out at the water, Ray had joined her, and between them they'd decided to say nothing for now. Monitoring the situation at Sayes Court and keeping DI Tulloch safe had to take priority for the next few hours. She'd report it once Dana was safe.

'They're opening the big warehouse doors,' she said. 'The car's driving into the building.'

In the centre of the river, a passenger ferry went past at speed, one of the first daytrips heading towards Greenwich. The wash came towards them and Buckle turned the dinghy to face it.

'Two people got out of the car,' said Lacey, after a few seconds. 'That makes seven people in the building, including DI Tulloch.'

The woman came back for Dana exactly an hour later. After dressing and eating, Dana had watched the morning news on television. When she heard footsteps, her hand went up to the locket as though clutching at a talisman, but when the door opened, she was standing ready, her breakfast tray in her hands.

'Go ahead.' The woman took the tray from Dana. 'Down the stairs. Next floor down.'

Dana did what she was told.

'Next door on your right,' said the woman,

as Dana arrived at a door that wasn't properly closed. 'Go straight in.'

'OK, so the house population has increased by two,' Lacey told her colleagues. 'There are seven people in there now. One on the top floor, one on the ground. DI Tulloch and her guide are on the first floor, as is someone who might still be asleep because he or she hasn't moved since last night. There are also two in the room that DI Tulloch seems to be heading for.'

She paused, there were a few moments of static, then more information.

'OK, DI Tulloch's in the room on the first floor with two others, her guide's left her there and is heading back down the stairs.'

Turner's eyes dropped; Buckle stared straight ahead. They were picturing the layout of the house, as she was. Seven people: one on the top floor, two on the ground and four on the first, three of whom were now in the same room. Remember that. If they had to go in suddenly, they didn't want any surprises.

'This could be it,' said Anderson over the radio. 'Stand by, everyone.'

'Hello, Maya,' said the thin white woman standing behind the desk. 'Welcome to the

United Kingdom. We're so happy to see you here.'

'I'm Doctor Kanash,' said the young Asian man by the window. 'This is Nurse Stafford.'

The doctor will see you tomorrow. Kanash and Stafford. Real names? Remember everything you can. Kanash is about thirty-five, has a tiny scar just above his upper lip on the left side, and his very dark skin and eyes were making her think Sri Lankan rather than Indian or Pakistani. Stafford is older, maybe early forties, thin hair cut into a bob, mousy brown but with strands of grey. She's wearing a wedding ring.

'Thank you,' said Dana, knowing something was expected of her. 'Thank you very much.'

It was OK to look round, wasn't it? Any woman would look round the room nervously. A couch pushed up alongside one wall, with a long runway of tissue paper along its length. A height measure and weighing scales. A blood-pressure kit on the desk. A box of surgical gloves. Some sort of electronic scanning equipment.

'You had a long trip, I know,' Kanash was saying. 'A very difficult trip, but it's over now.'

'Have some tea.' Stafford had moved from behind the desk and was now beside an urn of hot water. 'We have jasmine, or peppermint?'

They were being nice to her. Should that make her feel better, or worse?

'Please, I am very — I don't know the words. What will happen now?'

'We completely understand,' said Kanash, as Stafford gave Dana a smile. 'Everything is very new. But there's nothing to worry about. We have a very nice job waiting for you. A very nice couple who want someone to look after their house, especially when they are travelling. It's a beautiful house. Not so much to do. You'll be very happy.'

'Thank you. Do I go today?'

The two exchanged a glance. 'I'm afraid not,' said Stafford. 'There is much to sort out first. Lots of paperwork. Work permits and visas and immigration papers. The British need so much paperwork. But while it is being sorted out, you will stay here with us and we will take very good care of you.'

'Thank you,' said Dana.

'Hold still a moment.' Stafford had picked up a camera from the desk. As Dana stared at her, she pressed the button. 'Just for your file,' she said. 'So we don't get you mixed up with one of the other ladies.'

'How are you feeling after your trip?' asked Kanash. 'Any health problems we should know about?'

Dana shook her head, knowing she looked scared and that it was probably exactly how every other girl in this room had looked.

'Right,' said Kanash, and Dana had a sense he'd got to the end of his stock repertoire of pleasantness. 'Let's get you on the scales, shall we?'

'She's on the move again,' Lacey told the crew. 'She's being escorted back upstairs.' She looked at her watch. 'Better part of an hour,' she said. 'What was all that about?'

She hadn't expected an answer. 'She must know something after that,' she said. 'We could go in now.'

'She's still fine,' said Buckle. 'They said twenty-four hours.'

'Lacey, are you there?' Anderson's voice sounded agitated.

'I can hear you, Sarge,' she replied.

'Has a boat or vessel of any kind gone up Sayes Creek in the last fifteen minutes?'

'Negative, Sarge.' Lacey saw her own puzzlement reflected on the faces of both Buckle and Turner. 'No one's been in there since we came on shift.'

'Well, there are eight people in the house now and nobody else arrived by car.'

'Are you sure?'

'Course I'm bloody sure. DI Tulloch and one other on their way back upstairs. Two in the room she's just left, that's four. One more on that floor who hasn't moved since we started surveillance, and one in the room next to DI Tulloch's on the top floor. And two characters on the ground. So how did number eight squeeze in? Teleportation?'

'We didn't see anything, Sarge.' Beads of sweat burst on Lacey's temples as she began to scan the water around them.

Back in her room, Dana went straight into the shower. She ran the water as hot as she could bear and stood beneath it, telling herself to calm down.

They'd done nothing except carry out a perfectly ordinary, if extremely thorough, medical examination. She'd been weighed and measured, against a background conversation of how she was a little on the slim side but still very attractive. Kanash had listened to her chest and pronounced her heart and lungs perfectly healthy. He'd taken her blood pressure and seemed quite happy with that, too. She'd been sent into a toilet cubicle and asked to provide a urine sample. They tested it there and then, finding no traces of sugar or protein, which was good, apparently, but explained that it would need to be sent away for further testing. Then Stafford took blood, but did it so smoothly and expertly that Dana barely felt the needle go in. Kanash had put headphones on her and asked her to listen out for tiny pin-pricks of sound. They'd asked her to read from a card on the wall, a card with pictures on it, for women who couldn't read the Latin alphabet. 'Boat,' Dana had said. 'Fish, tree.' She'd mimed apple and scissors for good measure.

Then she'd been asked to lie on the couch. At this point, Stafford took over, although Kanash remained in the room, hidden from sight behind the drawn curtain. Dana had been asked to undress to her underwear, and when she'd looked reluctant, Stafford had explained that the British government would only issue permits to people who were perfectly healthy.

'Have you ever had a child?' Her fingers had roamed over Dana's stomach, pressing and probing. 'Ever been pregnant?' She'd mimed a bump over her stomach, in case Dana hadn't understood. 'Lie back and bring your heels towards your bottom.' The look on her face told Dana that this was the part when it usually got difficult.

Gasping, her skin stinging, Dana turned off the shower and let the cold air flood over her. What did it matter if they were watching? It wasn't as if she had anything else left to hide.

It had been a cervical examination, that was all. She'd had them before. They were unpleasant, you gritted your teeth, relaxed as best you could and waited for it to be over. They didn't last long and there was absolutely no need to be such a wimp about it, but for the love of God, why had they had to do all that to her? What was going on here?

She stepped out of the cubicle and found a towel. She wrapped it around her shoulders and waited to stop shivering. From the next room came the sound of the lavatory being flushed. Then a low-pitched moaning.

78

Pari and Dana

Someone was tapping on the pipes again. Pari lowered herself down until she was kneeling on the tiled bathroom floor. Three taps. The sound of the cistern died away. Pari pressed her face against the wall. There had been people in the room next to hers before now, but no one had tried to talk to her before.

'Hello,' she heard, in English.

She said nothing, waiting to see if the voice would speak again.

After a few seconds, it did. 'I'm Maya. Are you OK?'

Pari understood OK, it was international language. She started to speak, but the sound that came out was somewhere between a moan and a gasp.

'What's wrong? Are you ill?'

'It hurts.' Finally, Pari was able to talk.

'Where do you hurt? What happened to

you? What's your name?'

The English words were coming too fast. Pari took a second to process what she'd just heard. 'I'm sick. In pain. My name is Pari.'

Silence, as though the woman on the other side of the wall was thinking. Then, 'Have you told the nurse? The woman who brings us food?'

Crouched over like this, the cramps were too painful. Pari got to her feet.

'How long have you been ill?'

'I don't know. Many days.'

'How long have you been here?'

'Many days.'

People in the corridor. Pari heard quick footsteps in the room next to her own. Then the other bathroom door being pulled shut.

Dana moved quickly back to her bedroom. There was a knock on the door as it began to open. Nurse Stafford was standing outside, together with the woman who brought her food and a heavy-set, middle-aged man whom Dana hadn't seen before. He, too, was wearing scrubs, pale blue like the woman's. His right hand was tucked into his trouser pocket.

'Sorry to disturb you, Maya.' Stafford stepped into the room towards her. 'There's just one more thing. Was there something you forgot to mention downstairs?'

The other two followed her in and the door closed behind them. Dana's hand flew to her locket as the woman in blue scrubs approached her. The man pulled his hand from his pocket. Dana flinched, before realizing he was holding a small glass vial containing red liquid. Her hand hesitated, for just a fraction too long. The woman took hold of one arm, the man the other. She could no longer reach the locket.

'Of course, it's possible you didn't know.' Stafford was a couple of feet away, looking steadily into Dana's face. 'The levels we found were very low, but it does raise an interesting question. How could a woman who's spent the last few weeks on the road from Afghanistan, closely guarded and protected every step of the way, be in your condition?'

Dana shook her head. 'I don't —'

'It's a very simple test,' said Stafford. 'We do it as a matter of routine. We've just never had a positive result before. But congratulations, Maya, if that's really your name. You're pregnant.'

79

Lacey

Lacey got back to the yard shortly after two in the afternoon. Neither she, Buckle nor Turner had wanted to leave their post by Sayes Creek, but Chief Inspector Cook had insisted. If anything happened, they'd be called back, he'd said, but Dana wasn't due to be pulled out until midnight and there was no way he was going to be involved in a difficult and dangerous rescue operation with a knackered crew. It had been impossible to argue.

Out of habit, she looked for the officer who was keeping an eye on the yard. The ice-cream van that was his temporary home was empty. Nor was there any sign of him wandering around.

Her own boat was empty, too. She popped back up and went to find Eileen. No plain-clothed presence on her boat either.

'Where are the bodyguards?' she asked.

Eileen pulled a don't-ask-me face. 'They had a call-out that took priority. They'll be back later.'

'Better hope our neighbourhood psycho needs the cover of darkness, then,' muttered Lacey, although privately she was relieved. Being alone for a few hours felt like a good idea.

She'd pulled off her sweatshirt when her phone started to ring. Not her usual phone — that had been lost in the river along with her canoe. The one she'd used to contact Nadia.

'I've remembered something. I thought I should call you straight away.'

Lacey sat down and pulled a pencil and notepad towards her. 'Go ahead.'

'I think I can remember the way they took me, when I left the house,' said Nadia.

Lacey reached across to the chart table and found the Thames Pilot Book.

'I've been thinking about it ever since I spoke to you,' said Nadia, when Lacey asked her to go ahead. 'I bought a map of the river and tried to work it out. I've even been down to the water's edge.'

'Nadia, we know where you were kept.' Lacey had found the chart with Sayes Creek. 'It's a house very close to the river. We're watching it at the moment, but anything you can tell me will be useful.'

'I can show you.'

Lacey looked at her watch. She had to be back at Wapping by ten o'clock. The chances were that the exact details of Nadia's exit from the house weren't that important any more. On the other hand, it wouldn't hurt.

'OK, where are you now?'

'By the water. A place called St George's Stairs. I remember passing them that night. And the pier just up-river.'

Lacey looked at the map. St George's Stairs was an access point to the river very close to the South Dock Marina. The pier Nadia was referring to was Greenland Pier, a busy mooring point for passenger traffic.

'OK, I'll come and pick you up.' She looked round for her car keys. 'It will take me about half an hour to drive round to you.'

'But it will not work in a car.'

'I'm sorry?'

'I've tried to walk the route and it isn't possible. There are places a car can't go.'

'I think you'll find a police warrant card opens a lot of gates.' Lacey checked that she had hers.

'And there was a building. I was taken to it before they said goodbye. I can't find it on land, I've been looking all day, but I

554

think I might be able to in a boat.'

'You want us to go on the water?' No. Memories flooding back. The head appearing out of the dark water. Strong hands pulling her under. She did not want to go out on the river.

'Lacey, I'm still afraid of it,' said Nadia. 'But I think it might be the only way.'

80

Dana

Dana was being marched downstairs again.
She was pregnant? How could they tell that
quickly, it had been barely more than a day.
Christ, she didn't know whether to smile or
scream. They'd reached the first floor, the
woman nudged her along the corridor. The
treatment had worked! The egg she'd seen
on the scan had popped out of its follicle.
One of the several million donated sperm
had found it and the two of them had
decided they might just have a future
together. There was a baby growing inside
her. And she'd put them both in danger.

She couldn't panic. She still had the
locket. The team would be watching everyone in the house very closely. They'd be
here in minutes.

Helen would kill her. Oh, please God, let
her have the chance.

They were back at the examination room.

The door was pushed open. Someone new was standing just in front of the window, holding up a file to the light. In the top right-hand corner was a small, startled photograph of Dana herself. The man — tall, dark-haired, wearing a well-cut suit — was studying it closely. Then he turned. Alexander Christakos, her fertility consultant.

'DI Tulloch,' he said. 'What an interesting turn of events.'

Dana's hand shot to the locket. She pulled hard as the three staff members who were still flanking her all pressed in to stop her next move.

'This is a police operation and you are all under arrest,' she said. 'My colleagues are surrounding the building.'

Christakos picked up the phone and held it out. 'In that case,' he said, 'I suggest you invite them in.'

'Detective Sergeant Anderson, a pleasure to meet you,' said Christakos several minutes later, as Anderson burst, red-faced and puffing, into the room. 'Actually, I think I've heard quite a lot about you from a young friend of mine, but we can get to that. Do have a seat.'

He sat down behind the desk and gestured

557

to the chair in front of it, exactly as he had in the clinic in town. He was dressed as immaculately, was as smoothly handsome as ever. Anderson ignored him, addressing Dana instead.

'Some sort of clinic, Ma'am. Five people in the building other than ourselves. Mr Christakos here, three members of staff and a young foreign woman who looks like she could be a patient. They're all in separate rooms waiting for us to talk to them. Are you OK?'

Dana nodded. 'I'm fine, but the woman needs medical attention. She was in a lot of pain earlier this morning.'

As Anderson stepped to the door and spoke briefly to someone outside, Dana gripped the back of the chair. She desperately wanted to sit down and knew she couldn't do it. She had to look in control.

Christakos gave a small, polite smile. His hands were perfectly still on the desk in front of him. 'I'm not aware of any medical issues on the part of our guest, but thank you for drawing it to my attention.'

'What is this place?' said Dana. 'What happens here?'

'These are my private consulting rooms.' Christakos opened his hands as if to say *Take a look, I have nothing to hide.* 'This is where I see patients who don't want to attend a busy London clinic. I've only been here for a few months, so we're not quite up to speed, but I hope in time we'll be able to carry out simple procedures here.'

'What sort of procedures?' said Anderson, from the doorway.

Christakos glanced at Dana, and let the corner of his mouth turn up in a small, knowing smile. 'A variety. But largely concerned with assisted pregnancies. A number of our sperm donors come here to donate. It's more convenient than our clinic in town for those who live south of the river.'

'What are the girls for?' said Dana.

He blinked again. 'Girls, Detective Inspector? I don't employ girls. I have a number of women on my staff. There is Nurse Rachel Stafford, for example. And Kathryn Markova, who is a sort of office manager, although she, too, has some medical training.'

'There is a young woman in a room upstairs who I'd put money on being an illegal immigrant,' said Dana. 'From what I could tell this morning, she is seriously ill. I'll ask you again, what are the girls for?'

Christakos gave a small, sad smile, as though she were missing something important, before standing and turning to the window. The glass in front of him was clear, and Dana could see the building immediately opposite. Five storeys high, with rectangular windows, a flat roof and cast-iron balconies. Christakos had apparently gathered his thoughts.

'Detective Inspector, many years ago, my sister and I entered this country as immigrants. I won't say illegally, but things weren't as strict back then as they are now. We've done well here, so occasionally we like to help others who need our assistance.'

'What does that mean exactly?' said Anderson.

'Very occasionally, if we hear of young people — not necessarily women — who need help settling into a new country, we sponsor them. We give them a place to stay, assisance in learning English, and eventually we help them find employment.'

'And you inform the authorities when you do this?'

'The UK Border Agency has been less than helpful in the past,' said Christakos. 'We find we can manage very well without them.'

There was a knock on the door and the uniformed sergeant poked his head around it. 'A moment, Ma'am.' Behind him, Dana could see Mizon's blonde hair.

'There's a discrepancy,' the sergeant said, when she and Anderson joined him in the corridor. 'The surveillance equipment told us there were eight people in the building, including you. One left by car just before you called us. So we should have been looking for six, apart from yourself. Trouble is, what we were seeing on the equipment got very confused. We lost track of where everyone was. We've checked the entire building, top to bottom, and there are just five people. We've been in the basement and up on the roof. Only one young foreign woman, in a room on the ground floor. She's a bit dopey, but she looks fine. Certainly doesn't seem to be ill or injured.'

'There was someone in the room next to mine overnight,' said Dana. 'A girl called Pari. In a lot of pain. Check again.'

'We stopped the car that left here earlier on the approach to London Bridge,' said Mizon. 'The driver claims he's called Kanash and is a doctor working at the Thames Clinic. He had a meeting here with Dr Christakos this morning and is on his way back to work. They're taking him to Lewisham.'

'I take it they searched the car,' said Dana.

Mizon nodded. 'There were two industrial-sized containers in the boot that he says are cryo-storage vessels. He claims they're empty but that the clinic are waiting for them.'

'Come again?' said Anderson. 'Cryo what?'

'Fertility treatment relies upon preserving gametes and embryos for use in the future,' Dana told him. 'Sperm, eggs and fertilized embryos can be frozen in liquid nitrogen and kept until needed.' She turned to Mizon. 'Gayle, we should have them delivered, but I want someone to see exactly what's inside them. In fact, can you try and get hold of Mike Kaytes for me?'

Mizon stepped away down the hall and pulled out her phone. The sergeant resumed his search of the building.

'Get him brought in, Neil.' Dana nodded her head to the room where Christakos waited for them. 'He's not telling us everything.'

81

Lacey

'Don't have a good feeling about this,' muttered Lacey ten minutes later, as she steered Ray's motor boat out of the entrance to Deptford Creek and turned up-river.

Lewisham Control had been unable to send support. 'We're absolutely up to our eyes in it,' the dispatcher had told Lacey. 'RTA on Lewisham High Street and an armed hold-up in Barclays Bank. Can you hold on till things clear up a bit?'

Reluctant to call her own colleagues and divert them from the far more important job of keeping an eye on Dana, Lacey had decided to meet Nadia alone. If what the Afghan woman had to show her was largely irrelevant, it could wait till she reported in later. If it turned out to be important, she could call it in immediately and insist upon back-up. She had a radio, a phone, even a torch, safely tucked inside a waterproof bag in the bottom of the boat. It was broad daylight and she was in a properly equipped boat. What could possibly go wrong?

'Let someone know where I've gone if I don't call you in an hour,' she'd told Eileen, who had promised to do exactly that.

She steered wide as she neared the entrance to Sayes Creek, not wanting to give the surveillance team any reason to worry about her presence on the water. She half expected them to hail the boat and pull it over, even if they didn't recognize her at the helm, but she didn't even see the dinghy close to the wall, and the RIB must be further downstream.

Past Sayes Creek, she steered close to the bank again, and after a few minutes saw Nadia waiting for her on St George's Stairs.

'That way.' Nadia pointed up-river, once she'd pulled the life-jacket over her head and climbed into the boat in front of Lacey. 'This is the way we went when I left the house. It was dark, but I remembered last night.'

Lacey set off again, keeping close to the bank, steering up-river towards the city.

'I remember that.' Nadia pointed to the entrance to South Dock Marina. 'I thought we might be about to go in there, but at the last minute we moved on past.'

Lucky for you, thought Lacey, thinking of the corpses lying weighted on the marina floor. She steered the boat around Greenland Pier, keeping a lookout for the fast vessels that used it to moor up, and then past the entrance to Greenland Lock. Nadia was intent on the south bank.

'There.' She was pointing at a gap in the wall. 'They took me in there.'

'That's a sewage outlet.'

'It leads to a room. It looked like a room for machinery. Very old, but beautiful. There were flowers in the ironwork. And huge great columns.'

Lacey looked at her watch, then downriver again — she could still see no activity outside Sayes Court — and finally at her police radio in its waterproof bag. 'Nadia, why didn't you tell me this before?'

'I told you, I never think about that night. I only let myself remember when I realized how important it was to you.'

'I can't take you in there.' Lacey looked again at the tunnel entrance. 'The tide's getting quite low, we could get stuck.'

'OK, just steer to the wall,' said Nadia. 'There is something you need to see.'

'What?'

'A ring fixed into the side. I think it's what

they tie the girls to. They tie them to the rings and then, when the water comes up, they drown.'

The wound around the corpse's neck. It was a detail that had never been made public. Oh God, that was horrible. To be tied up in a tunnel, watching the water coming closer. 'How far in is it?'

'There are several of them, but the first is just inside the entrance.'

Lacey steered the boat the final few yards that took them to the embankment wall and just inside the tunnel entrance. By keeping the engine in gear and the revs low, she was just about able to hold the boat in position.

'Just here.' Nadia was pointing further into the tunnel. 'A little more in.'

Ray's boat had a deeper keel than the dinghies the Marine Unit used to patrol these tunnels. Already, they'd moved further in than felt wise. 'Nadia, I really can't go any further. I need to get you back on shore and then call this in. What? What's the matter?'

Nadia had stiffened, was sitting bolt upright in the boat, her eyes going from side to side.

'Lacey,' she said, in a small voice. 'I think there's someone here.'

Instincts kicking in, Lacey put the engine

into reverse and looked back over her shoulder to steer out. A sudden screech. The boat rocked. She looked round in time to see Nadia falling backwards into the water.

82

Dana

'I'm sorry, Dana,' said Kaytes, 'but I think the clinic's clean.'

They were back at Lewisham police station. Three hours had gone by since Dana and her team had left the house in East Street. Christakos had said nothing beyond what he'd told them already and Kaytes and a team of detectives had just finished as thorough a search of the Thames Clinic as they could without a court order.

'We've lost a young woman.' Dana was finding it impossible to sit down. 'There were six of them in that clinic when he allowed me to phone my colleagues and by the time you arrived there were five. He knows where she is. He may have even killed her. He is not getting away with it.'

'Of course not,' said Kaytes. 'But his licence from the HFEA clearly permits him to . . .'

'Sorry, what's HFEA?' Anderson interrupted.

'Human Fertility Embryology Authority,' Kaytes told him. 'It's the regulatory body for fertility treatment in the UK. You should check with them, see if there are any complaints or investigations outstanding against Christakos. But to be honest, I'd be surprised.'

'Is it big business, fertility?' asked Anderson.

'God, yes. People will practically bankrupt themselves to have a baby. Mind you, most kids bankrupt their parents in the end, so I suppose it just saves time.'

'So what would a clinic like that turn over in a year?'

'Millions. Take donor insemination, for a start.'

Dana made herself sit down.

'A woman might pay up to a thousand pounds a cycle,' he went on. 'Let's say she takes six cycles to get pregnant. Six grand, and what has the sperm cost the clinic? Pin money for some medical student who's not that squeamish about having a wank in a hospital cubicle.'

'Fascinating,' said Mizon, after the moment's silence that seemed called for. 'So we can assume Christakos is successful.

That he's making money.'

'I'll say,' said Kaytes. 'The Thames Clinic has an international reputation. It was one of the pioneers of the egg-sharing scheme back in the 1990s, and that's a real money spinner.'

'Do we need to know what egg sharing is?' asked Anderson.

'Probably not,' said Kaytes.

Egg sharing? Dana started to get up, told herself to wait, to be sure.

'It can't hurt,' said Mizon. 'Don't we need to know as much as possible about what he's up to?'

'Well, it's a clever idea, really.' Kaytes settled himself on a desktop. 'It brings together women who've gone beyond the age of being able to produce viable eggs, with couples who can't afford the huge cost of IVF. Basically, the older, richer couple fund IVF treatment for the younger, who in return agree to share the eggs produced.'

And that's what it was all about. 'Thank God we sent for you, Mike.' Dana was on her feet again.

'Glad to be of service.' Kaytes looked flattered but surprised.

'There's an acute shortage of donor eggs, isn't there?'

Kaytes nodded. 'Very much so. Women

who are donating eggs have to undergo almost full IVF treatment. They have daily injections, drugs to shove up their noses. Then there's the surgical procedure itself, under general anaesthetic. It's a lot to ask a woman to go through. And usually for the benefit of a perfect stranger.'

Something lit up behind Kaytes's eyes. He'd got it. The rest, on the other hand, were getting twitchy.

'Give me a second, guys, I am going somewhere with this,' said Dana. 'Mike, in other countries, the USA most typically, egg donors are compensated financially, right?'

'They are here,' said Kaytes. 'But only a few hundred pounds. In the US, couples pay thousands of dollars for eggs from a good donor.'

'And what makes a good donor?'

'Young, healthy, intelligent and good looking. And a physical resemblance to the receiving parent is a decided advantage.'

'What are you two getting at?' said Anderson.

Dana crossed to a spare computer and typed into the search bar. 'OK, this is more than I would normally share, but it'll become blindingly obvious soon anyway. The fact is, Helen and I are hoping to start a family.'

Of the faces around her, only Kaytes didn't look surprised.

'But given our particular circumstances, we're going to need a bit more help than the average couple,' she went on. 'Come and look at this.'

The others gathered round.

'Sperm bank,' said Stenning, with what sounded like distaste in his voice.

Dana stiffened. 'You know what, Pete? When the time comes for you and some unfortunate young woman to breed, I really hope you can manage it in the time-honoured way. But if you need a bit of medical help, you're going to have to lose some of that squeamishness about bodily functions.'

Stenning shook his head. 'No, you've just reminded me that I did it myself a few years ago. When I was at Hendon. A lot of us did. For the money.'

'You were a sperm donor?' Mizon had taken a step away from him.

'Me too,' said Barrett. 'Kept me in beer and ciggies for two years.'

Dana shook her head. 'That is information I really could have done without just now. But getting back to the point. This is how we choose. Look.' She found the screen where the listings of available donors appeared and the little blue, yellow, green and pink icons popped up.

'So, there are umpteen little Stennings and Barretts running round the place,' said Mizon.

'Gayle, would you focus for a second?' said Dana. 'This is a sort of online catalogue of available sperm. With some very basic information about the donors.'

'I wonder if I'm still on it.' Barrett leaned closer.

'Not umpteen.' Stenning turned to Mizon. 'There are regulations governing how many families an individual donor can supply. And how old are you, twelve?'

'Stop it,' said Dana. 'This isn't about sperm, it's about eggs. Mike, am I right in thinking there isn't an equivalent site that couples who need donated eggs can go to?'

'Definitely not,' said Kaytes. 'We have an acute shortage of egg donors in the UK.'

'For all the reasons you just told us about. So if a couple have plenty of money but no viable eggs of their own, what do they do?'

'Oh my God.' Mizon had got it too, now.

'Quite a lot go abroad for their eggs, to countries where the authorities aren't quite so squeamish about paying donors,' said Kaytes. 'There are international egg banks. Frozen eggs can be shipped over, but the best results come from fresh eggs. Typically, that means the recipients will arrange for the donor to travel to them, so cycles can be coordinated. You can imagine how bloody expensive that gets.'

'Unless the women are smuggled in through cheaper, less orthodox channels,' said Mizon. 'And especially if they don't even know their eggs are being taken from them.'

It took a second for the men to catch up.

'These women are egg donors?' said Anderson.

'I think they could be,' said Dana. 'They've been smuggled in for something and we've more or less ruled out the sex trade. So what else do young, attractive women have to offer?'

'Their fertility,' said Mizon. 'You think this bastard Christakos is stealing their eggs?'

'When people choose a donor, whether sperm or eggs, they're looking for someone who looks like they do,' said Dana. 'Most couples with the money to spend on egg donation and who are OK with it ethically will be white. They'll be looking for a white donor.'

'But these girls are from Afghanistan,' said Stenning.

'They're Pashtuns,' said Dana. 'Lacey's

been banging on about it for days. Light-skinned, pale-eyed Asians. Fertilize one of their eggs with white British sperm and you're going to get a white-British-looking baby.'

'Well, not guaranteed,' said Kaytes, 'but I agree, the chances are pretty fair.'

'And because these girls are being paid nothing, because they don't even know what's going on, the profit margin for Christakos is massive,' said Dana. 'Why else was Nadia talking about medical treatment? She was on an IVF programme without even knowing about it. Sahar wasn't pregnant, she'd had her body pumped full of IVF drugs.'

'So how and why are some of them ending up in the Thames?' said Mizon. 'How come Nadia was fine?'

'The woman strung up on Lacey's boat had no trace of IVF drugs in her system,' said Kaytes.

'Why would Christakos kill his golden geese?' said Stenning.

The incident-room door opened and one of the clerical team looked in. 'DI Tulloch, I'm sorry but we've just had a call from the front desk. Someone has just pranged your car.'

Dana stared at her. Of all the moments to

pick. 'You're kidding me.'

'Really sorry, Ma'am. They need you to go down and swap insurance details.'

Dana got to her feet. 'Gayle, while I'm out, can you look up egg donation? Get an idea of just how much people are prepared to pay for donated eggs. Neil, I want the Thames Clinic's accounts seized. I want to know how much money's coming through the books and where it's coming from.'

Dana's car was at the end of the line. The left tail light had shattered. Pieces of white and red plastic lay around the ground. A green Ford Mondeo with its engine running was parked just a yard or so away. She set off towards the driver's door, but as she drew level with the car someone grabbed her firmly by the upper arm. At the same time, the rear door opened and she was shoved inside.

As Dana twisted round, getting ready to fight and scream, her captor flung himself on to the back seat beside her and the driver stepped on the accelerator. They turned left along Lewisham High Road. Dana fell back against the seat.

From what she could see in the rear-view mirror, the driver looked vaguely familiar. No doubt at all, though, about the identity of her kidnapper. There were few people in the world she knew better.

'What the fuck have you done with Lacey?' said Joesbury.

83

Pari, Lacey and Dana

Touch was the first of Pari's senses to come back to her and it came wearing a thick, red mantle of pain. Her brain seemed to be swelling, pressing hard against the bones of a skull that had become as brittle and fragile as china. She was breathing, but every breath felt like ground glass scraping against raw flesh. And she was so hot. Her body was covered in a slick sheen of sweat and there was no air left in the world. Her throat was burning. No one could feel this bad and live. And yet she did. A second later she was still alive, and a second after that. After many, many seconds she could start to think beyond the pain.

She was lying face down. The hard iron surface she could feel against her right temple was causing most of the pain. If she could move a fraction, free her head, it would help. But her brain was sending messages that her limbs couldn't hear. And there was so much mud in her head. Her thoughts were weighed down, struggling to form themselves and make sense. Was this real mud? How could it be when she was so hot?

Everything lurched. The world surged high into the air and fell again. The ground beneath her was moving. She focused for a few seconds on the rocking, pitching, rolling motion. She was on water.

'Nadia!'

No reply. Even the water had stopped moving. Knowing she couldn't risk taking the boat any further into the sewer, Lacey tied it to the mooring ring. Straddling the hull for balance, she stretched up, not quite able to stand upright.

Nadia had been wearing a life-jacket. She wouldn't just sink. Someone had to be holding her under.

'Nadia!'

She reached for the bag that kept her radio and phone dry, knowing she'd screwed up badly, that Nadia could lose her life now.

The bag wasn't there. The only explanation could be that Nadia had reached out for it, clutching at anything to avoid being pulled overboard. Trying not to give way to panic, Lacey scrambled out of the boat on to the ledge. No sign of disturbance, just gently moving water. Then a splash, a cry, about twenty yards further in.

'Nadia!'

She should get into the boat and go for help.

If she did that, Nadia would die.

Trying to push away the memory of the creature that had tried to drown her the night before, of the human shape she and Ray had seen in the creek, and without even the benefit of a torch, Lacey set off into the tunnel.

'I can't believe you're doing this. Screw up your own life if you must, but stay the hell out of mine.' Dana turned from Mark to the man at the wheel. 'And who the hell are you?'

A man in his late sixties. Thinning hair, thin build, sun-tanned skin. The only eyebrow she could see in the rear-view mirror raised fractionally. 'Let's just say I'm your driver for the afternoon,' he told her.

'Like hell you are. Take me back right now. In fact, stop the car, I'm getting out. And you'd better be good at quick get-aways, because I am phoning this in the minute I'm out of —'

'Will you fucking well shut up?' Mark told her.

Back to the man at her side. 'You pranged my car, you asshole. I can't believe you did that. And in case it's escaped you, I'm in the middle of something bloody important. Where the hell are we going?'

Mark sighed. 'Dana, we're driving round the frigging block. If you'd calm down and stop screaming for a second, you'd spot that for yourself.'

She stopped shouting; gave herself — and him — a second. 'What do you mean, what have I done with Lacey?'

Mark was close, invading her personal space. He never normally did that. 'Ray phoned me an hour ago. This is Ray Bradbury, by the way.' He nodded towards the driver. 'He lives on the next boat to Lacey. She came home after her early shift, borrowed Ray's boat and went out on the water, telling his wife to sound the alarm if she didn't come back in an hour. She's not answering her phone and Wapping can't get hold of her either. Given everything that's been going on lately, that didn't seem good. And while we're on the subject, I'm in the middle of something bloody important too, so if anyone's career is being screwed up right now, it's mine.'

It took a moment for Dana to take in what he was saying. 'But, I thought . . . we all thought . . .'

There was no humour in her best friend's face. He was angry with her; disappointed. 'Yeah, thanks for that.'

'You're not? You haven't? You're still —'

He nodded, gave her that peculiar half-smile that she'd often thought she could fall in love with, were she remotely that way inclined. 'Yeah, just about. I think.'

84

Pari, Lacey and Dana

When she swam back into consciousness, Pari could hear again. The slow, steady slap of water. Gulls screaming. The distant hum and chug of river traffic. A jet engine over-head.

The stench around her seemed alive. She could almost feel it wrapping its damp, slime-ridden folds around her body. Her nostrils were smarting with the acid sting of it creeping its way inside her head. It jabbed at her stomach like the dull blade of a knife, lay in her mouth like vomit she couldn't spit away. She'd never imagined a smell this bad and wondered, for a moment, whether it might be the stink of her own rotting body that was surrounding her.

And why couldn't she see? Did she still have eyes? Those were gulls she could hear. What had the gulls done to her, while she'd been lying here?

Wait. Wait. She could feel her lashes striking the upper part of her cheeks when she blinked. She still couldn't see anything but blackness, only now she understood why. She was wrapped in something. Shrouded.

Panic gave her the power to move again. She tried to push herself up, but her hands were tied behind her back. She tried kicking, but she was bound hand and foot.

That cold slipperiness against her face was black plastic, kidding her that she was blind, keeping the air from her face. She tried to open her mouth and found that it was taped shut.

And then, as though the effort had exhausted her, Pari slipped away again into oblivion.

Lacey carried on, past a lantern-shelf that offered no promise of light, past a ladder that would take her up to the surface, if being on the surface would help at all, and further still.

Ahead of her, the tunnel came to an abrupt T-junction. To take the right-hand fork, she would have to jump into the water and there was no way she was doing that. She went left, now moving parallel with the river, and after a few minutes heard a squeal, which could have been made by a rodent but somehow sounded bigger, more human. She opened her mouth to call for Nadia and found she didn't dare. The light was all but gone and ahead was blackness so dense it looked solid.

It was solid. A wall. The tunnel curved to the right and then opened out into a much bigger chamber. There was light in here. Not much, but enough to tell Lacey that she was, apparently, alone. She followed the ledge and was surprised to find the light growing. Still very dark, still far too many shadows, but even completely out of reach of the light from the sewer entrance she could see where she was going.

A little further in, she could see the source of the light. Three small tunnels at roughly waist height. Sewage outflow pipes. There would be a pumping station behind them. She might have found the building that Nadia had talked about.

She reached the first of the pipes and peered through. Hardly more than a metre long, and daylight beyond it. Jumping at the chance to get out of the sewer, Lacey climbed into the pipe. A few seconds later, she was in the pumping station.

Two storeys high, the lower floor was underground. She knew that because the boarded-up windows and the large double door were all much higher in the walls. The light was coming from several skylights.

No sign of Nadia — or anyone else, for that matter.

Running along the opposite wall were three recessed arches. She didn't think anyone was hiding in them, but it was difficult to be sure. Between her and the arches were three iron plinths. Lacey had no great knowledge of engineering, but guessed that they would have held the pumps, back when this station had been operational. There were hiding places behind each. And not far from where she was standing, she could count four weights, with handles, that looked exactly the same as the ones holding down the corpses at South Dock Marina.

Something caught her eye and, carefully, she crossed the tiled floor. On a shelf, high above the damp-stained tiles, were folded sheets. Linen sheets.

There's someone here.

Who? Who had pulled Nadia overboard?

Movement behind her. Lacey started to turn. She sensed, rather than saw, someone loom over her. Then nothing.

'OK, so now we've lost two young women, one of whom should bloody well know better.' Dana faced the occupants of the

586

small room at Lewisham. She'd gathered the smallest team she'd dared, the only ones she could trust with the knowledge that Mark was back in the fold. Anderson, Stenning and Mizon. Together with Mark himself and his new best mate Ray Bradbury, they were a group of six.

'Lacey took a phone call at two thirty this afternoon,' Anderson said. 'In fairness, she called for assistance, but there was a lot kicking off in the area and they couldn't get anyone out to her. From Mrs Bradbury on the next boat, we know she then went out on to the river, in Mr Bradbury's boat, to meet Nadia Safi, who we are similarly unable to trace. So strictly, Ma'am, three young women.'

'It just gets better,' said Dana. 'Oh, and does everybody know, we also have a mermaid at large on the Thames.'

'Come again?'

Dana gestured impatiently for Ray to fill everyone else in on what he'd told her and Mark in the car. That whoever had been stalking Lacey for the past couple of weeks was moving around by water, possibly in a small boat, but swimming at least some of the time. He told them about the heart shape in glass and pebbles that Lacey had said nothing about, assuming it to have been left behind by Mark. And he told them about the voice calling Lacey's name, about the tapping on the side of her yacht, about the night they'd both gone out in his boat and seen someone in the water.

'I'm not saying one way or another.' Bradbury was repeating himself now. 'It was dark. We were both a bit spooked. All I'm saying is that from the neck up, at least, it looked human.'

'Why didn't she say something?' asked Mizon.

'Would you?' Mark turned to Ray. 'And she saw it again, this morning?'

The other man nodded. 'She got up just before dawn. I heard her climb out of our boat, although that dozy bugger in the main cabin didn't. She was on the deck and saw it in the water.'

'Male? Female? What did she see exactly?' asked Anderson.

'Human head,' said Ray. 'Too far away and too dark for her to recognize features, but she did see what she thought was long hair floating around, suggesting a female. It just sank below the surface before she had chance to raise the alarm.'

The door opened and David Cook came into the room. His eyes narrowed when he saw Mark but he said nothing, focusing instead on Ray. 'We found your boat, Ray.'

The room fell quiet.

'It was spotted a few minutes ago down by the barrier. It had obviously overturned. Sorry, mate.' He turned to the rest of the room. 'Sorry, everyone. It's not looking hopeful.'

Dana closed her eyes.

'Nope,' said Ray.

Dana turned to him. Probably because she couldn't bring herself to look at Mark.

'Lacey's a bloody good swimmer,' he said. 'I've not known a woman as strong or with as much stamina since my wife was young. She knows how to handle boats and she knows the river. Also, according to Eileen, she went off wearing a life-jacket. Wherever she is, she didn't have an accident on the water.'

'I hope you're right, Ray, but the most experienced skippers can get taken by surprise,' said Cook. 'I've got as many offi-cers as I can spare looking for her.'

'Is it possible Lacey got a lead on what happened to this other girl? Pari, did you say she was called?' said Mark.

'If she did, she should have called it in,' snapped Dana.

'She bloody well tried.' Mark sighed. 'Let's look for this Pari girl. Maybe she'll lead us to Lacey.'

'And Nadia,' said Mizon.

Dana dropped her head into her hands. Just how many bloody women were they going to be pulling out of the Thames before the day was done?

85

Pari, Lacey and Dana

When Pari came round again, she knew she was on the big river, the Thames. She also knew she was amongst rubbish. The foul stench hadn't gone. It was the smell of rotting garbage. Coming from a city where there'd been no official refuse collection, Pari found it familiar enough. She could only assume that, here, people stored their rubbish on the river.

Why was she here? She'd been in her room at the clinic, been talking to a woman on the other side of the wall. There'd been commotion in the next room and then everything had fallen silent. Not for long. Two of the clinic staff had come back. They'd seemed unusually hurried, anxious. She remembered them coming towards her, then . . .

Nothing. Maybe a faint memory of being carried down the stairs. And had she felt sun on her face for the first time in weeks? After that, nothing.

Pari tried to relax, to concentrate on the rocking, pitching, rolling motion beneath her. The wind seemed to have picked up. The water was rough. The tide was rolling in or out fast. Impossible to tell which. But she couldn't be moving, because she would hear an engine. She was on a moored buoy. It was a hiding place and a temporary one at that. It was probably still daytime. At nightfall, they'd come back. She'd got until nightfall to get away.

It was the tang of blood in her mouth that brought Lacey back to herself again, that salty, metallic taste, both comforting and terrifying at the same time. She licked her lips, fought back an urge to throw up, and opened her eyes.

Nothing was clear. The darkness felt like a friend, softening the impact of the swirling shapes and repeated images. She closed her eyes again and took stock.

She was on the silt-covered floor of the sewage tunnel, that much at least she was able to take in. There was light, which meant she probably wasn't too far from the pumping station. She didn't need to be able to see to know that she was sitting in several inches of water and probably had been for some time. She was freezing cold and in a great deal of pain. Much of it came from the injury to her head, some from where her arms had been pulled behind her back and tied together. The rest of it came from the rope fastened tightly around her neck. She tried to lean away from the wall but the rope stopped her. She turned her head and her worst fear was confirmed. She was tied, around the neck, to one of the mooring rings in the sewage tunnel wall. She couldn't move far, she probably couldn't stand up. And when the tide came back in, she'd be helpless.

'Do you recognize this woman?'

The orderly from the clinic, Kathryn Markova, looked down at the photograph.

'She does.' Stenning was watching the interview on the screen. 'Did you see her? Classic double-take. Keep at it, Gayle.'

'She will,' Dana told him. 'I think Markova looks surprised though. Didn't expect to see what she just did.'

Markova was shaking her head.

'We call her Sahar. It's a reconstruction,' said Mizon in the interview room. 'She was too badly damaged when we pulled her from the river. But this one wasn't.'

As Mizon slid the other photograph across the table, there was no doubting the shock on Markova's face.

'It can't be,' she muttered to herself.

'We found her three days ago,' said Mizon. 'She'd only been in the river a matter of days, so I'm guessing she was with you early last week. Did you look after her? Serve her meals? Take her down for treatment? Did you kill her?'

'She was fine,' said Markova. 'She was with us for a few days and then she left. Nothing happens to them when they're with us. We look after them. We aren't doing this.'

'Somebody is,' said Mizon.

86

Pari, Dana and Lacey

It was working. The sharp metal cleat Pari had found by fumbling around had cut a hole through the bag. It helped enormously, letting in fresh air and reducing the claustrophobia that had been threatening to send her over the edge. Now the same weapon was working its way through the tape around her wrists. The bastards had wrapped it round many times, but she was getting through it.

She had to keep going. It didn't matter that she felt like death, she couldn't stop. The problem was, the swell on the river had picked up and the pontoon was pitching about like a toy boat in a toddler's bath. If she threw up with tape round her mouth, she'd suffocate. So every few seconds she had to stop, rest and breathe.

'I think you'll find that donating eggs is

perfectly legal in this country, Detective Inspector,' said Christakos.

Dana stared back. 'I think you'll find that taking body parts without consent is illegal in most countries. Murder certainly is. You'd better hope that abduction, imprisonment and assault are the most serious offences you're charged with before the day is out.'

'These women all came willingly into this country. They were free to leave my clinic at any time. And they all signed consent forms.'

'I don't believe that for a moment,' said Dana.

Christakos looked smug.

'Where are these forms?' Dana realized she'd boxed herself into a corner.

'In a filing cabinet in my office. Along with receipts for money the women were given when they left the clinic. A comparable amount to paying a British donor expenses.'

No, he was not going to wriggle out of it that way. 'The trouble is, some of them left via the Thames,' said Dana. 'The underwater route.'

'I know nothing about that,' said Christakos. 'They were all perfectly well when we said goodbye to them.'

'Even if they were forced or tricked into signing something,' said Dana, 'it proves nothing. How many of them can even read English?'

'The procedure and its implications were explained to them very clearly. Most of our guests speak Pashto or Dari and I am fluent in both.'

'Do you think they'll say that in court?'

'I doubt this will ever come to court,' said Christakos. 'For one thing, you'll have to show a direct link between eggs or embryos in my clinic and women you know have spent time with us. And given the extremely sensitive nature of the organic material we store in the clinic, I'll be surprised if any court gives you permission to confiscate and test it.'

'Donated gametes leave a trail.'

'But if, for the sake of argument, gametes were obtained improperly,' said Christakos, 'then the trail wouldn't be there. I'm sorry, Detective Inspector, but the only charge you can legitimately lay at my door is the one of carrying out medical procedures in an unlicensed building, and that's not even a criminal offence. I'll probably lose my licence, but as I'm less than five years from retirement, that hardly seems a major issue.'

'Where is the young woman who was in the room next to mine last night?'

'I have no idea who you mean.'

'Do you have any idea of the whereabouts of Constable Lacey Flint?'

For a second he looked shocked. 'I had no idea Lacey was missing.'

Dana's phone was ringing. It was Barrett, who was in charge of the search of East Street. She excused herself and left the interview room.

'We've done this side of the river, Ma'am,' Barrett told her. 'I'm just outside a place called Sayes Court. Big house, right at the top of the creek. Anyway, turns out Alexander Christakos lives here with his sister.'

Dana turned to look through the window of the interview room. Christakos had his eyes closed.

'Does he indeed?' she said.

'Has done for years, according to the sister. Nice old duck. We didn't spot the connection immediately because she owns the house and it's in her name, which is different. Seems Alex Christakos isn't his real name, it's one he adopted when they moved here, because he felt a Greek name would be more acceptable to the medical establishment and patients than one from South Asia. Guess what? They're from Afghanistan.'

Christakos had dark hair and blue eyes, spoke both Afghan languages. He was a pale-eyed Pashtun, like the women he'd imported.

'So I guess that explains how he slipped past us to get to the clinic this morning,' Barrett was saying. 'He must have used his sister's boat.

'Could also be how they got Pari out,' replied Dana. 'With some sort of heat-concealing cover to fool the surveillance equipment. This lot are people-smugglers, remember.'

'More interestingly,' said Barrett, 'both of them know Lacey.'

I had no idea Lacey was missing.

She'd let that one go. Christakos had opened his eyes and was looking directly at her through the window. Dana couldn't help feeling that he knew exactly what she was saying. She turned her back.

'Know her how?' she asked Barrett.

'Christakos's sister just said she and her brother are friends of Lacey's. Getting quite upset as well. I've got one of the PCs making her tea.'

Dana looked at her watch. 'Tom, I'm sending a team over,' she said. 'They obviously got the girl out via the creek and that house. I want it searched.'

The tide was coming back. Much as she'd

have liked to pretend otherwise, Lacey knew she hadn't been as wet half an hour ago. She couldn't see her watch, had no idea of the time, but knew the tide would have been due to turn some time in the early afternoon.

Less than a year ago, she'd been pulled headlong into the river, had come within a frantic gasp of drowning. She remembered all too well the paralysing cold, the swirling, dense blackness, the complete helplessness of being at the mercy of fast-moving water. It was going to happen again.

Unless something serious had taken place, the operation in Sayes Creek would still be under way. All her colleagues' eyes would be upon it. She wasn't due back on shift until 10pm and wouldn't be missed until then. Her only chance was Eileen.

The water in here wouldn't be fast like last time. It would creep towards her, slowly, torturously, knowing she couldn't escape.

Her neck was bleeding. She'd tried pulling at the rope to untie it, or even dislodge the mooring ring. She'd tried turning her head to gnaw at the knot, but whoever tied it knew their knots. It wasn't budging.

Twice in the last year she'd found herself at the mercy of the Thames, the second time by choice. She'd leapt from a Marine Unit

Targa in a rash attempt to save the woman she now knew as Nadia Safi. *Got you,* the rushing water had whispered, as its folds had closed over her head and she'd felt the barnacle-encrusted hand of panic reaching up from the river bed. She'd beaten it that time, had saved herself and the terrified Afghan woman. Had she really, stupidly, thought that she and the river had made some sort of truce?

And now a rat was paying her more attention than she felt comfortable with. How long before it plucked up the courage to climb down on to her shoulder and get closer to the blood seeping out of the wounds on her neck?

You can't ever drown, Marlene had said. *That's the legend among watermen. If you cheat death in the water, the river loses its power to harm you.*

Claptrap, Thessa had snapped back. *Of course you can drown. Don't you dare take silly risks.*

She'd taken an unforgivably stupid risk coming here, bringing Nadia here. And now, it seemed the only question remaining was which would get to her first: the tide or the rat?

87

Dana and Pari

'Sahar's real name was Anya Fahid,' Mizon told the rest of the group. 'The body we found on Lacey's boat was that of Rabia Khan. Both from Afghanistan. Both smuggled into the country illegally. Markova's adamant, though, that none of the girls are harmed in any way. When the treatment cycle is over, they're placed with people who are genuinely offering jobs and homes. There's a network of Afghan families in London who help out. She thinks the egg business is a small price to pay for a new life.'

'Is she telling the truth?' asked Barrett, who'd just arrived back.

'I think she might be,' said Mizon. 'She seemed genuinely upset. Although I can't help feeling she's not telling us everything. She's very vague about when and how these women leave the clinic. Says she doesn't get involved with that side of things.'

'If Kaytes is right, then the treatment they're being subjected to, whilst unpleasant, won't actually kill them,' said Mark.

'It doesn't kill them,' said Dana. 'These women are drowning. There's something else going on. Christakos has no need to kill these women and plenty of reason to keep them alive. He doesn't want to draw attention to himself, nor does he want to run unnecessary risks. I think he's a people-trafficker. I think he's exploiting vulnerable young women and defrauding childless couples, and I think he's an all-round sleaze bag, but I don't think he's a killer.'

'So who the hell is?' said Anderson. 'The mermaid?'

The tape was more than half cut through. Pari tried to tear the rest, but it was too strong. On with the pulling, sawing action. Almost there. Pull again. Backwards and forwards and she was free. She tore the plastic apart until she could pull it up over her head and breathe fresh air again.

Darkness. A darkness with stars and the lights from the city, but darkness all the same. A whole day had passed while she'd been tied up and they'd be coming back. She pushed herself on to her knees and looked round. Not too far from the middle of the river. She was moored fifty yards or so off the north bank, on a rubbish barge, as she'd guessed.

There were eight large skips on the barge and she was in one of them. The skip wasn't full, and anyone passing in daylight, even coming quite close, wouldn't have seen her.

Pari twisted round until her ankles were touching the metal cleat and started sawing again. It wasn't so easy with her feet, but she had her hands to guide her and every few seconds she looked up to see if a craft was approaching. Nothing, though. The water was quiet tonight. Keep sawing.

'You know who she is, don't you? The woman who's killing these girls.'

Christakos stared back at Dana with his large, dark-blue eyes. Hours in custody were starting to take their toll. His face looked strained, and the lines around his eyes seemed to have deepened.

Dana leaned forward, resting her arms on the table between them. 'The woman who swims as though she was born in the water. The one who's been seen in the river from time to time, by watermen who just assume they're overtired or have had one drink too many. The one who gave rise to the legend of the Creek mermaid.'

Christakos raised his eyebrows and gave a little start. He was good, just a fraction too slow for the surprise to be convincing.

'She attacked Constable Flint a couple of nights ago,' said Anderson, while Dana was still thinking about her next move. 'At the same time that we apprehended two men heading towards your East Street premises with a young Afghan woman. She's got a bit of a thing about Lacey, been hanging round her boat, playing tricks, trying to frighten her. Then the other night, she upturned Constable Flint's canoe and tried to drown her. All this happened in the South Dock Marina, where we found two more bodies.'

'Detective Sergeant, I don't mean to sound flippant, but if young women frolic in the Thames in the small hours, they can expect to find themselves in difficulties.' Christakos stifled a yawn. 'I still don't see what any of this has to do with me.'

'Two young women whom we can definitely connect to your clinic, because your assistant has recognized them, were pulled out of the river this summer,' said Anderson.

Christakos closed his eyes.

Dana decided to throw him a lifeline. 'I don't believe you intend to harm any of

605

these women. I think in your own way you're doing your best to protect them. But she gets past you somehow. How does she do that?'

His eyes snapped open again. 'I look forward to the press conference when you announce to the nation that the killer you're hunting is a mermaid. Weren't you looking for a vampire earlier in the year? They're going to have you working on *The X-Files*, Detective Inspector.'

'We're not looking for a mermaid, we're looking for a good swimmer.' Anderson jumped in before Dana could react. 'We have a man upstairs who's been swimming in the river for forty years. Constable Flint's been doing it all summer. It's perfectly possible if you stay close to the bank, respect the tides and watch out for traffic. How does your girl do it? Discreet flotation device? One of those big mono fins you see the free divers wearing?'

Christakos shook his head, as though there were no end to the nonsense he was expected to listen to. He looked tired, a patient man who'd been pushed to the limits of professional courtesy. He'd be convincing in a witness box.

'I've been speaking to your sister,' said Anderson. 'She's quite upset. She likes

Lacey. But you knew that, didn't you? She told us the two of you have met her. That Lacey's visited you at your house.'

'I am extremely fond of Constable Flint. I would not dream of harming her. I haven't harmed any of the young women who've been in my clinic.'

'Possibly. Possibly not,' said Dana. 'But what you need to be worrying about is how long it's going to take before we decide one way or the other.'

'What do you mean? Where is my sister now?'

'You think the worst that can happen is losing your licence and your reputation,' Dana pressed on. 'Ultimately, you may be right. But your assistant has identified two of our victims. We've got more than enough to charge you with murder, and unless we find Lacey and the other two missing women in the next few hours, that's exactly what we're going to do. You're an immigrant with a habit of travelling abroad. No magistrate will give you bail. You'll be stuck in a British prison for the next six months while we get ready for a trial.'

She waited, giving Christakos a chance to take in what she was telling him, and then went in for the kill.

'What will she do, do you think, without

you to keep her in check? What will she do tonight if she has any of these young women? What will she do to Lacey?'

88

Pari

As soon as Pari's feet became free, she scrambled to the edge of the skip. The rubbish was several feet deep and once she started moving she began to sink into it, but she made it over the side and dropped to the floor of the barge.

And now she had to drink or she would die for sure. If necessary she'd lean over the side and lap up the Thames. She spotted an upturned plastic tub with perhaps an inch of water in the bottom. She lifted it, tasted it and poured the rest down her throat. Better.

Her thirst assuaged, Pari glanced to the north bank. She couldn't swim, had never learned to swim. There might be something on this barge that could help her float, but the water was moving so fast. She stood upright, or as upright as she could manage on the constantly shifting underlay of rubbish, and looked around. Maybe there'd be a boat that could help her.

'Help!' she yelled.

And then, as though her longing had had the power to conjure up rescue from the ether, she heard the gentle hum of a small outboard engine.

'Help!' she yelled again, into the void that was the black river.

'For the love of God, be quiet,' replied a voice in her own language.

89

Lacey

The water had reached Lacey's waist. She couldn't stand upright, the rope around her neck was too short. She'd tried everything she could think of and there was no way she could get her face higher than the water line on the bricks opposite. She had less than an hour.

Once already — it could have been minutes or seconds ago, she couldn't be sure — she'd lost it completely. She'd screamed until her throat felt as though it were bleeding, but the only answer she'd received had been the gentle lapping of the returning waves. And now panic was building again. Her chest was growing tighter. She couldn't think, couldn't plan, couldn't be calm. All she could do was scream.

Except that wasn't her voice. That sound, winding its way through the darkness, wasn't even a scream. More like a moan. Or an echo of a moan.

'Hello! Is someone there?'

For a moment, only the sonorous mumblings of the water answered her. Then,

'Lacey?'

'Nadia?' Hope surged through Lacey's body. She wasn't alone. 'Nadia, I'm over here. Where are you?'

'Lacey, I can't move.' Nadia sounded ill, exhausted. Hope died. 'Lacey, they've tied me up. The water. Come and get me. Please.'

'Where are you?' Lacey was spinning in the water, the rope cutting like a blade into her neck, trying to locate the source of Nadia's voice and knowing she was planting cruel and hopeless ideas of rescue in the other woman's head.

Sounds of hands slapping hard against water. Then Nadia cried out again, reverting to her own language in her terror. She wasn't anywhere close. Lacey took hold of the rope again and pulled hard. It held as firm as ever.

Nadia was screaming now. And that was the sound of someone choking. Wherever Nadia was, she'd been tied up closer to the sewer floor than Lacey and the water had reached her already.

The screaming and the struggles and the

choking went on. Lacey closed her eyes tight and would have given anything to close her ears, too, so that she wouldn't be able to listen to the sound of another woman drowning. After a few more seconds she realized she didn't need to. The sound of her own sobbing was masking just about everything else.

It takes a long time, she learned, for a strong young woman to drown.

90

Pari

Pari stared out across the water. The voice had come from the direction of the furthest bank. 'Who's there?' she called. 'Who is it?'

The sound came hissing back towards her, soft and urgent, sibilant. 'Shhh!'

Pari rubbed her eyes. Something was making its way towards her. A small craft, without lights. As it grew closer, Pari could see the pale, carved wood of the hull and then the driver, an old woman wearing a black hood and cloak and with only her large, pale face visible. She was struggling with the current. It was almost taking her past, sweeping her away downstream, but she managed to toss the rope and Pari caught it.

The woman stared up at her. 'You need to get in,' she said in Pashto. 'Quick, there isn't much time.'

'Who are you?' Pari was suddenly reluctant to leave the relative security of the barge and climb down into that frail-looking boat. 'Are you taking me back there?'

'I'm taking you somewhere safe. Where no one can hurt you again, but you have to hurry.'

'Are you the one who sings to us?' Pari was trying to match the voice she was listening to with the one she remembered coming from below her window. 'The one who helps us get away?'

'Ai, ai!' The old lady pointed up-stream. 'Will you look? They're coming. Don't you understand? They'll throw you in. Me too, if they catch me.'

Pari followed the woman's stare. Sure enough, there was a pin-prick of light on the water, heading towards them.

'Who is it?' she asked.

'If you're not coming, I'm going without you. I daren't let them catch me.'

It was the woman's terror that convinced her. And the light was getting bigger, heading directly towards them. Pari swung both legs over the rail and lowered herself into the boat. At a nod from the old lady, she loosened the rope and pushed hard against the barge.

The distance between the boat and the pontoon grew quickly and Pari realized the old lady was steering them out to the middle of the channel. 'Where are we going?' she demanded. 'Get to the bank.'

The woman was looking up-stream. 'I can't. That's the way they're coming.'

She was right. The oncoming boat was close to the north bank. They had no choice but to cross the river. Pari turned round, trying to judge how far it was.

'The tide's taking us,' her companion said. 'Can you row?'

Pari had no idea, but the lights from the approaching boat were getting bigger. She picked up the oars and pulled as hard as she could. Ignoring the pain in her head she did it again. And again.

She kept pulling. The old lady clung to the tiller, as though sheer force of will could make the engine work harder, but as they moved closer to the centre of the river Pari wasn't sure how much more she had to give. Each stroke was getting harder. But every time she looked up, the lights on the pursuing boat were closer to the rubbish barge, closer to discovering she'd gone.

The waves were bouncing over the side of the boat, soaking them both, and too much water was gathering in the bottom, but every stroke took them closer to the opposite bank. Pari carried on rowing, her eyes fixed firmly on the planking of the boat, dreading to see the lights of the pursuing boat almost on top of them.

'The current's easing off now,' said the old lady at last. 'You can probably stop rowing.'

Pari looked up and round. They were drawing close to the bank. She pulled the oars out of the water and tried to get her breath.

'Are you all right?' said the old lady. 'I'm Thessa, by the way. You must be Pari. I've seen your name in the books.'

Pari managed to nod. With a stab of alarm she saw the pursuing boat at the pontoon. It was big, with lots of lights. It wasn't a boat that seemed to be aiming for stealth. And there seemed to be another, drawing up behind. She watched people climb out and start making their way around the skips. Looking for her.

As the engine slowed and the face of her driver screwed up in concentration, Pari spun round on her seat. A black gap in the river wall had appeared before them. The river water was pouring into it.

'We can't go in there.'

'It takes us to a ladder.' Thessa swung the boat wide and aimed it directly at the outlet. 'You can climb out.'

Oblivious to Pari's whimpered protests, the boat travelled in beneath the arched roof of the sewer and the night became even darker. Pari blinked furiously. A few yards of brickwork on either side was all she could see.

'Your night vision will kick in properly soon,' said Thessa. 'Close your eyes for a second or two.'

Pari closed her eyes for a second. She didn't make it to two. It's hard to keep your eyes closed when someone very close is screaming.

91

Lacey and Dana

The rats had been growing in number. As the water had risen, creeping up the sides of the tunnel, so the eyes had appeared all around Lacey. Eyes that jumped, darted, stabbed at her in the darkness.

She was on her feet, the water at chest height, struggling to keep her balance, the wound around her neck raw from her attempts to pull free. She had another twenty minutes, she reckoned, before the water covered her completely. The rats knew it too. They knew their time was running out.

They'd gathered on the ledge, just above her head. Nostrils twitching, tails flying, ears twisting to every new sound, scrambling over each other in a never-ending quest to be close to her, a writhing mass of plump bodies and thick tails. The eyes were the worst though, eyes that never seemed to leave hers.

One of them sprang, its needle-like claws stabbing her face before it clambered into her hair. More of them coming at her.

Screaming, thrashing, she dropped into the water to get them off. Water in her throat. Her head banging against the wall. Bites in her scalp. Her hair being pulled. She couldn't breathe. Something was striking at her head. Someone yelling, threatening.

Not her voice.

Lacey struggled to her feet and spat out water. She shook her head like a terrier with a rat in its mouth but no small, cruel creatures clung to her. A short, thin girl with long black hair was standing in the bow of a boat, slamming an oar down hard against the ledge, the wall, even occasionally Lacey's head, and yelling in a language Lacey didn't understand. She would have been a terrifying sight, except the rats had gone. She'd scared away the rats.

'She says she hates rats,' said a voice behind her. 'It was always her job at home, to scare the rats from out of the back yard. This is Pari, by the way. I'm helping her escape.'

As though exhausted by the effort, Pari collapsed into the bow of the boat. Thessa's boat. Thessa herself was at the stern, a black cloak drawn around her head and shoulders. She looked at Lacey in astonishment.

'My darling girl,' she said. 'What on earth are you doing here?'

Dana sat opposite Christakos and uttered the formalities that would continue the interview. She was conscious of Mark, standing immediately behind her, his hands gripping the back of her chair. She should tell him to sit down, if she fancied wasting her breath.

'There was no sign of Pari on the river,' she told Christakos. 'Our officers have just got back.'

Christakos's skin had turned several shades paler in the few hours he'd been in custody. 'She has to be there. We've used it before when we've had to hide girls for a short time. They're perfectly safe.' He sounded as though he were trying to convince himself. 'Did you look properly?'

'I searched every inch of that bloody barge myself,' said Mark, before Dana could open her mouth. 'I found parcel tape in one of the skips that could have been used as a restraint. Other than that, nothing.'

Christakos dropped his head into his hands.

'Who is it?' said Dana. 'Who has taken her?'

He seemed to shrink in front of her eyes. 'My sister,' he said. 'My sister got to her first.'

92

Lacey and Dana

Thessa was giving the two women in her charge medical attention. She had insisted on doing so, in spite of the surroundings. She'd given them both fresh water and wrapped a scarf around Lacey's neck wound. She was helping Pari to escape, she explained. They had to go further into the sewer, to find a ladder that would take them safely to the street. She and Pari had been on their way when they'd heard Lacey screaming.

According to Thessa, who was well and truly in charge at the moment, there wasn't room for three of them in the boat, so Lacey would have to swim holding on to the side, and to do that she'd need to be feeling a whole lot fitter than she was. Thessa had produced a flask of something that tasted a little like brandy, only thicker and sweeter, and made them both drink some of it.

Lacey drank and tried to get her head back together again. The water and the brandy helped. She wasn't going to drown, not just yet. Her head hurt and her throat felt as though it had been ripped open, but she was going to be OK. The rats had gone. The water was rising, but they were safely out of it — she crouched on the ledge, the other two still in Thessa's pretty, silly boat.

A boat that somehow seemed to cast a pale, silvery light around itself. Or maybe that was just the light from the strange, old-fashioned lantern that Thessa had switched on.

The boat rocked and Lacey's eyes went to the young woman in the bow. Since her very vocal attack on the rats, Pari hadn't spoken. She was curled up on the narrow seat and looked as if she was in pain, as well as exhausted. In the dim light, Lacey took a proper look at her. Young, slim, long dark hair, pale eyes.

Lacey gave one more look around to make sure there were no rats. Then, 'Thessa,' she said, 'was Pari in that building on East Street? What happens in there?'

'We need to go.' Thessa was reaching for the mooring line, untying it. 'The water will get too high soon to take the boat any further. Lacey, can you get back into the water, do you think?'

'You said you were helping her escape. How did you know she needed to?'

'She sings to us,' interrupted Pari. 'She sings songs from home, so that we know we can trust her, and then she helps us get out. I've seen her.'

Someone else had talked about a woman singing. Nadia. Good God, how could she have forgotten Nadia?

'Lacey, are you OK? Look at me. Focus.'

Lacey forced herself to look Thessa in the eyes. Nadia was dead. She'd heard her drown. First the cries of terror, then the screaming, the choking and finally the silence.

'Lacey!'

She couldn't help Nadia. It might not even be possible to retrieve her body until the tide went out again. In the meantime, Thessa was right. The water was getting very high.

'What's happening to these women?' she asked.

Suddenly Thessa looked terribly tired. Tired and sad. 'Lacey, I don't know. All Alex will tell me is that the girls are trying to escape from a terrible life. He helps them.'

Alex? This was about Alex?

'I hear them crying as I go past in my

boat. I hear how sad they are, how frightened. I hear them in pain, like this little one here.' She turned and smiled at Pari.

'Some of them aren't just in pain,' said Lacey. 'Some of them are dying.'

Thessa nodded. A big, fat tear wobbled at the corner of her eye and began to roll down her cheek.

'Thessa, who's doing it?'

And finally, Thessa's face collapsed into grief. 'My brother. I'm so sorry, Lacey, but Alex is killing them.'

'It was about a year ago when the first woman vanished from the clinic,' said Christakos, as Anderson pulled out on to Lewisham High Street and stepped hard on the accelerator. As they picked up speed, he switched on the blue light. Dana was in the passenger seat. In the back, Mark was cuffed to Christakos.

Minutes earlier, they'd discovered that Christakos's sister was no longer at her house in Deptford. Upon hearing the news, Christakos had been able to think of only one place she might be. They were heading for the river. She owned an old Victorian pumping station, he'd explained, which she'd tried to keep secret from him. Whilst impossible for her to access from land, he believed she might be able to use her boat to navigate the sewer system.

'Jamilla Kakar was her name,' Christakos went on. 'We were baffled. We said good-night to her, locked the door of her room, as is customary, and then the next morning she just wasn't in it. There was no trace of her at all. The bars on the window made climbing out impossible. Her room was still locked. It was like — magic.'

Dana twisted round in the seat. 'Did you report her disappearance?'

Christakos might have taken a blow but he wasn't all out of arrogance.

'Of course I didn't, Detective Inspector. Let's not waste time with point-scoring. My first thought was that it was someone on the staff, but they denied any knowledge and it seemed unlikely somehow. They've been with me for many years. We put it down to carelessness. Someone had accidentally left keys around, Jamilla had taken advantage and left. I don't know whether you will believe this or not, but I hoped that she was all right.'

Anderson overtook a stationary car, putting them directly in line with an oncoming bus.

'But that wasn't the end of it?' Mark wasn't wearing his seat belt. Neither was

Christakos. None of them were. Had she been reckless, agreeing to this high-speed dash to an abandoned building on the river-bank?

'Sadly, it was just the beginning.' Christakos was speaking directly to Mark now. 'Not long afterwards, another woman vanished in exactly the same manner, even though we'd changed the locks. I couldn't put it down to carelessness a second time. Some-one had let her out. All the staff pleaded ignorance. I could hardly threaten them with the authorities. Besides, something told me they were telling the truth. I know my sister very well.'

Traffic, for the most part, was letting them through. They were in Deptford already, not far from the river.

'Excuse me pointing out the obvious,' said Mark, 'but from what I understand, your sister is in a wheelchair. How did she man-age to make her way round that three-storey house, helping young women escape and smuggling them safely away?'

'You'd be surprised by what Thessa can achieve.' Christakos looked oddly proud. 'She never let her disability stand in her way. She was always the strong one. I realized she'd been accessing confidential docu-ments on the computer. I've never managed to devise a password that she hasn't guessed. But she left a trail, of course. I could see that documents had been accessed when I'd been out of the office. Only she could have done that. And she started going out in that boat of hers at all hours. She smuggles keys to them somehow and then takes them away by water.'

'Did you challenge her?'

Christakos shook his head. 'She wasn't comfortable with the clinic, I knew that. If it made her happy to help one or two women leave sooner than they might otherwise have done, I was willing to live with that. I wasn't sure how much longer I was going to keep going anyway.'

'You were willing to let her take these women and drown them?'

Christakos twisted round to face Mark directly. 'I had no idea they were coming to harm. It was only just over a week ago, when you found Anya in the Thames, that I realized what was happening.'

'You realized she wasn't helping them escape at all?' said Dana gently.

Christakos shook his head. 'No. She was killing them.'

93

Lacey and Dana

'Alex is in custody.' Thessa steered the boat through the channel of the sewer. She and Pari were still on board, Lacey was clinging to the stern. They couldn't risk the engine, with Lacey being so close to the propeller, so Thessa and Pari were using the oars as paddles. Lacey was pushing against the wall to keep them moving, hating every moment of being in the water.

'He was arrested this morning,' Thessa went on. 'The staff of the clinic are all at Lewisham police station too, but there are other men involved. The ones who bring the girls here in the first place. He'll have given them instructions to go back for Pari once it was dark. Alex doesn't know I own the pumping station, but they could easily decide to look in the sewer.'

They were back at the fork in the tunnel, but other than a faint gleam in the darkness, Lacey could see nothing of the opening on to the Thames. Thessa turned the boat to follow the right-hand fork. 'Not much further. On the right-hand side. Nearly there, girls.'

Lacey looked up at her. In the darkness of the tunnel, Thessa's eyes looked huge. 'How long have you known? About Alex?'

Thessa didn't break the slow, steady rhythm of paddling. 'I've known about the clinic for a long time. I wasn't comfortable but I've always trusted Alex. He was always the strong one.'

'You didn't say anything to him?'

Thessa seemed not to have heard, was telling the story in her own way. 'I started singing to them as I went past in the evenings. I thought it would help, to hear a song from home, so I sang something I remember my mother singing to Alex and me when we were tiny. And then, one night, one of the women called out to me. Begging me to help her escape. I ignored her, just went motoring past, but all night I couldn't get it out of my head. I kept thinking, I could, I could help her escape. I could easily find keys, attach them to a ball of cork so they wouldn't sink, and throw them into an open window. After that it was easy. They'd creep down the stairs, let themselves out at the back, get into my boat and I'd bring them here. I gave them money and the details of some people I know who help them get settled.'

'Four nights ago.' Pari had twisted round to face the others. 'I heard you singing and I saw you throw keys. I saw someone leave.'

Thessa frowned and put her head to one side. 'No, dear,' she said, after a second. 'I think you're getting mixed up.'

'How many did you help get away?' said Lacey, as Pari began counting on her fingers. Thessa's arms seemed frozen in the act of paddling.

The question brought Thessa's attention back. She started paddling again. 'Only four. I'd have done more, but I could only leave the house when I knew Alex was out and not at the clinic. He doesn't leave me alone very much.'

Pari gave a little shrug and picked up her own paddle. Lacey paused a moment before asking the difficult question. 'Why are some of them dying?'

Thessa shook her head. 'I don't know. I didn't know they were until a couple of weeks ago. When I found Anya.'

'Who's Anya?'

'The body you found in the river, dear. When you were out swimming a week last

Thursday. I found her in South Dock Marina just days earlier. She'd broken loose of her weights, somehow.'

'I don't understand,' said Pari. 'Which of you found Anya?'

'Thessa did,' said Lacey. 'And then she left her somewhere she knew I'd find her. What about the woman on my boat? Were you responsible for her, too?'

'I'm sorry about that, dear, it must have been a dreadful shock. But you weren't getting the message. I thought the crabs might do it, or the boats — that you'd make the connection with the marina — but I guess I was hoping for too much.'

'How much further?' Pari was looking ahead again. 'I can't see any ladder. I have good eyes. I can't see anything.'

Pari had good eyes. Four nights ago, she'd seen Thessa rescuing one of the other women from the building on East Street. Two nights ago, someone, whom Lacey now knew to be Thessa, had strung the body of a freshly drowned young woman up on Lacey's boat. But Thessa had denied rescuing the woman. *No dear, I think you're getting mixed up.*

Suddenly Lacey was very conscious of being within striking reach of Thessa's paddle.

'I couldn't let it carry on, dear,' Thessa

was saying. 'Not when I knew the girls were being harmed. But it was beyond me, I'm afraid, to call the police about my own brother. I thought, if the bodies were found, if he knew the police were investigating, he might stop.'

'Why pick me?'

'I'd seen you swimming and in your canoe. And on your big, fast police boat. I knew you were the one.'

So it had been Thessa, in her little boat, who'd been visiting Lacey's yacht at night, Thessa who'd left hearts and crabs and, eventually, a corpse. In some ways, it made much more sense if the stalker had been trying to warn Lacey, rather than frighten her. Except —

'But the women are being brought here to die. Nadia told me. She told me they're tied by the neck to mooring rings and left to drown, just like I was. How can Alex be killing them, if he doesn't know about this place?'

'Nadia?' Thessa looked genuinely surprised.

'Nadia Safi. She was here with me today. She was at East Street, too.'

Thessa's big eyes opened even wider in astonishment. 'Nadia was here?' She turned back, to look along the long stretch of water.

'Yes, she brought me. I didn't want to say anything before because I didn't want to frighten you. She was attacked. Someone pulled her out of the boat. I think she's dead.'

'Nadia was attacked today? I'm not sure that's poss—' began Thessa.

There was a sudden sound, which none of them had made. The sound of something falling, or slithering, into the water.

Lacey drew her legs up beneath her, wondering if rats could swim. Thessa had stopped paddling, was sitting bolt upright, her eyes flicking from Lacey to Pari and back again. 'Put the oar down for a moment, Pari dear,' she said.

'We have to keep going,' Lacey countered.

Thessa ignored her, her attention still fixed on the noise they'd just heard. In the pale light of the lantern, she seemed to be changing. Her shoulders had drawn back, her head was up, her eyes shining again. She looked taller, younger, stronger. Then, too quick for Lacey to stop her, she reached to one side and caught hold of a mooring ring. In a flash, she'd pushed the boat's rope through it and pulled it tight. They stopped dead.

'Thessa,' said Lacey, as cold realization sank in. 'How could Alex have killed Nadia if he's been in custody all day?'

Fred and his crew were waiting at the jetty, the same one from which Dana had climbed aboard the traffickers' boat not twenty-four hours earlier. As they ran down the riverside steps to meet him, Anderson got a call on his radio. He held up a hand, indicating that they should all wait.

'Pete, Tom and Gayle are at the pumping station,' he told them, after listening for a few seconds. 'Uniform are on their way. As far as they can tell, it's empty, but they can't be sure until the door-breaking squad arrive.'

'How far is it?' Mark was looking round — back up the concrete steps, at the wide expanse of embankment, the nearby office buildings.

'About two hundred yards down-river.' Christakos used the hand that wasn't cuffed to indicate almost due south. 'The outlet that Thessa must use to access it is about twenty yards up-stream.' He pointed in the opposite direction.

Fred was looking grim. 'I'm sorry, Dana,' he said, before she could open her mouth. 'There's no way we can get in that tunnel until the tide drops a bit. Four more hours at least.'

Mark strode right up to his uncle. 'If they're not in the pumping station, they have to be in the tunnels somewhere.'

Fred didn't back down. 'Those tunnels are all but flooded. I've got a boat slap bang by the entrance and it can stay there till we know more, but there's no way I can risk any of my officers going in.'

'Give me a friggin' dinghy, I'll do it.'

'Not happening, my friend.'

Dana put a hand on Mark's shoulder. 'Get back in the car,' she told him. 'We'll drive round there.'

'How many women are we talking about, Mr Christakos?' Back in the car, moving too slowly around industrial buildings, Dana had a sense of needing to keep the conversation moving, if only to keep Mark from exploding. 'How many women did your sister help escape from the clinic?'

How many more corpses were waiting for them somewhere on the river bed?

Christakos closed his eyes, as though thinking hard. She heard him mutter the name Jamilla, then something that sounded like Shireen. Number four was a Yass, number five Ummu. Please let that be the last. They'd found five bodies. That was enough.

She could see the pumping station. A small, neat, but otherwise unremarkable brick building not far from the river. Christakos had named a sixth, a seventh, more. Good God, there were nine. Four more somewhere. Except . . .

'Mr Christakos, the third one you mentioned. Who was that again?'

Christakos opened his eyes. 'The third was Nadia Safi,' he said. 'A woman of twenty-eight. From Khost Province, in south-eastern Afghanistan. She vanished on the tenth of January this year, not long after she arrived.' A spasm of what looked like pain passed across his face. 'Is she one of the women you found? Is she dead, too?'

94

Lacey and Dana

'You said your brother has been with the police all day,' Lacey reminded Thessa. 'So he couldn't have been here. He couldn't have killed Nadia. He couldn't have left me to drown.' She looked round quickly, peering into the darkness, wondering how far away the ladder was and whether anything she'd been told in the last half-hour had been true.

'No,' agreed Thessa. 'He couldn't, could he? How silly of me not to think of that.'

'Pari, can you get out of the boat?' Lacey was moving again, making sure she was at least an arm's length from Thessa. 'Walk along the ledge until you come to the ladder, then climb it. I'll be right behind you.'

Confused, still frightened, Pari didn't move. She trusted Thessa, not Lacey. It wouldn't be easy to get her out of the boat.

'My brother is a good man, Lacey.' Thessa

unfastened her cloak and let it fall from her shoulders. 'A little misguided, perhaps, but a good man. I'm sorry for what I said about him.'

She was unbuttoning her blouse. Lacey opened her mouth to ask her what the hell she thought she was doing and realized it was hardly top of the list.

'Thessa,' she said instead. 'Did you kill them?'

Thessa was pulling off her blouse, revealing the flat, empty breasts of an old woman and the well-developed musculature of someone who had been swimming for years. 'Yes.' She stretched out her arms, rotating each shoulder, like a swimmer before a race. 'I am entirely responsible for their deaths. How's the water, dear?'

No, no, not her friend Thessa. Christ, she couldn't panic. 'Whatever you have planned, Thessa, I'm stronger than you are. You can't even walk.'

'True.' Thessa's left hand reached to her waist and unfastened her skirt. She unwrapped it, letting Lacey see what was beneath. 'But I can swim.' She gave a big, happy smile.

Lacey said nothing. She couldn't see much. She could see enough. Behind her, she heard Pari mutter something in her own language that sounded as though it might be a prayer.

'Well?' Thessa looked down at her own naked body, then back up at Lacey. 'Aren't you going to say, "What are you?" That's what they always say.'

'You're the mermaid.'

Thessa positively beamed. 'How sweet of you. I've always loved mermaids. Did you know Alexander the Great's sister was a mermaid called Thessaloniki? That's how I chose my name. My real one is quite different. But you'd know all about that, wouldn't you?'

Lacey was suddenly conscious of shivering violently. 'You know nothing about me. You killed all those women. You tried to kill me in the marina.'

The naked old creature at the stern of the boat smiled even wider. 'My darling girl, if I'd wanted to kill you I would have, trust me. I was simply trying to show you what you and your colleagues were incapable of finding for yourselves.'

As Lacey tried to process what she was hearing, Thessa sighed. 'But in the greater scheme of things you're right. About not really knowing you, I mean.' She nodded, then seemed to leap from the seat. A second later, she'd vanished.

'Pari, get out of the boat. Now!' Holding the bow in place against the wall with one hand, Lacey pulled at the terrified Afghan girl with the other. 'Come on. We have to find a ladder.'

As the other girl wobbled and scrambled to get from the small, unsteady boat on to the narrow, wet ledge, Lacey kept her eyes on the water all around them. Thessa was down there, probably very close. She gave one last shove on Pari's backside, kicked the boat away and prepared to pull herself out of the water.

Just as something dragged her beneath the surface.

The water was dark. She struck the smooth wood of the boat. As she pushed away from it, her shoulders bounced against the rough brickwork of the walls. She used it to navigate, to get herself to the surface, to start breathing again.

Pari was inching along the ledge, towards the ladder that would take her to safety, but her terrified eyes were fixed on Lacey. She wasn't moving nearly fast enough.

Lacey looked back at the tunnel. Nothing to see but the troubled water steadying itself. Nothing to hear but dripping from the arched roof, and the splash of waves against the walls.

Then a crippling weight had attached itself to her legs and was dragging her down again. Lacey went below the surface in an instant. Something was clawing at her, trying to get a tighter grip. She kicked hard and broke free for a second, before teeth sank into her thigh. Lacey almost forgot she was submerged in the instinct to howl. She bent herself double and struck hard with her right fist, her strongest hand. She hit hard and felt the grip on her loosening. One more, and she broke the surface again.

The ledge was close. Anything to be out of the water. She was on the point of reaching the slime-encrusted stone when two strong hands closed around her throat and she was going under for what felt like the last time.

This was it. She'd be the next body they found. Shrouded in white linen. Or maybe she wouldn't. Maybe she'd lie at the bottom of the river for all time. Thessa seemed to be everywhere, to have grown in size, to have numerous limbs, to be doubly strong. For a second, Lacey even wondered if there were three of them in the water, if Pari had jumped in to help. Yes, definitely three of them — she was being held by more than two hands. Then one pair of hands let go and the body that they might belong to — almost impossible to tell — had flung itself at the third person. It was one mass of wriggling, kicking, biting limbs. In a last effort to be free, Lacey twisted round like an eel.

And she was loose. Feet away, Pari was still crouched against the tunnel wall, her hands clutched to her face in horror. Her clothes were dry.

Lacey gave the biggest leap she was capable of. With Pari clutching her shoulders, it was the work of moments to haul herself on to the ledge and stagger to her feet. On impulse, she reached down into the boat and pulled out the nearest oar. A weapon of any kind felt like a good idea right now. Pressed against the slime-damp wall of the tunnel, she tried to get her breath, cough out river water and locate the woman who'd attacked her, all at the same time. At her side, Pari was pointing at something.

There she was, not three yards away, head rising out of the water, hair spreading out in every direction. Shoulders that looked impossibly wide and strong. A terrifying creature, teeth bared in a snarl, staring at her with the huge eyes of a mad woman, climbing out of the water, staggering to her feet on the ledge, getting ready to attack again. A woman who — and this was just about impossible to process in the circumstances — was most definitely not Thessa.

'Nadia Safi was a very troubled young woman,' said Christakos, as Anderson drew up on the concrete embankment by the pumping station. Two patrol cars and an unmarked Toyota that Dana recognized as belonging to Mizon were already parked next to the building.

Dana had altered the seating arrangement in the car, mainly to separate Mark from Christakos. She was now in the back seat, cuffed to their prisoner. She nodded for him to go on.

'We could see that from the moment she arrived,' he said. 'We put it down to her exceptionally traumatic journey, even by the standards of what our guests usually have to undergo.'

'Are you talking about her arrest?' said Anderson, an edge in his voice.

'I'm talking about the fact that she nearly drowned that night,' Christakos countered. 'Your officers made the people bringing her panic. They tried to flee, their boat overturned. Nadia nearly died. She was still having nightmares about it when she came to us.'

'She didn't die, because PC Flint leapt in

after her and pulled her to safety,' snapped Mark. 'Risking her own life in the process.'

'Was that Lacey?' For the time it took to blink, Christakos's face lit up. 'I had no idea. But back to Nadia. We soon realized it was more than the shock of recent events. This was something that ran very deep. How much do you know about my country, Detective Inspector?'

Out of the corner of her eye, Dana saw Stenning and Mizon get out of their vehicle. Both Anderson and Mark opened their doors. She held up her hand for them to give her a minute. 'I've visited India several times,' she said. 'I have family there. But I've never been to Afghanistan. I just know what I've heard on the news.'

'Then you'll only really know about events in Helmand Province. Khost is on the Pakistan border. It's unusual among Afghan provinces because many of its men go abroad in search of work, typically to Pakistan, sometimes further afield, leaving the women at home to raise their families and tend the farms. Nadia was the oldest of a family of girls. Her father worked away until he died, and, as is the tradition in that area, she was brought up as a boy.'

As she awkwardly followed Christakos from the car, Dana saw that both Anderson and Mark were looking puzzled. She straightened up and turned to Mizon. 'Talk to me.'

'We can't see anything inside, Ma'am. Windows all boarded up. And we haven't heard anything, but I wouldn't like to say one way or another.'

'How long before the trolls get here?' asked Mark.

'Few more minutes,' Stenning told him. 'Those big wooden doors are old. We should be able to go straight in.'

'Tell everyone to wait,' said Dana. 'But keep listening and let me know the second you hear anything.' She turned back to Christakos. 'What do you mean, brought up as a boy? Nadia didn't say anything about that to us. We have her on tape talking to Lacey, saying that she married young, into a good family, but her husband divorced her because she had three daughters and because there were some spurious doubts about her virginity. It was a very convincing story.'

'Nadia had never had a child,' said Christakos. 'I'm quite certain about that. She was still a virgin when she came to us. I'd go so far as to say she would never have been allowed to have a child. Her village treated her as a man, you see. She was expected to work in the fields like a man, provide for her family, make decisions, help govern the village. She even dressed as a man.'

'She told us nothing about that.'

The sound of a diesel engine reached them. A police van was approaching. Anderson went over to talk to the sergeant in charge as several uniformed officers jumped out.

'Her story came out over the course of several weeks,' said Christakos. 'She became quite friendly with Kathryn Markova. Frankly, it didn't surprise me. Given how prized sons are in Afghan families, how relatively unimportant girls are, it's quite common in some areas for girls to be brought up as boys from a very young age. Some of them don't even know they are girls until puberty hits and the bodily changes become evident. Quite what psychological damage has been imparted by that stage, I really couldn't say.'

95

Lacey and Dana

'Nadia?' No, she wasn't seeing things. That was Nadia, crouched on the ledge by the boat. Nadia, not dead after all, not a rapidly bloating corpse tied by the neck to a mooring ring, but very much alive. Those big, silver-grey eyes hardly seemed to blink in the half-light.

A scuffling noise at her side told her that Pari was moving deeper into the tunnel. With Nadia blocking the way out, it was the only sensible thing to do.

Where was Thessa? Were the two of them in this together?

Lacey set off in Pari's wake, her back pressed against the damp bricks, forced to stoop by the low, curved ceiling, constantly afraid of missing her footing. She side-stepped as fast as she dared, occasionally glancing ahead, more often looking back, watching the woman who was coming after them.

Nadia came steadily, but slowly, as though not wanting to risk falling back into the water or to get close to the oar Lacey was still holding. Or maybe she just knew they couldn't get out. Lacey risked another look forward. If Nadia and Thessa were working together, Thessa could be waiting further up the tunnel.

'Think about what you're doing, Nadia,' she called. 'If you kill us, you'll never see your children again.'

Nadia paused and spat some angry words in her own language.

'She says she has no children, you idiot,' translated Pari. 'She never did. She never had chance.'

'Go, Pari,' said Lacey. 'Find that ladder. There'll be one. There always are in these tunnels.'

Pari hesitated. 'What about Thessa?'

Bloody good question. Where was Thessa? *What* was Thessa? Had she been in the water just now? Had she pulled Nadia away from Lacey?

Pari started moving again and Lacey followed. Nadia matched their pace, stalking them through the tunnel. She was like a cat, waiting for a wounded bird to scrabble out from beneath the bushes.

The tunnel curved, taking away the pale light of Thessa's lantern. They would have been in complete darkness were it not for the occasional ventilation grids in the roof. So far, it seemed exactly the same as the tunnel she'd searched with Fred and Finn.

At last, Lacey felt something hard and cold jar against her right shoulder. Yes! A ladder up to street level. Pari, driven by panic, was already several rungs up.

Unsure how to follow her — as soon as she took away the threat of the oar Nadia would be upon her — Lacey stayed where she was. Then a sudden flurry of movement behind Nadia caught the attention of them both.

Thessa was moving quickly towards them through the water, swimming butterfly, a stroke particularly suited to her anatomy. Without thinking, Lacey raised the oar and shoved Nadia hard in the back. As she fell into the water, Thessa was on top of her instantly. The two swimmers disappeared in a fountain of black, foam-topped water.

'Lacey, I can't move it.'

Pari was at the top of the ladder, had reached the manhole that blocked their escape route. Lacey took another step up the ladder and stopped. She couldn't leave Thessa. She jumped back down on to the ledge, her feet splashing noisily in the water that had by now completely covered it.

Directly in front of her, a head and shoulders broke the surface of the water. Nadia was back.

'Women like Nadia have no real place in the world,' Christakos was saying as the uniformed team unloaded the tubular steel reinforcer that would break open the door of the pumping station. 'Their position is worse than that of servants, of slaves even. They are like the ghosts of slaves.'

'I don't understand,' said Dana.

'They are not men. They might be taught to fight, to handle guns and defend their families, but they'll never be accepted among the men. At family gatherings and weddings, they have to stay with the women. But they're not proper women either. They're not allowed to marry, have children, wear feminine clothes. Other women treat them as freaks. They're called *narkhazak*. It means eunuch. Children throw stones at them in the street. They don't fit in anywhere and if they come to the attention of the Taliban, they're likely to be executed.'

For once, Dana really didn't know what to say. There was an explosion of sound as the steel ram banged into the warehouse doors. The doors held.

'There was an incident shortly before Nadia left Afghanistan. It was the catalyst for her leaving in the first place.'

'What happened?' Dana asked. The team at the door were about to try again.

'The Taliban saw her out in the street unveiled and arrested her. They chained her in a storm drain and left her there. It was dry, but they knew, and she knew, that once the rain started the empty drain would become a torrent and she'd drown. She was left there for two days, chained by the neck, waiting to drown. None of her friends or family helped her. In the end, it was men working for me who helped her escape and come here.'

The doors fell inwards and the officers disappeared inside, Mark in the lead. Stenning, Anderson and Mizon followed. Dana could see beams of light as torches were switched on and shone around. She and Christakos stepped forward until they were at the entrance of the building.

She was looking down, that was her first surprise, although she'd been told the pumping station was half underground. The pale bricks and tiled interior reminded her of Victorian public baths. There were lots of hiding places: stone columns, arched recesses, huge iron plinths. The team were moving cautiously, even Mark was keeping his head, but Stenning was still, his torch-beam fixed on something on the ground. He looked up at Dana and she saw his lips form a single word: blood.

With a growing sense of dread, she un-locked the cuffs and released Christakos. 'Go first.' She indicated the stairway down. 'Slowly. Stay close to me.'

'It's clear, Ma'am.' The uniformed ser-geant came to meet them before they were halfway down. He looked up, his face all angular shadows in the dim light. 'No sign of anyone, but there's water on the floor, and one of your colleagues has found what could be —'

'I know.' Dana had reached the bottom step. Mark was at the far side of the room, peering into the first of three large outlet pipes. She hadn't noticed before, but he'd brought one of the life-jackets from Fred's Targa with him. Shit.

'Ma'am, there are weights here.' Mizon was at one of the arched recesses, looking up at a shelf. 'Just like the ones we found in the marina. And I'm pretty certain these are linen shrouds I'm looking at. This is where the bodies are wrapped and weighted.'

'But not drowned.' Mark was wearing the

life-jacket now. 'That's happening some-where else. Lend us your torch, Pete.'

'No!' Dana strode over to the outlet pipe as the torch was passed from one man to the other. 'No one is going into the sewer. It's too bloody dangerous.'

He shook his head. 'I'm not one of your officers, Dana.' He pointed back over her shoulder. 'You need to keep talking to him. Ask him if that sister of his really is a cripple. Because if she is, there's no way she can get into this place. Have a look around.'

For a second, he fooled her. She took her eyes off him, to look round at the doors high in the wall, at the steep iron staircase lead-ing down, at the precarious ladders, at the three outlet pipes that were the only access to the sewer. In the seconds it took her to realize he was right, he'd gone.

'No!' She held up her hand to stop Sten-ning, who'd been on the verge of following him. 'I am not responsible for what DI Joes-bury does. You, on the other hand, are stay-ing here. Gayle, get hold of Chief Inspector Cook. If the sewer has to be searched, his officers will have to do it.'

She walked back over to Christakos. 'We finished searching the South Dock Marina,' she told him. 'In addition to two more bodies, we found the weights that we believe were attached to Anya Fahid and Rabia Khan. Nothing else.'

He stared back, not really taking in what she was saying.

'You mentioned nine women,' she said. 'It is just possible that four of these women are still alive. That your sister really did help them escape. Alex, in your opinion, was Nadia Safi capable of violence?'

Christakos thought for several long seconds before speaking. 'I'm no psychologist, but what struck me about Nadia was that, although her lot in life had been dictated by men, it was women she hated. Other women — particularly young, attractive women, those who were desirable — they engendered feelings of absolute rage in Nadia. When we realized quite how disturbed she was, we decided to release her without further treatment. Then she vanished. We were worried, of course, but not entirely sorry to see the last of her.'

Christakos took a deep breath. 'Detective Inspector, I think I've been a complete fool. My sister isn't a killer. She just set one free.'

96

Lacey

'Keep going,' Lacey hissed to Pari as she scrambled up the ladder towards her.

More loud breathing, little gasps of distress. Pari wasn't strong enough.

'Give me some room.' Lacey started climbing again, moving upwards until she and Pari were side by side on the ladder. She reached up and the two women pushed at the grille together. Finn had had trouble with a couple of these covers. Mud, dirt and debris got caught and stuck. You just had to push hard and not give up. She felt it move. She could do it. She could get them out. And then a sound below turned her heart cold.

Nadia was climbing after them. In a few more rungs, a couple more seconds, she'd be able to reach Lacey. All she'd have to do would be to grab hold of Lacey's foot and take her own weight off the ladder. They'd both plummet to the water, and Lacey really wasn't sure she could fight the woman off a second time.

Lacey pushed again on the iron grille above her. She climbed up another rung, partly to get her legs further from Nadia's reach, partly to give herself more purchase to push against. The grille moved. The ladder was shaking with the weight of the woman climbing it and Lacey could hear laboured breathing below her. Any second now, she'd be within reach.

The cover came loose at the exact moment that Pari gave a furious shriek. Lacey glanced down to see her kicking at Nadia, trying desperately to keep her at bay. Lacey pushed again and the grate slid free.

'Pari, now!'

Pari shot up the last couple of rungs and into the street above them. Lacey was about to follow when a strong, wet hand clamped around her ankle. She looked down to see the snarling face getting closer. Then Nadia herself was the one screeching in pain. Below her, Lacey could see Thessa, who'd raised herself from the water somehow, clinging to Nadia. The three of them were dangling like a human rope, and only the grip Lacey had on the ladder preventing them from tumbling down.

'Lacey!'

Pari's face was above her, her arms lowering the grille again. For a second, Lacey didn't get it. Then she took one hand off the ladder, felt the other almost wrenched apart by the weight it was holding up, grabbed the grille and helped Pari guide it through the hole. She let it fall.

'Thessa! Get out of the way!' she yelled.

Nadia's grip broke. She gave the heavy grunt a body makes when all its air is expelled at once and fell backwards. But she twisted as she fell, and the grille continued falling. It hit Thessa too, and took her down. When Lacey jumped back down on to the ledge of the sewer tunnel, neither Nadia nor Thessa were anywhere to be seen.

■ ■ ■ ■

THURSDAY, 3 JULY

■ ■ ■ ■

97

Lacey and Dana

Industrial units filled the skyline in front of them. There was a chain-link fence several metres high almost at the water's edge, a fleet of white vans visible beyond it. They were heading for a spot on the south bank, a mile or so downstream of Greenwich. Some time overnight the weather had broken. Cloud upon cloud had banked up overhead and the wind humming down the Thames felt like winter. Or a normal English summer.

On the narrow, rock-strewn shore, six people were waiting. The pathologist Mike Kaytes, three members of the Marine Unit's tactical team and two SOCOs. Something lay on the stones behind them. Lacey could barely make it out, and that was probably deliberate on their part.

Behind her in the dinghy, Finn Turner was talking on the radio. 'Did you catch that?'

he said, when he ended the conversation.

Without turning round, Lacey nodded. The body of a young woman, found in the Thames by Cleopatra's Needle early that morning, was now at Wapping police station and had been identified as that of twenty-eight-year-old Nadia Safi. After her fall from the ladder, the tide had swept her up-stream and she'd become trapped between two boats.

'What you probably didn't hear is that she had a connection with South Dock Marina,' Turner said. 'Her employers kept a boat there. Nadia went down there to clean it, stock it for weekend trips. The small motor boat they also kept there is missing.'

Almost there. Turner cut back on the throttle, relying upon momentum to carry them the last few yards. One of the tactical team stepped into the water and caught the rope. The dinghy stopped and Lacey climbed out. The first pair of eyes she met belonged to the pathologist.

'Good to see you, River Police.' There was something about his scowl that wasn't quite as rigid as normal. That made her think he might actually mean it.

'Thank you for waiting.' She let her eyes travel past him to the small, pale form on the bank. 'Is that — her?'

Tight-lipped, he nodded.

'We were identical twins,' said Christakos, once he'd taken his seat in the interview room. 'Which of course means we were the same sex. My brother was named Mujeeb, but because of his condition he never felt comfortable being male. He didn't have a penis, you see.'

Christakos turned to Anderson. 'And it's impossible to consider yourself male without a penis, wouldn't you say, Sergeant?'

'I can't say I've ever given it much thought,' said Anderson. 'But I don't imagine it would be easy for a boy.'

'When we were in our early teens I first saw the signs of his veering towards the feminine,' Christakos said. 'He grew his hair longer, started wearing looser clothes, in brighter colours. Just before we left Afghanistan, he started calling himself Thessaloniki, Thessa for short. It was a joke on me, you see. Alexander the Great's sister was reputedly a mermaid of that name. Not that he thought I was great — it was more of a comment on my arrogance.'

Arrogance, thought Dana, looking at the broken man across the table, which had vanished completely. It was as though his sense of self had died along with his twin.

'What exactly was his condition?' she asked.

'Sirenomelia,' said Kaytes. 'A birth defect characterized by an apparent fusion of the legs into one single lower limb. It's also known as Mermaid Syndrome.'

Lacey kept her eyes on Kaytes. She wasn't ready, yet, to see what the river had left behind on the south shore.

'I've never heard of it,' said Turner. From the blank faces around them, it seemed nobody else had either.

'It's very rare,' admitted Kaytes. 'And it's usually lethal. Most babies with the condition are stillborn. Few of them live more than a couple of days. There's nothing in the literature to suggest someone could live to this age. Or indeed be quite so strong.'

She was going to have to look some time. It was why she'd begged to be allowed to come here. There was a demon to be faced and it lay, cold and dead, just a few yards away.

'What causes it?' asked one of the SOCOs.

'No one really knows,' said Kaytes. 'For a while it was thought to be linked to maternal diabetes, but that's more or less been ruled out. From what I could gather, and I didn't have a lot of time to read up, there's an abnormality in the umbilical cord that prevents proper development of the lower limbs and a number of abdominal organs. Typically, the kidneys don't develop and so the baby dies of renal failure.'

'Nobody expected Mujeeb to live,' said Christakos. 'Babies with that condition almost never do. But it wasn't quite so severe as some of the cases you hear about. He had one kidney that performed perfectly well and another that was weaker but still functional. And, significantly, he had a perforate anus. He could process food and dispel waste products. He lived.'

'It can't have been easy for him,' said Dana.

Christakos gave her a look that suggested she had no idea. 'Afghanistan in the 1950s,' he said. 'And our parents didn't take the care of him they probably should have done. There were a number of incidents when we were small. Other children from the neighbourhood. It didn't always start and finish with name-calling. A favourite game was to throw him into the lake and watch him swim. Of course he could, instinctively, but the games got rougher. One time, I really thought they were going to drown him.'

■ ■ ■ ■

'Sirenomelia,' said Lacey. 'Sirens sang, didn't they? They sat on the rocks and sang to sailors. The women in the clinic could hear Thessa singing to them.'

'Mythology's not really my thing, River Police,' said Kaytes. 'I'll do my best to tell you how he died, but beyond tha—'

'I killed her,' said Lacey. 'She was trying to save me and I killed her. I dropped an iron grate on her head. She fell back into the water and if she wasn't dead by then, she drowned.'

Silence. She could sense the nervous glances flying around above her head.

'Well, that should save me some time,' said Kaytes.

'Over the years, I actually started to think of her as my sister, not my brother,' said Christakos. 'Without any sex organs, she never experienced puberty. There was no body hair growth, no deepening of the voice. But strangely, she did grow quite tall and very strong. Her swimming ability was really quite remarkable. She swam, quite literally, like a fish. And when she wasn't swimming, she was always out in one of those silly little boats. She used to say it was only on the water that she felt really at home. She almost became the thing she most dreamed of being — a mermaid.'

Thessa lay curled on her side, almost as though she were asleep. Her long hair, still damp, streamed out behind her on the shore. Her face could only be seen in profile, and was mushroom pale against the mud. Lacey stepped closer and the group on the shore, who'd stepped away to let her through, watched.

Above the waist, Thessa's torso wasn't so dissimilar to Ray's. Broad swimmer's shoulders, arms that were both thin and strong. The empty breasts were simply the result of pectoral muscles wasted by age.

Below the waist, Thessa's body bore no resemblance to anything human.

'I'll know more when I can get her back.' Kaytes was standing very close behind Lacey. So was Turner, come to that, as though they were afraid she might fall. 'But from what I can see, it's not just a question of two legs joined by skin. There's an actual fusion of the long bones. She had one long, strong lower limb.'

'It doesn't really look anything like a tail, does it?' said Lacey, feeling an unfamiliar dampness in her eyes.

Thessa's lower limb was wide at the hip before tapering sharply. It was several inches shorter than one might have expected her legs to be, judging from the length of her torso. There was no knee joint that Lacey could see, but a mechanism for bending the limb must surely exist. How else would she have been able to swim so well? She had almost perfectly formed feet, they were simply joined at the ankle.

'Not in broad daylight,' said Kaytes. 'It looks like what it is. One of the numerous imperfections the human race should have come to terms with over the years. But at night, at a distance, in the water — well, I can see how gullible, romantic types might start fantasizing about mythical creatures.'

'Tide's getting close,' said one of the Marine Unit officers. 'We really should . . .' He left the suggestion hanging.

'Are you done here, Lacey?' asked Kaytes. She nodded, and stepped away while they lifted Thessa and placed her gently in a body bag. Turner had returned to the dinghy, was coming towards her now carrying a cone of cellophane. He pulled it away from the flowers within and handed them to Lacey.

'They're lilies,' she said to no one in

particular. 'She and Alex were born in May.' She bent and put the five stems on the shore, where the outline of Thessa's body could still be seen in the mud. 'Should be Lily of the Valley, really. But you can't get it this time of year.'

She stood up, sniffed and wiped her eyes.

'It was her birth flower,' she explained. 'Mine's Larkspur.'

FRIDAY, 18 JULY

98

The Mermaid

On the bow deck of her boat, Lacey lay in the sun. In the two weeks since Thessa and Nadia had died, her Bollywood tan had faded. She'd decided, though, that she rather liked herself with a golden glow. And who knew, maybe one of these days there'd be someone else around to admire it.

Eileen's large bare feet came into view along the deck. 'Post for you, Tracey.' Lacey sat up and refastened the strap on her sea-green bikini.

'You know perfectly well what my name is.' She took the assorted bundle of envelopes. 'You're just winding me up.'

Eileen walked away, back towards the cockpit. 'Don't know what you're talking about,' she muttered. Then she stopped and turned back. 'Couple of those were from estate agents. You selling up?'

Reluctantly, Lacey nodded. Dry land.

That was what she needed right now. It was a pity — she loved her boat, she loved the people she'd come to live amongst — but she'd never be able to look out at dark water, at dreary shores again, without thinking of what she'd lost. Of the friend she'd destroyed. Her fingers tore open the first speculative letter.

'One from Belmarsh as well,' said Eileen, just before she disappeared.

Belmarsh?

Discarding the estate agents' letters, Lacey found the envelope at the bottom. The address was handwritten, the postmark Belmarsh Prison.

My dear Lacey

We are all defined by the physical shell that carries us around. In this place where so much time for reflection is allowed me, I find myself dwelling increasingly upon what my twin might have become, had it not been for the minor defect in antenatal programming that stunted and twisted the normal formation of limbs, and thus, of a life. She had a rather brilliant, if wayward mind, but I guess I don't need to tell you that.

I am only too aware that, technically, what I did was a crime. I make no excuses for myself. Except to say that insofar as the clinic is concerned, we did no harm, and that the women we brought into the country left us to lead happier lives. I will be accused of exploiting the vulnerable for the sake of greed, and it is a charge I must accept. My conscience was salved, a little, by the number of women I helped escape from a regime far harsher than anything this country has to offer.

I'm so glad you are safe. If any part of conscious thinking remains to her, then Thessa most certainly will be too. You may think her mermaid obsession foolish, but it was born out of a need to feel complete; not a product of a defective accident of birth and the prejudice of bigoted minds, but a creature of purpose, whole and splendid. (She and Nadia had more in common than either would have imagined.)

She was always drawn to female physical perfection and you rather dazzled her. She told me once that she could see into your heart and that it was cold, but true as silver and strong as steel. She hoped that one day you would be able to return to your own name, to throw off the heavy veil that is Lacey Flint and find the purity within. I hope so, too.

Yours truly
Alexander Christakos

Seconds went by, and then minutes. And the sound of a mobile phone ringing found its way into Lacey's head. The estate agents' letters lay on her lap still, but without knowing, she'd torn them into a dozen pieces. She lifted her hands and let the breeze take them, up and out, over the water. The caller was Dana.

'I just heard from the UK Border Agency,' she said. 'They've decided to grant visas to all three women and, in time, process their applications for residency. Looks like they're all going to be able to stay.'

It was good news. Jamilla, Shireen and Ummu, the three women who, in addition to Nadia, had been helped by Thessa to flee the East Street clinic, had been found alive and well. Jamilla worked as a seamstress, Shireen was already married and Ummu had started her own baking business. None had shown any desire to go back to Afghanistan. None had had anything negative to say about Alex and his clinic staff. As an experience it had been boring, a little bewildering, even uncomfortable at times, but more than worth it in the end. Even when told about the possibility that their eggs had been illegally taken, they'd been sanguine. Different world, different priorities.

Pari was in hospital, recovering quickly from ovarian hyperstimulation syndrome, and already causing consternation among the hospital staff by regularly joining and surpassing the teams of ward cleaners.

In the coming weeks, Dana's team would begin the process of tracking down all the women who'd passed through Christakos's unofficial clinic. Lacey wouldn't be surprised if they weren't all in similar positions to the three that Thessa had liberated.

'Lacey, there's something else. Very hush-hush, but I thought you should know. There's been a confidential bulletin round. SO10 have just completed a long-running undercover operation. Over a dozen people have been arrested in south London. It's been their biggest success in years.'

Lacey took a deep breath.

'It's over, Lacey. I wouldn't be surprised if you have a visitor any time soon.'

When Dana had hung up, Lacey stood and climbed on to the next boat. The tide was almost at its peak and from Ray and Eileen's boat, so much bigger than her own, she could just about see the tip of the old dredger.

'Eileen.' She strode quickly back to the cockpit. 'Can I borrow your binoculars?'

Back on deck, she focused on the top of the old crane. Something new. A piece of fabric blowing in the breeze that never, even on the hottest day, left the creek in peace. A flag. A white skull standing out in relief on a black background. Two crossed swords beneath it. The Jolly Roger. The pirates' flag.

Her canoe was long gone. Ray's motor boat was still in the hands of the crime-scene investigators. It would take far too long to drive round.

'Eileen,' she said. 'I'm going for a swim.'

Good God, but the creek felt cold without a wetsuit. Several quick strokes of front crawl to stave off the shivering and then, on impulse, she switched to the undulating movement of a stroke she hardly ever used, wasn't even that good at, it just seemed right, somehow. Butterfly. As she rose from the water, her arms high and straight, she could see Eileen's shadow. She was standing on the port deck, watching her swim away, and Lacey knew, without turning round, that the older woman was smiling.

She swam on, towards the tall male figure that had appeared on the deck of the dredger, knowing that whatever happened, this strange, forgotten, watery wasteland was her home now.

She was staying. And she would swim. The creek was going to keep its mermaid.

AUTHOR'S NOTE

Please do NOT swim in the tidal Thames. Lacey Flint is a fictional character and a reckless one at that. The Thames is deep, fast and dangerous. As is Deptford Creek. It is a fascinating place to visit, and I thoroughly recommend the guided walks run by the Creekside Education Trust, but even at low tide nobody should venture into the Creek unaccompanied.

The stories told by Nadia, Pari and the other women from Afghanistan are all based on real events and are inspired by the book *Dear Zari: Hidden Stories from Women in Afghanistan* by Zarghuna Kargar.

Sirenomelia is a real condition, although it is unusual for people born with it to survive into adulthood.

ACKNOWLEDGEMENTS

My grateful thanks to:

Derek Caterer, Mike Katesmark, and Adrian Summons, who try (quite hard at times) to keep me grounded in reality. Also the staff of the Creekside Education Trust in Deptford and Anthony Hammond of the Environment Agency.

My friends at Transworld, in particular Sarah Adams, Alison Barrow, Chrissy Charalambides, Lynsey Dalladay, Elspeth Dougall, Larry Finlay, Gavin Hilzbritch, Katy Loftus, Kate Samano, Bill Scott-Kerr, Claire Ward and Bella Whittington.

My friends at St Martin's Press, especially Kelley Ragland and Elizabeth Lacks.

My hardworking and endlessly patient agent, Anne-Marie Doulton, and her equally wonderful colleagues, Peter, Rosie and Jessica Buckman.

Nick Blake for the brilliant video trailers and my son, Hal, for bringing Barney Roberts (of *Like This, For Ever*) to life. Finally, Eleanor Bailey, who is wise beyond her years.

ABOUT THE AUTHOR

Sharon Bolton (previously S. J. Bolton) is the author of six critically acclaimed novels: this is her seventh novel and features the popular DC Lacey Flint and DI Mark Joesbury.

She has been shortlisted for the CWA Gold Dagger for Crime Novel of the Year, the Theakstons Old Peculier Crime Novel of the Year and the CWA Dagger in the Library.

Sharon lives near Oxford with her husband and young son. For more information about her and her books, or to check out her addictive blog, visit www.sharonbolton.com. You can also join her on Facebook at www.facebook.com/SJBoltonCrime.